CAST
IN
SECRETS
AND
SHADOW

CAST
IN
SECRETS
AND
SHADOW

ANDREA ROBERTSON

PHILOMEL BOOKS

PHILOMEL BOOKS
An imprint of Penguin Random House LLC, New York

First published in the United States of America by Philomel Books,
an imprint of Penguin Random House LLC, 2021

Visit us online at penguinrandomhouse.com.

Library of Congress Cataloging-in-Publication Data
Names: Robertson, Andrea, 1978- author.
Title: Cast in secrets and shadow / Andrea Robertson.
Description: New York : Philomel Books, 2021. | Series: Loresmith ; book 2 | Audience: Ages
14 up | Audience: Grades 10–12 | Summary: "After suffering betrayals and losses, Ara, Nimhea,
Lahvja, and Teth must try to come together and find the Loreknights across the kingdom"—
Provided by publisher. Identifiers: LCCN 2021015485 | ISBN 9780399164231 (hardcover) | ISBN
9780698174139 (ebook) Subjects: CYAC: Fantasy. Classification: LCC PZ7.1.R598 Cas 2021 |
DDC [Fic]—dc23
LC record available at https://lccn.loc.gov/2021015485

Manufactured in Canada

ISBN 9780399164231 (HARDCOVER)
10 9 8 7 6 5 4 3 2 1

ISBN 9780593403068 (INTERNATIONAL EDITION)
10 9 8 7 6 5 4 3 2 1

FRE

Edited by Jill Santopolo and Kelsey Murphy
Design by Ellice M. Lee
Text set in Amerigo BT

TO KATIE, FOR WORLDS IN THE WOODS

SAE
FJERI
Well of the Twins
Ice Coast
Elke's Pass
Ruins of
Ice Mountains
Fjeri Highlands
Senn's Fury
Rill's Pass
Teth's Camp
Wellseeker's Landi
Darkfern
Silverstag
Port Pilgrim
Wuldr's Grove
Alderspring
Shepherd's Rest
Fjeri Lowlands
Bridgegate Cross
Westport
Oakvale
Foxgate
Hunter's R
Echir
Siva
DAEFRIT
Aerindross
Zeverin Gorge
Dothris
Marik
Ghost Cliffs
Ofrit's Cavern
Zeverin Delta
Punishing Desert
The Bone Forest
Butcher Crow
Fortress of the Sands
Handar
The Great Mines
Southern Sea
Isar
Zyre
Salt Coast
Blinding Cape

Forgotten Coast
KELDEN
NAVA'S IRE
FENMYR
LIFLAMYR
KAENMYR
ALLOMYR
FIVE RIVERS
PORT AMBER
THE GREAT MARKET
NAVA'S BOUNTY
SOLA
NAO~NIAS
NAO~HORSA
TRIBRIDGE
The Gash
NOMIS
MER
JAN
VIJERI
THE TANGLE
LAST LANDING
ERLAON
Serpent Coast
Shrouded Cape

❖ PROLOGUE ❖
THE VOKKAN INVASION OF SAETLUND

inning the war left a bitter taste in Captain Liran's mouth. The conquest of Saetlund could hardly be called a war; it had been a rout. Too short and too easy. What forces King Dentroth sent against the invading Vokkans were pitiful, lacking in training and discipline. On the plains of Sola, Saetlund's forces had melted before Liran's advance once the storied Loreknights had fallen.

Foolish tales.

Liran believed in gods; rather, he believed in one god, Vokk the Devourer. He'd seen Vokk with his own eyes—a visage he wished with each breath he could forget—and knew it was that god who had kept his father alive all these centuries. People speculated that Fauld the Ever-Living wasn't truly immortal, but Liran knew the truth. For so long as Vokk sustained his father, the emperor would not die.

To Liran, Vokk was all-powerful and terrifying. It was Vokk's army that had consumed all the world but this last kingdom, Saetlund.

But Liran did not love his god.

And this war . . . it was meant to be the last. Saetlund was the final conquest. Liran had been told that the kingdom held this honor due to lore of old, which the captain put no stock in. All that mattered to him was the idea that after Saetlund there was nowhere else to claim, and as far as Liran could see that meant soon the world would starve.

What of the Devourer then? Would Vokk abandon his people and find a new world to consume? Liran worried the god would consume his worshippers before abandoning this realm.

Saetlund claimed to have its own gods, but those same gods were supposedly responsible for the champions—so-called Loreknights— Liran's foot soldiers had cut down with ease. They'd been the opposite of legendary: only adequate with their arms (which showed no signs of being magical, as myths claimed) and lacking in honor. Three of the Loreknights had tried to flee when they saw their fellows laid low. Liran's cavalry had run them down in a matter of minutes.

Liran had heard it said that the empire delayed its attack on Saetlund because these knights were nigh invincible. It seemed Emperor Fauld had waited centuries for no good reason. When the Loreknights fell, an audible groan swept through King Dentroth's army. Chaos ensued.

Soldiers stopped obeying their officers' orders. Their ranks split, faltering. The Vokkan commander seized this advantage by sending his troops through these breaks to flank the enemy. The Vokkan forces so outnumbered Saetlund's that Liran soon had the bulk of the king-dom's army surrounded. After a third of Dentroth's soldiers had fallen, the remainder surrendered, opening a path to the capital city of Five Rivers.

The Vokkan army had prepared for a siege. They needn't have. Five Rivers had devolved into frenzied panic. When word spread in the capi-tal that King Dentroth had fled rather than fight, its citizens poured out of the city, attempting to flee and surrendering in droves to the advance troops sent to scout positions.

While the commander managed the hordes of Saetlunders suddenly on their hands, Captain Liran led a contingent of his troops into the city to make their assault on the palace. To Liran's chagrin, his brother Zenar insisted on accompanying them into the city. There was someone in the palace he wanted to capture, someone other than the king. Zenar's demand had surprised Liran. Aside from the spells they maintained to fortify Vokkan soldiers, the ArchWizard and his followers didn't trouble themselves with banal events like war, but this time was different.

At the palace gates, they faced the most resistance. Unlike Saetlund's army, the palace guard fought hard, falling back only when forced to, then establishing new defensive positions and fighting on.

Their efforts, though honorable, were futile. Bit by bit their numbers diminished. Liran's forces took the palace with only a few losses, where the palace guard were slaughtered. Liran's targets were the royals, but Zenar begged a portion of his brother's soldiers to hunt down the palace blacksmith. Liran would have refused but for the mad gleam in his brother's eyes. When Zenar became rabid about an issue, Liran knew better than to thwart him. And Zenar's strange request was in a way a gift to the captain, because the ArchWizard's presence would have posed a problem for the work to come. Liran couldn't have his brother interfering with his plans for the king and queen.

The fight outside the royal quarters was ferocious. Liran led from the front, cutting men down with sword and blocking their attacks with shield. The captain wished these last guards would surrender, but knew they would fight as long as they could. They were the type of soldiers Liran wanted in his army; that they fought for a coward who hid behind walls and doors rather than face his enemies was a tragedy.

When the king's guard had been defeated, Liran strode into the royal chamber. Dentroth and his queen, Kalhea, cowered together behind the bed, as if its four posters offered a defensible position. A final guard stood between Liran and the royals. They sparred briefly, but Liran was the superior fighter and the other soldier fell. When Liran approached the king, Dentroth stayed on his knees while the queen wept.

"Mercy." Dentroth went so far as to try to grip the hem of Liran's surcoat.

The captain's lip curled up in disgust, but he said, "You shall have it."

With two swift sword strokes, Liran opened the throats of Saetlund's rulers.

He knew the king hadn't been begging for death. Dentroth was too much of a coward to perceive his demise with anything but sheer horror. But Liran had given the king and queen a gift. Death was mercy.

Turning to his men, he said, "The last of the king's guard did this. He'd been ordered by the king to kill them before letting them be taken."

Liran's soldiers nodded. They understood their captain's motivation and agreed with it—that was the reason he'd selected them for this mission. It was also why he'd been glad Zenar had a separate purpose after entering the palace. His brother would have wanted the king and queen alive.

That was why they had to die.

1

raitor. Coward.

The landscape slipped past Eamon in a blur. He didn't see the vast fields of Sola that stretched to the east.

Wretched. Worthless.

Eamon didn't notice the fountains of green that sprung from the soil in some of the fields, nor did he notice that many lay barren. The famed black earth of Sola in those empty spaces had turned chalky gray and spun up in funnels when the wind caught it.

Doomed.

His horse jogged along, at times turning its head to peek at its rider, who hadn't moved in the saddle all day. Had it not been for the other horses trotting before, alongside, and behind, Eamon's mount would have wandered into those fields to feast on tender early summer grasses.

Eamon wasn't sure how he stayed upright in the saddle. He didn't feel like he was inside his body. He had no sense of time. He knew he sat astride a horse and that he held the reins, but it seemed like he was somehow apart, watching himself travel north, surrounded by Vokkan soldiers. To passersby he probably looked like an important person being escorted to Five Rivers, but Eamon knew he was a prisoner.

Even the worst episodes of illness Eamon experienced didn't compare to the physical and mental anguish he felt now.

I had to do it, didn't I?

He couldn't answer his own question. He wasn't even sure what it was he'd *had* to do.

Did he mean he had to collaborate with Vokk's wizards? Or he *had* to leave the others?

Doubts festered inside him, oozing like infected wounds that leaked their poison into his blood and made his stomach heave.

When Eamon first agreed to ArchWizard Zenar's proposal, he'd never imagined it would end this way—with him scribbling a pathetic note to his twin, Nimhea, in the middle of the night and creeping out of the camp like the craven he was. In countless daydreams he'd seen Nimhea on the River Throne flanked by Prince Zenar and himself. The ArchWizard's promises still tugged at Eamon's heart. All he'd ever wanted: Nimhea secure, protected by the Vokkans, Eamon himself finally rid of the chronic illness that plagued him. He'd made himself believe that if not for his secret alliance, Nimhea's attempt to regain the throne would be forever thwarted. The Vokkans were simply too powerful to be overthrown by that ragtag group that called themselves the Resistance. He'd done everything for the sake of giving Nimhea her crown.

It's the only way.

He'd managed to convince himself that Ara would understand what he'd done—once he had the chance to explain his reasoning. He hadn't been too worried about Teth. Eamon decided the thief would happily return to his life in the Below. So long as the kingdom was thriving again, a rightful ruler restored to the throne, the Low Kings would be satisfied. Nimhea would have her throne, the ArchWizard would gain the secrets of the Loresmith. Saetlund would thrive again in peace and prosperity.

But Lahvja. Lahvja the Summoner. Everything had changed for Eamon the night she drove away the wizards' hounds.

An irksome little voice in Eamon's head reminded him that he'd been relieved to see the hounds gone. He'd been horrified when they appeared. It meant the ArchWizard doubted him. Or thought Eamon didn't have the strength and will to see his mission through.

The sight of those menacing shadows twisted Eamon's gut so tightly he thought he would faint from the pain. It was too soon. Far too soon. Zenar's impatience was foolish. Had the prince captured his quarry that night, everything would have fallen apart. Their prize forever lost.

Wicked.

Whenever Eamon looked at his hands he saw blood. It made his head swim and his skin feel too tight, like his soul was being wrung out. However unpleasant, the sensations brought him a measure of reassurance. They reminded him that despite what he'd done, he wasn't evil. He would never have chosen this type of magic, but he hadn't any of his own—only that which he'd been taught by the ArchWizard's agents. The ritual required to maintain communication with the wizards repulsed Eamon. It was the first thing that planted a seed of doubt about his decision to ally with Prince Zenar.

It isn't right. It can't be right.

He often wept before whispering the verses that would draw nearby creatures to him. In the forests it was rabbits and squirrels. He hated what he had to do, but they were small, so he could force himself through the motions.

I always said, "I'm sorry."

The apology didn't make the visions of bloodstains on his hands go away. Nor did the scars that crisscrossed his arms take away the pain and guilt that haunted him.

Eamon's worst episode was at the caravan. His call had drawn a kid goat, likely untethered because its owners assumed it wouldn't stray from his mother. He'd tried to chase it away. But the little goat was ensnared by the spell and wouldn't leave Eamon's side. The wizards hadn't taught Eamon how to stop the ritual once he'd started it. It was only a matter of time before the kid's owners came looking for it. Eamon couldn't return to the caravan with a baby goat dogging his every step.

He let the goat sit in his lap, as he did with all the animals he summoned. Eamon wanted to spend time petting the kid, scratching behind its ears, speaking to it in a quiet voice, but with the caravan nearby he couldn't risk taking the time. He pushed the baby goat off his lap and onto the ground; it didn't resist or struggle, simply continuing to gaze adoringly at Eamon. At least he knew how to make the kill swiftly and, he hoped, with the least amount of pain possible.

As always, the blood poured out. Eamon hated the blood, but he needed it. Blood and entrails. They made him vomit. He'd learned not to eat before undertaking the ritual, so he dry heaved as he opened up the goat's abdomen and dug out its intestines. Pushing the gutted animal aside, Eamon arranged the entrails into the required shape—a spiral sitting in the goat's pooled blood. Then he spoke the words that would call Zenar.

No visage of the ArchWizard appeared. Only his voice, as clear as if the Vokkan prince were sitting beside Eamon. Eamon would give his report—where they were, what progress they'd made on the Loresmith's quest. He never lied, but he did omit. The ArchWizard's moods were easy to gauge even though Eamon had only the voice to go by. He'd learned that he needed to give enough information to make Zenar content—not necessarily happy, but at least satisfied that Eamon was performing the tasks he'd committed to. The one time Eamon had failed to do so, Zenar had sent the hounds after them. After that terrifying night, Eamon spent much more time composing his reports to the ArchWizard, rehearsing their delivery in his head until he felt sure Zenar wouldn't intervene.

At least that was Eamon's hope. But the ArchWizard's unexpected and unwanted interference planted seeds of doubt about his dreams of the future. As their journey continued, those seeds had sprouted, spreading like thorny weeds that tore at his insides. He didn't stray from his path, sending updates to Zenar, trying each day to convince himself that despite his growing fears, this plan would work. It had to work. The alternative was unbearable, for it meant every step of the way, Eamon had made the wrong choice, had shown the worst judgment.

That was why he'd finally made the choice to leave. Putting the words to paper in the note to his sister had rent his heart, but he saw no other way forward. He couldn't gamble with Nimhea's and his new friends' lives when he was this uncertain. He would face the ArchWizard and discover for himself the true nature of that man. Should Zenar give Eamon the assurances he needed, he would continue working with the ArchWizard toward their common goal. If his hopes had been misplaced in allying with Zenar, he would do what he could to protect Nimhea and the Loresmith.

Traitor.

Eamon broke from his stupor when the riders crested a rise, and suddenly it was there: the lake. It covered the horizon, a velvet expanse of blue broken only by the island at its center.

The lake didn't have a proper name; it had many names. Solans and

Daefritians called it the Gods' Lake. To the peoples of Kelden and Fjeri it was the Rivers' Lake. No one was sure what the Vijerians named it due to their penchant for silence and secrets.

Gazing at its rippling surface, Eamon decided the lake had no need for a name. Awesome in size, it drank from three rivers and fed the two that flowed south. The lake simply was.

The small island sitting in the middle of the vast waters did have a name: Isle of the Gods. The place where the gods drew people from each of the provinces to meet one another and give them the gift of a shared language. The Kingdom of Saetlund was born on that island.

Eamon shuddered at the thought of its holiness . . . and its power. He wondered, and feared, what Zenar and his wizards had discovered there. The same feelings that overwhelmed him while he'd journeyed with the Loresmith crashed into him now. A longing to know secrets of the isle, the belief that they would make him strong in mind and body, countered by disgust at his craving for whatever magic he could find. It wasn't a simple curiosity, nor an admiration. It was a raw wound desperate for a salve without which he would never be whole.

That constant ache saved Eamon from despair. Despite his guilt, despite his horror at what he'd done, Eamon guarded a tiny hope that the end of this journey would offer him a taste of the power he dreamed of. That he would be healed and given strength. He'd defied the ArchWizard, which blunted the stabs of anticipation in his stomach, knowing the chances that his wishes would be granted were few. His dream that Nimhea would understand his choices, be grateful for how he'd tried to bring her the ultimate prize, was swiftly dying as well.

Eamon had no idea what would come next. He guessed the soldiers would take him to the Temple of Vokk in Five Rivers, and not the palace. While it was military men who escorted him now, Eamon belonged to the wizards. The temple was the first building Emperor Fauld had erected after the conquest. The Devourer's holy site rose while the shrines of Saetlund's gods were razed. Rumor had it that the ziggurat of mammoth onyx crystals was the twin of the original temple on the distant Vokkan continent. The emperor had built the same temple after each of his conquests. With Vokkan rule came mandatory worship of a new god.

Little was known about Vokk, except for his insatiable hunger and his people's success at gobbling up the world kingdom by kingdom. Saetlund had been the last free kingdom. Eamon wondered how Vokk would sate his appetite now that he'd claimed every continent of the globe.

His stomach gurgled, then snarled. He vaguely remembered the soldiers forcing him to drink water while in his stupor, but he had no memory of food. Suddenly he was ravenous.

"Water?" Eamon croaked at a guard. "Something to eat?"

The guard handed him a skin of water and a hard, dense rectangle that Eamon guessed was some type of soldier's ration. He drank first, then bit into the rough-textured substance. It felt like eating sweetened gravel, but he forced it down.

Eamon straightened in his saddle and stretched. His horse flicked its ears, wondering if it needed to be wary of its newly wakened rider. Having satisfied his hunger and thirst, Eamon felt better. In fact, he felt more than better. Keenly alert and filled with an unfamiliar sense of strength, he wondered what in addition to actual food might be in the hard blocks.

Glancing at the four soldiers around him, Eamon tried to pull more memories from the last . . . How long had it been? Days. No, if he could see the lake, they had reached central Sola. They'd been riding for a week and then some.

Panic seized him without warning. *My satchel. Ofrit's scroll!*

His heart pounded until he saw his belongings tied behind the saddle of one of the soldiers' mounts.

Safe enough. He would have preferred to carry the satchel himself, but doubted such a request would fall on friendly ears.

The day wore on. Dusk came, then night. Still they rode. Stopping only to rest and water the horses—who were given chunks of food that looked almost identical to the soldiers' rations.

When hunger stirred again, Eamon ate another ration. The fatigue that had crept into his limbs melted away. His mind focused.

They traveled at that grueling pace day and night, never stopping in a village or city until they reached Five Rivers. The walls that ringed the city were mostly intact. They passed through what had once been the city gates. Eamon wanted to scour the capital with his gaze. He'd been born here. Five Rivers should have been his home.

But Eamon couldn't tear his eyes away from the Temple of Vokk and the spire rising from it that glistened in the sunlight. Taller than any other structure in the capital, the temple had been visible for hours before they'd reached the city. Its black crystals had glittered in the distance. Once Eamon's eyes had found the ArchWizard's dwelling place, he couldn't bring himself to look away.

Vokk presented a piece of the puzzle that Eamon wasn't sure how to fit with the rest of his dream. In the lore, Vokk had left Saetlund untouched out of love for his siblings—the gods who watched over the kingdom. But somehow that had changed. The Vokkan Empire had overrun Saetlund, and while Eamon hadn't heard any rumors of Vokk's presence in the conquest, it was hard to believe that Fauld the Ever-Living had attacked without the blessing of his powerful deity.

He watched the temple loom larger with each mile, a stepped

rectangular building topped by a pyramid. It stretched to an impossible height, its sharp apex seeming to pierce the sky. Eamon almost expected to see a wound in the sky above the spire's tip. A rip in the heavens through which the stars would bleed down. The Temple of Vokk dwarfed everything around it, even the palace, which crouched nearby like a supplicant.

The soldiers dismounted and pulled Eamon from his saddle despite the fact that he wasn't bound. They took him into the temple in the same formation of their travels, surrounded, leaving no chance for escape. The doors opened to a long hallway. The soldier at Eamon's back had to push him forward when he gaped at the walls. They were glossy black and covered with an oily fluid that didn't drip onto the floor. Instead, it streamed upward, disappearing into a gap where the wall met the ceiling.

Ebony doors trimmed with red lacquer interrupted the glistening black walls at regular intervals. A massive set of double doors awaited them at the end of the hall. The doors swung open for them.

A man stood at the center of the room. He was tall and had a long, sharp face. His chiseled features and sensuous lips made him as beautiful as poisoned fruit.

Eamon wondered if he was about to die. He wished he didn't deserve to.

The soldiers dropped Eamon's satchel beside the man then fell back, leaving Eamon alone with him. He heard the doors close.

"Prince Eamon." The man steepled his fingers in front of his chest and smiled.

Eamon stood before Prince Zenar and waited for the ArchWizard to announce his fate.

2

ra heard the breaking of waves where she stood, in a hollow behind tall, grassy dunes, though the ocean was hidden from her sight. She drew tight, shallow breaths, and her heartbeat struck hard and sharp against her breastbone. She kept her silence, waiting for an answer, while her eyes followed the boy to whom she'd put the question. It was a struggle to keep still, knowing Teth's future—and her own—hung in the balance.

When she'd crossed the bridge that connected the realm of the gods to her world, Ara found herself sitting exactly where she'd been—gazing into the campfire. Eamon's note was in her hand, but when she examined it she found that his tearstains had vanished. The signs of his sorrow for betraying his companions had taken on a new form. Ara's heart gave a heavy thud as the weight of Eamon's leaving hit her once again. She clung to the memory of what had happened at the Loresmith Forge, believing that somehow the transformation of Eamon's tears into the weapons of the first Loreknight was a sign that Eamon was not altogether lost to them. That he had not fully given himself over to evil and the Vokkans.

Teth was breaking down his tent when Ara called to him and asked him to walk through the dunes with her. He came to her immediately, lifting his hand to her cheek and rubbing his thumb over her skin.

"Where did this come from?" he asked with a chuckle, gazing at the soot he'd cleaned away. "Have you been playing in the campfire? I didn't know ash was good for the complexion."

Rather than answer, she asked, "How long have I been gone?"

Teth stared at her, frowning, and she realized that no time at all had passed for him while Ara had been smithing in a world apart from this one.

She told him about her sudden transport to the Loresmith Forge, Eni reappearing as the old woman from the forest, and the wonder of the forge itself. Last, she told him the weapon she'd forged belonged to him. That Eni had chosen Teth to become the first Loreknight of this age.

Then she waited.

Teth gazed at her. A smile broke across his face and he began to laugh, but his mirth died when the solemn expression on her face didn't waver.

Cursing softly, he looked at her. "No."

Ara didn't know how to respond. Conflicting impulses chased after one another: to apologize, to reach for him, to try to explain. But nothing felt right.

Teth paced back and forth beside a driftwood log, tension bringing the carved lines of his long, lean muscles into relief. His sandalwood skin gleamed in the morning sunlight as he ran his hand over the tightly wound tufts of dark hair that crowned his head. He kept his eyes forward, gazing at nothing in particular, his brow furrowed as he considered what she'd told him. Every so often he cast a glance at the bow and quiver, regarding the weapon with a mixture of curiosity and suspicion. He reminded Ara of an animal contemplating a snare, wanting the bait but sensing the trap.

It was different now, watching him. When she saw his taut

shoulders, her own muscles tensed. She felt more than sympathy. This was Teth—who'd appeared uninvited one night in their camp, a thief ready to pluck whatever valuables he could from Ara's sleeping companions. That night felt like a lifetime ago. The boy who'd set her teeth on edge so many times in their early travels had become a confidant, friend, and something more. She wanted to go to him. To take his hands and look into his eyes. To kiss away his doubts. She wanted to tell him to confess his hopes and fears and put his trust in her. Ara's heart ached for that.

But something stood between her and her desires. A change within herself. As she watched Teth, Ara felt she was split in two. The girl who'd fallen for this thief wanted to hold him and comfort him. The Loresmith could not.

The events in Ofrit's Cavern and smithing her first weapon at the gods' forge had forever changed her. Her thoughts were no longer only Ara's thoughts; neither did her feelings belong to her alone. Everything in her mind and heart was confronted by the overarching purpose of the Loresmith that whispered to her like a wizened chorus. What came into conflict with that purpose had to be put aside.

Ara hadn't expected this and chafed at the demands of her new duty. It wasn't that she couldn't physically put her arms around Teth, nor that her tongue refused to speak the words that came into her mind. She remained herself and yet she was aware that something new infused her. A heightened sense of being. An altered relationship to time and history. Most of all, she understood that she was no longer simply Ara, nor were her friends simply friends. They had been called to become new players in a very old story, and it was the Loresmith's place to guide them as they found their roles.

Teth was the first.

"Explain it to me again," Teth said as he passed Ara for the twentieth time.

She understood his need to dissect every moment of her time with Eni at the Loresmith Forge. Taking on the mantle of Loreknight was no small thing. She still grappled with the truth of her own role in their ongoing quest.

"Eni chose you." Ara knew that wasn't enough, but she struggled to find a sufficient explanation.

"Can gods be wrong?" Teth asked with a nervous laugh. "Not that I don't have many exceptional qualities."

"You do," Ara said quietly. Her emotions were a quagmire. Pride. Fear. Hope. Doubt. Beneath it all a warmth like firelight she was not ready to give a name to.

A smile played at the corner of his lips as he read the feelings in her eyes. "Don't distract me."

He briefly touched the pendant that hung from his neck, the one bearing the god of roads and travelers' symbol, and said, "No offense to Eni, but Loreknight is not a title I aspire to. Sticking to thievery is fine by me."

"Eni's exact words were 'Not all knights wear shining armor.'"

"Thank gods for that," Teth muttered. "It'd be difficult to climb trees in plate armor."

Ara laughed, imagining him cocooned in steel with his arms and legs wrapped around a tree trunk. The rush of affection for him swept away the Loresmith for a moment. She went to him, and he opened his arms to her. Teth bent to kiss her. His lips touched hers as his hands settled onto the small of her back, pulling her against him. A tiny gasp slipped from her throat. She felt Teth's smile against her mouth, then he kissed her again. Deeper. With hunger. Ara felt her body rise in reply.

She wanted to reassure him. She wanted more than that. Heat rippled through her limbs. His hands slid up the sides of her body.

And stopped.

Teth pulled away.

"What's wrong?" Ara asked, heart sinking. She thought she already knew the answer.

He hesitated, then said, "What does it mean for us?"

A chill rippled down her spine. She had replies for any number of his questions, but not that one. She walked away from Teth, troubled, starting to pace where he'd left off. She missed the warmth of his body against hers. The touch of his lips. She wanted them back with a fierceness that almost frightened her. With not a little effort, she pressed those sensations away.

When she'd crossed over from the Loresmith Forge, her thoughts had been completely focused on Teth. How would he react to the news she brought? Ara felt an overwhelming responsibility for him and sensed that this protectiveness bespoke the relationships between a Loresmith and her Loreknights. How closely connected they were. As they were chosen, she would watch over them, guide them in their service to the gods.

But Ara had not considered that Teth becoming a Loreknight could stand in the way of the romantic feelings that had grown between them. Feelings that had nothing to do with fate or legend.

Returning to him, she drew a long breath and shook her head. "I don't know what it means."

What she did know was that if Teth answered Eni's call, he would be changed, too. They would both be connected to the thrum of an ancient pulse that accompanied their every step.

"I had a feeling you'd say that." Teth rubbed the back of his neck.

A sudden ache settled in her chest at his concern. She felt like kicking herself for not asking Eni when she had the chance, while also cringing at the idea of doing so.

Eni, thanks for offering to make Teth a Loreknight, but does it mean I have to give him up?

Whatever her feelings for Teth, gathering the Loreknights to aid the rebels had to come first. She knew that, but Teth had to reach his own conclusion.

He walked to the driftwood log and gazed at the bow, quiver, and arrows.

"That's the smallest quiver I've ever seen." He frowned. "There are only five arrows."

"Five arrows for five tears," Ara said. "Its name is Tears of the Traitor."

Teth looked at her sharply. "Eamon?"

She nodded.

He crouched beside the weapon and stayed there, quiet for several moments.

"I don't know why you chose me, Traveler." His eyes were closed, and he spoke so softly Ara could barely make out the words. "But I accept."

When his hand touched the bow, a sound like the beating of a thousand wings filled her head, followed by the deep toll of a bell.

Ara already had a strong attachment to Teth, but now she felt something new. A thread connected them, alive with the knowledge of their commitment to each other and to a greater calling.

He met her eyes, and she saw the awe in his gaze.

She nodded. There was no need for words.

Teth drew an arrow from the quiver and examined the shaft.

"It's the same material as Ironbranch, isn't it?"

"Yes."

"No fletching." He nodded his approval. "I prefer Keldenese black goose feathers. I brought plenty with me. I can fletch these arrows when we're back at camp."

He slung the quiver over his shoulder and smiled. "I can barely feel it, but I also know that it's mine. I can never lose it. It won't slip off. The arrows will never leave the quiver unless I take them out." With a brief shake of his head, he murmured, "Incredible."

"I know," Ara replied.

Picking up the bow, Teth gave a low whistle. "Also light, but the balance is perfect."

He drew the bowstring a few times, even notching a featherless arrow.

"I get that the arrow tips came from Eamon's tears," he said. "But I can't figure how having only five is a good thing."

Ara knew why, and a smile flickered over her lips. "I don't want to spoil the surprise."

Ara and Teth were only halfway back to camp when she heard Nimhea shouting. Ara broke into a sprint, hoping that whatever new disaster had befallen them, it was less heartbreaking than the last.

When they reached the campsite, Ara expected to see an intruder, but only Nimhea and Lahvja were there, standing next to their partially filled packs.

"I can't believe I let you comfort me," Nimhea snarled at Lahvja. "You could have stopped him."

The princess looked nothing less than a vengeful goddess. Drawn to her full height, she rippled with strength and radiated fury. The fiery roots that had grown since they'd dyed Nimhea's hair framed her bronze face like a coronet of embers burning against her darkened curls.

Lahvja lifted her hands, trying to pacify the princess. "It wasn't my place. Only Eamon could reveal what was in his heart. I knew he would make a choice, but not what that choice would be."

"But I could have helped him." Nimhea's anguish tried to break beneath the rage, but she forced her grief back. "He was my brother. He didn't need to be alone in his struggle."

"It was his burden to bear," Lahvja said quietly. "And he's still your brother."

Nimhea glared at her. "He betrayed me, and he won't be forgiven. But he was right about one thing. You're worthless. All you do is talk in ridiculous puzzles without any meaning."

Lahvja shrank back as if Nimhea had struck her.

The cruel words stole Ara's breath. She waited for Nimhea to stop attacking and apologize. But the princess plunged on.

"You're as much a traitor as he is."

A gray cast painted over Lahvja's olive skin.

"Nimhea!" Ara put herself between the princess and the summoner. "That's enough."

Nimhea's eyes blazed, her entire body trembled, and Ara could see her rage was born of sorrow. But no matter its source, it would only do harm here. The princess's features were so contorted with anguish Ara barely recognized her. A sick twist of foreboding took hold of her stomach.

"It's time to go." Ara put her hand on Nimhea's shoulder, trying to tear her from the storm of anger she was lost in. "Help me ready the horses. Teth, finish packing up the camp with Lahvja."

Teth nodded, but looked at Nimhea as if she'd turned into a three-headed ice wyrm. He glanced at Ara with concern. She gave a slight nod to indicate that it was okay to leave her alone with Nimhea.

To Ara's relief, Nimhea didn't resist her gentle push in the direction of the horses. She glanced back and saw Teth talking to Lahvja, who was weeping. Ara bit her lip. It was so much to take in: Eamon's betrayal, Nimhea's misguided rage, Teth's new role. She didn't know how they would face so much change, so suddenly. But they had to.

The horses stirred when Ara and Nimhea approached, snorting and tossing their heads, sensing the volatile moods of the young women. Nimhea went to her mount and put her arms around the horse's neck. She didn't cry but stood there trying to calm herself. Her horse shifted uneasily, but then bent its head to snuffle in Nimhea's hair. Ara stayed nearby, watching the princess closely.

When Nimhea's breath had slowed, Ara asked, "What started that?" She tilted her head toward the camp.

"I came to my senses." Nimhea wore a twisted smile. Her gaze held a challenge that Ara decided not to take up. She would press Nimhea about her treatment of Lahvja, but not now.

The princess shifted her weight and abruptly averted her eyes. "I don't want to tell the Resistance about Eamon. Not yet."

Ara had been so focused on Teth becoming a Loreknight her thoughts hadn't yet considered all the consequences of Eamon's betrayal.

Of course they had to tell the Resistance. Its leaders—Suli, Edram, Xeris, and Ioth—expected and needed to be informed of what has transpired on their journey—both for good and ill. Eamon could compromise everything the Resistance had achieved. He could name key players, share their plans. If he confessed all to the Vokkans, Saetlund's rebels could be rounded up and executed. He also probably knew where the Loresmith quest led next, putting Ara and her friends at risk for capture as well.

But instead of saying all that, Ara asked, "Why not?"

She sensed that Nimhea needed to face what she was feeling. That there were words that must be spoken out loud.

"Because they'll kill him," Nimhea said after a tortured silence. "Even with what he's done—" She groaned and put a hand on her stomach. "I feel sick whenever I think about it."

"So do I," Ara said, reeling from the truth of Nimhea's statement. Of course the Resistance would want Eamon dead after what he'd done. But like Nimhea, Ara couldn't bear the idea of Eamon being hunted down and killed.

"I condemn Eamon's choice," Nimhea told Ara. "But I cannot mark him for death." She paused, then added, "Not yet."

Ara leaned against Cloud, finding reassurance in the gelding's solid form. The punishment for a traitor was always death, but her heart shouted against that fate for Eamon. At the Loresmith Forge she had borne witness to his sorrows and transformed his tears into something wondrous.

"We'll have to discuss it with the others," Ara said. She thought it better not to speak Lahvja's name until Nimhea's anger had more time to settle.

The princess frowned, but said, "I suppose we do."

They finished saddling the horses and returned to the camp.

"The packhorses are ready for whatever you've finished up," Ara said.

"We're nearly there," Teth called out. He sat cross-legged on the ground, fletching his arrows. Lahvja was gathering their rolled tents and buckled packs.

"I think you mean Lahvja's nearly there," Ara replied.

Teth held up an arrow. "Can you blame me?" The rounded feathers at the end of its shaft gleamed, throwing off hues of green and blue within the black.

"I suppose not." Ara crouched beside him.

"You didn't seriously expect me to leave without trying this first?" Teth finished the fletching on the last arrow.

He picked up his bow, notched an arrow, and let it fly to thunk into a stump about one hundred paces away.

"Hmm."

"You sound disappointed," Ara said.

Teth shook his head. "The balance and power of the bow is the best I've ever used. And the speed of the arrow is uncanny, but I thought the stump would, you know, disintegrate or something."

Laughing, Ara said, "What do you have against the stump?"

He made an impatient sound. "It just doesn't seem very magical."

"Keep shooting," Ara told him.

After he loosed two more arrows, Teth sighed. "Still no magic. The bow is exceptional, though."

"Keep shooting," Ara repeated.

Frowning at her, Teth obliged. The fourth arrow. The fifth. All clustered in a tight grouping in the center of the stump.

"Again," Ara said.

"I've used all my arrows," Teth countered.

"Have you?"

Puzzled, Teth reached for the quiver. His eyes widened when his fingers brushed the fletching of another arrow.

"How?"

He pulled the quiver over his shoulder and stared at it. Five arrows remained inside. He looked at Ara, brow furrowed with suspicion, then slipped the quiver back in place. He began to shoot again.

Soon there were ten arrows in the stump. Then fifteen.

"Gods," Teth whispered.

"The tears never stop flowing." Ara's throat tightened. She crossed her arms over her chest and looked away.

How could you, Eamon?

Teth was silent. He lowered his bow and reached for Ara's hand. She held it in a light clasp, feeling the dual connections between them. Teth to Ara, the embers that smoldered between them, and Loresmith to Loreknight, a profound bond that Ara had hardly begun to understand.

Would it be too much? When the next Loreknight was chosen, this bond would no longer be for the two of them only. Eventually, they would be eleven: ten Loreknights, one Loresmith. Ara couldn't imagine what she would feel when linked to ten companions. She worried it would overwhelm her spirit, leaving no room for the connection she had with Teth.

"Hey!" Teth broke through her tense thoughts. "What about all my magic arrows in the stump? Anybody could come along and steal them."

"Now you think thievery is a problem." Nimhea walked up to them. "What's this about magic arrows?"

"When your arrows hit a target, they become mundane," Ara told him quickly. "Should someone come across that stump, they would find ordinary arrows. And evidence that someone really hated that stump."

She'd been so wrapped up in the situation with Eamon that she'd neglected to tell Nimhea what had transpired at the Loresmith Forge.

"There's other news," Ara said.

Nimhea lifted her eyebrows.

"Teth is the first new Loreknight."

"What?" Nimhea's voice was like the crack of a whip.

Ara caught Lahvja watching them, then the summoner returned

to lugging their packs to the horses. Ara sensed that she knew exactly what was happening as well as what Teth had become.

Nimhea's eyes fixed on Teth's bow, then moved to the slim quiver at his back. She blanched, then reddened, and began to shake her head.

"*No.*" Nimhea was looking at the ground, as if telling the world it was wrong. "He's a—he can't—he doesn't—"

"I'm going to help Lahvja before you start forming full insults." Teth hurried away.

Nimhea lifted her gaze; her eyes bored into Ara. "Tell me it isn't true."

Ara expected to meet renewed anger in the princess's eyes, but instead encountered uncertainty tinged with something that resembled grief.

"I can't." Ara hadn't anticipated Nimhea's reaction. "The gods name Loreknights, and Eni chose Teth."

"Does he even want to be a Loreknight?" Nimhea asked slowly.

"He accepted Eni's decision," Ara told her. "But he's still getting used to the idea. We both are."

Nimhea opened her mouth to say something else, then snapped her jaw shut and went to the horses without a word.

When they had all mounted, Ara held her hand up. "Before we go, we need to decide how to handle Eamon's . . . departure. Nimhea would prefer we wait to tell the rebels until we know more."

"If we tell them, they'll have him killed," Nimhea said in a flat voice.

Teth frowned. "I can't argue with that, but you're forgetting something." He turned to Lahvja. "You said Eamon was going to his masters."

Lahvja was careful not to look at Nimhea when she answered. "I can't be completely certain, but I believe he'll be taken to the Temple of Vokk. There lies the heart of the wizards' power in Saetlund, where they work their blood magics and torment the innocent who resist Vokk's control."

"And therein lies the reason you can't hide this from Suli and the others," Teth said. "The Resistance has an agent operating inside the imperial ranks. As soon as word spreads that Prince Eamon is in Five Rivers, the agent will pass that information to the rebels."

Nimhea sucked in a hard breath. "Then Eamon is dead."

"Don't kill Eamon yet," Teth said sharply. "He's alive until he isn't, and if we decide we want to keep it that way, then let's focus on that."

Blinking rapidly, Nimhea asked, "How?"

"Your best bet is the Below, specifically Lucket, because of my personal ties to him. We need to contact him as quickly as possible; time isn't our friend," he continued. "I guarantee he'll know where Eamon is before the rebels' agent, and if we get word to him first, we'll win his favor for keeping him ahead in the game. He might be able to influence the rebels' decisions."

"This is not a game," Nimhea growled. Her horse pranced nervously.

"In the Below everything is a game, especially life and death," he told her in a flat tone. "Lucket can smooth things over for us with Suli."

"I agree with Teth," Ara said. "Lucket is our best option."

"Any objections?" Teth asked.

Nimhea and Lahvja stayed quiet.

"Good." He put his heels to Dust. "Let's get to Marik."

3

'll go into town and make contact with the Below," Teth said. "Marik is a large enough town that the Below will have runners. It should be no more than a day or two before Lucket gets our message."

Ara nodded, but her jaw clenched. There was no way of knowing if that would be fast enough. The possibility that Eamon might already have given the Vokkans sufficient information to find the Resistance as well as hunt down his former companions put a terrible strain on her spirit. She needed something else to focus on.

"While you're gone, we'll figure out where we're going next," Ara said decisively. "Eamon may already know what that destination is. Whether he does or not, we have to do everything we can to get there first."

They'd taken refuge in a loft above abandoned stables set on the outskirts of Marik. Moldering behind a working farm that boasted newer, pristine stables, their ramshackle hiding place was just outside of the town proper. Hay and must suffused the air.

Teth smiled wistfully. "I'd be delighted if it turned out to be Marik and we didn't have to go anywhere."

Lahvja leveled a gaze at Teth that made him laugh nervously.

"Sorry. Bad joke." He cleared his throat. "Any special requests when I go for provisions?"

"I need a few things," Lahvja told him. "I'll make a list."

She rummaged for a quill and ink in her pack.

Teth's brow furrowed. "I can only carry so much."

"Nothing I need is large or heavy," Lahvja said as she scribbled.

Ignoring the conversation, Nimhea examined the space, unpacked her bedroll, and found a place for it in a far corner of the loft. Ara noticed when Lahvja's jaw tightened.

Ara eyed Nimhea, noticing again the telltale flashes of red and gold at the roots of Nimhea's darkened hair grew more obvious each day.

With a wave at the princess's head, Ara said, "We need to cover that up again."

Teth nodded. "I'll get dye with the other provisions. Keeping our identities secret is more important than ever. Imperial patrols will no doubt be actively searching for us now that Eamon is in the capital."

"Wonderful," Nimhea muttered, wincing at the mention of her brother's name.

"I'll try to do a better job with your hair this time," Ara promised, hoping to distract Nimhea from thoughts of Eamon.

Handing her list to Teth, Lahvja said to Ara, "Let me do it. Vijerians dye their hair frequently. I have practice."

Relieved at the offer, Ara grinned. "I'd be delighted for you to take over."

"If Teth provides the basic dye I can add herbs that will make it look more natural and more flattering," Lahvja added.

Nimhea threw her the barest of glances. "The way Teth and Ara did it is fine. Don't bother."

Crestfallen, Lahvja began, "But—"

"And I'd prefer Ara dye my hair," Nimhea finished.

"Very well." Lahvja's lips set in a thin line.

Up to this point, the summoner had been distressed by Nimhea's behavior, but Ara could see frustration and a hint of anger at the corners of Lahvja's eyes. As for herself, Ara was about fed up with Nimhea's attitude. It was time to decide what she was going to do about it.

Teth coughed to break up the awkward silence. "I'll try not to be gone too long."

After Teth departed, Ara guessed ten words passed among the three women in the loft. Nimhea descended to the stables, supposedly to spend time with her horse. Lahvja took the scroll Eamon had left and began to read it. Left to her own devices, Ara attempted a nap with mixed results. Her body and mind ached with exhaustion, but thoughts intruded every time she began to drift away.

Abandoning her bedroll, Ara climbed down from the loft and headed outside. When she passed the horses, she glimpsed Nimhea curled up in the back of her mount's stall, fast asleep. Or at least she appeared to be.

She gets to sleep, but I don't? How unfair.

For a moment Ara wished Nimhea's horse would poop on the princess's head. She quickly took back the wish, knowing that a head covered in manure would only make Nimhea's mood worse.

Still, the image in Ara's mind was hilarious, and she had to cover her mouth until she got outside and could let laughter burst from her chest.

It was a fine day, and the fresh air revived her. She didn't roam far. The stables were surrounded by what might have been gardens but had been reclaimed by native plants and wildflowers. Ara closed her eyes and lifted her face to the sun. Bees buzzed in the meadow, and songbirds trilled their springtime melodies. Opening her eyes, Ara sat down, then lay back to gaze at the blue sky.

Sunlight warmed her skin, and a soft breeze that carried a tang of ocean salt bent the tall grasses.

Is the weather always this heavenly in Marik?

Rill's Pass had beautiful summer days, but they were scarce, and even the loveliest weather in the Fjeri Highlands didn't compare with this silken air flowing over her skin, carrying the perfume of unknown flowers.

A butterfly alighted on her bent knee, took off and danced a little jig in the air, then landed again.

Ara laughed at the butterfly's antics.

It took off, performed its dance again, and landed on her other knee.

She tilted her head, watching the creature with growing suspicion.

Eni? It could be. Eni can appear anywhere, in any form. Doubtless, they're still keeping an eye on us.

As she watched, the butterfly flitted back and forth, trading one knee for the other.

Aren't they?

Despite the possibility that the little being could be Eni, Ara couldn't bring herself to speak the god's name out loud. She knew that if it was the god, Eni would acknowledge her when directly addressed. They were too polite not to.

But she didn't want to take the chance that her visitor was not a deity, but simply a curious butterfly. She needed to believe that a greater being followed her steps. Even if she faltered, the knowledge that some-one was there, watching over her, brought much-needed reassurance. Especially now that Eamon was gone.

Ara had been trying not to think about it, but now that she was alone with nothing and no one to distract her thoughts, doubts that threatened to become panic slipped through the cracks in her courage.

Where do we go from here? How will we find our way?

The quest to become Loresmith, to face trials set by the gods, had always been daunting. Now the Vokkans would know what she was attempting and would doubtless do everything in their power to stop her. Ara didn't want to despair, but neither could she imagine how she could outrun or outwit Vokk's wizards and the empire's soldiers. She had faith in her companions, but they were only four young people.

Before Lahvja had joined their party, Eamon had been their link to the realm of myth and the lives of the gods. Ara still tied his breadth and depth of knowledge to the purpose of their journey . . . and of her fate. As a summoner, Lahvja was an intercessor between the gods and the human world, but she couldn't—or wouldn't—teach them in the ways that Eamon had. She hadn't devoted her life to the study of the Loresmith and Loreknights. He'd been gone less than a day, and Ara already missed his chatter and the random bits of erudition that peppered his conversations. But those small quirks she'd come to enjoy were nothing compared to the shattering reality that Eamon had known what she had to do and why. Without him, Ara felt like she'd lost the rope that would guide her through the blizzard of this quest. She had to lead the others, but Eamon had been the driving force behind their journey, his reasoning the map they'd followed.

That blow was terrible enough in itself, but the burden of his betrayal ran much deeper.

Ara and her friends had yet to talk about Eamon's departure in anything but practical terms. Shock was the main reason behind that fact, but if left long enough it could become a silence that hardened around them like clay in a kiln, sealing their emotions in a place they would sour and fester.

She couldn't shake memories of Eamon. His earnestness and sweet demeanor. Ara had believed Eamon, of all her companions, was the most committed to completing the Loresmith trials. She needed to put together the puzzle of his betrayal, to find some kind of reason behind it. The idea of condemning him without question, without any hope that, however twisted, his intentions might have been good, felt wrong.

But there was so much danger in what he'd done. Yes, he'd left them a scroll, which indicated he still wanted them to succeed. Yet, what if this seemingly helpful decision was another layer of subterfuge, put in place to lead them into some sort of Vokkan trap?

Nothing was certain. She had so many questions and conflicting emotions. She knew they all did.

Ara lifted up on her forearms and blew out a sigh. The rush of air sent the butterfly sailing off her knee. It fluttered frantically, beating its wings harder as if scolding her for creating the sudden windstorm.

"I'm sorry, friend," Ara said.

The butterfly circled her head one more time, then flew away for good.

She returned to the loft not knowing if she'd spoken to an insect or a god.

Teth returned with good news—he'd made contact with the Below's agents in Marik, and a message was on its way to Lucket. He also brought an abundance of provisions, including a freshly cleaned and trussed duck and a basketful of fruits Ara didn't recognize. The fruit gleamed like jewels—rubies, amethysts, citrines; they were round, oval, star-shaped, corkscrews. Some had smooth skin, others were rough, and a few even had spikes. Ara examined each one, marveling at their strangeness, wanting to taste them all.

As if he'd read her mind, Teth said, "If you eat them all, you'll have a very unhappy stomach."

"I know," Ara replied, but silently decided eating a small piece of each fruit would be all right.

Lahvja had taken a break from her studies to forage for greens and herbs. She came back to camp with her own basket and ordered Teth to clean out a partially tumbled-down chimney so she could use it as an oven. While he went to work, Lahvja rubbed the duck with oil and stuffed it with herbs and sliced bits of red and purple fruit.

After banking the fire in the chimney, Lahvja laid the duck on a stone slab to roast. She joined Teth and Ara at the small campfire Teth had built outside the loft and settled in to clean the greens that would accompany the duck.

Nimhea leaned against the doorframe of the stables, watching them.

"Come sit, Nimhea," Ara called to her. "It's time for us to talk."

The princess came without hesitation, assuming that their conversation would be about something Lahvja had found in Ofrit's scroll. And they would talk about that—at first.

When Nimhea was sitting next to Teth, Ara gestured for Lahvja to begin.

"I have good news and bad news," the summoner told them.

"Always start with the bad," Teth said. "It's a rule to live by."

Lahvja nodded. "The scroll is mostly gibberish."

Ara's stomach dropped. "Are you sure?"

She didn't want to insult Lahvja by suggesting Eamon could have understood the text when the summoner couldn't, but that was Ara's first thought. The second was that perhaps Eamon left the scroll because it was worthless to them.

"I've read it every which way," Lahvja said. "The scroll isn't written in an obscure language; the words are common tongue. Reading it isn't the problem. The content, however, is sheer madness. I've only found ramblings of a demented mind, even with the most generous of readings."

Ara considered that, chasing the spark of an idea. "It follows, though, in a way."

"How so?"

"In Ofrit's Cavern, Ofrit said to Eni, 'And they call me the mad one.' Isn't Ofrit reputed to have a tendency toward madness?"

"Yes," Lahvja answered. "But I don't know how that helps us determine where to go."

"What's the good news?" Teth asked.

"I'm not sure that it's good," Lahvja said. "But it's the only thing I've found."

Ara leaned forward. "What did you find?"

"Words and phrases that are repeated in the scroll," Lahvja said. "They don't make sense, but they appear often enough that I noticed."

She pulled a scrap of paper from her dress pocket.

"Keep in mind these aren't consecutive; they're scattered within the gibberish." She began to read from the paper. "'Seek the spiral. The spiral leads to darkness. Mad in the dark. Spiraling, spiraling. Down into the dark madness. The mad spiral goes down. Deep in the dark.'"

When she stopped reading, they sat in silence.

After giving a brief shake of his head, Teth muttered, "*That's* the good news?"

"I'm afraid so."

They went quiet again. Though she was frustrated, Ara let the words roll through her mind. She turned them over, examining them, searching for the key to their meaning.

Nimhea spoke up. "Ara, didn't Eni mention seeking something when we were in Ofrit's Cavern? I can't remember exactly what."

The question resonated with Ara. "That's . . . yes."

She closed her eyes, calling up the memory.

Ara, Nimhea, and Eamon had stood before Ofrit and Eni, who along with Ofrit's scrolls offered obtuse directions about the future of the Loresmith's quest.

"Eni said something like 'Seek out places,' and something else about mysteries in the dark."

"Okay," Teth said. "Dark places. That might be relevant." He cleared his throat. "Lahvja, I'm not trying to pry into your spiritual secrets . . ."

Lahvja drew herself up as if daring Teth to continue.

He dared. "You've known a lot about the gods and this quest up until now. You even knew Eamon might leave. Don't you have any sense of where we're supposed to go next?"

"No." Her shoulders slumped. "I believe the gods offered me their secrets as a means to join you and assist you, but now they've hidden themselves from me. I'm as lost as you are."

"You're not holding out on us?" Teth asked carefully.

Lahvja's violet eyes flashed. "Ask me that again."

"No." Teth scooted back from the fire, putting more distance between himself and the summoner. "I don't think I will."

"You know I don't need to physically reach you to have you in my grasp," she said in a deadly quiet voice.

"That's just mean."

She raised an eyebrow at him, then turned her gaze to Ara. "Did the gods say anything else?"

Ara kicked herself for not paying closer attention. Who doesn't give their full attention to gods? But the encounter with Ofrit and Eni felt like a dream. Her memory was gauzy and kept slipping out of her grasp.

"Hidden places," she blurted. "Ofrit mentioned hidden places where the gods' weaknesses dwell."

"Interesting." Teth scratched his chin. "Didn't know gods could have weaknesses."

"Hidden places. Spirals in the dark," Lahvja murmured. "The gods' weaknesses. I admit I did not expect any god to admit flaws."

Teth frowned. "We really haven't gotten anywhere."

"We're looking for a dark spiral that's hidden," Ara mused. "Ofrit gave us the scrolls—"

"Too bad Eamon took the translated page," Teth said.

Nimhea stiffened, and Teth winced.

"I'm sorry, Nimhea," he said. "I didn't mean—"

"Just drop it," Nimhea replied.

Ara frowned, wanting to press this subject, but she didn't want to lose the thread she was pulling at about Ofrit.

"Because the scrolls came from Ofrit, from his apothecary," she said slowly. "It must be his weakness we're facing."

"That follows," Nimhea said.

Lahvja nodded.

"Works for me," Teth said. "But what does it mean?"

"We sought Ofrit at his holy site," Ara said. "The hidden places must also be holy."

"Ofrit has another sacred place," Lahvja murmured.

"Not just Ofrit." Ara met her gaze. "All the gods do. And we have to find them."

Teth's brow furrowed. "How's that?"

"In order to become Loresmith, I must prove my worth to the gods," Ara told him. "They set trials that I have to overcome. I completed Ofrit's trial, and afterward Eni brought me to the Loresmith Forge. I think if I succeed in another trial I can visit the Loresmith Forge again."

Nimhea's eyes widened. "And smith another weapon for a Loreknight . . . the second Loreknight."

Ara nodded. "That's what I hope."

Hope flared in Nimhea's gaze. "The Resistance can build an army to challenge the Vokkans, but we'll never match them in numbers . . ."

"But if the stories of the Loreknights are true," Ara continued for the princess, "the difference in numbers won't matter."

Clearing his throat, Teth said, "I hate to stomp on dreams of glory, but I'm a Loreknight, and I don't think endless arrows will keep an army from stampeding me while I shoot."

"First of all, you won't be alone," Ara replied. "Second, in the tales, it was never individual Loreknights who triumphed over enemies. They fought together; united, they were a force beyond imagining."

"And I like a good story as much as anyone." Teth sounded apologetic. "But there were Loreknights in King Dentroth's court. They didn't stop the Vokkan conquest. From what I've been told, they were an embarrassment on the battlefield."

"Those were not true Loreknights," Lahvja interjected gently. "They were stooges of the king. Pretty courtiers chosen for political and personal reasons. The true method of selecting Loreknights, those who were champions of the gods, was abandoned long ago. When the kings and queens of Saetlund turned away from the gods to pursue their own gains, the power of the Loreknights was lost."

Teth suddenly grinned. "So I am the first real Loreknight in . . . centuries?"

After eyeing him warily, Lahvja said, "Yes."

"Well, isn't that a fine thing." Teth leaned back, resting on his elbows. "You're welcome."

Ara snorted and rolled her eyes. "There's another reason for finding the next trial quickly: we need another Loreknight to knock the gloat off Teth's face."

Teth waggled his eyebrows at her. "You know you can't resist my gloat."

Ara replied by throwing an orange at him.

"We should go to Vijeri," Nimhea broke in, throwing an annoyed glance at Teth. "Ofrit was first worshipped by Daefritians and Vijerians. His cavern is in Daefrit. My guess is the hidden place is in Vijeri." More softly, she added, "I only know that because of Eamon."

Whatever mirth had sparked among them faded at the mention of their lost companion.

Lahvja reached a hand toward the princess, but let it drop when Nimhea glared at her.

"We should take a ship," Teth said quickly, his eyes darting from Nimhea to Lahvja. "There's only one road to Jyn, and it's clogged with traders and patrols, but the empire has gotten lax about inspecting the harbor. Captains spread bribes around, and the city guards are happy to take them."

Lahvja grimaced. "The horses won't take well to a sea voyage."

"I know," Teth replied. "But it's a short trip, and if the weather holds, it shouldn't be too stressful for them."

Her mouth turned down with disapproval, but she stayed quiet.

"We'll go tonight," Teth told them. "I'll take you to the docks. I know the watering holes merchant captains frequent. I can buy us passage and a night aboard the ship. If we stay belowdecks until we're out of port, no one will know we're aboard."

Ara smiled. "I like this plan."

"That means the world to me," Teth said solemnly, then broke into a grin.

She punched his arm, laughing. He caught her eyes with his. Her heart fluttered, but she quickly looked away, afraid to indulge in a personal moment amid this crisis.

"Since that's settled," Ara said, "we should talk about Eamon. Not about the practicalities of his leaving us, but about the risks we now face and the loss we all feel."

She might as well have grown a horn in the middle of her forehead for the sudden silence and looks she got.

"I'll just say," she pressed on, "I miss Eamon. I'm afraid for him and of what he's done and could still do, and I'm worried about us without him."

Nimhea stood up. "Stop."

"Nimhea," Ara said, standing up to face the princess. "We have to talk about this. Eamon was our friend, your brother; ignoring what happened is ridiculous."

Nimhea's jaw clenched. "I can't. I won't."

Tears glossed over her eyes, threatening to spill onto her cheeks.

Lahvja scrambled up and started toward Nimhea.

Nimhea thrust her hand out. "Stop!"

"Let me—" Lahvja took another step, her own voice on the verge of breaking.

"Don't you dare!" Nimhea spoke in a harsh whisper. "Don't you dare."

Devastated, Lahvja swiped a tear from her cheek and left to check on the roasting duck.

Ara tried once more. "Would it be easier to talk about Eamon without Lahvja here?"

"Can we just leave it?" Nimhea sounded exhausted.

Ara nodded, but added, "For now."

"Fine," the princess snapped. "And tonight you're going to dye my hair."

4

ra strode the deck of the *Mermaid's Lament* on sea legs she'd never known she had. Anticipating her first time sailing, she'd worried every pitch and roll of the ship would turn her green and send her racing for the rails. Instead, her heart soared when the wind tore through her hair and salt spray crashed onto the deck. She'd never felt more alive.

The *Mermaid's Lament*'s captain and crew were Vijerian, giving Lahvja and Teth the chance to pick up gossip from the sailors and dig around for any clues to the location of Ofrit's hidden place. The second night at sea, they shared their reports with Ara and Nimhea while the four of them rested in hammocks that swung with the movement of the ship.

Lahvja rolled onto her side. "I had to ask several people before I got an answer—most swore and walked away—but a few mentioned a place known as the Tangle."

"That's the same name I got," Teth added. "Though no one wanted to say anything more about it. The name alone made them curse or say a swift prayer to the gods."

"That's comforting," Nimhea muttered. She lay on her back, staring at the ceiling.

"They have good reason to fear such a place," he replied. "Who knows what Ofrit's put there? Besides, the empire forbids worship of Saetlund's gods. Anyone who admits knowledge of this Tangle could be dragged off by Vokkan imperial agents."

"Did you have any luck regarding its location?" Ara asked.

Lahvja shrugged. "The depths of the jungle. That answer was consistent."

"You must have a more trustworthy face." Teth chuckled. "No one would tell me where it is."

"The depths of the jungle." Nimhea half growled. "Not exactly helpful when Vijeri is *all* jungle."

"It's not all depths," Lahvja countered. "Ofrit has to mean the innermost reaches. They're almost inaccessible. The few villages there don't welcome outsiders, but they would know the secrets of the jungle."

Nimhea gave her a cold stare, then turned to gaze at the ceiling.

Ara sighed. "And how will we convince them to share these secrets?"

Vijerians had drawn back from the rest of Saetlund after the conquest, using the terrain of their province as a natural barrier to the Vokkan armies. The empire attempted a march into the jungles, clearcutting a huge swath from TriBridge south, which became known as the Gash. They stopped just short of Mer, then abandoned the project, having decided the cost and labor required to build roads throughout the province was too much. Dismissing the villages as worthless in the eyes of the emperor, the Vokkans excused their failure by claiming their capture of the only major city in the province meant the entire province had been subdued. The Vijerians knew better, and Lahvja had told them that Vijeri played a key role in supporting the Resistance with supplies of weapons and other necessities.

"I hope the fact that I'm Vijerian and Teth is half Vijerian will work in our favor," Lahvja answered. "Or that because we're seeking a holy site, they'll know we are no friends of the empire. But you're right to be concerned. We'll have to go to Mer. It's the only village in the interior that regularly receives outsiders."

"Then we go to Mer," Nimhea said without deigning to look at them. "Now someone shutter that lantern."

Ara woke the next morning knowing she would not let the day pass without confronting Nimhea. The princess had a right to anger and grief, but her behavior threatened to fray the bonds of their group and undermine their quest. Though Ara was awake, the quiet, shallow breaths of her companions let her know they were still sleeping. She rolled carefully out of her hammock and felt her way across the cabin to the door.

On the ship's deck, the bright sun of late morning greeted her, and she realized how tired they must all have been to sleep so long, cocooned in the darkness belowdecks. All of them except Nimhea, who stood at the rail gazing out at the Southern Sea.

"How long have you been up?" Ara asked, joining the princess.

Nimhea glanced at her. "Why do you care?"

"Because you're giving me an answer like that," Ara replied, watching sea swells lift the ship then recede.

The princess's only response was a huff of breath. She pushed off the rail and began to walk away.

"You are not leaving." Ara grabbed Nimhea's arms, turning the princess to face her. "We are going to talk about Eamon—even if I have to throw both of us into the sea to make it happen."

Nimhea shook her off. "That's ridiculous."

When Ara continued to hold her with a flat stare, Nimhea made a disgusted sound.

"Fine. We can talk."

"Tell me how you are," Ara said quietly. "How you *really* are."

"How am I supposed to be?" Nimhea shot back. Then she looked away, seeking something, anything, to focus on other than Ara, her eyes finally settling on a group of seagulls that circled the mainmast. The birds' shrill cries punctuated the tension between the two women.

"Stop it," Ara told her, fighting to regain Nimhea's attention. "I am not your enemy."

Nimhea was quiet a long time. Tears began to slip from the corners of her eyes. She swiped at them angrily, then laughed. It was an ugly sound.

"I'm being punished, aren't I." Nimhea made it a statement rather than a question.

"Punished by who?" Ara asked, startled by the harshness of Nimhea's tone.

Looking abashed, Nimhea wrapped her arms around herself and rocked back on her heels. "By the gods."

"You think Eamon leaving was the gods punishing you."

"No," Nimhea replied. "My failure was Eamon leaving. Don't you see? Eamon was my test. I was supposed to save him. He's the person closest to me in the world, and I was blind to his suffering. If I'd been the sister I should have been, Eamon never would have entangled himself with the wizards."

After considering that, Ara said, "I don't think the gods are doling out punishments. Even if what you're saying is true, it would mean the gods aren't only punishing you, but Eamon as well."

"But . . ." Nimhea pressed her lips together.

Ara gestured for the princess to continue.

"I should have been the first Loreknight!" The words burst out of

Nimhea. "Teth is a thief. A thief! Yes, I like him, but a Loreknight? It was supposed to be me. How else can I know that I'm meant to seek the throne?"

"You're seeking the throne because you're the heir," Ara said gently. "You want to be Saetlund's queen. A good queen." She paused, then said, "Loreknights serve the kings and queens of Saetlund, but I don't know if a monarch has ever also been a Loreknight."

Nimhea's face fell.

"You never considered that, did you?" Ara felt for the princess.

In truth, until that moment Ara hadn't considered it either. The only reason Eni's choice made sense was because of Teth's personal allegiance to the god, but if she'd had to guess who the first Loreknight would be, she would have named Nimhea.

"I just . . ." Nimhea's voice was shaky. "The idea of the Loreknights, the kingdom's champions. I'm a warrior. What could be more of an honor?"

"You would rather be a Loreknight than queen?" Ara asked, deeply curious about how Nimhea would answer.

"I always thought I could be both."

They both fell silent and turned back toward the sea.

"Eamon's leaving wasn't the work of the gods," Ara said at last. "Eamon alone is responsible."

Nimhea grimaced. "I don't know how to accept that my twin brother is evil. That sounds like a line out of an overwrought players' drama."

With a soft laugh, Ara said, "It does."

She leaned over the railing, watching the waves swell and recede beneath the ship. "I don't think Eamon is evil. He made a poor choice for reasons that I don't think we can fully grasp. That doesn't mean he's inherently wicked."

Nimhea rested her hip against the rail and folded her arms. "I wish I could believe that."

"You can," Ara told her. "You're choosing not to."

"Why would I do that?" Nimhea's eyes clouded with anger. "I hate feeling this way."

Ara turned to face the princess. "Because it's easier."

"Believing my brother is evil is easier?" Nimhea scoffed.

Ara pressed on. "Think about it, Nimhea. If Eamon were evil you could write him off forever, disown him, arrest him, send him into exile without any doubt you'd done the right thing."

She paused, making sure Nimhea hadn't already dismissed what she was saying out of hand. The princess's expression had gone from angry to irritated, and she held Ara's gaze with hawk-sharp eyes.

"But if Eamon is a good person, as I believe he is," Ara continued, "all of this gets much more complicated. We're forced to face the whys of his betrayal. He made a choice we think is awful, maybe beyond forgiveness. We have to know what drove him to make that choice."

A tear slipped down Nimhea's cheek. "You really think he's not wicked?"

"I don't think he wanted to betray us," Ara said, taking her hand. "I believe he must have thought he had to."

"How can you be so certain?" Nimhea shook her head. "Why aren't you angry? Eamon's the one who dragged you into this."

"Eamon set me on the path to finding my true self," Ara replied. "I'm the Loresmith, and my purpose is to seek out the gods who will name the Loreknights. I don't have time to be angry."

Nimhea pulled her hand free. "You're making me feel like a child."

"Good," Ara said. "Because you're acting like one."

The princess lurched back as if Ara had shoved her, then she stared at Ara in silence for a long moment.

At last she let out a brittle laugh. "Gods, I have been, haven't I?"

"A bit," Ara answered.

"You don't sweeten your words at all."

Ara's lips formed a thin smile. "Not when it comes to matters like this. I can't afford to. None of us can."

"So what do I do?"

"You focus on the task at hand, like I've been trying to do," Ara told her, then added, "And you start being nicer to Lahvja."

Nimhea swallowed and looked away. "That's hard."

"You didn't seem to think so before Eamon left."

"But that's why he left," Nimhea lashed out. "I was so caught up in Lahvja that I ignored my brother to the point that he left us." Shaking her head, Nimhea finished, "I won't be distracted again."

"Fine," Ara said. "Don't be distracted. That doesn't give you permission to be cruel to someone who cares about you."

Nimhea nodded slowly.

Teth emerged from belowdecks. He stretched and blinked against the bright light. Walking over to them, he called, "Did I miss anything?"

The first shout came before Ara could answer.

"Land ho!" The first sailor's cry was followed by others. Ara, Nimhea, and Teth ran to the ship's bow. In the distance was a tiny wall of green so bright it appeared to be glowing.

"The Serpent Coast," Ara murmured. "I never thought I'd see it."

Nimhea gave her a sidelong glance. "You must be doing a lot of things you never thought these days."

"Was that a joke, Princess?" Teth asked, his eyebrows going up.

With a shrug, Nimhea answered, "It have might been."

Despite the protection of oiled canvas cloaks, the travelers arrived at the village soaked to the bone. Raindrops were far sneakier than Ara had imagined. They crept inside the tiniest gaps between fabric and flesh and took advantage of movement however slight, a shift in the saddle, a shrugging of shoulders, the turning of one's head, to bypass the barriers set against it. Beneath the heavy cloak, Ara's sodden clothes had pasted themselves to her body. Her skin felt slimy. She was miserable and wondered if the others were faring any better. They'd given up speaking shortly after the rain began, as the torrent drowned any attempts at conversation.

The road widened very slightly to reveal the village. One moment there had been a narrow trail barely discernible among branches and vines of the dense jungle, the next a settlement appeared as though emerald curtains had been drawn back. Its buildings balanced on stilts, and the dwellings themselves were camouflaged within the tree canopy. Steep railed ladders stretched from the ground to offer entrance, and bridges linked the buildings to one another; an entire community floated above their heads.

Ara glanced around the spaces beneath the elevated walkways. She spotted gated platforms linked to hoists that could be used by anyone for whom the narrow ladders weren't feasible or to raise heavy goods, but she couldn't imagine getting the horses onto the lifts. Fortunately, underneath one of the largest buildings squatted a long, broad structure that appeared to be stables. She nudged Cloud with her heels and led the group on a zigzagging path to negotiate the myriad stilts.

The stable keeper was a spindly man with hair that fell down his back in an orange-and-black plait. Teth haggled over the price, while Ara blinked up through the rain at the tavern.

Lahvja came to stand beside her.

"Have you visited this village?" Ara asked.

Lahvja shook her head. "I was born in TriBridge and spent my childhood there."

She paused, turning a half circle to regard the community above. "The interior of Vijeri is a mystery—even to the rest of the province."

Though she felt a stir of unease, knowing they would have to traverse country unknown even to the province's inhabitants, Ara found reassurance in the fact that there would be no more likely place to find Ofrit's hidden site.

Looking at Ara, Lahvja continued, "The jungle makes travel difficult and frustrates many who imagine they'd like to build here. But as you can see, those who live among the vines and trees make an art of it."

Lahvja pointed to the ladder. Up close, Ara saw that its rails were carved with figures that looked like a language, but not any she recognized. She ran her fingers over the symbols, tracing their shapes.

"What is it?"

"Poems," Lahvja answered. "In Old Vijerian."

"People still speak Old Vijerian?" Ara asked with surprise. The old languages of the province had faded long ago, or so she'd thought.

Lahvja laughed. "Speak and write. Vijerians take pride in keeping the language alive. With few outsiders venturing into the depths of the province, people living in the interior speak it more often than the common language."

"I had no idea," Ara said.

"You aren't meant to know," Lahvja told her. "It's one of the things we Vijerians keep to ourselves."

Ara peered at the railing. "Can you read some to me?"

Smiling, Lahvja read:

> *Deep, deep*
> *strange, my love falls*
> *into me*
> *for an infinite*
> *moment.*

Something in Ara stirred at the words. She looked back to the stables, searching for Teth. He caught her staring and raised a teasing eyebrow. Ara turned away, a flush creeping up her neck. At the swift movement, the vine hanging beside Ara shifted.

A head appeared.

The snake, its skin the same jade hue as the vines and leaves surrounding it, stared at her. Its tongue flicked out, tasting the air mere inches from her face.

Ara didn't know whether to scream or giggle madly. The snake's mouth curved up, making it appear that the creature was smiling at her. She stood frozen, not even daring to breathe.

A soft cooing sound came from behind her, and Lahvja's hands stretched toward the snake. "Oh, aren't you darling."

Ara still couldn't bring herself to move. To her horror, it was the snake that began to slide forward. Closer. Closer to her face. Its tongue continued to flicker in and out. Then its head was resting on Lahvja's palm.

"I'm delighted to meet you," Lahvja told the snake. It slid over Lahvja's skin, circling her wrist, making its way up her arm.

Ara watched its body stretch from the trees. It was so long. So terribly long.

The snake's tail appeared only after the rest of its body hugged Lahvja's right arm and both her shoulders. Ara felt a little sick.

Noting her stricken expression, Lahvja laughed gently. "You needn't fear this one. She's a friend, and I'm sure she's well known around the village."

It took Ara a moment to find her voice. "I didn't know snakes could be friends."

"Excellent friends." Lahvja beamed at her, then the snake. "They eat disease-carrying vermin, and they gift us with ingredients key to the work of Vijerian apothecarists."

Still mortified, Ara asked, "Aren't you at all afraid?"

"I have nothing to fear." She tickled the snake's throat. "Most snakes aren't venomous, and their bites rare. If you're bitten by a snake, it means you've done something wrong."

"How do you know what snakes are dangerous?" Ara wasn't ready to give random snakes the benefit of the doubt.

Lahvja considered her question. "If you see red, yellow, or purple skin, or any combination thereof—stay far away."

"Are they all so big?" Ara pointed to Lahvja's snake friend.

Lahvja's laughter did not put Ara at ease.

"This one is hardly big," the summoner said, making Ara groan inwardly. "There are massive snakes in the jungle, but the largest serpents are shy and don't trouble themselves with people."

Ara made herself speak the question that jumped into her mind. "Are any of the big ones dangerous?"

"The only serpent rumored to be man-eating is the amethyst python," Lahvja replied. "And it's deep in the jungle, far from any settlements."

"Deep in the jungle," Ara repeated. "You mean where we're going."

Lahvja opened her mouth to answer then stopped herself, brow furrowing. "Ah. Yes, I see how that's troubling. Quite troubling, actually."

Ara swallowed the hard lump in her throat.

"If it helps," Lahvja continued, "it's believed there are very few amethyst pythons in existence. There isn't enough sizable prey to sustain a large population."

At *sizable prey* Ara had stopped listening.

"Gah!" Teth's exclamation announced his arrival.

He jumped back from Lahvja. His cry made Ara jump, too.

"Look," Lahvja scolded. "Now you've made her irritable."

Somehow the snake's stare did appear cross.

Teth gaped at Lahvja. "You let that thing climb on you voluntarily?"

"Of course." Lahvja stroked the serpent's throat.

Teth made a strangled sound.

Lahvja frowned at him. "Teth, I'm beginning to doubt your Vijerian roots."

Nimhea appeared behind Teth. "What's all the yelling about—oh . . ."

Her eyes widened when she saw the snake entwined with the summoner.

"That's incredible," she said.

Teth and Ara exchanged a look of disbelief.

"Is it your magic?" Nimhea came closer to Lahvja.

Lahvja shook her head. "Not at all. Would you like to meet her?"

Taking in a small breath of wonder, Nimhea nodded.

"Lift your hand, move slowly," Lahvja told the princess. "Let her take your scent."

Nimhea smiled as the snake's tongue flicked out, and then the snake bumped its blunt nose against her fingers.

"She likes you," Lahvja said.

Clearing his throat, Teth interjected. "I'm going to take the packs to the inn. I'll just . . . be there."

He scampered up the ladder, forgetting the packs altogether.

Ara took one more look at the snake and the two women it had ensorcelled, then hurried after him.

5

he way ArchWizard Zenar moved reminded Eamon of snakes: sinuous, elegant, and potentially deadly. When he looked at the prince, even his smile was serpentine.

"It's quite the surprise, seeing you here."

Eamon bowed deeply, trying to keep his fear hidden. "I know, ArchWizard. My deepest apologies for breaking from the plan we'd agreed on. I'm honored to make your acquaintance in person at last."

Zenar's mouth quirked in acknowledgment of the greeting.

"You're a clever young man, Eamon." He walked around Eamon in a slow circle. "Surely you have reasons for leaving your companions."

"I assure you, I do." Words rushed out of Eamon. "I bore witness to impossible things, and I retrieved an item. Something unbelievable; I had to bring it to you immediately."

Zenar tilted his head. "You've piqued my interest. Come, let's have a drink and relax. You must be tired from your long journey."

He ushered Eamon to a divan wrapped in gold silk. Grateful, Eamon sat. He marked himself fortunate, as he hadn't been beaten or threatened since his arrival, but he knew he was nowhere near safe. Zenar's every movement, gesture was made with care that seemed orchestrated, as though Eamon was meant to watch some sort of drama unfold. Only he was a major player in this performance who had no idea how to fulfill his role.

The ArchWizard went to a cabinet and withdrew two silver chalices and a crystal decanter. He brought these items to the side table next to the divan. Eamon peered at the substance in the decanter. This was something more than wine. Its color was an unnatural red, too bright and far too opaque for fermented grape juice. The ArchWizard poured himself a cup of the same liquid, surprising Eamon.

Lifting his cup, Zenar said, "To the unexpected."

They drank.

Zenar sank into a high-backed leather chair opposite the divan and took another sip from his chalice. Eamon felt obliged to do the same. The liquid burned on his tongue and had a sour aftertaste. Warmth in his mouth spread into his throat and through his neck, making his skin hot. His head tingled in a not unpleasant way, though the tingling occasionally felt like an itch.

Trying to keep a grasp on himself, Eamon attempted to analyze the sensations that intensified with each passing moment. The tingling overtook his entire head, making it feel as though his skull was expanding.

He encountered his own mind and marveled at its vastness. At the same time, he became incredibly focused. He took in the minutiae of everything. The grains of wood, the threads in the carpet. He followed the path of a single drop of water down the wall on the opposite side of the room. So beautiful. All the tiny bits that made the world. Gratitude for being witness to it surged through him. And he was desperate to talk about everything he felt.

He hadn't noticed that amid his reverie Prince Zenar had drawn a tiny vial of blue liquid and tipped it into his own chalice. The wine in the ArchWizard's cup turned to a translucent purple.

"How do you feel, Eamon?" Zenar asked.

"Extraordinary." A quiet but firm voice in Eamon's mind urged caution, reminding him of the strange red drink he'd consumed. And yet he could barely keep himself from blurting every thought that jumped into his mind. He wanted to talk. He was desperate to talk.

"Good." Zenar leaned back in his chair. "Now tell me all the things that happened to you."

Eamon had hoped to tell the ArchWizard part of the story but not reveal all, holding certain details back that might shield his sister and his friends. But words streamed out of his mouth like a river driven by an inexorable current. The colors and contours of the room distracted him and made it difficult to pay attention to what he was saying, much less control the conversation.

He told Zenar everything about the Loresmith. Beginning with his and Nimhea's abduction of Ara in Rill's Pass, Eamon took the ArchWizard through their journey from the Fjeri Highlands to Ofrit's Cavern. Zenar listened with impatience, having little interest in the appearance of a lowly thief or their time in Silverstag—he'd already known about the arrangements to meet with Resistance leaders—hurrying Eamon through the mundane progress of their travels to linger on Lahvja's appearance and defeat of the wizards' hounds.

"You shouldn't have sent them," Eamon said, surprised by his own audacity.

"I beg your pardon?"

"The hounds were a mistake," Eamon continued; anger crept into his words. Just as he couldn't stop himself from confessing everything, neither could he hide his feelings. "It served no purpose other than to terrorize us, and it brought Lahvja to us. When she joined us, all my plans began to fall apart. She knew too much of magic, of the gods. She threatened to displace me."

She did displace me. Eamon ground his teeth.

Zenar regarded him curiously. "You don't like this summoner."

"It's not about liking or not liking," Eamon said in a huff, ignoring that it was only half true. "I was the source of lore and arcane knowledge until she arrived with her mystical abilities. She communed with the gods, where I recited what I'd read in books. And Nimhea was infatuated with her."

"Indeed?" Zenar smiled slowly. "That could prove useful."

Eamon bit his tongue. He hadn't meant to bring Nimhea's budding romance into the conversation. He didn't begrudge his sister's feelings, but he couldn't stand that she'd fallen for someone who represented everything Eamon wanted to be but had been denied. Lahvja was, well, full of vitality. And she had power. Real power. She embodied all the reasons Eamon had made his deal with the Vokkans.

With her arrival, Eamon's dread that his role would be rendered obsolete had grown day by day. Feelings of inadequacy had plagued him for as long as he could remember. Friends of the Dentroth dynasty who'd harbored them in the Ethrian Isles after the conquest had made it clear that Princess Nimhea was the twin who mattered. Eamon was no more than a hanger-on.

His life had been that of a recluse until the day that two of their friends approached him, speaking in whispers of a dire warning that his sister's path led to her doom. Of a Vokkan prince who wanted to help the twins. Then they'd said the words that gave Eamon the purpose he'd longed for: *Only you can save her.*

That day set Eamon upon a new path. A path that had led him to this place.

Continuing his tale, Eamon recalled joining the caravan and its plodding pace across the Daefritian grasslands and the horrible night of the raid.

"Did you send the soldiers, too?" Eamon shot an accusing look at Zenar.

Zenar returned his gaze calmly. "I'm afraid I don't know what you're speaking of."

Not able to discern if the ArchWizard spoke the truth, Eamon said, "A conscription squadron raided our caravan. We were almost captured."

"How resourceful your friends must be to have evaded the soldiers," Zenar said thoughtfully. "Imperial recruiters are reputedly dogged in their work."

Eamon still waited for an answer.

With a sigh, Zenar told him, "That was army business. I have nothing to doing with the army; that's my brother's realm."

After considering Zenar's words, Eamon decided he wasn't trying to deceive him. It didn't make him feel any better.

Eamon explained their arrival at the Bone Forest and Ofrit's Trials, briefly wondering if the ArchWizards would send his followers to the place. No wizard would make it past the judgment of the butcher crows, but Eamon suspected Zenar would send them anyway. The ArchWizard was particularly interested in the path through Ofrit's Labyrinth and the Bridge Between Worlds that had transported Eamon, Nimhea, and Ara from Ofrit's Cavern to his apothecary.

Eamon had just begun to describe what transpired in that place when Zenar jumped to his feet.

"Impossible!"

The ArchWizard's shout stunned Eamon into silence.

"You're lying." Zenar began to pace, his face reddened to resemble the liquid in Eamon's chalice. The contrast to his usual pallor was shocking and frightening.

"I'm not," Eamon answered quickly. He couldn't have lied if his life depended on it, which it probably did. But he sensed that Zenar's knowing Eamon spoke the truth was what had so disturbed the ArchWizard.

Zenar sucked in a breath through clenched, bared teeth. "You encountered a god. Ofrit himself."

"Ofrit and Eni spoke to us," Eamon said quietly.

"Eni." The god's name was a snarl in Zenar's throat.

Eamon swallowed hard. "Both gods, the Alchemist and the Traveler, were there."

Zenar stared at Eamon for an uncomfortably long time; then he went to a cabinet and withdrew a vial of honey-like liquid, pouring a measure into his chalice. The ArchWizard downed the cup's entire contents in one swallow.

When he returned to the chair beside Eamon, Zenar's pupils were dilated and he was noticeably calmer.

"What, pray, did these gods do in your presence?" he asked.

When he reached the point where Ofrit gifted him the scrolls, Zenar's eyes went wide.

"You have these scrolls?"

Eamon pointed at the satchel lying on the floor between them. Zenar picked it up, opening it carefully. He withdrew Ofrit's scroll, cradling it in his hands.

"May he be sated," Zenar murmured.

Eamon didn't understand the meaning of the phrase, but it sounded like the ArchWizard was pleading for forgiveness.

"The scroll is why I came to you," Eamon hurried to say. "I knew you needed to have it. I couldn't leave it with that summoner."

Nodding slowly, the ArchWizard said, "Perhaps you made the right decision after all. Where is the other?"

Eamon swallowed the sudden lump in his throat. "I left it."

"Why?" The word came out deadly quiet.

Knowing he might be about to condemn himself, Eamon answered, "They need to find the site of the next trial. Without one of the scrolls, they'd have no chance."

Zenar's jaw twitched. "You helped them. And then came to me."

Eamon's unwelcome temper flared again. "You need Ara to succeed. You want the power of the Loresmith. She won't have it without completing the trials."

Zenar trapped Eamon with a hard gaze. It was a long time before the ArchWizard spoke again.

"Yes," he murmured. "But to you I pose this question: Does it serve me best to let your young friend continue on her quest unimpeded or to intervene?"

He rose. When Eamon moved to do the same, Zenar laid a hand on his shoulder, pressing him back onto the divan.

"Rest here. I'll have food sent to you while I make arrangements for your stay."

He went to the door, pausing to say, "I'll be interested in your answer to my question."

Zenar left the room, taking the scroll with him. Eamon watched him go, knowing that no matter the man's words, the only answer the ArchWizard was interested in was his own.

6

fter settling into their rooms—Ara and Nimhea in one, Teth and Lahvja the other—and changing out of their drenched clothes, they sought dinner. The tavern was attached to the inn, a round building with a high-peaked roof that the rain sluiced off in torrents. The covered walkway saved them from another soaking.

The inn had been clean and sufficient. The tavern was the balm to days riding in the rain. Chandeliers hung from the high ceiling. Instead of burning candles, they held glass globes filled with a substance that glowed golden as sunlight. The beams supporting the ceiling were decorated with Vijerian script. Cheery fires burned in small, tidy hearths. Low, round tables studded half the room, where cushions upholstered in silk made fine substitutes for chairs. Rich savory scents and spices floated in the air.

Ara's stomach didn't growl so much as roar. Soggy food held little appeal, and she hadn't eaten since breakfast.

They found a table and settled onto the cushions.

"Let me order," Lahvja said. "They'll have Vijerian specialties that I think you'll enjoy."

Teth gave her a wide smile. "If it's anything like your cooking, I'll eat it."

"I like how Teth thinks," Ara said.

Nimhea remained silent.

Lahvja waited an extra beat to allow for Nimhea's reply. When none came, she went to the long bar that separated the kitchen from its patrons. A few minutes later, she returned bearing a silver platter with four tiny cups and a decanter. Lahvja placed a cup in front of each of them, then carefully poured measures of a bright red liquid from the decanter.

Joining them at the table, Lahvja gestured to her cup. "This is *fali*; it's a mixture of local fruits and a Vijerian spirit called *ro*."

Ara lifted the cup to her lips and drank. The *fali* was at first pleasantly sweet and cool, but a moment later, fire kissed her belly and her head began to hum.

"Well now." Teth set his cup down. "That's quite the concoction."

Lahvja smiled. "It would be unwise to have another before we've eaten."

Nimhea took the decanter and refilled her cup with slow deliberation. She downed the *fali* in one gulp and refilled her cup.

"Save some for the rest of us." Teth grabbed the decanter and refilled his glass, but didn't drink it.

He passed the decanter to Lahvja so she could refill her cup and Ara's.

Nimhea scowled. "We can order more."

"Only if you don't plan on getting out of bed tomorrow," Lahvja told her.

"I can hold my own."

Lahvja covered Nimhea's hand with her own. "But you don't have to."

Nimhea met Lahvja's gentle gaze, hesitating for a moment before she drew her hand away. Ara noticed. It was a tiny thing, but still, it was something.

The food arrived, preventing the exchange from progressing

further. Ara's eyes widened as dish after dish was set on the table. Stews, skewers of meat, vegetables, and even fruit—most of the latter two she didn't recognize. There was a soup that smelled slightly of lemon and another where chunks of fish floated in a delicate broth. Braided rolls and flatbreads accompanied the meal. Sweet cakes scented with herbs were presented for dessert.

"I may have been too enthusiastic when ordering." Lahvja blushed, but she was beaming. "But I haven't been in Vijeri for such a long time. I couldn't resist."

Ara knew they'd never eat it all, though at the moment her grumbling stomach assured her she could do that very thing on her own. Her mouth watered.

Lahvja named all the dishes for them, gave warnings about those that lit a fire on your tongue.

"The other purpose of the *fali*," she said, "is that it will cool your mouth if any dish is too hot. But be careful not to drink too much. The breads will also counter the heat."

They dove into the feast. No one attempted to start a conversation. For the time being, food was all that mattered to them. Each dish was surprising and scrumptious; some flavors Ara could identify, while others were completely unfamiliar. All melded perfectly. Heady scents filled her head, and a menagerie of flavors danced on her tongue—so much so that she could have sworn a spell had been cast upon her. In that dreamy state, she picked up a slim, curving vegetable that reminded her of the skinny yellow beans that grew on stringy vines in Fjeri, dipped it in an herbed cream sauce, and took a bite . . .

"Ara?" Lahvja's voice came from very far away. "Ara, can you hear me? I've ordered you a drink made of fruit and yogurt. I don't think *fali* will be enough after what you just ate. For now, try to breathe and be still."

Ara opened her mouth to speak but could only draw a wheezing gasp, suddenly aware of the heat blazing from her face and neck and the sweat beaded on her forehead. Most of all, the roaring furnace inside her mouth.

Nava's mercy, I think I'm dying.

Her burning head felt like it would soon lift off her body and float away.

Teth had come to crouch by her side. His arm slid around her waist, his eyes full of concern. "I'm right here. Lean on me if you need to."

Resting in the curve of his arm, Ara tried to thank him, but her voice refused to come.

Turning to Lahvja, he asked, "Will she be okay?"

"She's fine," Lahvja answered. "Just a bit . . . stunned."

Ara tried to speak again but only succeeded in coughing while tears poured from her eyes.

"I'm sure it will get better soon," Teth said, pressing a brief kiss to her temple.

She managed a nod. A wooden cup was shoved in front of her.

"Drink this," Lahvja said.

Between coughs, Ara managed to get in sips of the sweet and creamy mixture, which quenched the fire in her mouth and throat. Her coughs began to subside and breathing became normal.

Nimhea watched her with an apprehensive gaze.

"Senn's teeth, what happened to her?" the princess asked Lahvja.

Pointing at the half-eaten vegetable Ara had dropped onto the table, Lahvja answered, "You aren't meant to eat that. It's a garnish." She frowned at Ara. "I'm fairly certain I mentioned that when I described the dishes."

Rather than answer, Ara kept drinking the yogurt.

When they'd eaten as much as their bellies would allow, Ara and Teth went to the bar.

"Now that you're recovered," Teth said, sliding a smile at her, "should I describe the expression on your face when you ate that pepper?"

Ara's returning look threw daggers. It only made his smile wider.

"Maybe later then," he teased.

Turning his attention to the tavern keeper, Teth said, "My friend and I are looking for a guide."

The woman's brow furrowed. "To where?"

"A place sacred to Ofrit," Ara told her. "Called the Tangle."

The tavern keeper blanched, taking a step back. "That is a place of death and should not be spoken of."

"I have no choice but to go there," Ara replied, though her heart had skipped a beat.

The other woman gave her a long, assessing look, then said, "Ask, if you must."

She gestured toward the open room.

Ara took a step away from the bar toward the center of the space and cleared her throat.

"Excuse me!" She raised her voice, and in the sudden quiet it seemed deafening. "We are seeking the Tangle. If you know of this place, we'd be grateful for your aid."

Though the room had gone silent, no one bothered to look up. Nor did anyone volunteer information.

Ara bit her lip in frustration, but she could hardly blame the tavern patrons. Who was she to appear in this remote village, demanding forbidden knowledge? The locals would be within their rights to run her out of town.

"That went well," Teth muttered.

"You're not helping." Ara searched the room anxiously, willing someone to glance her way or beckon for her to follow them to some quiet place where their conversation wouldn't be overheard.

Eamon, why aren't you here to tell us where to go? A sudden pang gripped her chest.

Movement in a shadowed spot where the firelight couldn't reach caught her eye.

Someone or something rose.

The shape seemed much too large to be a person. It reminded her of a bear rising from all fours to its full height.

Whatever it was filled the corner of the room from floor to ceiling.

The hulking shadow became a man. A huge man. He came toward them, and Ara could swear she felt the floor tremble with each of his steps. When he drew near, she had to tilt her head up at a steep angle to look at him. She'd never encountered such a tall person. He looked as if he'd been hewn from the trunk of one of Wuldr's mighty oaks.

"You seek the Tangle." His voice was a low rumble. "I know the way."

Ara couldn't place his features; they could almost be called Fjerian, but not quite. He had a pronounced jaw, broad cheekbones, and a face cut in sharp lines. His eyes were ice blue and his hair the color of summer wheat. Most striking were his clothes, or rather, the lack of them. He wore a leather kilt with side slits that revealed his log-like thighs, and a matching harness crisscrossed his broad chest. All the rest was skin baked golden by the sun. Muscles like boulders. Muscles in places Ara didn't realize one could have muscles.

What cobbler crafts boots that big?

And he was shiny. Too shiny. Ara thought it must be a trick of the firelight because his skin glistened as if it had been oiled.

"Who leads you?" The man looked from Ara to Teth.

"I do," Ara answered.

He looked her up and down, but in his gaze she found neither approval nor disapproval.

"Then I speak with you only."

Ara could sense Teth tensing behind her. She made a small gesture, hoping to ease his worry. While the stranger cut an intimidating figure, Ara didn't fear him. As far as she could tell, he wasn't armed, though his body was probably weapon enough. Even so, should anything go awry, her friends were near enough to help.

"How do you know of the Tangle?" Ara asked.

The man smiled broadly. "I have business with one of the gods; it sometimes puts me in the paths of the others."

"What god do you serve?" Ara asked, surprised that he spoke so openly of the gods.

"Wuldr."

The Hunter. Ara considered that, and a smile played on her lips when she observed that this man could have been Wuldr in human form. But Wuldr didn't play those sorts of games. It put her at ease that the stranger had dedicated himself to Fjeri's god. The god of her homeland.

Without prompting, the man said, "You will need a guide. I will take you to the Tangle."

"I appreciate your offer." Ara wished she could take a few steps back so her neck didn't cramp from looking up at him. "Would you mind if we get to know each other a bit more before I accept?"

"Ale," the man said.

"Excuse me?" It wasn't the response Ara had expected.

With a grunt of disapproval, the man addressed Ara as if she was a child. "You are asking for my time. To share in cups is a gesture of respect and the only honorable way to begin a negotiation."

His tone gave Ara the distinct impression that this negotiation had already gotten off to a poor start.

She wasn't familiar with the tradition he'd described. In Fjeri you provided food and drink to visitors in your home, but not to strangers on a first meeting.

Who is this man? Where is he from?

"Then I shall buy you ale," Ara said, not wanting to give further offense. It wasn't as if there were volunteers lining up to show them the way to the Tangle.

The huge man pointed at a table. "There."

He walked to the table and sat down. Ara stared after him in disbelief.

He didn't even tell me his name.

Baffled but intrigued, Ara ordered two ales from the tavern keeper. She would have preferred a different drink but didn't know what kind of insult or provocation it might be if she ordered something else for herself. She carried the ales to the table where the man sat quietly, noting that Teth, Nimhea, and Lahvja were watching anxiously from their own table a few feet away.

The stranger also noticed. "Your friends seem reluctant to leave you. Do they not trust in your ability to negotiate?"

"They trust me." Ara bristled at the question. *It's you they're concerned about.*

Ara set one of the ales in front of him.

He took the cup in his hands, turning it slowly.

"It should be *skirva*," he murmured.

"Did you want something else?" Ara asked. She'd barely heard him, but thought perhaps his negotiation included the sharing of a wide range of cups. She sent a silent plea to Wuldr that it was not. More than two mugs of ale would set her head to spinning.

He shrugged. "Never mind."

Lifting the cup in one hand, he said, "Fair dealing and friendship."

"Fair dealing and friendship." Ara raised her cup in kind. The sentiment was one she could agree with.

"Now we strike our cups on the table twice, exchange cups, and drink." The stranger's voice had saddened. In his eyes she saw a vast loneliness.

His eyes met Ara's. Following his lead, she hit the table twice, timing her strikes with his. They traded cups and drank.

Ara took one gulp and set her cup aside. It didn't make her head swim like *fali*, but the taste was horrid by comparison. The stranger drained his cup with relish.

"Good!" He slammed his cup down. Then he turned a smile on Ara that was so broad and bright she could hardly believe the same person was sitting across from her.

Did that brief ritual make him so happy?

"I am Joar," he continued. "And I will take you to the Tangle."

"My name is Ara."

"Ara." Her name rumbled in his throat. His heavy brow furrowed. "You are a small creature."

"And you're a very large creature," Ara shot back.

"You take offense at my words, but you should not," Joar told her, shaking his head. "The deadliest beasts of the world come in all sizes. In Vijeri, the sting of the waterfall wasp will kill you in moments. Metildi's spider is no bigger than your smallest fingernail, yet its bite will paralyze even the largest of men and render them helpless while they are cocooned by the attacker's thousand nest mates. The ruby viper would barely bracelet your wrist with its gleaming red skin, but if it struck you with its tiny fangs, you would be raving mad two days later with no known remedy to save your mind."

Ara was fairly certain he'd meant this invocation of perils as a compliment, but it only put her on edge about their imminent journey into the jungle's depths. She did not want to be cocooned by a tiny spider's nest mates, and she could barely keep herself from shuddering at the thought.

She'd presumed Joar was much older than herself, but sitting across from him, she could tell he had a young face. His size belied his youth.

"Why would you help us?" Ara asked.

Joar signaled for another ale. "You chase a secret of Ofrit. That means either you are fools or you serve a great purpose. I will always aid those who are in service of the gods."

"And if we're fools?"

"Then you will meet whatever fate Ofrit fashions for you," Joar stated in a flat voice. "And I will know you deserved it."

"Aren't you worried that you'll die with us?"

Joar frowned at her; then a slow smile overtook his face. He laughed as his eyes danced merrily. "No."

Ara stopped herself from shuddering, barely.

"I am also helping you because no one else will," Joar continued, still grinning. "The Vijerians don't like others delving into their mysteries."

"I can hardly blame them," Ara muttered, then said, "I'd like my friends to join us now. Is that acceptable?"

Joar nodded. "Now that we have raised our cups and spoken our words, it is right that I meet my new companions."

She beckoned for Joar to follow her to the table where her friends sat with the remnants of their dinner. Making room for the chair Joar dragged over, they watched him with varying degrees of curiosity and apprehension.

Lahvja spoke first. "We still have plenty of food. Would you like some?"

"I am grateful," Joar told her, and immediately tucked in to the dishes.

He picked up the same pepper that had rendered Ara senseless and, before she could warn him, popped it into his mouth. She waited for heat to overwhelm him, but Joar chewed and swallowed, then continued eating with enthusiasm.

Ara caught Teth's eye and his brow lifted, expressing his own puzzlement at their new companion's seeming imperviousness to the wicked vegetable.

"So you're friendly with Wuldr," Teth said to the huge man. "I can respect that."

Joar spared him a glance, obviously more interested in food than conversation. "You know Wuldr?"

"*Know* would be an exaggeration," Teth replied. "But I've made my home in his forests for quite a while now."

"Hmmm." Joar ate. They sat and watched. He ate until all the food was gone.

Pushing back his chair, he patted his belly and let out a satisfied sigh. Then he stood, his gaze sweeping over the four of them.

"Meet me below the inn at dawn."

He walked away without another word.

"Friendly guy." Teth watched him leave. "Who else is excited to travel with him?" Teth raised his hand while the others sat staring at him.

"Yeah. That's what I thought."

7

hen they returned to the walkway between the tavern and the inn, the rain had become a light mist. Nimhea and Lahvja walked side by side, talking quietly, while Ara and Teth hung back.

Ara was about to offer him a reluctant good night when he took her hand. His touch sent a tendril of warmth curling through her.

"Come with me."

Her breath hitched slightly at his words. They held an invitation and a promise that stirred her to the point of being unsettling. She let him guide her to the ladder. He gestured for her to descend first. With reluctance she let go of his hand and climbed down. He walked between the tall beams supporting the inn and toward the jungle.

"Wait," Ara said. She had no desire to leave the safety of the village for the unknown wilds at night. Joar's description of Metildi's spider and the ruby viper were still fresh in her mind.

"I promise it's safe," Teth told her. "And it's not far."

Teth took her hand again, and her heart skipped. He moved with confidence despite the darkness. She marveled at his silent steps and the sinuous flow of his limbs. The moon was up, lighting the jungle in a manner adequate for thieves but that left Ara wanting a lantern. It was incredible that Teth could find his way so easily. Maybe someday he would teach her how to navigate the shadows. Their sessions training with the Loresmith staff had stalled once they'd reached the Zeverin Gorge. She missed the time they'd been able to spend alone. More than the skills she learned, Ara wanted more stolen moments when they could laugh and trade playfully barbed quips. Heat flooded her limbs as she remembered the way Teth would stand behind her, his strong hands on her hips, adjusting her stance. Those same hands sliding down her arms to her wrists until he changed her grip on Ironbranch.

Now Teth had found another means to steal time for the two of them. Quite the thief.

A minute later, the trees and vines opened up to reveal three pools. Ara's breath caught in her throat. It was beautiful. The water gleamed with reflected moonlight. Iridescent lanterns on tall posts encircled the springs. Their light didn't compete with the moon's bright shine, but they gave off a sharp, herbal scent that Ara couldn't place.

"The tavern keeper told me about these," Teth said quietly. "They're spring-fed, keeping them cool and refreshing."

Cool and *refreshing* were two of the best words Teth could have uttered in this hot, sticky place. Smiling, Ara unbelted her tunic, then paused. With a polite cough and a roguish wink, Teth turned away from her. Her skin prickled with heat as if he hadn't turned away. She imagined what it would be like to have his gaze following her every moment, the revelation of bare skin that she'd offered no other but wanted to give to him. The very thought of it brought white heat low in her body, making her toes curl.

She loosened the plait in her hair with her fingers until it fell in waves over her shoulders; the waves were like satin brushing over her heated skin, making her shiver. She pulled her tunic overhead so she wore only the undershirt that skimmed her thighs, wondering if she should remove it as well.

"Are you okay?" Teth asked, hearing her sigh.

Blushing, Ara stood undecided, half of her wanting to tell him to turn around and see her in this state of undress, to watch his expression as he took her in. The rest of her was uncertain she was ready.

"I'm fine." Deciding she could remove her undershirt later if she desired, she climbed down a bank of smooth, round stones to enter the pool.

As promised, the water flowed over her skin like cool silk. She sank to her shoulders.

"Mmmmmm." It was heavenly. She leaned back, dipping her head into the pool to soak her hair.

"Good?" Teth asked, slowly turning.

"Very." She lifted her head, and water sluiced over her scalp and down her neck.

His gaze found her, and his jaw tightened. Something Ara couldn't recognize passed through his eyes. Then he grabbed the hem of his shirt and pulled it over his head.

It had occurred to her to turn around, offering him the same privacy he'd afforded her, but her eyes refused to leave the sight of his lean torso. Torchlight danced off his bronze skin, shadows finding the contours of his muscles.

The bracing cold of the water no longer held the rising heat of her blood in check.

Teth tossed his shirt aside. Catching her gaze, he looked at her for a long moment, as if considering something. His expression told her nothing.

Then a slow smile curved his lips.

"Would it offend you if I took everything off?" he said casually. "I'd rather not wear my trousers into the pool."

Heat climbed up into Ara's cheeks and down her body. "I don't mind."

When he reached for the button of his trousers Ara quickly turned away, heart hammering against her breastbone. She swam to the center of the pool.

Though she resisted sneaking a glance over her shoulder, her rebellious mind tried to conjure an image of what Teth would look like without any clothes. She shut her eyes as if it would stop the vision and swore under her breath. The feelings rippling through her were wild, beyond her control, thrilling and frightening her.

She heard a quiet splash, and the pool rippled around her. She dared to turn around.

"Ahhhhh." Teth swam toward her, grinning, but stopped a few feet away. "I know I'm supposed to be from here, but I much prefer the weather in Fjeri. Even the winters. I can't take this mucky heat."

"Neither can I," Ara said, relieved that their conversation avoided anything about Teth being naked. She couldn't see his body beneath the waterline, but simply knowing that he'd shed all of his clothes set her heart to racing.

Why would we say anything about him not wearing clothes? She cursed her ridiculous thoughts. *Because it's all you can think about*, her own mind answered. She groaned inwardly.

"And that rain," he continued with a shudder. "I didn't think it could be possible to drown atop a horse, but I believe it now."

Ara's laugh sounded a little too loud to her. Despite her attempts to concentrate on Teth's face, she kept stealing glances at his bare shoulders and the top of his chest where the moonlight made his skin gleam.

How can he be so calm?

"Lahvja seems happy to be here," she said, trying to add something to the conversation despite her inability to concentrate.

She hadn't anticipated how difficult it would be to stop herself from reaching out to Teth. To touch him. Pull him close. To beg him to touch her.

Nava's mercy, what is wrong with me?

"I'm glad Nimhea's eased off on her," he continued in an infuriatingly mild voice. "That was hard to see. I understand why she was angry, but none of this is Lahvja's fault."

"It must be hard for her," Ara replied, unable to keep her gaze from flicking down to the surface of the water where the rest of his body was hidden. "To be caught between her friends and the gods."

"I'm glad it's not my job." He leaned back, looking up at the moon.

The movement revealed his upper torso. Water droplets formed on his chest, rolling down his skin. Ara longed to reach out and touch one, to let her fingers follow its trail over his body. The urge to reach for him was unbearable.

He sighed. "Though I'm not exactly sure what my new job entails. Probably a lot of godly oversight, huh?"

"I couldn't say," Ara murmured.

He sank back into the water. "I know we still have to sort out the rules of a relationship between the Loresmith and one of her knights," he said.

"Yes." *Right now that feels like the most unreasonable thing I've ever heard.*

"But I want to kiss you."

Ara went silent, though her pulse jumped.

Teth swam closer. "What do you think of that?"

"Just one kiss?" *Only one? Not enough. That would never be enough.*

"If it's what you want." His voice was as quiet as the gentle ripples in the water.

Ara didn't want to think about what she should or shouldn't do. But she was here in this moment. With him.

"Yes."

He closed the space between them. She realized he could stand, while the water was still too deep for her to touch the bottom. His arms slid around her waist and drew her against him. She could feel all of him. The hardness of his body pressing into hers. A little gasp escaped as she was suddenly aware of how much he wanted her.

She wanted to wrap her legs around him, but denied herself that desire, sensing that there was a point at which she wouldn't be able to stop herself from doing everything she wanted. And she wanted so much.

He brought up one hand to touch her face. "I'm sorry, but this is all I can think about."

"Don't be sorry," she said, relieved that she wasn't alone in her wanting.

She parted her lips when he bent to kiss her; the touch of his mouth was like velvet. Driven by instinct, she crushed herself against him, hungry for more. Teth groaned. The arm that was holding her tightened. His fingers dug into her hip, rocking her body against his, and Ara gave in to the sensations that took hold of her. Exquisite, silken heat.

Teth's other hand moved from her cheek to her neck. His fingertips trailed over her throat and down, lightly tracing her curves, learning the shape of her, making her gasp against his mouth while he kissed her.

It was heady torture to revel in how much he wanted her, how much she wanted him.

Why can't I have this? I need this. I need him.

She'd started to believe that one kiss could last forever, and she wanted it to, but Teth gently pulled away. He rested his forehead against hers. His breath came hard and fast. She could feel his heart racing; its pace matched her own.

"Teth." Her voice was shaky. "I want—"

She didn't know how to finish the sentence. She didn't want them to stop. She needed to know what came next, what the relentless urges building within her meant, where they would lead. She wanted *him*— no matter the consequences. She was about to tell him so when he spoke first.

"Ara." Teth's voice tightened, as did his hold on her, but the quality of his touch had changed. "Stay still."

"Why?" She stiffened in his arms, aware of a new, unwelcome tension in his body.

I did something wrong. I went too far.

Wrenching disappointment and a sickening humiliation swept over her.

"Snake," Teth whispered.

"What?" That was not anything Ara had expected him to say.

She'd been clinging to him with abandon. Now her fingers gripped his shoulders in panic as the implications of that single word became clear.

Her voice went shrill. "In the water?"

"No, they're on the bank, watching us," Teth whispered. "But thanks for putting that image in my head."

"They?" Ara had a hard time being still. She wanted to thrash her way out of the pool, while at the same time she felt paralyzed. She wrapped her arms tighter around him.

"The first one apparently invited a few friends."

Ara shut her eyes tight, swallowing hard. "What color are they?"

Please not red. Please not yellow.

"It's hard to tell in this light," he said. "But they look like the snake Lahvja made friends with."

Making herself take a deep breath, Ara told him, "They probably aren't venomous. What do you think they want?"

"I think they want a bath." Teth hadn't relaxed. His arms were like iron bands around her waist. "I'd rather not share."

Nava's mercy. "Please. No sharing."

"I'm going to pull you to the opposite bank," he said quietly. "Please tell me if any snakes show up there."

Ara's gaze swept the side of the pool she faced. "No snakes."

"Good."

She kept her eyes locked on the empty bank as Teth drew her away from the center of the pool.

"Oh gods." His fingers dug into her sides.

They had almost reached the bank. "What?"

"Just don't look back. When your feet hit the edge of the pool, climb out and go for the village. I'll be right behind you."

"They're in the water, aren't they?"

He didn't answer.

Ara had the urge to bite Teth's shoulder so she wouldn't scream, but that didn't seem very fair. She held her breath instead. Her heel brushed solid ground. Without hesitating, she scrambled up the bank and stumbled along the path. Dripping water, she ran, no longer caring that it was hard to see. She didn't stop until she reached the ladder below the inn.

When she turned, Teth was there as he'd promised. He'd pulled on his trousers and had a rumpled pile under his arms.

"I got our clothes."

They stared at each other for several moments.

Ara began to giggle. Teth chuckled. She let herself fall against him. While Teth held her, they laughed until they were crying.

"That wasn't exactly how I imagined this evening going," Teth said when they'd regained control of their laughter.

Ara swiped tears from her cheeks. "I hope the snakes appreciate what we did for them."

They fell into laughter again.

Eventually their mirth faded, and Ara was suddenly aware of how little she was wearing. Her undershirt was soaked and clung to her skin. Her legs were bare.

Teth had gone still, as if he'd read Ara's mind and paused while sifting through options before he made a choice about what to do next. He held her lightly, and his fingers began to stroke the line from the nape of her neck to the center of her shoulder blades.

Though she'd stopped laughing, her breath continued to be quick, shallow sips of air. Her heart rabbited beneath her ribs. When she'd leaned against him, her elbows had been trapped at her sides and her hands were fists against his collarbone. She flattened her palms against his chest, reveling in the warmth of his skin and the hard lines of his torso.

Teth slipped a finger beneath her chin and tilted her face up. He bent his head and brushed his lips over hers ever so gently. The caress was too brief, a whisper of a kiss, compelling Ara to slide her arms around his neck, wanting him closer, needing a kiss that was longer, deeper. But Teth caught her wrists and moved her hands away. His lips feathered over the spot where her jaw met her earlobe.

"Let me look at you," he whispered. "Please."

The words stole her breath. He was quiet and kept very still until she nodded. Ara drew a shaky breath as he released her wrists and stepped back. Though self-conscious, she wasn't embarrassed, nor did she avert her eyes from his face. She watched Teth as his gaze moved slowly over her, drinking in the sight. His limbs grew taut and his jaw clenched.

In his eyes she saw wonder, tenderness, and, beneath that, smoldering heat. Seeing the stoking fire in his gaze set her own blood alight.

"Teth." She wanted to close the gap between them. She wanted his hands on her.

"Close your eyes." His voice was rough.

She did.

"Lift your arms over your head." The closeness of his voice told her he'd taken a step forward. It was a strange request, but Ara complied.

Her eyelids snapped open when she felt fabric slide over her arms, settle on her shoulders, and cover her thighs. Teth had slipped her tunic over her body, covering her wet undershirt. She felt a stab of disappointment that Teth easily read on her face.

His hand curved around the nape of her neck and he leaned in to kiss her. This kiss spoke to her. His lips lingered on hers and she tasted his desire. A longing that mirrored her own.

Ara wrapped her arms around his waist and closed the small space remaining between them. Her skin felt feverish. She kissed him hungrily. Her body molded to his, but somehow it wasn't close enough.

Teth's hands moved to her shoulders, and he very gently pushed her away.

"We should return to the inn," he said in a strained voice. "And go to bed."

Ara's heart skipped a beat, and she bit her lip. "Together?"

He looked away, making a sound that was something between a growl and a groan. "Senn's teeth."

Forcing himself to meet her questioning gaze, Teth spoke quietly. "I don't think . . . not yet. Not when I know you're worried that it, that we . . . might be violating some ancient rule set down by the gods."

The combined force of relief and regret hit Ara hard. She didn't know what to say. Or what she truly wanted.

"And I have to say," Teth continued, looking chagrined, "I don't want to let Eni down. I never imagined an honor like this could belong to me."

His voice had thickened, and he paused to clear his throat. "I'm a thief. A scoundrel. And I was perfectly happy that way. But now . . . to be a Loreknight . . . it's so much more. I feel a weight of responsibility, a sense of duty I never would have imagined I could feel."

Ara reached out to caress his cheek, a sudden tightness in her chest. "I know . . . I *know*."

She retrieved her trousers from the ground where Teth had dropped them. He turned away to put his shirt on as she wiggled them up her damp legs and hips.

They climbed the ladder and entered the inn, but when they stopped in front of the door to Ara and Nimhea's room, Ara hesitated, frowning.

"Nimhea and Lahvja seemed to be reconciling. What if they ended up in the same room?"

Teth shook his head. "They didn't."

Ara raised a skeptical eyebrow.

"If they had, they would have made sure we knew," he told her. "They'd leave a note or some other sign to make absolutely certain they weren't . . . interrupted."

Shifting her weight from one foot to the other in her sudden discomfiture, she asked, "How can you be sure?"

"Because it's what I would do." There was a dangerous glint in Teth's eye, and his smile made her knees weak.

He pressed two fingers to his mouth and then rested them on her lips. "Good night, Ara."

Teth moved past her to the door to his and Lahvja's room and went inside.

Ara stood outside her room's door for a long while, wondering what she was going to do about the thief who was on the verge of stealing her heart.

8

he cell wasn't the worst of it. The cell Eamon could bear. He wasn't chained. He didn't share the space with rats or other vermin. The cell was spare, but clean. Servants brought meals three times a day that tasted fine, kept his belly full, and didn't play games with his mind. His simple cot verged on comfortable, and his chamber pot was cleaned twice a day.

The "arrangements" Prince Zenar had made for Eamon were tolerable, but his heart was sick over his helpless, humiliating confessions to Zenar. He'd revealed so much. All the ways he'd hoped to protect Nimhea had crumbled the moment he'd drunk the ArchWizard's vile concoction.

The only bright spot in that ordeal hadn't been because of any triumph on Eamon's part. No, Zenar's greed and singular focus when it came to magic and Saetlund's gods caused him to ignore salient facts that would have been to his great advantage to know. He had failed to press Eamon on the details of their time in Silverstag. Most importantly, he'd had no interest in Teth, dismissing the thief out of hand. Because of that, Zenar didn't know about the deal struck between the Below and the Resistance. That vital fact remained a secret. Eamon could only hope that Zenar didn't mull over the conversation and decide to revisit the meeting in Silverstag in a second interrogation.

His cell was located deeper into the Temple of Vokk, partway down a great staircase. When Eamon laid eyes on the steps spiraling into darkness, he knew what true fear was.

He was certain death waited for him at the bottom of that staircase.

But the guards did not march him to the bottom. They followed only a few turns before reaching the cell that Eamon now occupied, and they'd left him. Left him without saying a word in a place that felt like indecision. He was neither welcome in this place nor condemned.

That could have driven him mad, but it didn't.

What broke him were the children.

He could hear them far below. Their cries, whispers, and whimpers floated up like the echoes of ghosts.

At first he'd believed they were ghosts. Whether those ghosts haunted the temple or simply existed in his own mind, Eamon didn't know.

It wasn't until the first line of young ones—some so small they had to be carried—marched past his cell, continuing down the spiral stairs, that he knew they were real. Their hands were shackled, and they were chained to one another. Dirty and disheveled, wearing frightened and bleak expressions, they descended step by step in utter silence. Their cries didn't reach him until later, after the guards had left.

Eamon tried to peer down the spiral, but only darkness stared back up at him.

Down there, he thought, *are the* real *cells.*

But why were the Vokkans taking children? It could be a second, secret Embrace being slowly enacted. Eamon remembered talk of missing children in Silverstag, and the agreement between the Below and the Resistance to try to get to the bottom of why Saetlund's children were disappearing from their homes.

Eamon didn't know why, but now he knew where the children were being taken.

At least they weren't being tortured, as far as he could tell. They cried, but the sounds were those of fear, not pain.

Those far more innocent than he disappeared into the dark, and he was certain an unimaginable horror lurked there.

That became his torment.

9

he rain that plagued them from the coast to Mer gave way to vine-filtered sunlight that crept into Ara and Nimhea's room with the dawn. The air remained heavy and saturated with moisture; when Ara drew breath it swam in her lungs. Damp heat clung to her hair and skin, compelling her to plait her hair in a slender ring around the crown of her skull to keep it from plastering itself on her neck. She abandoned her usual long-sleeved tunic for a sleeveless linen undershirt that she belted at the waist. Instead of leather trousers, she pulled on raw silk tights that served as an extra layer in cold weather. They were opaque enough to be modest and would at least let her skin breathe.

Nimhea made a similar change in her clothing. As they left the room together, Ara noticed that Nimhea's hair color had been improved significantly with the addition of Lahvja's herbs—though Ara had decided to keep to herself the choice to take the summoner's advice when mixing the dye—its hue was now darkest auburn instead of a muddy, grayish brown. From the way Nimhea kept touching her hair, the princess seemed pleased by the improvement.

Teth and Lahvja were waiting for them in the hall. When Ara smiled at Teth, she immediately blushed and silently cursed herself for it, but she couldn't stop the flashes from the previous night that sprung into her mind's eye, making her toes curl.

Senn's teeth, Ara, get control of yourself.

Teth's returning smile was crooked and impish. It did nothing to quell the bubbling warmth beneath Ara's skin simply from being in his presence.

Joar awaited them below the inn, slathering oil on the broad swaths of bare skin he seemed to favor.

He really does oil himself. Ara covered her mouth to hide her giggle and marveled at how vain he must be to do such a thing.

With the sun out, Joar's body shone. He wore the same leather harness and kilt as the night before, and it was even more obvious that he was nothing but blocks and ropes of hard muscle. Only now there was an addition that stifled Ara's laughter and turned her blood icy.

Hanging from a strap on his back was the skull of a butcher crow, but it had been altered. Ara could see steel fittings and leather straps that transformed the bones into a helmet. Attached to the helmet, neck armor flowed down and out, enough to cover his shoulders and upper chest. The armor had been crafted of overlapping scales in shining ebony; it was a material Ara didn't recognize, but that at the same time was somehow familiar.

"Gods." Teth appeared beside her. "That can't be real."

Ara had to swallow a couple of times before she could speak. "I think it is."

"Who wears a butcher crow skull for a helmet?" he muttered.

Teth's skin took on a slight grayish cast as he walked up to Joar.

"You didn't happen to find that lying around in the desert." Teth made a show of examining the skull.

Joar's laugh was close to a roar. "What manner of trophy would that be?"

"A lucky one?" Teth replied.

"You are a strange man." Joar frowned at him. "Only a coward would do what you suggest. I took the skull of a crow that attacked me in the Ghost Cliffs."

"Mmmm." Teth nodded. "How nice for you."

Joar smiled. "It is nice, for it makes a very fine helmet."

To demonstrate, Joar fitted the helmet on his head. "You see?"

Ara's hand flew to her chest, certain her heart had stopped. The giant wearing a butcher crow helmet was a terrible amalgam of beast and man. A monstrosity sent by the gods to punish the wicked. The armor covering his neck and shoulders melded to his body, transforming him into a creature of the air and sea. Otherworldly and terrifying.

Teth hadn't stopped nodding, but he looked like he might be sick.

"Impressive." Nimhea strode forward, admiring Joar's trophy-helmet. "Tell me about the fight."

Joar pulled off the helmet and grinned at Nimhea. At the same moment, Teth snapped out of his daze and grabbed Ara's arm, pulling her out of hearing distance.

"I don't know about this guy."

"Why?" Ara asked.

Teth stared at her.

She spread her hands. "Okay. I get that he's . . . overly enthusiastic about the hunting thing. But the Tangle is a dangerous place. Don't we want to have someone who killed a butcher crow on our side?"

"The obvious answer is 'yes.'" Teth gazed at Joar and Nimhea, who were talking and laughing like old soldiers sharing war stories.

"But—"

"But," he continued, "I don't know anything about him."

Ara shrugged. "It doesn't seem strange to not know about one person in an entire kingdom."

"You don't understand," he told her. "The Below knows about everyone, especially anyone unusual. Joar is someone we would have noticed. We keep far more accurate records of births, marriages, deaths, disappearances than any monarch ever did. We should have a record of Joar, but as far as I know we don't."

"Because you've memorized all the records in the Below."

Teth pointed a finger in Joar's direction. "His record I would know. He's an outlier. There is no one else like him in Saetlund. There's no way the Low Kings haven't tried to hire him."

"Hire him? You mean as an assassin?" Ara asked with apprehension.

"No," Teth replied quickly. "Someone of Joar's . . . stature isn't suited to assassin's work. Assassins should be invisible."

He glanced in Joar's direction and coughed to cover a nervous laugh. "Joar is what we call a bruiser. Bruisers are meant to be a spectacle." His jaw twitched. "I can't stand not knowing who someone is."

"You didn't know who I was," Ara said. "That worked out."

His expression softened. "You've got me there."

The look in his eyes made her wish she could fold herself into his arms and melt against him.

Taking her hand, he blew out an exasperated breath. "I can't help but feel he's someone."

"We need him." Ara settled for squeezing his fingers, which was hardly adequate. "There's no one else to guide us."

In truth, they didn't have time to try to find another guide. Not knowing what information Eamon had given to the Vokkans, any delay in finding Ofrit's hidden site could prove disastrous. Ara didn't know what awaited at the Tangle, but that place held the key to continuing the Loresmith quest.

"I know," Teth said. "But I'm keeping my eye on him."

With a nod, Ara said, "Fair enough."

Teth's suspicion didn't worry Ara. As a thief he was inclined to be wary. But she was surprised that she didn't have more reservations about Joar. She knew little about him. Teth couldn't supply any clues to shed light on Joar's past. She should be more anxious about a stranger not only joining them, but leading them into the depths of a jungle.

Like Teth, Ara sensed something odd about Joar, but unlike her friend, what she felt didn't alarm her. Instead, the feeling irked her, like a familiar tune she couldn't name.

When Lahvja set her packs down beside the others, Joar shook his head.

"You have all brought too much. Get rid of everything but what you need to fight and for sustenance."

Nimhea folded her arms across her chest. "What about our tents, our bedrolls?"

"I have sleeping gear you will use," he replied. "Do not bring your tents."

"But we need our tents," Ara protested. "How will we have protection from the rain?"

Ara imagined trying to sleep while pellets of rain slapped her entire body. It made her want to scream.

"You will have protection," Joar said, though it did little to reassure her.

Teth had pulled a few things from his pack and began stuffing them into a satchel.

"We won't need the packhorses, but I'll get our mounts." Lahvja started to walk away.

"I'll help you," Nimhea offered.

"No horses." Joar stopped them. "Horses are worthless in the deep jungle."

He paused, rubbing his chin. "Except to give you a chance at escape. Many things will stop to eat a fallen horse while you are running away. I would not treat an animal thus, but it is your decision."

Teth stared at Joar, as if trying to decide whether the huge man was serious or making a terrible joke.

"We won't bring the horses," Ara said.

"Hmmm." Joar grunted, assessing their group. "Can all of you fight?" He pointed to Nimhea. "You look like a warrior."

"Good." Nimhea smiled at him. "Because I am."

When his eyes fell on Lahvja, he frowned. "You do not."

"She has other talents that aid us," Nimhea said quickly. Lahvja threw her a grateful smile, blushing a little.

When Nimhea smiled back at her, an open, affectionate smile, Ara's worries about the pair faded away.

"What do you do?" Joar turned to Teth.

Teth said in a flat voice, "I have a magic bow."

"Hmmm." Joar squinted at him. "You want me to think you are jesting, but I think you are not. May I see this bow?"

"Maybe later," Teth answered.

Joar held Teth's gaze a moment and then laughed. Teth didn't join him.

To Ara, Joar said, "I told you last evening that being small can be an asset. Are you an assassin?"

Ara choked on her own breath. *An assassin?! I can't attack anyone, let alone kill them!*

Lahvja and Nimhea burst into laughter, while Teth smirked.

"Ara is like me," Lahvja answered with a smile that wanted to become a laugh. "She has other talents."

"But I'm not an assassin," Ara blurted, having regained her composure.

Joar looked at Ironbranch. "A quarterstaff is more than a walking stick. Were you never taught to fight with it?"

"It's complicated." Ara turned to pull necessities from among her belongings.

Teth came to her defense. "She's skilled with the stave. You needn't worry about her."

Ara gave him a sidelong glance, once again missing the lessons he'd given her.

Apparently satisfied, Joar dropped that line of questioning. Instead, he pressed an oxblood leather waterskin into her hand.

"Spread this on any bare skin," he said. "The rest of you should do the same. The insects are vicious in the deep jungle."

Pulling out the stopper, Ara sniffed, and a bright herbal scent filled her nose. It seemed familiar. She poured a little of the contents into her palm and winced, not because the liquid stung, but because it was the oil she'd seen Joar rubbing on his skin.

Her stomach tightened. *I thought he was glossing his muscles out of sheer vanity, but instead it's protection.*

She should have known better than to pass judgment upon someone she hardly knew.

"The villages heat this oil on posts that ring its boundaries," Joar continued. "It keeps the swarms at bay."

That's how I know the scent, Ara thought, remembering the posts that circled the pools she and Teth had visited. Memories of the night before flooded her, making her hands tremble.

Joar gave her a puzzled look, and Ara rid herself of thoughts of Teth—his hands, his lips, *gods*—as quickly as she could.

"Thanks for this," she told Joar.

Ara hadn't noticed any insects on the ride to the village, but that was probably due to the rain. This oil spared them from buzzing and bites in the village. She wondered just how bad the swarms would be once they were beyond its boundaries.

While Ara applied the oil to her skin, the others went to rearrange their packs.

"Don't forget the ears," Joar told her. "It would be very bad if something crawled inside to lay eggs."

She closed her eyes for a moment, willing those words forever out of her mind.

When they'd finished changing out their supplies, Joar whistled. It was a bright, warbling sound, the perfect imitation of a bird's song. Loud rustling came from the trees to their left, followed by a flash of white fur. Where Joar had been standing alone, a great wolf now sat beside him.

"An ice wolf," Ara breathed.

Larger than the wolves of Fjeri's forests, ice wolves roamed the mountains and coasts of the inhospitable north, elusive and wary of humans. Only the few people who'd glimpsed them could confirm their existence outside of myth. But here an ice wolf sat companionably with Joar, watching them with its silver eyes. Its gaze wasn't threatening, but curious and intelligent.

"By the gods, how is this possible?" Ara asked the huge man.

"A pair of cowardly and cruel trappers baited barbed hooks and put them into the den where her young pups were hidden." Joar's voice thickened with emotion.

Lahvja drew in a quiet gasp of horror, and Ara's stomach twisted at the wickedness of such a snare.

He continued, "The pups had no chance of survival, but the trappers used them to draw out the pack. Fools they were, thinking that even a small pack of ice wolves could be bested by a pair of men."

With a grimace, he said, "The pack returned and found the pups. But even in their rage, they eluded all the snares the trappers had laid for them. They killed the men, ripped them to pieces, and left their bodies in the snow, not eating a single scrap of flesh. Ice wolves would not taint themselves thus. But the mother, who had the most fury, must have reached the trappers first, and was dealt a fatal blow from one of their knives."

Joar paused and looked at the wolf beside him. "I believe only Wuldr's hand stayed the other wolves from killing her as they normally would, preferring swift mercy to a lingering death."

"You found her?" Ara asked. The tale mesmerized her, and her voice was barely more than a whisper.

He nodded. "In a pool of her blood mingling with that of the trappers. I carried her until I found a cave to shelter in. It took many weeks to nurse her back to health. When she was restored, I expected her to seek her pack, but she would not leave me."

The wolf gazed up at him, and he turned to meet her silver eyes. "That was many years ago."

The back of Ara's neck prickled as she tried to take the measure of this man who wore a butcher crow skull for a helmet and had won the loyalty of one of the most elusive creatures in Saetlund.

"That's who you are!" Teth smacked his palm against his forehead.

The wolf bared her teeth at his loud exclamation.

"Easy, easy." Teth lifted his hands and glanced at Joar. "Can you tell her I'm a friend?"

Joar's brow furrowed. "You are not yet a friend. Only an acquaintance."

Groaning, Teth said, "Could you ask her not to do that?"

With a shrug, Joar replied, "She will not harm you unless you attack me. Her teeth only mean she finds you annoying."

"Well, that hurts my feelings." Teth folded his arms over his chest and turned to Ara. "Could you tell her Eni likes me? Maybe that would help."

Ara's glare told him he'd said more than she should.

"Eni?" Joar asked. "What does the annoying one have to do with Eni?"

"Nothing," Teth answered quickly. "It was a joke."

A growl joined the wolf's bared teeth.

"I promise to be less annoying," he said to the wolf.

She stopped growling and lay down, resting her head on her forepaws.

Nimhea looked from the wolf to Teth and jerked her thumb at Joar. "What did you mean you know who he is?"

With a wary glance at the wolf, Teth said to Joar, "You're Koelli, aren't you, one of the people of the Ice Coast."

Ara drew a sharp breath. *That's why I thought I knew the armor.*

Some of Imgar's old stories told of Koelli warriors who wore armor crafted from the near-impenetrable scales of the great sea monsters that lived in far northern waters—farther than Saetlund's fisherfolk dared to sail. It was the sort of armor any blacksmith would give a fortune to lay hands on and search for the secrets of its rare workmanship.

Before Joar could answer, Ara said, "But they're all gone. Only a few stayed through the conquest, and those that did were killed along with the Hawk's rebels."

At the mention of the Hawk, Joar's eyes glittered. "My father returned to the Northern Isles, but my mother remained to fight beside the Hawk. She was a fierce warrior and did not want to return when an enemy marched on the horizon."

To Ara, he said, "I am Koelli. When the Vokkans came, I still toddled on my feet. It would be another three years before I could wield an ax or draw a bow without aid."

An interesting measure of time, Ara thought.

"Your mother?" Lahvja asked quietly.

Joar's voice was solemn. "She died as she wanted, on the field of battle. The other Koelli died alongside her. They sent word to my father to return and take me to the Northern Isles, but he never came."

He sounded neither sad nor angry.

"After the conquest, I was taken in by one of the rebel fighters who survived the Vokkan invasion. He brought me to his village in the forests to the west of Wellseeker's Landing and raised me as his own," he continued.

Ara's heart warmed toward Joar. Wellseeker's Landing was on the eastern edge of the Fjeri Highlands, which meant his homeland was also hers.

"I'm from Rill's Pass!" she exclaimed, then bit her lip, wondering if she'd revealed something she should not have.

Joar smiled at her. "You have a northern look about you."

Ara thought it was probably the endless sweating and blotchiness she suffered in this hot place that gave her away.

"I consider Fjerian highlanders my kin." He clapped her on the shoulder. She had to steady herself against the weight of his arm. "You are my sister."

She couldn't stop her smile. "Thank you."

Lahvja knelt beside the great white wolf. "Does she have a name?"

"Is it 'wolf'?" Nimhea asked with a sideways glance at Teth.

"Why would I call a wolf 'wolf'?" Joar snorted. "All creatures deserve the honor of a name."

Teth grumbled under his breath.

Nimhea burst into laughter. Lahvja tried to hold her laughter in, failed, and threw Teth an apologetic smile.

Ara leaned over and whispered, "I'm sure Fox doesn't mind."

Joar rested his hand on the wolf's head and scratched behind her ears. "Her name is Huntress, for she has dedicated herself to pursuing with me my quest for Wuldr's blessing."

"Why would she do that?" Nimhea asked.

"That same question troubled me," Joar told her. "I thought perhaps it was because I saved her life, and that may be part of the reason, but I am more inclined to believe her service is not to me but to Wuldr. She carries the weight of grief. I wonder if she does not also carry guilt. Wolves do not usually leave their cubs alone. The omega wolf remains behind to guard them. But her pack was small and needed all its hunters to make a kill. Believing the cubs would be safe in their den, she left them. She sojourns with me to make amends for that choice."

Teth raised a skeptical eyebrow. "That's quite a bit of projection— don't you think?"

Huntress growled at him.

"It would be better if you did not talk so much," Joar said.

Grumbling again, Teth fell to the back of the group. The wolf caught Ara's curious gaze. Those silver eyes were shining, as if full of laughter.

10

hether or not it was true, the jungle acted as though it wanted no visitors. Their pace through the dense forest felt glacial. They followed what Ara assumed were game trails, as she, Nimhea, and Eamon had done when they left Rill's Pass, but the paths along which Joar led them were almost invisible. Snaking vines and twisting roots caught at their feet. Branches and broad leaves reached down to block their way. It was too easy to imagine the nightmare it would have been to attempt this trek without a guide.

We would have been lost here forever.

Ara became disoriented. The jungle canopy, in its endless shades of green, hid the sky. She had no sense of direction and a likewise uncomfortable relationship with time. She found it difficult to track the sun's progress through the day. Hunger was the only thing that hinted to her what the hour might be.

As they walked, conversations were stunted. Perhaps it was because of Joar's presence and their decision to keep the full nature of this journey to themselves, or that the narrow path forced them to walk single file, but Ara suspected it had more to do with the way they were captives within a net of trees and vines, or possibly captivated by the myriad sights and sounds all around them. The song of the jungle fascinated Ara. Birds, insects, monkeys, and creatures she could not name poured their calls out ceaselessly. With every trill and whistle, she wondered what creature this or that voice belonged to.

Joar's oil worked as promised, keeping insects at bay, though Ara didn't notice an abundance of them.

She still wasn't certain of the time when Joar stopped walking. He looked up, then turned in a slow circle, keeping his eyes on the forest canopy.

A moment later, he said, "We camp here."

It was earlier in the day—at least Ara thought—than she'd expected to stop and make camp. She took in their surroundings, trying to discover what made this particular spot suitable for camping. The trail was slightly less overgrown, but there was nothing resembling a clearing or a place to set up tents. Not that they had tents.

Joar took off his pack, opened it, and pulled out three tightly rolled bundles of fabric.

"I will show you how we will sleep," he said.

He shook out one of the bundles, which separated into two pieces. He picked up the larger piece, unrolling it along the path. It was leaf-shaped, wide in the middle and narrowing at each end, and longer than Joar if he'd lain beside it.

Leaning down, he found a seam in the middle of the fabric and opened it to show the hollow inside.

"You rest in here," he told them, "like seeds in a pod. Or a caterpillar in a cocoon."

Lahvja crouched beside the pod. "I've heard of this, but never seen it. They're woven from plant fibers, yes?"

Joar nodded. "A weave tight enough to keep water out, but allowing one to breathe. They are very useful."

"What do you have against tents?" Teth asked, half joking.

"Tents take up too much space," Joar answered. "And in heavy rain they flood. These will not."

He picked up the pod and stretched it between two trees, tying it off with ropes so that it was suspended about five feet from the ground.

"So it's basically a covered hammock," Teth commented.

"It is much more useful than a hammock," Joar replied. "Hammocks are for leisure."

"What's wrong with leisure?"

Joar ignored him and continued, "After you climb inside you will need to button the flaps at the end of the pod to close yourself in. If you do not, curious snakes might visit in the night."

"What a pleasant thought," Teth murmured.

"We've had enough of snakes," Ara said to him quietly.

He winked at her. "Isn't that the Twins' truth."

Taking the second piece of fabric, Joar stretched it between four limbs and secured it a foot above the cocoon, creating a barrier between the forest canopy and the sleeping pod.

"You will be protected from rain."

The concept is sound enough, thought Ara, despite the disconcertingly organic appearance of the pods. *And it can't be that different from the way we slept on the ship.*

"I could afford the space for only three," Joar told them as he shook out the other bundles. "You will have to share."

Ara glanced quickly at her companions. There was no missing the sudden tension.

Sharing would be *very* different from the way they'd slept on the ship.

Meeting Teth's eyes, a flurry of emotions coursed through her mind. Hope. Fear. Desire. Trepidation.

It was Nimhea who spoke first. "If Lahvja is amenable, I'll share the sleeping cocoon with her."

Lahvja's eyes widened slightly.

Nimhea blushed, then said quietly, "Only if you like."

Pressing her lips together, Lahvja only hesitated a moment before saying, "Yes."

Nimhea's blushed deepened, and a small smile crept onto her lips. "Good."

"Yes, good." Joar looked at Ara and Teth. "You will share the other cocoon."

Neither Ara nor Teth answered.

Joar frowned at them. "Do you not wish to share? I would offer a place in my cocoon, but I take up too much space for another to sleep there."

"It's fine," Ara told. "We can share."

Her heart was sputtering with joy and panic.

"Then it is settled," Joar said, and continued setting up the other two cocoons.

Teth sidled up to Ara, murmuring, "Are you sure about this?"

His hand rested lightly on the small of her back, sending tendrils of heat through her limbs.

"Do you want to separate Nimhea and Lahvja?" Ara replied, dodging the question while at the same time working to keep her voice from trembling. His fingers began to make small circles at the base of her spine.

Withdrawing his hand, Teth gave a little bow and said, "Whatever my lady wishes."

It was his slow smile that sent a thrilling shiver.

When Joar had finished hanging the cocoons, he said, "There is a task you must complete while I am gone."

"Gone?" Nimhea said with disbelief.

Joar continued, "Build a large fire, large enough for two spits. You will find dry kindling in my pack. The fire will keep predators at bay, and we will need it to roast the meat."

"What meat?" Lahvja asked.

Joar smiled and signaled to Huntress. The wolf bounded into the jungle. "I will return soon."

He melted into the dense green a moment later, though to Ara it seemed impossible that he could disappear so completely and silently, given his size.

The only person who hadn't built a wet-wood fire was Nimhea, which irked the princess no end. She and Ara collected fallen wood while Teth set about constructing two greenwood spits. Lahvja had gone into the jungle in search of medicinal plants that could only be found in Vijeri.

"I don't understand why my Ethrian trainers didn't teach me any survival skills," Nimhea muttered while they gathered deadfall.

Ara was careful to check for crawling things before picking up a log. "I think they must have imagined you living with the rebels, not trekking through the jungle."

Nimhea was silent, then said, "I don't want to admit it, but I understand I was being handed off from one group of protectors to another. Neither my friends on the isles nor the Resistance wanted me to live outside of their bounds."

"That's only because you're important," Ara said. "They want to keep you safe."

Nimhea gave her a sharp look. "I think if I hadn't insisted on being trained as a fighter, they would have been happy to ply me with jewels and silk dresses. That's what their idea of a queen is. I'm pretty sure the only reason they let me have my way is because a girl who can swing a sword might be more inspiring to a conquered people than a pampered princess. But they never wanted me to actually fight. And you saw how the Resistance reacted when I chose to join the Loresmith on her quest instead of remaining with them."

"The kings and queens of Saetlund haven't been warriors for decades," Ara replied with a sigh. "It's fair that the Resistance would have . . . underwhelming expectations of you."

"Underwhelming." Nimhea laughed bitterly, but her eyes were sad. "Do you think anyone believes I can be something other than a figurehead?"

"I do."

Nimhea held Ara's gaze for several moments, as if waiting for her to qualify her answer.

"Thank you," the princess said softly.

"Of course."

As dusk set in, the true value of Joar's body oil revealed itself. While there had only been some insects flying around them during the day, the evening air was alive with buzzing creatures. The drone their masses created was a constant reminder of their presence and their wish to swarm over the bodies of the campers.

"That sound could drive you mad," Ara remarked as she and Teth balanced the deadwood in a ring around the kindling.

He grimaced. "Yes, it could."

Nearby, Lahvja was sorting through the many plants she'd foraged. "Try not to think about it. Or pretend it's music."

"Okay," Teth replied, waiting a beat. Then he said, "I don't like this music."

Lahvja laughed.

"If it makes you feel better, I'm not enjoying the music either," Nimhea said.

She'd been watching Ara and Teth work at building a fire in wet conditions.

"You light the kindling," Ara told the princess. "Then you have to keep feeding it. Eventually the small fire will dry the logs, and they will catch."

"Do you want to try your hand at the next fire?" Teth asked. "I'll oversee your work."

Nimhea gave him an irritated look. "I'll build the second fire. I don't know that I need you to oversee."

"We'll find out." Teth grinned at her.

The princess's first attempt at arranging the deadfall collapsed onto the kindling. She shot a warning glare at Teth before he could say anything. He returned her look with a bland smile.

The second time, Nimhea stacked the wood correctly, and before long two large campfires were burning under the greenwood spits.

Not long after, they heard rustling from the trees. Joar emerged with Huntress at his heels. He had a deer slung over his shoulders, but it was unlike any deer Ara knew. From head to tail it was blanketed in green.

When he laid the deer on the ground, Lahvja eyed the large beast critically. "We don't have the means to preserve the meat. It's a shame that some will go to waste."

Joar gave a dismissive grunt. "There will be nothing left but the hide and head, and the creatures of the jungle will make use of that."

Ara came over to take a closer look. She could see the deer's brown hair peeking through the green in places, but only a few. Curious, she reached out and touched the strange substance. It was springy and slightly damp under her hand.

"Is this moss?" Ara asked Joar.

Joar nodded. "This is a moss deer, common to the jungles of Vijeri. And this type of moss only grows in a moss deer's hair. The moss helps the deer by camouflaging it from hunters, and the deer helps the moss by giving it a place to live. When I learn these secrets of nature, I am comforted. I know that no matter how humanity destroys itself, nature will go on."

"Tell me how that's comforting," said Teth.

"Nature does not seek to hurry its own end, whereas humans always chase their doom," Joar answered. "Though I've kept myself apart from people as much as I could these past years, I hear news from villages of barren fields and empty stores. I've seen the result of humans' slashing and burning—the Gash. And I hear of suffering. People's suffering caused by other people."

He looked down at the glassy-eyed deer. "There is blood and death in nature, but not the greed nor the sadism that thrives in the human heart. I would sooner see the wilderness survive than people."

"But Saetlund wasn't always like this," Nimhea objected. "Before the conquest—"

Joar raised his hand. "It is always easier to lay the blame at someone else's feet. My adoptive father taught me the history of this land. Saetlund was already corrupted and on the same path as the Vokkans; the empire was simply faster."

Nimhea looked away.

"Maybe," Ara said. "But Nimhea is right; before the rule of succession and the dynasty, Saetlund thrived and its people lived in peace as the gods directed."

"That was so long ago it does not matter," Joar said with a heavy sigh.

"For all our sakes, I hope you're wrong," she replied.

She held Joar's gaze for several moments. He was the first to look away.

The deer had already been dressed, and now he knelt beside the beast and began to butcher it. He first carved several choice pieces and tossed them to Huntress, who wagged her tail in thanks. Soon her silver-white muzzle was bloodied, a sight that was more than a little unnerving.

There is blood and death in nature. Joar's words left Ara shaken, but she couldn't believe all humanity was inherently wicked. If what Joar said was true, then the Loresmith quest would be pointless. But the gods themselves had sent her on this journey. Unlike Joar, the gods had not condemned all humanity, and neither would she.

Lahvja came to Joar's side with her satchel of herbs, and the two of them fell into deep discussion about the best ways to season venison. It became evident that Joar relied on foraging local fresh herbs and roots to flavor his meals, and Lahvja was eager to chat about the flora of her homeland and its culinary properties, introducing him to edible plants he wasn't familiar with.

Soon both spits were full of skewered meat, and fat dripped into the burning wood, sizzling and crackling. They took turns rotating the spits and tending the fire.

Ara turned to Joar. "How did you come to believe what you do about people and nature? You said you're on a quest for Wuldr."

"My journey is sacred," Joar told her.

She perked up with interest, wanting to know more, but without giving away too much about her own quest.

"How did this quest come about?" Ara asked.

Joar went silent.

From where he turned a spit, Teth quipped, "I guess you're forbidden to talk about it."

Regarding Teth for a moment, Joar said, "No."

"Then by all means share," Teth said. "Our dinner isn't going to be ready for a while."

"Very well." Joar settled in beside Huntress, who rested her head in his lap. He scratched behind her ears absentmindedly as he spoke.

"On the eve of my tenth birthday I had a dream. I sat before a fire not unlike this one. Wuldr and Senn sat beside me."

Ara shivered, recalling her own dream about Wuldr and his massive hound hunting in the forests of Fjeri.

"Wuldr looked at me," he continued, "and asked two questions: 'What does your heart want most? What does your soul long for?' My reply: 'To serve you and to find my true home.' I loved the Fjerian family who raised me, but my spirit was restless and could not settle.

"Wuldr said, 'The wild and hidden places of this land, those places most feared by mortals, hold the key to your happiness. Your journey will be long and your trials many, but I will be with you in the hunt.

"'When you wake, tell your family what I have said. They are my children and will understand why you must go.'"

He gazed at the flames, lost in memories. "Wuldr was right. My father only asked that I wait until he had forged me an ax for my journey and that I would one day return it to him."

"Your father was a blacksmith," Ara said quietly.

She and Teth exchanged a look. Nimhea had been focused on feeding the fires, but she paused in her work to listen more closely to Joar.

"On the day the ax was finished, I bade my father farewell and went into the mountains," Joar continued.

Startled, Ara said, "You went into the wilderness alone when you were only ten?"

"For Koelli, ten years is a child's coming of age," Joar explained. "I believe that is why Wuldr came to me on that occasion."

She shot a worried look at Teth.

He shrugged. "When I was ten I was already a full-fledged—" He cast a wary glance at Joar before he continued. "Artisan."

Nimhea snorted at his choice of word.

Ignoring her, Teth turned his attention to Joar.

"You started with the mountains? I take it you're not one for easing into a sacred journey. 'Cause you went full bore."

Joar chortled. "That may be true for most people, but the mountains were familiar to me, and I do not balk at snow and cold."

"I take it you had more clothes then." Nimhea smirked from where she crouched beside the fires.

Joar didn't react except to say, "Wherever I have gone, I have worn the clothing most suited to its climes."

Chagrined, Nimhea ducked her head and said, "Fair enough."

"Most Vijerians wear silks that breathe in the heat," Lahvja interjected. "I know none who've adopted your bare-skinned style."

Joar cleared his throat, and Ara spotted a blush washing over his pale cheeks. "I did try to dress as Vijerians do. But the wraps and knots were too frustrating. I gave up."

Lahvja stared at him, waiting for him to say he was jesting. When he failed to, her eyes sparkled with mirth, but she simply nodded and said, "Please continue your story."

"I spent two years in the Mountains of the Twins, learning the patterns of nature and how to survive all its moods. During that time, I met Huntress, and she became my companion. From there I went to the Fjeri Lowlands because to the east are Kelden and Sola, where the wild places have been turned into orchards, farms, and grazing lands. As before, I passed the next two years in the lowland forests. As the time to depart drew close, a fellow traveler crossed my path and asked to share the safety of my campfire. When I agreed and also offered him food and drink, he revealed himself to be a bard and asked to pay for my hospitality with grand tales.

"He spoke and sang of wondrous places hidden in Saetlund and the strange creatures that dwelled therein. When he finished I asked if any of his tales were true. He advised me to seek that answer for myself."

Joar stood up and said to Teth, "Let me take on this task for a while."

"Not going to say no to that offer." Teth grinned. "Turning a spit isn't the thrilling pastime I thought it would be."

"Lahvja, would you like me to trade places with you?" Ara offered.

Lahvja shook her head. "I prefer to stay close to the cooking. The scent of the meat lets me know if it needs more seasoning."

"Nimhea?" Ara asked the princess.

"Thanks, but no," Nimhea answered. "I'm still learning how to keep the fires hot."

Teth sat beside Ara. He took her hand in his, lacing their fingers, and she was filled with a warmth that had nothing to do with the fires.

"Shall I continue?" Joar asked.

"Please," said Ara, wishing she could snuggle into the curve of Teth's arm, but she wasn't yet comfortable with such an open display in front of her companions.

"The bard's tales had been so fascinating, I was eager to hear more," Joar said. "But I slept so deeply he was gone by the time I woke the next morning."

Hearing Joar's story, Ara was convinced his bard had in truth been Eni in disguise. It bore too many similarities to their visit from the old woman in the Fjerian forest for her not to be suspicious. It made her all the more curious about Joar. First Wuldr, then Eni. What designs did the gods have for this hunter?

Teth's grip tightened on her hand. They exchanged a look, and she knew he believed Joar had had a visit from Eni, too.

"When the time came for me to leave Fjeri," Joar continued, "I set my path toward Daefrit and the Ghost Cliffs, a place the bard had sung of. He had described its dread creatures in such a way that they came alive in my mind.

"Despite my urge to rush there, I took my time going south and lingered in the Daefritian grasslands for two years. I knew I must understand all types of wilderness. To favor only those with infamy would not be the way of a true hunter but that of a man of greed seeking trophies and fame."

An unbidden memory of corpses impaled on the thorns of bone-white trees crept into Ara's mind, a cold reminder of the reward such trophy-seekers could expect from the gods.

Joar continued, "The grasslands were kind in their temperate climes, but posed a challenge. Though brimming with game, there is little cover for a large hunter. I had to find ways to conceal myself in order to stalk the herds that are always alert, always expecting an attack. Wild dogs and great cats were my competitors. I struggled to live in peace with them.

"In the dry season I was challenged to exist without fire, for a single errant spark could set the plains alight. The only thing with greater hunger than wildfire is the Devourer himself."

He made a sign over himself, unfamiliar to Ara but what she guessed must be a ward against evil.

"When the next winter approached, I traveled to the Punishing Desert by way of the Ghost Cliffs."

"What did you make of the Bone Forest?" Ara asked.

"The bard bade me stay out of the Bone Forest," Joar replied. "He said to enter that holy place would be to gamble foolishly with my life. Everything he'd told me about the Ghost Cliffs proved to be true, so I contented myself with walking its perimeter."

He gestured to the helmet sitting atop his pack. "Though it was in sight of the Bone Forest that I faced my greatest battle. I stood atop a cliff, gazing upon the bleached trees. Tempting dreams of striding into those woods and besting what lay within crept into my mind. It was then I heard a fierce cry and looked up to see death's shadow about to engulf me. I only escaped by throwing myself off the cliff to a ledge below. The butcher crow pursued. We fought for what must have been minutes but felt like hours. Each time I met its eyes I saw my doom, but also the choice to beat it back. I hoped the crow would tire and abandon the attack, but it became clear that the spirit world waited to claim one of us. In the end, I feigned injury, appearing to collapse, and the bird became too confident in its imminent kill. When it reared back, ready to drive its beak through my chest, I buried a spear in its heart."

Joar lowered his head, breathing out a long sigh.

"You regret killing it?" Teth blurted in disbelief.

"I live and thrive in the deepest wilds of Saetlund to honor Wuldr," Joar told him. "I hunt only to eat and kill only when attacked. I took no pleasure in the demise of such a magnificent creature. Though I am grateful for the protection it gifted me after our battle."

Teth looked at Joar as though the hunter had grown a beak. "You're a little mad, aren't you?"

Joar shrugged, then turned his gaze to the roasting spits. "Is our meal ready? I'm ravenous."

Lahvja examined the cuts of meat turning over the fires. "Soon."

He gave a grunt of disappointment.

"Did you spend two years in the desert as well?" Ara asked.

With a nod, Joar said, "It was the most difficult part of my journey thus far. I am a child of the north, of the cold seas. The desert is a place I still struggle to understand. Its sun put a torch to my skin, its moon stung me with cold. The absence of water was a bane to my spirit. My sustenance came from creatures I'd never considered hunting before. Snakes, lizards, insects. Wuldr made stark my assumptions about game and food. I learned not to despise things simply because they were unfamiliar and that disgust is used as a disguise for ignorance."

"That's true," Lahvja said as she sprinkled additional seasonings onto the meat. "Though I could never eat a snake. Snakes are friends."

Teth shuddered, and Ara smiled at him.

"What was your favorite thing to eat in the desert?" Nimhea asked.

"Bats," Joar answered. "The wings crisp up, and the meat has a good chew." He glanced skyward. "If you'd like, I could net some for us another night. The bats in Vijeri can get very large."

Teth shuddered. "Let's stick with deer."

Joar frowned at the thief, and Teth lifted his hands.

"I admit my ignorance. But can we leave it be for now?"

Ara didn't understand Joar's comment to Lahvja about none of the deer being wasted until he began to eat. And eat. And eat.

Everyone else had finished their dinner long before the hunter swallowed his final bite.

Teth finished licking his fingers, then whispered to Ara, "Do you think if I ate like that I'd get taller?"

"Sorry. That's not how it works," she whispered back.

"A fine meal." Joar slapped his stomach, then let out a loud belch.

"I don't think they heard you back in the village," Nimhea said, then she belched even louder.

Wrinkling her nose, Lahvja said, "When I'm cooking, I expect better manners."

"Apologies to the cook." Nimhea winked at her.

Joar belched again. Huntress growled at him.

"She's on my side." Lahvja reached over to pet the wolf.

Joar gave Huntress an accusing look. "You never objected before."

Huntress replied with an indignant sniff.

A light wind stirred the trees. Huntress sniffed again, while at the same time Joar stood up and took a deep breath.

"We should get into the cocoons," he told them. "It's about to rain."

"How do you know it's about to rain?" Teth asked.

Joar ignored him.

Ara's heart began to beat so hard it seemed impossible that the others couldn't hear it.

You will have to share.

She stole a glance at Teth, who seemed perfectly at ease as he helped Joar quench the fire.

"Do we need to set a watch?" Nimhea asked.

"Huntress will keep watch for us," Joar told her. "You can rest without trepidation."

Nimhea nodded, then took Lahvja's hand, and the two of them walked to one of the sleeping pods. Ara watched Nimhea help Lahvja into the cocoon and wondered if either of them felt the frenzy of emotions that she did. They looked so calm.

"Are you ready?" Teth was at her side.

Ready for what?

"Of course," Ara replied in tight voice.

"Sleep well," Joar bade them.

She tried to smile, but it felt like a grimace.

Teth gave Ara a leg up while she found the opening of the cocoon and then scrambled in. She held the cocoon open while Teth levered himself inside. He buttoned the flaps, and darkness swallowed them.

Clearing his throat, Teth asked, "Do you mind if I sleep with my shirt off? It helps with the heat, and I can use it as a pillow."

"I don't mind," Ara said, knowing she wanted to take her tights off, but she decided to keep that to herself.

What followed was an awkward bumping into each other in the cramped space as Teth took off his shirt while Ara attempted to discreetly peel the tights from her legs. Every movement set the cocoon to swinging.

Ara smoothed her tunic so it covered her to mid-thigh and stretched out on her side, then unbraided her hair, waiting for the cocoon to still. She felt Teth lie down beside her, and the light touch of his breath on her skin let her know he was facing her. She turned toward him and settled on her side.

When the cocoon stopped swinging, they lay in silence. His scent was all around her. Notes of pine and river stones mixing with the lush green of the jungle.

"Ara," Teth said quietly. He reached out, twining his fingers in her hair and gently pulling his hand through the loose waves.

She could hear in his voice the same thing she felt. That it was unbearable to be so close and keep apart. "I know."

They kept still, their breath mingling. Every inch of Ara's body thrummed, aching with the need to be in Teth's arms. It felt like a cruel trick of the universe that only last night, they'd decided it was too soon to share a bed and now here they were, in the smallest space Ara had ever tried to sleep in, let alone share.

Raindrops began to bounce off the canvas stretched above the cocoon. Sporadic at first, the rain grew to a downpour that drummed all around them.

"Joar was right," Ara said.

"Of course he was," Teth grumbled.

Ara listened to the steady rhythm of the rain. "Do you think the rain would hide any sounds we make?"

"I don't—" The sound of giggling followed by a loud shushing cut through the drum of raindrops.

"There's your answer," Teth whispered.

While Ara didn't like the idea of anyone hearing things she liked to imagine doing with Teth, she couldn't take the simmering tension in her body.

She murmured, "What if we're very, very quiet?"

"Is that possible?" he asked, a smile in his voice.

"I'd like to find out," she answered softly. She lifted her hand and rested her fingertips on his cheek.

There was a pause, then Teth spoke with a new roughness in his voice. "I'm game."

"Keep still." Very slowly she traced the shape of his face. She let her fingers trail over his lips and chin, then along his throat. Her hand moved over his bare shoulder and upper back, feeling his lean, taut muscles. Her breath quickened. She brought her hand back to his shoulder and slid her palm down his arms.

When her fingers touched his wrist, Teth caught her hand.

"My turn," he whispered.

"I'm not finished," she objected. "I've barely begun."

"I promise you'll have another chance," he whispered. "But I need to touch you. Let me."

He released her hand, and Ara kept still. He began by mirroring her exploration, touching her face first. He cupped her cheek in his hand, and his thumb traced the shape of her mouth. His fingers ran down her throat, then his fingertips played along her collarbone. He stroked the back of her neck, making her shiver.

Leaving her tunic in place, Teth ran his hand down the side of her body until he reached her upper thigh. There he slipped his hand beneath the hem of her tunic. He went very still when his fingers discovered her bare skin. Her lips parted, and a tiny gasp escaped. Not wanting Teth to think the sound was one of alarm, she moved closer.

Teth carefully slid his hand up to her hip, stopping there. His palm curved around the rise of her body, and his thumb stroked her hip bone. She trembled with each new sensation.

"More?" he whispered.

She could barely get the word out. "Yes."

His fingers drifted from her hip to her abdomen, caressing gently. He moved his hand over her navel to her sternum. When he began to explore further, Ara had to bite her lip to stay silent. His touch was exquisite agony.

She reached for him, her lips touched his, and he drew her into a kiss. Her breath came fast, and she ran her palm over the planes of his chest and stomach as her body demanded more. Her fingers toyed with the waistband of his trousers. She started to unbutton them, but suddenly Teth broke off their kiss and grasped her wrist.

"You don't want—" Ara's heart pounded.

"Yes, I want." Teth sounded like he spoke through clenched teeth. He drew a ragged breath, then continued, "But we decided last night that it's too soon. What I want isn't . . . gods, this is hard . . . it isn't what we should do."

He rested his forehead against hers. "Not until we're both sure of it."

She wanted to argue. Her body shrieked its frustration, but she drew her hand back and threaded her fingers through his. "You're right."

They stayed like that, hands clasped and leaning into each other. It took a long time for Ara's breath and pulse to slow.

Teth let out a long sigh. "Are you ready to sleep?"

"Yes," she lied. Her heartbeat may have calmed, but her limbs were still taut with the memory of his touch.

"Turn over."

When she did, Teth pulled her close, fitting her into the curve of his body. With his arm curled around her and the length of his body pressing against hers, Ara doubted she'd sleep at all. But in time her eyelids grew heavy and the tension in her body eased. Her mind drifted into the world of dreams.

11

ra could have sworn she'd barely fallen asleep when something tugged hard on the cocoon, startling her awake.

"Dawn," Joar's voice boomed. "We must depart."

Beside her, Teth groaned and stretched.

"Did you sleep?" he asked.

"A little," she said. "You?"

"I'm not sure," he replied. She could hear the smile in his voice as he nuzzled the back of her neck. "You may have to fill me in on whether what I remember was real or a really good dream."

Ara laughed softly. "You're terrible."

"But that's why you like me." He pulled her close and kissed her ear.

She laughed again and unbuttoned the cocoon flap.

They passed two more days and nights in the depths of the Vijeri wilderness. During their nights in the cocoon, Ara and Teth agreed they should try to sleep right away. But while she was curled against him, Teth's fingers sometimes began to wander. His lips found her neck and shoulders. She reveled in his touch until she could bear no more, then lay awake for what seemed like hours, waiting for sleep to come.

Midmorning on the third day, the jungle noises began to fade until they vanished completely. After days of traveling through ceaseless cacophony, the silence made Ara's skin crawl. Despite the quiet, she couldn't shake the feeling that they were being watched.

Joar paused on the trail. "Something has changed."

Ara pushed past Nimhea then Joar to take lead of the group. The trail had abruptly widened to become a true path. It curved to lead them along a pond covered in green scum. Ara caught sight of a moss deer feeding in the far shallows, its camouflage so perfect she could only tell it was there when it bent its head to take another mouthful of swamp grass. Beyond the swamp, the path opened further to where light blazed forth. The jungle shrank from it. As they approached, the light became so bright Ara had to shade her eyes with her hand.

They entered a clearing, and as her vision adjusted, Ara realized the source of the light was the sun. A perfect circle had been carved out of the otherwise impenetrable green. Nothing grew in the clearing save vines that snaked across bare earth to climb and cover an object at its center. As it was cloaked by vines, Ara couldn't tell what the structure was made of, but its dome shape suggested a hide or hut.

"So this has to be it, right?" Teth asked quietly.

"Seems likely," Ara replied. Her heart knocked sharply against her ribs.

They'd found the Tangle. She tried to calm the sparks of nerves beneath her skin, but her mind threw images from the Bone Forest at her: the horror of the bodies impaled on stark white branches, the hulk of butcher crows staring down at them, the traps in the labyrinth. Before they had reached Ofrit's Apothecary, death had been waiting at every turn.

What waited in the Tangle?

To all of them, she said, "Stay close."

She led them cautiously toward the dome, ever searching the clearing for signs of movement or danger.

The jungle remained silent. The air perfectly still. Waiting.

Despite being close to the dome, Ara still couldn't make out how it had been constructed. Vines covered every inch of it except a single arched opening. As she circled the squat structure, Ara guessed she'd be able to stand at full height once inside, but none of the others would. She doubted Joar would fit at all.

"I'm going inside," Ara decided. "Nimhea and Lahvja will come with me. Joar and Teth should stay here and keep watch."

Joar nodded. His expression told her he had no interest in entering the cramped space. Teth's face was unhappy, but he nodded.

She smiled at the two other women, despite sharp wariness that set her teeth on edge. Sword and sorcery—the pairing seemed the wisest choices for exploring a god's realm. A strange echo of the past swept over her. The last time she'd ventured into such a place, her companions had been sword and scholar.

Oh, Eamon. How much you would have wanted to be here.

Ara shook off the sharp pang of his absence, his betrayal . . .

She stepped through the opening.

Behind her, Nimhea gave a sudden shout. Turning, Ara saw vines growing at impossible speed, separating her from her companions. She threw herself at the opening, tearing at the vines, but to no avail.

"Ara!" Teth called. "Are you all right?"

"I'm fine," Ara replied, running her hands over the thick web of green where none had been a moment ago.

Through the vines she caught the glint of steel.

"We'll cut through," Nimhea said.

"No," Ara told her after a moment's hesitation "I think this means I'm meant to go alone."

It wasn't what she wanted, but what was required.

No sooner had the words left her lips than Nimhea began to shout again. Then all of her friends were shouting. Huntress howled.

"What's wrong?" Ara called.

She tried to peer between the vines that had trapped her inside, but was startled to discover they were still growing, cutting her off from the outside world.

"Nimhea! Teth!"

Their voices were muffled, but it sounded like a struggle ensued outside the dome. Then she couldn't hear them at all. Ara beat her fists against the green wall, desperate to get back to her friends. The vines were unyielding as iron.

"No!"

The only remaining openings in the dome were gaps in the ceiling where sunlight speared through, but they were just wide enough to fit her fingers between. She couldn't even wedge Ironbranch into the gaps and use it for leverage.

Infuriated, Ara let out a cry and dropped to her knees on the dirt floor. She'd been willing to enter alone, but having her companions forced away and in peril where she could not help them, didn't know what was happening to them, was too much.

She screamed again, but the vines had no pity.

Ara bowed her head, drawing deep breaths. Rage only served to give her a raw throat. She needed a solution.

Making herself slowly take in her surroundings, she saw what her anger and fear had masked. The dome wasn't a vine-covered structure built of wood or earth; the vines *were* the structure. Woven together, twisting around one another, they had created this hollow.

"The Tangle," Ara breathed. "I'm inside the Tangle."

The hairs at the nape of her neck prickled. Though she'd been separated from her friends, she was still where she was supposed to be. She had to set her fears aside. There would be another way to reach her companions. There had to be.

But where could she go? There was nothing here but the prison of vines and a dirt floor.

A dirt floor with a hole in its center that Ara swore hadn't been there a moment ago.

She crawled on her hands and knees to the edge of the hole, which proved to be more of an opening in the ground than a simple hole. Large roots had pushed dirt aside to create a passage that led into the earth. The roots crossed over one another, twisting together in ledges that weren't exactly steps, but were obviously a way down. And there was nowhere else to go.

The only way out is through.

The passage was very dark. Ara could only see a few feet in front of her, but every few steps there came a shifting of earth in that space ahead and a brief rain of dirt and stone, after which a new shaft of sunlight appeared to encourage her forward. The passage spiraled down, down. The air was soft and cool. The scent of rich earth surrounded her.

How much time has passed? An hour? More? Ara wondered when the ground finally leveled off and she stepped into a broad cavern. *What is happening to the others?*

Her heart gave a painful wrench, but she forced herself to focus on the present, sensing that she would not be reunited with her friends until she'd faced whatever waited for her in this strange place.

Spears of sunlight entered the hollow through gaps between roots high above, rendering the space a patchwork of light and dark. She stayed still, listening. The only thing she heard was an occasional quiet susurration that she took for air moving through the cave. For all she could tell, the room was empty, but her instincts screamed that it was not.

The earth trembled beneath her feet for a moment, and the space grew a bit brighter. She turned to find more sunlight filtering from high above, but the passage that had brought her to this place was gone. Across the room she could make out a pile of rocks, and beyond that—

No. It can't be.

But it was. The passage that Ara had traversed was now on the opposite side of the room.

She shook her head. What kind of sense did that make?

A scrabbling sound, coming from a corner cloaked by shadow, drew her gaze. Her mouth went dry with fear. She couldn't see what was in the darkness and gave a little yelp, jumping back when a figure scuttled across the cavern. It was hunched over, dressed in rags, its long white hair tangled and matted. As quickly as it had appeared, it melted into shadow once more.

"Who's there?" Ara called. She gripped Ironbranch tightly. Her pulse roared in her ears.

What is in here with me?

"Who's there?" a creaking voice echoed. "Who's there? Who's who? Who? Who?"

"Come out where I can see you." Ara slowly moved toward the voice, holding Ironbranch across her body in case anything leapt at her.

An earsplitting sound, half laugh, half cry, pierced the air, and all the hairs on Ara's arms stood on end.

The figure dashed forward. Rather than running at her, it ran around her in circles.

"Someone's here! Who's someone? We're someone! No! Not us! Not us? Someone else."

She tried to follow the movement, turning in circles in an attempt to keep whoever it was in front of her so she couldn't be attacked from behind, but her efforts were useless. The thing moved with inhuman speed. Her heart pounded and her lungs burned as she whipped around in circles.

"Stop!" Ara cried out, gasping for breath and stumbling from dizziness.

Whoever it was listened to her plea and slowed to a shuffle, finally stopping beneath a ray of sunlight.

"Why have you come to visit?" The voice was familiar, and curious rather than menacing. "No one visits us here."

The figure lifted its head, and between the tangles of white hair Ara could make out a face. It was a face she knew.

"Ofrit," Ara breathed, hardly believing it could be true. But it was. A god stood before her. A god in ruins.

His features were the same, but the light of wisdom she'd seen in his eyes at the apothecary was now a frenetic gleam; his hair and beard that had been long and glimmered with starlight were dulled by grime. His dark skin was caked with gray mud.

"She knows our name." Ofrit's eyes rolled back in his head, and he shuddered. "The girl knows us."

"Of course I know you," Ara said gently, though her jaw clenched. She hadn't known what to expect in this place, but she never would have anticipated this.

What had befallen the god to bring him to this wretched state? He bore almost no resemblance to the arrogant deity she'd met in Daefrit.

Ofrit snarled, but the sound wasn't directed at her. "How can she know us when we don't know ourself?"

He hissed. "Quiet!"

What can I do?

She reached back to memories of her previous encounter with the god. She'd had to prove her worthiness by passing the judgment of the butcher crows and then solve riddles to reach Ofrit's Apothecary. Only then had she, Nimhea, and Eamon received the scrolls that revealed the remaining path of the Loresmith quest. And only after earning the blessing of Eni had Ara been taken to the Loresmith Forge.

Like the apothecary, this place belonged to Ofrit, who loved puzzles. So there must be a puzzle or several to solve. Would she be judged again? All Ara could do was explore the cave.

"I'll be right back," Ara told him, carefully stepping away. She didn't know what to do about the frenetic deity, but hoped she could at least keep him calm.

"Careful!" Ofrit's voice was shrill, each breath he drew rattled. "Mother is irritable today."

He pointed at the pile of rocks on the far side of the space and did a little jig while cackling.

The pile of rocks began to move.

Ara's throat closed.

What she'd taken for rocks was alive. And enormous.

As it moved, it passed through pockets of sunlight and glimmered in pale and deep purples.

It was an amethyst python. It had to be. The giant predator Lahvja had suggested might only be a myth was all too real, and it was here.

Her stomach lurched, and she thought she might vomit. The snake was massive; coil upon coil of thick muscle rustled as dry scales slid across one another, rising in a heap that was taller than Ara.

"See! See!" Ofrit dipped down and picked up a stone. With a gleeful cry, he hurled it at the giant snake.

"No!" Ara cried out as he scampered away and capered around the space.

To her relief the rock missed the python and hit the wall behind it. Nonetheless, at the movement and sound, the snake lifted its head and hissed in their direction.

"Senn's teeth. That thing could eat a warhorse," Ara hissed.

"Or you!" Ofrit giggled. "Or me!"

Somehow Ara doubted the god was in danger of being eaten, but she was another matter.

She shrank back, then tried to place herself in shadow between the spots of light.

"You can't hide," Ofrit said in a singsong voice. "She can smell you. She can see the heat of your body."

Whatever hope Ara held that the darkness might cloak her from the snake evaporated along with her plans to search the cavern.

Ara stayed still for several minutes while Ofrit gibbered nonsense and sometimes sang.

The python showed no signs of moving toward them. Taking her eyes off the snake, Ara's gaze moved to the relocated passage beyond it.

The only way out is through.

Her body drooped. "That's the way out."

"There's a way out?" Ofrit keened. "Oh. Oh please. How we would love to get out."

His face abruptly changed, anger flashing in his eyes. "There is no way out. She lies."

"I'm not lying," Ara shot back.

"Don't listen to him," Ofrit whimpered. "He wants to stay. He makes us stay."

Tearing at his hair, then scratching his face, he snapped, "She lies. There is no other place. This is the only place. Our place."

Ara swayed on her feet as she began to comprehend what her trial must be. Ofrit—the sad, frightened Ofrit—wanted to escape this place. She would have to get him out. But how?

To reach the passage, they'd be forced to pass the snake. Ofrit was too unpredictable for that.

Then what?

And what had happened to the god she'd met only a few weeks before? Who was this iteration of Ofrit? Maybe it wasn't the god at all, but some kind of trick.

No.

Beneath the grime and the wildness, Ara could sense the god. She knew he didn't belong here, but why couldn't he free himself?

And they call me the mad one.

That was what Ofrit had said to Eni in Ofrit's Apothecary.

Ofrit was a god of contradictions. The god of healers and assassins, of scholars and prodigies. Genius and madness.

In the old stories, that was what made Ofrit dangerous. His unpredictability. His great and terrible mind. His was a power that teetered between control and chaos.

In the far north, there was a kind of madness that came with the winter. The long darkness brought despair that crawled into one's mind on spidery legs and nested, weaving webs that snared light and hope, keeping them away from one's heart. The madness touched everyone, but some felt it more keenly and could become lost in it. That deeper madness used its webs to bind a person within themselves, cutting them off and hemming them in until they believed they were utterly alone. Unreachable.

In this place, madness had taken control, and the god was lost in the vastness of his own mind. Cut off from his divine siblings, from his people, from the world. Ofrit himself was the puzzle.

I have to bring him back.

Ara seized Ofrit's shoulders, trying to force him to look into her eyes. Upon touching him, her skin hummed and crackled with an inhuman energy. She dreaded taking physical hold of a god—how could it mean anything other than death?—but she knew it was the only chance she had to free him.

"Ofrit!"

He hissed at her, eyes rolling back into his head.

"Leave, leave, leave," the god simpered. "You don't belong here. This is my place. My place!"

Ara's heart slammed against her ribs as she gripped him tighter and gave a hard shake.

"I am here for you! I am the Loresmith."

She thought her eardrums would burst when he let out a keening wail, but she only held him tighter.

"I'm not ready," Ofrit panted, looking anywhere but at Ara. "I will fail."

"You are ready," Ara said. "I've seen who you are. Brilliant and formidable. But you must be whole again."

Ofrit became still.

"You've seen me," he whispered.

Ara softened her voice. "I have. You showed me the immensity of the universe. I was and am still in awe of you. The Loresmith cannot defeat Vokk without your aid."

Ofrit threw his head back and screamed. The sound tore through Ara's body and felt as though it shattered her bones. But she did not let go. Lightning crackled along the god's head and limbs, spreading over Ara's skin, searing her inside and out. Her lungs were on fire. It was too much. She was mortal, unable to bear this kind of power. And yet she knew she could not let go. Not even if it cost her life.

The wretched old man began to blur, then change, until he vanished entirely, replaced by the Ofrit Ara knew from his trials in the Bone Forest. The dirt had been scrubbed away; the white hair was still wild, but it was clean and free of tangles. He gleamed with a god's aura, and she felt power radiating from him.

"Ofrit," Ara murmured. "You have been freed."

"Very good, Loresmith." Ofrit squinted at her. "Perhaps you won't die after all." He paused and winked at her. "You know the way out."

Then he was gone, too.

12

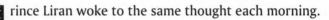

rince Liran woke to the same thought each morning.

Will today be the day?

The question circled his mind until he swatted it away like a pestering insect. He didn't know how long he had to live, not because he was ill nor because he adhered to some sage belief about the inevitability of death.

No, his burden was one of the many belonging to an heir to the Vokkan emperor:

Forty-nine Lirans had lived and died before his birth, and twenty-one Zenars existed before his younger brother took on the name. It was the same for the hundreds of sons of Fauld the Ever-Living bearing other names. The Emperor of Vokk only tolerated his children so long as they served his purpose. They could become powerful, but not too powerful. Their father never allowed his offspring to become potential threats to his rule. Fauld had been a father many times over, but never a grandfather.

No child of Fauld made it past the age of forty. While there was no proof that these untimely deaths were the fault of the emperor, Liran could find no other feasible explanation. He was also certain that he couldn't be the first of Fauld's sons to reach the same conclusion—but none had managed to avoid the ultimate outcome: their own demise.

Though history determined he would one day meet an untimely end by some machinations of his father, Liran wanted to escape that fate, and at long last he was in a position to do it.

Emperor Fauld only produced sons, a fact that Liran—and many others—found suspect. He didn't want to speculate about what happened to the girls who must have been born over the centuries. They were a mystery, as were the women who bore Fauld's children.

Liran had no memory of his mother, only a parade of nurses and tutors who raised him. Nor did he know who Zenar's mother was, though it was plain that the same woman hadn't birthed them. Their birthdays were only eight months apart. Both brothers had inherited their father's formidable height, sharp cheekbones, and heavy-browed, piercing eyes, but that was where their similarities ended.

Liran had hair like dark honey and eyes that were a frosted blue. His skin was lighter in the winter but tanned deeply in the summer months. Not only was he tall, but he also had a broad chest and strong shoulders. His arms and legs were wrapped in thick rope-like muscles.

Zenar matched his brother's height, but where Liran boasted bulk, the younger brother had long, slender limbs. His hair was the color of straw, his eyes a preternaturally bright green. His narrow face featured a pointed nose and full lips set in skin so pale as to appear translucent in certain light; skin that the sun turned an angry red within minutes of exposure. Liran sometimes wondered if Zenar's sensitivity to the sun had driven him to a life in shadow or if his love of shadows had transformed sunlight into his enemy.

Tutors oversaw Liran's education, and military officers undertook his martial instruction. Zenar followed a different path. Liran couldn't be sure how Fauld knew his younger son had innate mystic talent, but the two brothers weren't schooled together. Zenar never set foot in an armory or on a practice field. Instead, he was drawn into the wizards' circle at an early age. Liran went without seeing his brother for days at a time. When he did, Zenar was distracted and often babbled about things that Liran didn't understand. Things that sometimes frightened him.

Messages from Zenar came with more frequency these days than at any other point in their shared lifetimes. That fact brought Liran no joy, though he sometimes experienced twinges of regret that his brother was an adversary rather than an ally. He walked at a fast clip from the military offices that occupied the former palace to the Temple of Vokk. It was a relatively brief trip; the two buildings were separated by a courtyard dominated by a garden and glasshouse, where the wizards cultivated the ingredients for their myriad elixirs and potions.

He crossed the threshold into the side entrance of the temple. The place always smelled wrong to him. He could tolerate the glossy, ever-moving viscous black walls and the garish splashes of gold, but it was the temple's odor that most unsettled him. It was a noisome mixture of char and something metallic laced with a cloying floral scent that made his stomach churn.

Liran waited while a servant opened the door to announce his arrival and then hurried out of the commander's way. Zenar stood next to the wall nearest his desk, holding a silver chalice in one hand. He made an odd gesture with his free hand, and a stream of black liquid slithered off the wall and settled into the chalice.

"Brother." Zenar returned to his desk and took a seat. He motioned for Liran to do the same before taking a sip from the chalice. When he set the cup down, black slime clung to his lips, which he licked away with relish.

What is that? Liran had asked the first time he'd seen his brother quaff the stuff.

Power had been Zenar's answer.

"I have troubling news," Zenar said.

The tenor of his voice caught Liran off guard. His brother did sound troubled, and that was surprising. Zenar was very rarely unnerved.

"What's the problem?" Liran asked.

Zenar ran a hand over his hair—another surprising quirk, Liran thought; his brother believed himself above physical tells—then folded his arms across his chest.

"Saetlund's gods are taking an active role in the Loresmith's quest."

Liran pressed his lips together. He wanted to laugh, but knew that would be a bad idea.

"You'll have to say that again."

Obviously annoyed, Zenar spoke slowly, as if his brother were a child. "The gods of this kingdom are helping the Loresmith."

Liran cleared his throat. "How do you know that?"

"The boy," Zenar replied with a disgusted twist of his mouth. "Prince Eamon. He returned to us with vital information regarding the Loresmith."

"What do you mean he returned to you?" Liran asked, a steel fist closing around his heart.

"I mean he's here."

Liran reeled as if he'd caught a punch to the gut. He hadn't bothered to report Zenar's claims about his influence over the lost heirs of Dentroth. Long gaps between his correspondence with the rebels wasn't unusual. They kept their exchanges few and spare—it was far too risky to do otherwise. Liran kept them informed of Vokkan military strategy and movements as well as the status of ongoing rebellions in other parts of the empire. Both Liran and the rebels were waiting for a critical juncture of numbers and unrest that would allow them to move against the empire. But the rebels had never offered news of nor inquired about the missing royal twins or the mythical Loresmith. If such things were afoot, surely they would have alerted him to these facts. Had they, Liran might have paid more heed to Zenar's ramblings about folktales and legends.

He couldn't deny that knowledge of Eamon's choices would frighten and infuriate the rebels, but until now he'd doubted his brother's claims of influence over the young man and even more so that one of Dentroth's heirs would actively collude with Vokkan wizards. Zenar was prone to self-flattery and exaggeration. Liran had assumed that Zenar's minions had managed to track down Dentroth's heirs and keep tabs on their movements, but nothing more. He'd even wondered if the pair of youths who'd landed on Saetlund's shores were the prince and princess at all. Plenty of imposters would be happy to ingratiate themselves with a son of Emperor Fauld.

For that reason, Liran hadn't alerted the resistance leaders to Eamon's potential treachery without proof beyond his brother's words. This turn of events shook him to the core. Yet even now, with Zenar claiming Eamon was in his custody, Liran didn't completely believe it. But if it was true, he'd severely underestimated his brother and feared what that might cost his secret allies.

Despite Liran's aversion to all business involving the wizards, the presence of the young Prince Eamon in Five Rivers demanded his immediate and close attention. A part of him was relieved that no word from the Resistance had come regarding this turn of events, for he believed it would include only one order: assassinate.

He believed in the rebels' cause because the Vokkan conquest not only meant control of the kingdom, but would also ultimately lead to the destruction of the land as it had in each territory the empire claimed. Liran had borne witness to it many times over. The world was being devoured by Vokk's insatiable hunger. Its fields were barren, its people starving. Saetlund was the final conquest, and Liran had come to realize that the end of Saetlund would become the end of the world. So he had allied himself with the Resistance, but he was a soldier, not a murderer. That wouldn't change.

"Under what circumstances did you obtain this information?" Liran knew better than to directly question the verity of Eamon's identity, but there were other ways to fully grasp the situation.

Zenar scoffed. "I didn't torture him, since it's obvious that's what you're asking. I gave him a potion that loosened his tongue. Nothing more."

"Why would you trust what the boy says?" Shaking his head, Liran went on, "He abandoned the task you gave him to come here. What if the pressure became too much for him and he simply ran away? You've told me how fragile he is."

He was glad to learn the young prince hadn't been harmed. As much as his father and brother favored it, Liran had never believed torture provided truth.

"His body is fragile, plagued by chronic illness," Zenar shot back. "But he has an incredible mind. That's why he's been useful."

He steepled his fingers and stared into the space behind Liran. "As to why he came here . . . I'm still not sure. He claims it's because he encountered Saetlund's gods and believed we needed to know immediately."

"There are no gods but Vokk," Liran replied out of habit. He'd seen no evidence of the existence of other deities, but Vokk had demonstrated many times how very real he was. His gut twisted at the memory of horrors he'd witnessed, things he tried to lock away in the recesses of his mind.

"Don't behave like a dullard, Liran." Zenar scoffed. "You may be more comfortable dealing with problems of a material nature, but it's time to put aside these pedestrian notions you cling to. Saetlund's gods are very real, but until recently all signs pointed to their having abandoned the kingdom well before we conquered it. Unfortunately it seems they've taken an interest in recent events. An active interest."

"What proof do you have beyond this boy's words?" Liran had long been immune to Zenar's insults.

Zenar tsk'd as he stood up. "Come around the desk."

Liran had paid no notice to what occupied Zenar's desk, but his brother now unrolled a length of vellum until it covered the entire surface and placed weights to hold the scroll open.

"What is it?" Liran asked as he joined Zenar behind the desk.

"A scroll from one of their gods," Zenar replied in a reverent tone. "Specifically, Ofrit, known as the Alchemist. He is the god of wit and wisdom, worshipped by scholars, inventors, healers, and assassins."

"Healers *and* assassins?" Liran frowned.

With an impatient sigh, Zenar said, "Some of the same plants that have healing properties can also be used to kill." He snickered. "Ofrit is also the god of contrariness."

"How did the boy come by this scroll?" Liran glanced at the parchment. Two-thirds of it was covered with writing, the other third featured a map of Saetlund.

"It was placed in his hands by the god himself," Zenar replied. "A guide for the Loresmith on her quest."

Liran looked at his brother sharply. "The Loresmith is a woman?"

"A girl." Zenar didn't bother to hide his disgust. "The daughter of Dentroth's blacksmith. *He* died in the conquest, if you recall, but being of his line, *she* has the inherent ability to become the next Loresmith."

"Wait, become the Loresmith?" Liran folded his arms across his chest. "Is she or is she not the Loresmith?"

"I'm not going to confuse you by explaining how she is both," Zenar snapped. "All you need to know is that we now have the means to intercept her. As troubling as the appearance of Saetlund's gods is, Prince Eamon has given us a great gift."

Grinding his teeth, Liran said, "You're going to kidnap this girl? Why not just kill her if she's such a threat?"

Liran didn't want the girl to die, but he needed to know what Zenar was planning.

"There is a vital conversation I must have with the Loresmith." Zenar pinched the bridge of his nose. "And it must take place before she completes her quest."

He stabbed a finger at the map. "According to Prince Eamon, there is no other map like this in existence."

Liran bent over the map. It resembled other maps of Saetlund save large markers naming locations he'd never heard of: the Tangle, Senn's Lair, and Nava's Ire, among others.

Indicating the unusual markers, Zenar said, "These are hidden sites sacred to Saetlund's gods. The Loresmith must visit each of them to complete her quest."

His finger moved to the Tangle. "Given where Eamon parted ways from the group, it follows that this will be the first site they visit. I'm sending agents to the village nearest the Tangle in order to confirm my theory, but I believe the Loresmith may have already moved on." His finger traced a line north. "To here."

"The Great Market isn't a hidden site," Liran remarked. "It's arguably the busiest place in Saetlund."

"Indeed," Zenar said. "Where the Loresmith needs to go is Nava's Ire in Kelden, but without this map she doesn't know where it is. She'll be forced to seek clues as to its location at the Great Market—also known as Nava's Bounty, a sacred site of their fertility goddess. We've been meaning to root out a pocket of heathens still worshipping Nava there. This errand solves two problems at once."

His eyes narrowed. "It is an errand you shall run."

Liran stepped away from the desk. "I don't take orders from you."

"Please, brother." Zenar lifted his hands as if to pacify Liran. "This is not an order. It is a favor."

"So I'm doing you favors now." The hairs on the back of Liran's neck stood on end. Zenar wasn't like this. He closely guarded any operations his wizards undertook and regarded the military, including his brother, with contempt.

"You are . . . I hope." Zenar spoke carefully. "Because I have something for you in return. A way out."

A light flared in Zenar's gaze that made Liran's skin crawl. "I don't understand."

"I can save you. Save us both." Zenar's mouth stretched into a skeletal grin. "The time has come for the reign of Fauld the Ever-Living to end."

Before Liran could respond, there came a rapid knocking at the door.

"Come!" Zenar shouted.

A messenger ran into the room, practically falling on Zenar's desk. Zenar plucked an envelope out of the messenger's hand.

"You may go."

Though it hardly seemed possible, the messenger rushed out of the room faster than he'd entered.

After reading the message, Zenar turned to Liran with a placid expression, as if he hadn't just announced his plans to commit treason.

"This should be helpful for your errand," Zenar said, handing the message to him. "Apparently, they have a giant with them."

13

he god had vanished, but the snake was still there.

That wasn't what Ara had expected, and it was a problem.

Her hands balled into fists at the injustice of it.

I solved the puzzle! I freed Ofrit! So why am I still trapped in this cave with a giant python?

The snake should have disappeared with the god.

But it hadn't. And that had to mean her trial wasn't finished. There was another puzzle to solve here.

She groaned inwardly as her eyes swept the cavern once more.

Empty, but for herself and the deadly serpent.

The python lying between Ara and the only way out of this place. Unmoving, the creature had gone back to looking like a pile of rocks. The camouflage only made the snake seem more dangerous.

Ara crouched, shifting her weight from the balls of her feet to her heels as she turned ideas over in her mind.

Perhaps she could use Ironbranch to vault over the snake and into the passage.

No. The ceiling was too low for that.

Run past it and hope she was fast enough?

That seemed a poor option, too. There was space—five feet, give or take, between the snake and the side of the cavern—but rushing toward the snake, even if not straight at it, was likely to provoke an attack. She didn't like the odds of successfully defending herself against what had to be a master hunter.

A bittersweet smile crossed her lips as she imagined Joar encountering such a monstrous beast. In Ara's place he'd likely be ecstatic.

Then his voice was in her mind. *I kill only when attacked.*

Joar would admire the python and not want to harm it. How would he deal with this predator?

Ara knew not to provoke it, but she didn't know if that would be enough. If the snake was hungry or inherently aggressive, she stood little chance of getting by without a fight. She shuddered at the thought of being crushed in those massive coils of pure muscle. The idea of being eaten was too terrible to comprehend.

Would you really eat me? she asked the snake silently. *Lahvja warned that you're a man-eater.*

But that wasn't exactly what Lahvja had said, was it?

The summoner had told Ara the only snakes rumored to eat humans were amethyst pythons. Rumors were not always truth. When Old Imgar had taken Ara into the woods and taught her survival skills, he'd spoken of the forest's predators.

There are many fearsome tales about ravenous wolves and raging bears, he'd said. *But truth be told, it's rare for wolves to hunt a person or bears to attack. Most animals do what they can to avoid people, because more often than not people cause trouble where we go—troubles for nature's creature and for nature itself.*

The python was large enough to eat a person, but would that be its primary instinct? How likely was it that this snake had even encountered a human before? Ara and her friends had spent days tramping through the wilds, and they'd encountered no one. From the reaction of the villagers at the inn, it seemed like Vijerians kept away from this part of the jungle.

If I'm the first person this snake has seen—Ara didn't know whether Ofrit, being a god, counted—*there's a chance it won't regard me as prey.*

But it could think I'm dangerous. It could judge me a threat.

Judgment.

Her mind flashed to the Bone Forest and the trees laden with butcher crows. Their massive black wings and bright, shining eyes. The deafening caws that drove her to her knees.

Ara gazed at the snake with a new awareness. *This is not another puzzle. This is where I will be judged.*

With a shiver, she wondered if she would be found worthy this time.

Ara recalled Lahvja's playful exchange with the green snake in the village, and that the snakes at the springs had let her and Teth depart without incident.

I could never eat a snake. Snakes are friends, Lahvja had said.

I need to convince this python that I'm a friend. Or at least harmless.

Staying low, Ara crept to the side wall she would need to follow to reach the passage out. The snake lifted its head; its tongue flicked as she moved. Once against the wall, she went still.

If only Ofrit hadn't thrown those rocks. That certainly hadn't put her in the snake's good graces.

Ara tensed when the python began to move, but it wasn't coming toward her and seemed to be repositioning itself against the other wall.

Ofrit had called it *Mother.* Why?

Peering through the shadows, Ara noticed for the first time that the snake, while still giant, was made to appear even larger because it was coiled around something.

A nest. It has to be. Ara's heart stuttered.

If the python was protecting a clutch of eggs, that made her all the more dangerous. The most aggressive animals in the north were moose and bears guarding their young.

Ara let out a slow, shaky breath.

Mother.

She would have to show that she was threat to neither the snake nor her unborn. She must honor the guardian of this sacred place. Closing her eyes, Ara called on who she believed could offer protection in this moment.

Merciful Nava, bountiful mother, guide my steps in this place. Let there be peace between me and your blessed.

Opening her eyes, careful not to make any sudden movements, Ara forced herself to return Ironbranch to its sheath. She pressed herself against the wall, trying to make herself as small as she could.

She began to inch along the wall.

The python was instantly alert. Her coils rustled as she stretched up to watch Ara more closely.

"Forgive me, Mother, for this intrusion," Ara whispered fervently, her heart hammering. "In Nava's love, I mean you no harm."

The snake moved a foot closer to Ara, and she froze against the wall. Another foot. Another. The python had closed half the distance between them.

Merciful Nava, lend me your aid.

Ara gazed at the snake.

The snake stared back at her, forked tongue kissing the air. For several moments, Ara couldn't move. Her limbs refused to even twitch. She could barely draw breath. The only part of her body that seemed to be working was her pulse as it raced through her veins.

Finally gaining command of her muscles, Ara dared to edge a little farther along the wall. All the while, she fought for control over the wild, thrashing terror that threatened to overwhelm her.

The python's green eyes stayed locked on her, but the snake didn't come any closer.

Ara slid along the wall a few more inches. It was pure torture. Every instinct screamed at her to run or to attack. To strike at the danger before it could hurt her.

But she couldn't. She would be found wanting. She would fail this trial.

And she would probably die.

The snake remained still.

A bit more.

Breath eased out of Ara's lungs.

She won't leave the nest.

The python had moved as far as she could without abandoning her eggs entirely. She did not want to pursue Ara past that point, unless absolutely necessary.

Ara would show her that she needn't give chase.

Keeping herself pressed to the wall, Ara continued her agonizingly slow crossing of the cavern. She drew within a few feet of the passage and longed to dash for it, but running would make her look like prey. She couldn't risk the python's hunting instincts taking over.

At last she was there. She took care to back into the opening, making sure her eyes never left the python. And then she was out of the cavern and climbing the strange, spiraling root steps. As she climbed, the passage began to change. Roots gave way to stone. Instead of filtered sunlight, oil-burning lanterns hung at intervals, filling the staircase with a gentle glow.

Reaching the top of the stairs, Ara discovered a trapdoor. She pushed it open and gazed up into darkness. Given the changes in the passageway, she wasn't surprised the stone steps hadn't led her back to the Tangle, but a little light to reveal where the trapdoor led would have been a comfort.

The only way out is through, she told herself again, and crawled up.

The wind howled as it drove snow through the wintry air, but the fires of the forge kept the cold at bay. Old Imgar's smithy was exactly as it had been the night she'd been taken by Nimhea and Eamon. She wore the same clothes: her undyed soft wool shirt, covered by her leather apron with its scorch marks, and her butter-soft leather leggings. Her tools were laid out on the worktable.

Ara closed her eyes for several heartbeats. The wind continued to shriek in her ears, and the air held all the familiar scents of the smithy. She opened her eyes.

I'm home.

It was as if none of the events of the past month had taken place. As if it had all been wild workings of her imagination.

Her heart swelled as she went to the opening in the smithy's stone walls. The storm made it difficult to see her grandmother's cottage, but light from within it bobbed and winked at Ara like welcoming laughter.

With a cry of delight, she threw herself out of the smithy to run to the cottage.

"Grandmother!"

The shout left her throat at the same moment everything vanished, and she stood once again in the cavern of the Loresmith Forge, with its domed ceiling and endless stars.

Her heart leapt. She hadn't realized that part of her had missed this sacred place and longed to return to it. It hadn't changed . . . except that where the forge had stood was Imgar's smithy.

"As my brother said, very good, Loresmith," a voice boomed behind Ara. "Very good indeed."

Ara whipped around to find a figure, twice the size of Joar, standing before her. Wuldr, the Hunter. The god of her homeland. A silver-blue nimbus surrounded him.

"You've completed this trial." His giant hand enfolded hers. "Now you have work to do."

When Ara gave him a questioning look, Wuldr simply gestured to the entrance. She stepped back inside. Everything was as it had been. Her tools. The forge. The blizzard outside. The windows of her grandmother's cottage blinked at her.

With a tightening of her chest, Ara understood that this place must be significant to the task at hand. But how?

It might be a challenge of her will, requiring that she focus on her craft while she longed to be home or at least with her friends again. But the work of the Loresmith demanded her full attention, and it was work that she must complete alone, no matter what her heart wanted.

Is this meant to be a lesson about Teth, too? she wondered. *Could it be that solitude is the Loresmith's lot?*

She shrank from that idea and dismissed the thought. *Not always. I'm not always alone. Only at the forge. And even at the forge, I have a god for company.*

While the weighty memories of Imgar's smithy, of home, might challenge her, the reason Wuldr wanted her to work here was something else. As if in response to her musings, the wind called again and snowdrifts crested like waves.

Winter. The north.

Wuldr appeared amid the swirling blasts of ice and stepped into the smithy.

"Bracing." The god grinned at Ara.

She thought he must be teasing her, as she doubted he'd be touched by the cold.

He shouldn't have been able to fit into the space, but the building shifted to accommodate him. A horse-sized hound trotted into the smithy.

"My companion, Senn." The god reached out to scratch behind his hunting hound's ears. Senn wagged his tail. "Senn, meet Ara. She is the Loresmith, and vital to our cause."

Senn turned his gaze on her. Ara didn't know what to do other than act how she would with any strange beast. She lifted her hand to let him sniff. He obliged, then gave her a friendly lick that covered her entire arm. She tried not to wince. This was a dog she didn't want to offend.

Wuldr gestured to the forge. "I will see to all your needs whilst you toil."

The snow. The highlands.

"The weapon will be for your knight," Ara said, grasping the reason for the Fjerian god's presence and Imgar's forge.

The second Loreknight has been chosen.

He nodded.

Meeting his gaze, Ara traveled to her homeland in his eyes: forests, rivers, ice-capped mountains, a lonely coast filled with ruins. A storm of snow and ice flared in his eyes, and a song filled her head.

She knew.

Wuldr smiled when he saw she understood. "I leave you to your task."

Ara was taken aback by her realization. This hadn't been what she'd expected. Or rather who.

She went to the forge and collected iron ingots that she would need to create molds. This project would require two molds and ask much more of her than Tears of the Traitor. Wuldr's knight required two weapons, one for each hand. It would take days to finish. Her body thrummed with anticipation. She set to work.

While the molds were cooling, Ara gathered ingots of godswood she found stacked on the worktable in the smithy. She could have sworn none had been there when she first entered the space. As she inspected the unusual material, she speculated about its origins. It had qualities of both wood and metal. Was it mined or harvested? Woodsman that he was, Ara wondered if Wuldr supplied the gods with this precious material.

When she left the smithy, the gods' cavern changed to meet her needs. When she grew tired, a bed appeared for her to rest upon. If hungry, Wuldr was there with hot meals. They differed from those Eni had brought to her. Where Eni—as the old woman—cooked up comforting soups and delicious cakes, Wuldr's fare consisted of smoked and roasted game accompanied by wild greens with herbs and foraged mushrooms.

Wuldr maintained a respectful distance, always ready to answer Ara's questions as she crafted the weapons. But Senn was ever curious about her activities and often came sniffing around the forge.

At first the hound's presence set her on edge, but as days passed she grew comfortable with the great beast and came to enjoy seeing him bask in the warmth of the forge. It would have been perfect had she been able to convince Senn not to continue giving her his friendly licks.

Ara forged the blades first, then turned her attention to the hafts. As she worked, she became troubled by the aesthetic of using the same material for both haft and blade. There was no questioning that the godswood must be forged; she wanted a way to distinguish blade from haft. She considered several options before settling on silvering the blades.

The moment she had made her mind up, Senn came into the smithy and dropped two slobber-covered silver ingots at her feet.

Wuldr must approve, Ara thought as Senn lowered his head so she could scratch behind his ears.

Once silvered, the two blades shone with bold contrast to their dark hafts. She was pleased with the result, but her work felt unfinished. She looked to her past for a solution. All the work she had done for Imgar. The variety of techniques he'd taught her.

When business was slow or Ara grew tired of crafting endless horseshoes and farmers' tools, Old Imgar let her practice engraving and etching. She was infatuated with the contrast between the brawn required when working at the forge and anvil and the delicate work of creating images in forged metals. Both were essential skills of a master smith. Though she could use gravers to create letters or patterns, Ara worked the hardest to render scenes from nature. Flowering vines ringed the edges of steel plates she created for her grandmother. Her proudest achievement had been etching the scene of a hunt on the blade of a woodcutter's ax—a great stag running through the forest pursued by hounds and a man on horseback. This she presented to Imgar as a gift. She would never forget how pride shone in his eyes when he accepted it.

The bright blades before her wanted an image from the wilds, but not one she'd created before. She gazed into the ever-raging storm outside. Gusting winds, blasts of ice, and swirling clouds. Forces with more strength and power than the greatest warriors could claim. She imagined the blizzard streaming into the smithy and pouring itself into the steel blades.

Ara had no trouble finding the beeswax she needed to etch the blades. It appeared just as the godswood had. She applied the wax to the blades, creating the ground she required, and then became absorbed in carving the intricate image of a winter storm traveling across the blades. The screams of wind and hissing of ice outside the smithy encouraged her hand.

When the image was finished on both blades, she prepared the acid bath in which she'd submerge the ground. Though ready to continue the process, she paused. Within the sounds of the storm, another sound rose. A voice. Someone singing.

Setting the acid aside, Ara went to the smithy door and peered into the blizzard. A figure walked amid the storm. Wuldr. He lifted his hands to the sky, and his great booming voice sailed on the wind. Senn romped alongside the god, howling his delight. The song was joyful and exuberant, bolstering her spirit and filling her with determination.

Returning to her task, Ara removed the ground from each blade and then dipped the carved wax into the acid. She lifted the acid-covered grounds from the bath and carefully applied them upon the blades once more. As the images from the grounds were etched upon each blade's surface, Wuldr's song grew louder. It filled the smithy. She watched the acid work its way into the blades and sensed Wuldr's song infusing the godswood with his blessing.

With the etching completed, Ara cleaned the acid from the blades, then polished them. The storm on the blades looked alive, as if at any moment the etching would begin to move across the silver surface. She could hear the echoes of Wuldr's song. When she looked up she expected to see the god still striding through the blizzard, but he and Senn were gone. The faint music came from the blades. And though she had created them, she couldn't help but look upon them with wonder.

Ara took the finished weapons and left the smithy. She was unsurprised to find Wuldr waiting for her in the gods' cavern.

"What do you have for me, Loresmith?"

She held the pair of axes out for him to take. "Lord Wuldr, I present to you StormSong."

Accepting the weapons, Wuldr took his time to examine them, poring over the etched images, testing their weight, and taking broad swings that whistled through the air.

Senn barked and danced around the god's feet.

"Yes, my friend," Wuldr said to his hound. "These are worthy weapons indeed."

To Ara, he said, returning the axes to her, "Bestow them upon the one I have chosen."

"If I may ask," Ara said, "is it not strange that a Koelli should be named Loreknight and not another of my company?"

Her thoughts were of Nimhea and how this news would sting the princess. First Teth, now Joar. Would the time come for the heir to the River Throne? And if not, what did that mean?

"Though not born of Saetlund, he is a child of this land and has been called to serve its people," Wuldr told her. With a mischievous smile, he added, "Just as a thief could be asked to become a hero."

She felt the blush on her cheeks.

"There have been many surprises on this journey," she admitted.

Wuldr grinned. "And there will be more. But answer me this, Loresmith: What lesson did you learn in the Tangle?"

Ara considered his question, her mind retracing the events that had transpired since she stepped into the dome of vines. She thought of puzzle, trials, judgment, and worthiness. It all came down to choices: the choices the people of Saetlund and its rulers had made, the choices the gods had made, and now the choices she made.

A tragedy of poor choices, of selfish desires, had allowed the Vokkans to conquer Saetlund.

They had reached a moment when new choices could be made. When a lost kingdom could be restored.

"A new Loreknight is chosen when we face the god's inner nemesis," she told him. "Ofrit's brilliance is countered by madness and obsession that he struggles to control. I must overcome what drove each god from the people of Saetlund, so that they may return to us."

"Good." Wuldr nodded his approval. "You know your path. I have given you a hunter; now it is your turn to seek out the hidden places where the gods have locked away their dark secrets. Even mine."

He paused, a shadow passing over his face. "Saetlund's salvation lies in the restoration of its guardians. Both gods and Loreknights. The Loresmith stands at the heart of this truth."

Senn lifted his head and let out a howl that made Ara's goose-flesh rise.

In a voice so low she could barely hear it, Wuldr whispered, "Do not fail."

14

ra had hoped that Wuldr would do her the kindness of magicking her and her companions back to the village, but when she opened her eyes she was sitting inside the dome of vines. The spiraling descent had vanished, and she sat on a plain earth floor utterly unextraordinary except for the odd growth of vines around it. The opening on one side had reappeared. Outside the dome, Ara heard the ceaseless noise of the jungle, trilling birds, buzzing insects, chirping amphibians. And a new sound. Shouts.

Scrambling to her feet, Ara wedged her body through the slender opening of the dome. Free of the muffling dark, she could hear the cries clearly. Shouts of alarm, anger. An ax in each hand, she ran through the jungle as fast as she could, frustrated that her speed was hampered by snagging vines and rotting tree fall.

Where there first had been the shouts of multiple voices, Ara now heard only two voices. She recognized both. Joar and Nimhea.

Where are Teth and Lahvja?

Her muscles wanted to seize up with fear, but she forced her worst imaginings away and kept running.

The shouts were close now, loud.

She came around a corner on the game trail and stopped, staring at the scene before her with horror.

Beside the swamp, a tree had come to life and was attacking her companions. No, not a tree, but a creature that had perfect camouflage. Its long, narrow body resembled a tree trunk, but the knots on that trunk were moving, opening and closing. Mouths. It walked on broad, root-like appendages that splayed out around it, resembling a spider's legs.

One giant eye, bile yellow with a slit of an iris, stared from the conjunction of its trunk and limbs.

Instinctively she knew this was no child of Nava. Here was a creature spawned by Ofrit's madness.

The mouths shrieked as the tree creature's vine-covered limbs lashed out like tentacles. The tips of those limbs featured needle-like thorns from which yellow slime dripped.

Teth had found a perch in a nearby real tree and fired an endless barrage of arrows at the tree beast, but the arrows were deflected by whatever armored its limbs. Some of his shots had lodged inside the mouths covering the monstrous trunk-body, but the creature batted away most of Teth's arrows.

Wearing his butcher crow helm, Joar created a terrifying appearance barely outmatched by that of the tree beast. He looked like a nightmare brought forth from the same wicked realm as the horror he faced. He fought with his entire body, whirling, slashing, leaping over tentacles that attempted to knock him off his feet. His ax had better success against the beast than Teth's arrows. He methodically chopped at the swinging limbs, hewing thorns wherever he could.

The axes forged at Wuldr's behest belonged in Joar's hands. Ara was about to call out to him when she caught sight of Lahvja's body lying motionless beside Nimhea, who had taken up a defensive position alongside the helpless summoner. The princess's blade flashed out, slashing tentacles that reached for their prey. Huntress had joined

Nimhea in drawing off the creature's attempts to grab Lahvja's body.

With a low cry, Ara rushed to them, the Loresmith Forge and the purpose of the axes forgotten.

Startled by a newcomer's approach, Huntress spun around, snarling, but when she recognized Ara she gave a welcoming bark then returned to her sentinel post.

After a quick glance in Ara's direction, Nimhea asked, "How badly is she hurt? There's been no time—"

The princess jumped over a tentacle that swung low, then struck, shearing off its thorned tip.

The creature shrieked with pain, and its other tentacles shrank back.

Ara dropped to her knees beside Lahvja, setting Wuldr's axes aside. Lahvja was so still Ara couldn't tell if she was breathing. She pressed her fingers to Lahvja's neck, searching for a pulse. It was there. Weak, but there. Her dress was torn. Ara pulled back the ruined fabric to reveal a long but shallow slime-covered gash that ran along her left side.

"She's alive," Ara breathed. "But she's bleeding. I need to bind the wound."

"Do it," Nimhea told her. "I'll protect you."

Even as the words left Nimhea's lips, the creature attacked again, and Nimhea fended off the sweep of tentacles with ferocious sword strokes.

Ara tore the dress further so she could create bandage strips. Her heart pounded as she wrapped the cloth around Lahvja's body.

"Done," she told Nimhea.

Nimhea turned to look down at Lahvja. "Thank Nava."

"Ara! Nimhea!" Teth's shout pulled her eyes to the tree. "Look out!"

At the same moment, Huntress snarled a warning.

Ara sensed the attack coming a moment before she saw it. One of the limbs flew at her. She somersaulted backward and rolled away from the limb, its glistening thorns passing mere inches from her body.

Nimhea dove to the side, avoiding the tentacle, but was unable to recover in time to strike it with her sword.

Out of the beast's reach, Ara crouched low to the ground. She had yet to find her bearings when she heard Teth yell in pain. Her gaze flew to an object dropping from his tree. Tears of the Traitor tumbled through branches and hit the forest floor. She heard the sounds of snapping branches a moment later, but she didn't see Teth. His perch in the tree was empty, but the thief was nowhere to be seen.

With a strangled cry, she lurched toward the tree, while the swamp beast refocused its attack on Joar.

"Stop!" Nimhea grabbed Ara's arm. "We need you here. Defend Lahvja while I help Joar."

Ara shoved Nimhea away, wrenching her arm free. "I have to find Teth."

Then she was running. She ignored Nimhea's shouts that followed her.

Ara went to the place Tears of the Traitor had landed. She searched around the tree, looking for any sign of Teth.

"Teth!" she shouted. "Where are you?"

Nimhea was still shouting for her, but an irrational obsession had taken hold of Ara. The sounds of the battle seemed to fade away as her head pounded with a singular need:

I have to find him.

She circled the tree twice.

There was so sign of Teth.

Is the creature so fast it grabbed him and has already drawn him into the swamp?

A broken sob bubbled up her throat.

"Teth!"

Mind reeling, she fell back against the tree. A wave of dizziness swept over her, and she leaned her head against the trunk. Her gaze traveled upward.

A body was tangled in the vines. They formed a natural net into which Teth had fallen.

Relief spilled through her. He wasn't moving, but Lahvja hadn't been either.

How can I get him down? He's too vulnerable up there.

A scream shattered Ara's focus.

Nimhea.

She didn't scream a second time.

Shame pummeled Ara mercilessly as she realized how rash she'd been to leave the others for Teth's sake. The horror of Nimhea's sudden silence turned her blood to ice.

"Eni protect him," Ara breathed before racing back the way she'd come.

Nimhea was lying facedown beside Lahvja, while Huntress menaced any tentacles that came near.

"Nimhea!" Ara threw herself to the ground beside the fallen princess and turned her over.

She couldn't stop her own scream.

The tentacle had caught Nimhea at the left cheek, its thorn ripping through skin up to her hairline, catching the corner of her eye. The left side of her face and neck were covered with blood and slime.

Ara's gut twisted.

This is my fault.

There was no time to bind Nimhea's wound. If they were to survive, she had to help Joar: the warrior who now faced this monstrosity alone.

Guilt dug its claws into Ara. Joar was the second Loreknight. Getting the newly forged axes to him should have been her sole focus upon returning to the others. Instead, she'd let her emotions rule her with disastrous results.

From the moment of Ara's arrival, Joar hadn't slowed his attack, nor had he stolen a glance in her direction to discover what new events had transpired. His focus upon the creature never wavered.

He hacked ceaselessly, sending chunks of its flesh flying. All the while, Joar sang. The deep, bellowing melody was in a language Ara didn't understand. It was a choppy song, broken up by his puffing breaths and war cries, but that it was a song was unmistakable. Each note drove him forward, filling him with resolve.

With one last glance at Nimhea's prone form, Ara scooped up the axes and ran toward Joar. She waited for a moment when the creature retreated slightly from its assailant and screamed its pain.

"Joar!" Ara shouted.

He turned and she raised one of the axes overhead, dropping the other, so she could grip the first with both her hands. "This is Storm!"

She hurled the ax, watching it fly end over end. Joar dropped his own ax and caught Storm's haft with his left hand.

A boom of thunder shook the air.

Joar threw his head back and let loose a cry that rivaled the rumbling in the sky. Huntress lifted her muzzle and howled.

He stretched out his right hand. Ara picked up the second ax and threw it. "Song!"

When he caught Song, the booming was joined by a swelling chorus, distant voices carried on the wind, echoing the melody Joar had sung when Ara first came upon him. A silver-blue nimbus hovered over his skin and became a sphere within which raged a terrible storm. Music surged around him, accompanied by a gale filled with spikes of ice and needles of snow.

Ara staggered back, overawed by the power Wuldr had instilled within the axes. Joar was now the god's vessel, and she was there to bear witness. Her limbs shook with amazement, but at the same time she felt a deep sense of completion, of the fulfillment of her true purpose.

The creature bore down on him, lashing its thorn-tipped tentacles in a renewed attack. Joar answered the assault, swinging StormSong with the driving downbeats of the ethereal music. He surged forward, hacking limbs with each step. The storm traveled with him, assailing the creature with its frigid arsenal. Hunks of ice smashed into the monstrosity, and it sent up shrieks of rage.

Tentacles shot out at Joar, but they were fewer now, and he cleaved any that came within reach of his axes. The creature's cries became those of fear, knowing that once it had been the attacker but was now the attacked. It began to retreat into the water of the swamp, but Joar had no intention of letting the beast escape. He stepped into the swamp but didn't sink; the water beneath him had frozen instantly. While the creature's size only let it move slowly through the mire, Joar moved swiftly along a frozen path. As he approached the beast, the water surrounding its trunk turned to ice, trapping it in place. The creature shrieked again, its limbs thrashing. Joar raised both axes and hurled them. The creature's great single eye exploded, and the axes lodged deep within its body. It slumped onto the ice, unmoving.

The blizzard surrounding Joar faded, as did the song. Joar walked to the beast and dislodged his axes, pausing to rinse them in the swamp water just beyond the ice. He followed the frozen path back to shore; when he stepped onto earth the ice vanished and the swamp returned to what it had been. The creature's carcass floated atop the dank waters.

Joar came to Ara, holding up Storm and Song.

"What is this wonder you have wrought?"

But the spell that captured her while Joar fought had been broken and was replaced by a torrent of fear, grief, and guilt.

"I'll explain," Ara said, her voice on the verge of breaking. "But first we help the others."

He nodded gravely. "That is as it should be."

"Go to Lahvja and Nimhea," she told him, then bolted toward Teth and cursed under her breath. She'd had no choice but to leave him and help Nimhea, but she was terrified of what she might find.

To her surprise, he was crouched beside the tree when she reached him. He raised one hand and gingerly touched his swelling forehead.

"Teth." She reached for him, then stopped, suddenly arrested by shame. He'd been all she could think of from the second he'd fallen, and it had almost gotten Nimhea killed.

"That's going to be a big bump," he groaned. "Tell me my irresistible looks haven't been marred."

She smiled impulsively at the joke, but then Nimhea's torn flesh reared up in her mind's eyes and a vise closed on her ribs.

"Are you all right?" Ara knelt beside him, but kept herself slightly apart. "Aside from the bump?"

"I think so," he answered. "I had to jump out of the tree to avoid a tentacle, but I managed to jump right into a branch. Thankfully the vines were nice enough to catch me."

Ara flinched at the memory of staring up at Teth's body tangled in the vines. The way the need to help him had made her ignore everything else and what it had cost.

"I take it we won." Teth's gaze had found the dead creature in the middle of the swamp, and he grimaced. "What of the others? Is anyone hurt?"

Ara couldn't bring herself to speak about their fallen friends and gestured for him to follow her back to the others. They found Joar kneeling beside Nimhea, rummaging through Lahvja's satchel. Huntress trotted around them in circles, whimpering.

"You are well?" he asked Teth as they approached.

"Well enough," Teth answered.

When Teth saw Nimhea, he sucked in a sharp breath. "Nava be merciful."

"She was. They will both live," Joar said.

Ara looked at the terrible wound and thought, *Is this mercy?*

"I found what I needed in Lahvja's satchel." He handed Ara linen bandages. "Do what you can to stanch the bleeding."

When he poked silk through the eye of a long silver needle, Ara's stomach curdled.

"Her eye—" Ara began, when Joar's stitches neared the socket. The flesh surrounding Nimhea's eye swelled in sickly hues of yellow and green.

"I hope it can be saved," Joar replied. "I know only a little of healing, and this is the best I can do. The paste Teth is making should help with the pain and keep infection away. We will need to apply it to Lahvja's wound, too."

When he'd finished the stitches, Joar cleaned Nimhea's skin of blood and spread the green paste Teth had created over the wound. Ara helped him bandage the left side of Nimhea's head.

They then removed the makeshift bandages Ara had wrapped around Lahvja.

"Not deep enough to require stitches." Joar sounded relieved.

He applied the green paste to Lahvja's wound and then covered it with fresh bandages.

Staring at the two motionless women, Ara asked, "Is the poison still harming them?"

Gesturing to Lahvja and Nimhea, Joar said, "Its attacks were meant to maim, not kill. I do not believe its venom to be fatal, given what I've heard. Neither of our friends shows signs of fever or convulsions. They breathe freely."

He continued. "We should plan to rest here for the night. We'll need to build litters for our injured companions so we can carry them back to the village. They will be in pain for some time and will need rest as their wounds mend."

"You knew about this creature?" Ara asked, surprised he'd given them no warning about such a threat.

"There are tales about such a beast," Joar replied. "But I did not believe them to be true. I thought them no more than a story meant to frighten young children and keep them from wandering into swamps. Most stories about monsters are of that ilk."

Teth frowned at him. "What did you mean when you said it didn't want to kill them?"

"In the stories, this creature's poison renders its victims unconscious, and once they are in its clutches it waits for them to awaken before it consumes them."

Ara shuddered.

"That creature cannot be of this world," Joar continued. "Earthly predators do not feast on the suffering of their victims as well as the flesh."

"It was born of a god's madness," Ara told the hunter, and for a moment she was back in the cavern, staring at Ofrit's frenzied state. His awful suffering. "The god is now free of this madness, and the creature is slain. I believe the swamp will return to its natural state."

Joar's brow furrowed. "How can you know this?" He placed StormSong on the ground between them. "And what of these weapons? It was only by their power that I was able to defeat the beast."

"Senn's teeth," Teth murmured with a sharp look at Ara. "I didn't see that coming."

"I forged those axes," Ara told Joar. "They are a gift from Wuldr for you."

"StormSong." Gazing at the bright axes, Joar's face filled with wonder. "The storm on the blades is alive. The voices of my ancestors rise up when I wield them. I cannot fathom a weapon more suited to me."

He paused, then added, "Though, it grieves me some to know I will put aside my father's ax."

"You can still use it for regular tasks, like chopping wood," Teth suggested. "Think of the others as your special-occasion axes."

Ara rolled her eyes at him, and he flashed her a teasing smile.

"Why has Wuldr gifted me StormSong?" Joar said softly. "I have not earned such a blessing."

"Wuldr seems to think otherwise," Teth countered. "And I'd say your sojourn in the wilds is officially a success."

Regarding Joar thoughtfully, he added, "That's the good news. The bad news is, you now have a new quest."

Wuldr frowned at him. "A new quest is an honor. Such a thing could never be 'bad news.'"

He spoke the last words like they left a foul taste in his mouth.

"Guess we don't have to be worried about getting you on board then," Teth said. "That's more good news. Welcome, friend."

Teth clapped his hand on Joar's shoulder. Then gave the bulging muscle a tentative poke.

"What are you even made of?"

Huntress growled at him.

"Sorry." Teth pulled his hand away. "No offense meant."

"You are a strange man," Joar said with a rumbling laugh. "So very strange."

"I've heard worse," Teth replied.

Ara appreciated his attempt to lighten the somber situation they'd found themselves in, but she couldn't feign mirth. Her eyes kept finding Nimhea's bandaged face.

That is my fault. I failed her.

The truth of it gnawed at her ribs. It was for Teth's sake she'd abandoned Nimhea and Joar. He hadn't even been in real danger.

How could I have been so reckless?

By abandoning Nimhea, Ara realized she'd put their very purpose at risk. She felt a sickening twist in her stomach. Nimhea was the leader Saetlund's people would rally to. The Resistance had shown little interest in Ara's quest—it was Nimhea who was important to them, the future queen of Saetlund. To lose her would be to lose everything they fought for.

Ara had made a near-fatal mistake, and she was terrified of the moment when Nimhea woke up and she would have to tell the princess what happened.

I don't know if she'll be able to forgive me. I don't know if I can forgive myself.

"Tell of me this new quest." Joar's words broke through Ara's dark thoughts.

"You know of Saetlund's gods." Ara focused on the hunter. "But have you heard of the Loresmith and Loreknights?"

Joar nodded. "My father was fond of telling tales, especially the old legends."

His usual somber expression gave way to a sudden wonder, revealing the young man who lived beneath the mask of the solitary, hardened hunter.

"Our quest is to restore the Loreknights to Saetlund," she said. "So the Vokkans are driven from Saetlund, and the true heir to the River Throne will rule once again and heal this land and its people."

She gestured to the princess. "Nimhea is Dentroth's heir. She returned from exile to claim her throne."

"My father said the Loresmith line had been broken." Joar looked doubtful, but hope sparked in his wintry-blue eyes. "There can be no Loreknights to save the kingdom without the Loresmith."

"The line was broken," Teth told him, reaching for Ara's hand. "But things changed."

Glowering at Teth, Joar was clearly drawn to the mystery, but hesitated to embrace its truth. "If the Loresmith did not pass on his gift to one of his children, that magic was lost. What you say cannot be true."

"It can," Ara replied, lacing her fingers with Teth's. "Because of me."

15

he waif scurried down the street. A frightened mouse fleeing a cat.

She threw herself on Captain Brekk, who lurched backward and cursed.

"Please, sir," she gasped. "Help me."

It was close to midnight. Brekk and his men reeked of ale, but they straightened and made the best attempt at officiousness they could. Though the spindly girl was nothing to worry about, Brekk's men flanked him and kept their hands on their sword hilts. He'd trained them well. His patrolmen had lost teeth until they got it right.

"What's the matter, girl?" Brekk pushed the girl off him. He'd thought her a child, but when she looked up he saw she was nigh a woman, her wide eyes and rosebud mouth set in a heart-shaped face, and his attitude changed.

She sobbed. "A cutpurse stole my coins, and my mother has a fever. She sent me to fetch medicine, but now . . ."

"There, there." He took her hand. "I'll take you to the apothecary, and we'll get your mother's medicine."

"Oh, thank you, sir." The girl kissed his hand. "Thank you."

One of his men chortled. It sounded like Pole; the captain would remember that.

"What's your name?" Brekk took her chin in his hand. She had a pretty face and wide blue eyes. A strand of pale blond hair had slipped free of her cloak's hood.

"Violet." She smiled shyly.

The captain turned to his men. "Keep on the patrol route. I'll rejoin after I help Violet with her errand."

"Yes, sir." His sergeant saluted.

Brekk caught a few of the guards smirking. That he could let go, but the laugh—Pole would regret it.

Taking the girl's upper arm, the captain pulled her along the street until he could no longer hear his soldiers' voices. After a quick check to ensure the street was empty, Brekk steered her into the shadows behind a warehouse.

"Sir, the apothecary—"

"We'll get there soon enough." He pushed her hood back. Her hair tumbled out, fine as spun gold. "But first we need to discuss payment."

"I told you my coins are lost to a sneak thief."

"I have plenty of coin." Brekk stroked her hair, and she backed away until she bumped into the warehouse wall.

"What I'm looking for is gratitude, Violet," he continued, following her. "A show of appreciation for keeping you safe."

He leaned forward to whisper in her ear. "As you already know, these streets are dangerous."

The girl attempted to evade him again, but Brekk caught her wrist and tore her cloak away with his other hand. It was a shame she was so spindly.

"Please, sir," she cried. "I am grateful, but please don't hurt me."

Brekk grabbed her throat. "Be quiet."

Violet fainted.

With a snort of disgust, he let her body slump against his shoulder while he attempted to unbuckle his sword belt with one hand. He felt a prick on the back of his neck and scratched it absentmindedly. His sword belt clattered to the ground, and he reached beneath his tunic to unbutton his trousers.

Brekk's stomach began to gurgle.

Damn the kitchen at the Pig's Tail.

The gurgle grew louder, and he began to feel queasy. He dropped Violet, clutching his stomach. Cramps seized his guts, and Brekk felt as if his bowels would loose any moment. They did.

He groaned, struggling to get his trousers down before the next surge.

A wave of nausea sent Brekk to his knees as stabbing pain wracked his bowels. His stomach heaved, and whatever hadn't exited his ass surged up his throat.

Everything went dark. He hadn't passed out. Something was covering his face, tightening. He tried to vomit, but fabric pulled taut over his mouth. He choked on partially digested food and acid. He couldn't breathe. He couldn't—

The girl let Captain Brekk drop. Though it was rare anyone would be given the chance, with closer examination a person would know the captain had been mistaken: this was no girl on the cusp of womanhood, but a woman grown. She pulled his cloak off his face and threw it over half his body. Not the bottom, excrement-covered half.

"It's a good look for you, Captain."

She donned her discarded cloak and walked away.

When she reached the house, she slipped around the back. It didn't matter that she had a key to the front door. Habit drove her to find a way in that was unlikely to be noticed.

The woman dropped into the cellar. She didn't need a lantern to make her way between the shelves to the stairs. She'd taken this route many times before.

When she reached the top of the stairs and opened the door, bright light surprised her. Blinking against it, she stepped into the kitchen where her mother fussed over dishes.

"Welcome home, love." Her mother came over to kiss her cheek. "Everything go well?"

"Very," she answered, removing her cloak. She laid it over the back of a chair.

At twenty-five years old, the woman didn't need to live in her mother's house, but she preferred to. Not only was it convenient, but it also ensured that she would be at hand to keep her mother safe. She was all too aware what evils existed in the world.

"I'm delighted to hear that." Her mother pattered back to the hearth where a kettle hung. "Tea?"

"Please." A little frown appeared on the woman's face. Her mother wasn't in the habit of making tea in the middle of the night. The reason became clear when her mother carried a porcelain tea service into the parlor. There were three cups on the tray.

Senn's teeth.

Light from the kitchen spilled into the parlor, but the room itself was dark. With good reason.

I should have sensed he was here.

Her mother set the tray on a low table flanked by two velvet armchairs. One was occupied.

After pouring three cups, her mother announced, "I'll take my tea in the kitchen."

The woman settled into the second armchair and picked up her cup.

"Dagger," the man in the other chair greeted her.

She could hear the smile in his voice, and she ground her teeth. Stealth was the only subject he'd bested her in while they were at the academy. He took every opportunity to remind her of that.

Dagger took a dainty sip of tea. "Garet."

"We were busy this evening," he remarked.

"Knock it off," she said. "You were here. I was working. 'We' weren't doing anything."

She knew Garet only called them *we* to irk her, but she always took the bait.

"Of course," he said.

Dagger's eyes had adjusted to the light, and she could see him clearly. The same face she'd known from childhood, changing slightly as each year passed. Mousy brown hair he tied back with a strip of leather. Half Keldenese, half Daefritian, he had light brown skin. His eyes were dark, his cheekbones prominent, and his nose pointed.

"And who were w—you this evening?" Garet asked.

Dagger folded her legs beneath her and snuggled into the chair. "Violet."

"Violet?" he laughed. "I didn't know you had a penchant for flowers."

"I don't," she replied. "I like Violet because it's so close to *violent*. It's like a teensy-weensy warning that no one heeds."

Shaking his head, Garet laughed again. "Only you could come up with that."

"Thank you." Dagger finished her tea and set the cup down.

Garet sobered. "You know Lucket doesn't like it when you go off book."

"Just tidying the neighborhood."

"You know the rules," he said. "Never draw attention."

She tsk'd. "I never do. All that happened tonight was a captain known to be a drunkard drank too much and drowned in his own vomit."

Garet nodded slowly.

Dagger shifted to a cross-legged position. "I assume you're here about a mark."

She'd been tired when she entered the house, but a new job always made her antsy.

"I think you'll like this one." Garet drew a letter from his coat. "It's unusual and has ramifications beyond our usual assignments."

Ignoring his use of *our*, Dagger took the letter and began to read. She let out a hissing breath.

Dagger was rarely surprised, but this job was startling. It set her veins on fire.

Garet regarded her, wearing a half smile. "You should take it as a compliment."

She shrugged. "It's not a compliment. They need me because I'm the best."

The smile spread across his lips. "I know you are."

16

hile Teth built the litters, Ara and Joar set up camp. As they worked, she explained the events following Nimhea and Eamon's arrival at Rill's Pass, and her quest to become the new Loresmith. Joar asked few questions, accepting what she had to say mostly with solemn focus but sometimes awe.

When she'd finished, Joar turned to Huntress. "What say you, friend?"

Huntress gave a sharp bark.

To Ara, Joar said, "We are honored to join your quest, Loresmith."

Then quietly, as if only to himself, "It is more than I could have dreamed."

At nightfall, rather than attempt to hoist Nimhea and Lahvja into a cocoon, they tented oiled canvas over the litters. Huntress curled up between them to keep watch.

With the third cocoon free, Ara opted to sleep alone rather than continue to share with Teth. He tried to hide his hurt expression, but Ara could see how much her choice confused him. She knew he'd wanted to comfort her and take comfort in her after the awful events of the day.

As the evening wore on, she'd become more and more uncomfortable with his nearness. What should have been reassuring instead nagged her about her mistake. Whenever she checked on Nimhea and

Lahvja, she was reminded that she'd abandoned them for Teth's sake. At times she found it difficult to even look at him.

Sleep itself was fitful. In her dreams, Teth danced above her on vines, laughing, while half of Nimhea's face slowly peeled away. When the princess opened her mouth to scream at Ara, the creature's tentacles spilled out, grasping for her.

She woke covered in cold sweat and was unable to return to sleep.

The next day, Lahvja woke first.

Just after midday, the summoner moaned and her eyelids fluttered open.

Ara called for their group to stop. She'd been walking behind Lahvja's litter, which Huntress pulled along the trail. Joar and Teth carried Nimhea's litter, given her more serious injury, in the hopes that she'd be jostled less.

"Where am I?" Lahvja blinked into the jungle canopy.

Hearing her stir, Huntress lay down on the path to let the litter settle.

Lahvja tried to sit up, but cried out and fell back.

"Keep still, Lahvja." Ara crouched beside the litter. "You were injured. The wound is still fresh."

"The creature." Lahvja's whisper was full of terror, then panic. "Nimhea!"

Ara placed her hand on Lahvja's shoulder to keep her from trying to sit up again.

"You're safe now," Ara told her. "We're all safe. We killed the creature, and now we're on our way back to the village."

Joar joined them and offered Lahvja a waterskin.

Ara cupped her head to help her drink.

Her face crinkled at the taste.

"Something I brewed up last night," Joar explained. "For pain and to help you sleep. It smelled terrible when I made it, and I'm sure that's how it tastes."

With a weak smile, Lahvja said, "I appreciate the effort." She paused, pursing her lips, then said, "I taste breathroot and Bythum's Sorrow."

Joar nodded.

"Clever." She drank more, then signaled she'd finished.

Ara drew back, and Lahvja rested her head on the litter. A few moments later, her eyes closed and her breath grew slow and shallow.

"I think it best if they sleep until we reach the village, where they can be treated by a true healer. Their wounds are serious and require more skill than I can offer," Joar told Ara. "Until then they should be using all their energy to heal, not hike through the jungle."

"Agreed," she said, though she wondered if Nimhea would be as willing to return to slumber as Lahvja had been.

It wasn't until that evening, when they were making camp, that Nimhea stirred. Like Lahvja, she woke with sounds of pain. Ara rushed to the princess, her heart in her throat.

"Nimhea." Ara knelt beside the litter and took her hand.

Nimhea didn't try to sit up, but her free hand reached for the bandage wrapping her head.

"I'm wounded," she murmured, touching the cloth gingerly. "What happened?"

"Joar defeated the creature," Ara told her. "But you were injured. There was poison in its thorns that rendered you unconscious."

Groaning, the princess asked, "Lahvja?"

"She's healing, like you."

"My wound." Nimhea fingers searched for the boundaries of the cloth. "How bad—"

Dread bored through Ara's chest, but then Joar was there, catching Nimhea's hand, moving it away from the bandages.

"You must leave it, Princess. Drink this."

"You know who I am," Nimhea said. "Who told you?"

"I did," Ara said.

Joar's other hand tilted Nimhea's head up so she could drink from the waterskin.

She winced as her head moved. "It hurts."

"I know," Joar said. "This will help."

"Ugh," Nimhea blurted after taking a sip. "Tastes like swamp rot."

"I give you my word that it isn't," he replied. "Drink more. You need it."

She obeyed, but grimaced as she drank.

When he'd determined she'd had enough, Joar gently lowered her head.

"Try not to move," he urged. "Don't fight sleep."

"Where are we?" she asked. "Still in the swamp?"

"On our way back to the village," Ara said.

"Good," Nimhea muttered. "I hated that swamp." She yawned, grunting at the pain it caused. "My head."

She tried to reach for the bandage once more. Tears began to well in Ara's eyes.

My fault.

Joar seized Nimhea's hand, holding it until Nimhea went still. "Do not touch."

The princess made a grumbling sound that soon turned into a light snoring.

Joar turned to Ara to say something, but stopped when he saw her expression.

He reached over Nimhea's body to rest his hand on Ara's shoulder. "She will heal."

Not trusting herself to speak, Ara nodded.

The unbandaged side of Nimhea's face was serene, but Ara knew her own dreams would again be haunted.

They passed three more nights in the jungle before reaching the village. The progress was slow by necessity, but Ara chafed with impatience, not only wanting to get her injured friends to the healer sooner, but also worried about the next stage of their journey. She understood now that the trials led to the naming of a Loreknight. According to the legends, there were ten Loreknights in all; thus far, the gods had chosen two. While encouraged by the progress she'd made, Ara grappled with dread at the feeling that in no way could she gather all the Loreknights before the Vokkans caught up with her. They had too many resources. They had Eamon.

She was running out of time.

The village healer, Danik, took charge of Nimhea's and Lahvja's treatment, even insisting that they stay in his home until they recovered. Ara, Teth, and Joar returned to the inn.

During their return trip, Ara had been so focused on Nimhea that she'd paid little attention to the toll the journey had taken on her mind and body. Now that her injured friends were safely in the healer's care, every ache and twinge made itself known. She could feel the weight of her exhaustion.

Ara forced herself to use the basin of water and a cloth to scrub the grime from her body, then collapsed into bed, letting sleep swallow her whole.

She woke with no sense of how long she'd been absent from the world. Her limbs were heavy, but her mind was rested.

Fingers of light reached through the shutters of her room's window, but Ara didn't think it was sunlight. When she peered out, she saw it came from torches that glowed along the platform railings. She also noticed that light shone in the windows of the tavern on the next platform. Her stomach grumbled that it had been some time since she'd eaten.

Ara dressed and left her room. She considered knocking on Teth's and Joar's doors, but not knowing how late the hour was, decided against it.

The tavern welcomed Ara with a low din of conversation and savory scents that made her mouth water. Arching one eyebrow at her in greeting, the barkeep said nothing but nodded toward a table where Joar and Teth were digging into plates heaped with food.

Ara hesitated. She wasn't feeling particularly companionable. The sight of Teth called to mind memories that filled her with guilt. On the one hand, she didn't have to worry about Joar or Teth bringing up her mistake—neither knew of it. Joar had been battling the creature; Teth had been unconscious.

The only person who knew how she'd failed was Nimhea.

Should I tell them?

She didn't know if they'd condemn her or try to console her. Neither put her at ease.

No. She couldn't tell them. Too much shame stung her to even try speaking about what had happened.

Suddenly Ara didn't feel like talking at all. She decided to go back to her room, but Joar caught sight of her before she could leave.

"She lives!" His voice boomed through the tavern.

With reluctance, Ara waved and went to their table.

Chuckling, Joar jutted his chin at Teth. "This one worried you might never rouse."

Teth pushed a chair out for her. "Have a seat."

He gestured to the abundance of food on the table. "If you're hungry, we have enough to share. This is our second round of dishes, and Joar has already ordered, what?" He looked at Joar. "Fifteen more?"

"Not so many," Joar answered. "I say ten."

"Do you think that's enough?" Teth joked.

Frowning, Joar replied, "If she eats too much, I will order more."

"There you have it," Teth said to Ara. "He can order more."

Ara smiled weakly at him, and he signaled to a server for another plate.

"You never know," he continued. "You just might eat too much. When I woke up, I was ravenous."

"How long have you been here?" she asked.

"About an hour," he replied. "I slept most of the day, like you."

"Has anyone spoken to the healer?" Ara wondered if Lahvja or Nimhea had woken.

If I don't tell anyone what happened at the swamp, will Nimhea speak the truth? Will that be worse?

Joar wiped his mouth after downing an ale. "I did, in the early afternoon."

"And?" She tensed.

"Danik bade me not return until tomorrow afternoon," he said. "That our friends should not be disturbed before that."

That gave Ara the night and the morning before she could see Nimhea, and she had decided she must speak to the princess before anyone else. It wasn't only her guilt that compelled her. There was a new Loreknight . . . and again it wasn't Nimhea. As the Loresmith, Ara believed she should be the one to explain Wuldr's choice to the princess.

The double blow of Nimhea's wound and a virtual stranger being chosen instead of her made Ara dread the imminent conversation.

She ate quickly, bidding Teth and Joar good night as soon as she was full. Teth offered to walk her to her room, but Ara refused. Her guilt and confusion about Nimhea were tangled up with her feelings about Teth. She couldn't face both, and she wasn't ready to tell Teth what she'd done.

Back in her room, Ara undressed and crawled into bed. Despite sleeping through the day, her body still ached with exhaustion. She closed her eyes. As the well of darkness enfolded her, she hoped it would hold her fast and keep her dreams at bay.

At midday, Ara went to the healer. She'd stayed in her room through the morning, ignoring knocks at her door. When Teth called her name, her chest burned.

I'm not ready.

Not ready for what? To talk to him?

Ara knew it was more than that. She avoided Teth because their next private conversation wouldn't only be her confession. The more she turned over the events in the swamp in her mind, the more resolved she became that there was only one course of action she could take.

She was the Loresmith. Her duty was to all the Loreknights. To favor one over the rest led to disaster. The swamp had revealed that bleak truth. She only wished she'd understood that sooner.

Danik opened the door to his home and ushered Ara inside. The front area of the house was arranged as a work space. Shelves were filled with glass bottles and jars. Pungent odors filled the air; some Ara could identify within the miasma, most she could not.

The healer bade her wait while he went into another room. A moment later Lahvja emerged. Ara drew relieved breath, and joy fluttered through her seeing her friend whole and walking.

Lahvja came to embrace her, though she winced when Ara returned the hug.

"Oh!" Ara drew back. "I'm so sorry."

"The pain is little compared to a happy reunion with a dear friend," Lahvja replied with a kind smile.

"How are you?" Ara asked.

"Danik is a skilled healer," Lahvja answered. "I'm mending quickly. I also owe a debt to Joar. His poultices kept the wound from festering, and he was wise to keep me and Nimhea at rest."

When Lahvja spoke the princess's name, a cloud passed over her face.

"Is Nimhea awake?" Ara's hands began to tremble. She clasped them behind her back.

Lahvja nodded.

"I need to speak to her."

With a sigh, Lahvja lowered herself into a nearby chair. "She will not speak to anyone. Not yet."

A hard lump lodged itself in Ara's throat. She swallowed several times.

"Has she said anything to you?"

"A little." Lahvja pushed her long mahogany hair behind her

shoulders. She suddenly looked deeply weary. "But mostly to demand I keep all but Danik away."

Her gaze fell past Ara into some imagined distance. "She knows it can't stay this way for long. And that we will need to leave here soon."

She paused, then looked directly at Ara. "But I want to give her at least some time. To let her heal and adjust."

Ara bit her lip, then asked, "Has the wound improved at all?"

"I can't say, as I didn't see it before yesterday," Lahvja replied. "I know Joar did the best he could with what was available."

She went silent for a moment. "The scarring will be significant."

Though Ara had expected it, hearing Lahvja speak the words made her sway on her feet. "And her eye?"

"The soft tissue around the area was damaged, but not the eye itself," Lahvja said.

Thank Nava.

For some reason Ara's voice dropped to a whisper. "Has she seen the injury?"

"No," Lahvja replied. She offered nothing more.

Her heartbeat sped up, and Ara asked, "Did she say anything about how it happened?"

The question appeared to surprise Lahvja. "Only that she was defending me at the time."

"She said nothing else?" Ara countered, taken aback by Lahvja's answer.

Why didn't Nimhea tell Lahvja what happened?

Lahvja shook her head. "I don't think she wants to recall the fight. It's too close." Taking Ara's arm, Lahvja steered them toward the door. "Take a walk with me. I need the fresh air and for you to tell me what transpired within the Tangle."

It turned out that Ara wasn't the only one with a story to tell. After she'd recounted her ordeal with Ofrit and the python, and then at the Loresmith Forge with Wuldr, Lahvja related what had happened to the others from the point they'd been separated.

Their shouts of alarm had been provoked by the vines' sudden growth not only around the Tangle, but also outward. The vines spread, pushing Lahvja and the others back until they were forced from what had been the clearing. Facing knotted, dense jungle, there was no way to reach Ara. All they could do was wait by the swamp. That was when the creature had attacked.

"In all of my nightmares I've never encountered anything so vile," Lahvja spat as though she couldn't bear a taste in her mouth. "Everything about it was wrong. Wicked."

Ara made a small noise of agreement. The memory of the swamp beast still made her feel sick.

"I tried to evade its attacks, but its reach was so long and so swift."

"In the end it took down everyone but Joar," Ara said. "And he was only able to defeat it with the powers of StormSong."

Lahvja went quiet.

Ara spoke softly. "I know it will be hard for Nimhea to hear about Joar."

Nodding, Lahvja said, "It will, and it pains me to add another burden when she already suffers."

She glanced at Ara. "I would ask that you let me deliver this news. I believe that would be best."

Ara swatted away the knee-jerk desire to say no. As much as she wanted to speak with Nimhea, it would only be selfishness on her part to deny Lahvja's request.

"You should tell her."

"Thank you." Lahvja offered her a little smile.

Joar and Teth were waiting on the platform outside Danik's home when they returned.

"It's good to see you on your feet," Teth said to Lahvja.

She laughed. "Good to be on my feet."

"And you've been hiding," Teth teased Ara, but there was a weight behind his words that made her look at her feet.

"Joar." Lahvja took the man's giant hands in hers. "I am so grateful for the aid you've given me and Nimhea. And I rejoice that the gods have named you Loreknight."

"Thank you," Joar replied. "As for my attempts at healing, they were crude. I wish I could have done more."

"Do not belittle what you've done." Lahvja smiled at him.

"What of the princess?" he asked.

"More time," Lahvja said quickly. "She needs more time to rest. It's best we let her alone for now."

With suddenly drawn expressions, Teth and Joar offered silent assent.

Looking at Lahvja, Ara asked, "Could you eat?"

"I thought you'd never ask."

"I could eat," Joar added, his face brightening.

Teth lifted his eyebrows. "We'd better leave soon. The way Joar eats, the village will run out of food."

"I had not considered that possibility." Joar's expression grew troubled. "You are right. We should leave soon."

Groaning, Teth put his face in his hands.

At the tavern, Lahvja went to speak with the cook about preparing a light broth with specific herbs for herself in lieu of a heavier meal.

When she joined them at the table, Ara said, "As soon as Nimhea is able to travel, we need to continue our quest. There are eight more Loreknights to be found."

"So eager for shiny new heroes?" Teth teased. "But that makes me feel less special. Joar, too, I'm sure."

Ara rolled her eyes at him and Joar grunted, while Teth grinned at them both.

"I believe I can help," Lahvja broke in. "Given what Ara told me about the Tangle and her conversation with Wuldr at the Loresmith Forge, I think we must go to Nava's Bounty."

Teth gave a low whistle, his impish expression fading. "The Great Market? That's the busiest place in Saetlund. Exactly the kind of place we've been avoiding."

"I understand that," Lahvja replied. "But each of the trials has taken place at a holy site wherein the dark aspects of the gods dwell."

"But Nava's Bounty is the opposite." Ara frowned at her. "It's the place that celebrates her goodness, the gifts of fertility, the harvest, family."

With a nod, Lahvja continued, "And the Great Market was built around it. We've found the way to each trial by first visiting the sites where the gods are revered, known places where people once traveled to seek out the gods. The dark places are secret. Shunned."

"What about the scroll?" Teth asked. "That's what led us to the Tangle."

"I've been reading it while at rest," Lahvja said. "And I'm afraid it has no further direction for us."

"Ugh." Ara rubbed her temples. "The answers we need are with Eamon."

"They may be or not." Lahvja shrugged. "We cannot know what mysteries lie in the scroll Eamon has. Perhaps the scrolls only speak of Ofrit and were meant to help us begin our journey, but not direct us through the whole."

She paused, smiling. "If nothing else, thinking of it in those terms might ease your mind. Better not to dwell on what we cannot change."

Ara returned the smile grudgingly.

A server appeared with broth for Lahvja and an array of dishes for the rest of them to share.

"What do you expect to find at the Great Market?" Teth heaped steaming vegetables and sizzling meats onto his plate. "Besides a swarm of imperial soldiers?"

Lahvja lifted a spoonful of broth and blew on it. "In truth, I don't know, but I believe it is our best chance of finding Nava's hidden site."

Teth swallowed the food he'd been chewing, then took a lingering drink of water, before leaning back in his chair. "It's not just the Great Market I'm concerned about. The roads leading there are the most heavily patrolled in Saetlund."

"Could we join another caravan?" Ara asked.

"After the raid on the Below's caravan in Daefrit, I don't think we can risk it," Teth answered. "And the border of Sola and Vijeri north of TriBridge is a fortified imperial checkpoint. They'll search every caravan wagon."

"I suppose we could make our own path through the jungle with Joar guiding us." Ara tore off a chunk of bread and swiped it through the sauce pooling on her plate.

Joar grunt his assent without looking at her. Strangely, he hadn't touched his food.

"Lose your appetite?" Teth asked.

"Your words from before lie heavily upon me," Joar answered. "I think I must hunt to supplement the village's foodstuffs. It is unfair that I burden them."

Teth threw his hands up. "Joar! It was a joke. A joke!"

Joar frowned at him. "I think it is a serious matter."

Dropping his head back to rest against the chair, Teth stared at the ceiling, muttering to himself.

Ara thought to come to Teth's rescue, but then she caught the smile that crept onto Joar's lips and disappeared just as quickly. The she noticed Lahvja meeting Joar's gaze and quickly hiding her own smile. Teth, it seemed, had found a worthy opponent. Ara wondered how long it would take the thief to figure that out.

After recovering his composure, Teth continued eating for several minutes in silence. Joar dug into the food as well, and Lahvja sipped her broth.

When his plate was clean, Teth set his fork down and said, "We could save time by traveling through the Gash."

"The Gash isn't patrolled?" Ara asked.

As far as Ara knew, the Gash was simply the empire's failed attempt to build a war road to bring troops and siege weapons into Vijeri.

"It used to be," Teth replied. "But it turns out the Gash is a very unlucky place for imperial soldiers. Terrible accidents. Animal attacks. People going missing or losing their minds. At first these misfortunes made the Vokkans increase their patrols of the Gash, as they assumed insurgents were the cause. But no rebels were ever captured, and fatalities grew to the point of becoming intolerable. Eventually, the imperials decided a burned-over swath of jungle wasn't worth the trouble."

Ara paused between bites. "They never discovered the cause?"

"Not a viable cause," he answered. "But soldiers from the garrison that was eventually abandoned swore that the Gash was haunted."

"Hmph." Joar looked at Teth. "When I saw the Gash, I found no evidence of ghosts."

"But did you enter the Gash?" The tremulous question came from Lahvja, who had gone very still.

"I passed by the southern edge, but did not traverse the Gash itself," Joar admitted. He peered at her with concern. "What troubles you?"

Ashen, Lahvja spoke slowly. "It was not only soldiers who bore witness to the spirits that inhabit the Gash. Vijerians have stories of them as well. Frightening stories."

"But they are *stories*," Teth countered. "I've had no reports of danger in the Gash from the Below."

"And do members of the Below frequently traverse the Gash?" Anger flashed in Lahvja's eyes. The emotion was so uncommon in the summoner it made both Teth and Ara draw back.

Teth cleared his throat. "I can't recall specific details of such a journey, but someone must have. The Below are everywhere. We go everywhere."

"Not there." Lahvja's voice was hard and cold.

Teth opened his mouth to reply, but seeing Lahvja's expression changed his mind.

"Lahvja," Ara said gently. "I'm not questioning the truth of these stories, but if there are spirits, do you think they pose as much of a threat to us as the imperial patrols we'll encounter on the roads and at the border?"

Lahvja turned a sharp gaze on Ara, but a moment later her shoulders sagged. "I don't know. I can only say that the Gash is ground I hoped never to tread."

Shifting in his chair, Teth avoided looking at Lahvja when he said, "I say we avoid the roads. The empire has to be circulating our likenesses by now, and I'm guessing they know we're in Vijeri."

"We don't know that Eamon told them or that he gave them the scroll," Lahvja snapped.

"We don't know he hasn't," Teth replied in a measured tone.

"Joar?" Ara turned to the hunter.

He returned her gaze steadily. "You are the Loresmith. I follow where you lead."

She hadn't expected that answer, and his words made her skin prickle. The sensation grew stronger when Lahvja said, "Joar is right. The decision should be yours."

"Works for me," Teth said, returning his attention to the meal at hand.

Ara sat, aware of Joar's and Lahvja's eyes on her. While she was deeply honored by their trust, a stony fear settled on her chest.

The Loresmith should lead, but I made the wrong choice in the Tangle, and Nimhea paid the price. Who will pay if I make the wrong choice now?

They waited for her answer, and she hoped they took her silence for contemplation and not the fear it was. Ara knew this wasn't a responsibility she could shirk, but that didn't stop her throat from constricting.

She forced herself to swallow and take a long, slow breath.

"We go to the Gash."

Joar and Teth both nodded.

Lahvja closed her eyes. "So be it."

When they finished their meal, Lahvja excused herself to return to the healer's home to sit with Nimhea, and Joar announced his intention to hunt, leaving Ara and Teth alone at the table. They sat in silence for several moments, then Teth reached out and covered her hand with his. Ara clasped his fingers briefly, then pulled her hand away.

He watched her with a slight frown. "I can tell you're upset. A lot has happened. Do you want to talk about it?"

Words caught in Ara's throat. What could she say? Her feelings were a tangle of guilt for what had happened to Nimhea and the longing to be close to Teth again. The knot around her heart was so tight the sharpest blade couldn't cut through it.

She fumbled with her thoughts until she finally answered, "I'm not ready."

Teth's smile was so kind, Ara could barely hold his gaze. He stood up, then leaned down to brush a kiss across her forehead.

"I'll wait," he murmured.

17

imhea convalesced in Danik's home for the better part of the week, never allowing visitors aside from Lahvja. In that time, Joar kept his word and brought fresh game to the village tavern each day, making sure Teth spotted him carrying whatever boar, deer, or fowl he'd hunted. Teth would watch Joar wordlessly, then walk away, shaking his head. Whatever Joar's motivation, the cooks at the tavern were happy to take the meat.

Without demanding explanation, Teth adapted to giving Ara the space she needed. He left her to her own devices, making it unnecessary for her to go out of her way to avoid him. She was grateful for his unspoken acceptance. It unburdened her of one unpleasant conversation, but she still faced the impending encounter with Nimhea, which occupied most of her thoughts.

The night Lahvja announced over dinner that Nimhea would be ready to depart the next day, Teth surprised Ara by taking her aside after bidding the others good night.

"I know you've been worried about Nimhea," he said. "And I wanted to respect that, but seeing as she's ready to travel now, I thought I'd remind you that this is our last opportunity to brave the springs."

Ara stared at him, unable to speak. His interpretation of her aloofness was rooted in some truth—she was worried about Nimhea—but he had no idea of the other feelings that troubled her. All having to do with him.

He moved close, brushing his lips against her cheek. Desire curled within her, but her body remained rigid.

"Or if you don't want to trouble the snakes," he continued, "I could come to your room."

He kissed her, a gentle, caressing kiss. Heat bloomed over the surface of her skin, but she couldn't respond the way he wanted.

Teth pulled back, frowning. "Is something wrong?"

"Teth." She disentangled herself from his arms. "Something happened . . . I haven't told you . . . I haven't told anyone."

The furrow in his brow deepened. "What?"

Ara's heart rammed against her rib cage. Getting the words out caused her physical pain. "When I came back, you, Nimhea, and Joar were fighting the creature."

He nodded.

"I heard you cry out." Her voice was thick. "And I ran to you."

She squeezed her eyes shut against the memory, hating it. "Nimhea shouted for me to stop. She and Joar needed my help, but all I could think about was getting to you. I only cared about helping you."

Forcing herself to look at him, she found Teth watching her with wide eyes.

"Nimhea fell while I was looking for you." Ara's body was shaking. "That thing slashed her face, almost took her eye, while I was gone. She begged for my help, but I ignored her. I can't forgive myself. I don't think she'll ever forgive me."

"Ara." His voice was soft. "Ara."

He rested his hand on her cheek. "You made a hard choice. An impossible choice. I'm so sorry you had to do that."

After pausing for several heartbeats, he drew a long breath, looking deep into her eyes. "But I would have made the same choice."

"Teth—" He didn't understand.

"Because I'm falling in love with you."

The words struck her like a blow. She could feel cracks spreading along her breastbone, the brittleness of the bone itself, ready to splinter. Ready to spear her a thousand times and more.

"I can't," she whispered.

Teth pulled back, searching her face.

"How I feel . . ." Ara couldn't bear this.

But I have to. I have to.

She could still hear Nimhea's scream. The agony of it.

"I can't choose you over another Loreknight," she said. "Don't you see?"

His hand dropped to his side, and his face blanched. "No."

"I'm the Loresmith." Ara couldn't stop now. If she did, she'd never find the strength to finish. "I'm responsible for all the Loreknights. I must lead all the Loreknights. And I must lead them equally. When Joar took up StormSong and defeated that creature in the swamp, I felt the bond between Loresmith and Loreknight, the same bond I have with you."

Teth shifted his weight, her words obviously making him uncomfortable.

Ara bit her lip. She was doing a terrible job of explaining herself. "I don't mean that what I feel for Joar is what I feel for you, personally; that's something completely different."

He relaxed a little, making an attempt at a smile. "Well, that's a relief."

She felt her resolve waver as she looked as his face, into his amber eyes so full of care for her, but she forced herself to continue. "But that's what I was worried about when you became the first Loreknight. That I would treat you differently because of my feelings for you. After what happened to Nimhea, I'm sure of it."

Teth took a step toward her, reaching for her hands. Ara shook her head.

"Teth, I've been forced to realize that romantic love . . . I don't think it can be a part of the Loresmith."

Teth stared at her as if he were looking into the face of a stranger. "Is that what you really believe?"

Is it? Ara didn't know what she believed with any certainty. But she *did know* the guilt that gnawed at her ceaselessly. She *did know* that the scene in the swamp played out in her mind over and over, and with each remembrance, she knew she'd failed as the Loresmith. She'd made the wrong choice, and she'd made that choice because of her feelings for Teth.

She couldn't bring herself to answer him directly. "We can't—"

"Stop." Teth held up one hand. "Don't say anything else."

She didn't argue. There was nothing more to be said.

Ara let him walk away.

She stood alone on the platform, surrounded by the night song of the jungle.

The splinters in her chest buried themselves deep.

Dawn had yet to crest the horizon, and Ara expected to be the first at the stables. Instead, she found herself the last to arrive. The horses were saddled, and Joar was tying the last of their belongings onto one of the packhorses. Teth, Lahvja, and Nimhea were nearby, engaged in a lively conversation.

Ara stopped to watch them. She had passed a miserable night after speaking with Teth, but she'd set a boundary between them that needed to be in place. It was the choice she had to make.

At least that's what she kept telling herself.

Now she approached the second conversation she dreaded.

"Ara!" Nimhea called, spotting her and coming to meet her.

The left side of Nimhea's face was still bandaged, but she otherwise looked in good health.

Ara readied herself for Nimhea's outrage.

Instead, the princess pulled her into a tight embrace.

After momentary shock, Ara recovered and asked, "How are you?"

"Thankful to be alive and out of that swamp," Nimhea replied. She started to smile, then winced. "I have to learn to smile with only the right side of my face for a while."

Ara laughed weakly. She couldn't understand Nimhea's affable mood—it was the absolute opposite of what she'd been expecting.

What if she doesn't remember?

Ara hadn't considered that possibility and wondered what Nimhea did remember of the fight. If Nimhea had forgotten parts of the battle, then only Ara and Teth might know what happened. The thought might have provided a feeling of relief, but it didn't. Difficult as it may have been, enduring Nimhea's anger was what Ara felt she deserved. But now she would have to carry her guilt without any chance for forgiveness, unless she filled in the gaps in Nimhea's memory. But if she did that it would undoubtedly cause the princess more pain.

I've done enough to hurt Nimhea.

Except . . . what if her memory came back? Nimhea was still healing. She could very well start to remember more details of the fight, and Ara's choice.

If that happens, it might be worse if I don't tell her the truth. She'll think I've been hiding it from her.

Ara's stomach churned. She had no idea what to do about her predicament.

"I'm eager to continue our journey," Nimhea said, drawing Ara back to the moment.

"Did Lahvja tell you about Joar?" Ara asked, remembering another potential problem.

"She did." Nimhea rolled her shoulders back. "It was a surprise."

For the first time since Nimhea greeted Ara, her warm expression faded, and Ara saw something unpleasant flit across the princess's face. By the next breath it was gone.

She smiled, this time using only the uninjured side of her face. "You have two Loreknights now. Congratulations, Loresmith."

"Thank you." Ara shifted her weight, uneasy. She wanted to say more, to ask how Nimhea really felt about Joar becoming a Loreknight, but it wasn't the right time. She didn't know when it would be.

Joar joined them. "All is ready. We should be on our way."

Ara found Cloud standing next to Dust. Teth was already in the saddle. He didn't say anything when she approached.

After she settled onto Cloud's back, Ara turned to him. "Good morning."

She'd decided she wasn't going to avoid Teth or ignore him despite their unpleasant parting the previous night. Though she'd ended the romantic side of their relationship, Teth was still her companion—and she hoped her friend.

"Good morning," he replied. Neither his voice nor his expression conveyed his feelings toward her. His face was unreadable.

She felt a sudden chill.

As with Nimhea, Ara had expected hurt or anger from Teth, but the absence of emotion unsettled her deeply.

Joar and Huntress led them out of the village, taking the narrow road that led north, toward their next goal. She had passed the trial of the Tangle and forged StormSong. They'd won the battle against a horror of an enemy. Lahvja and Nimhea were well again—making their group complete.

It should have been a triumphant moment.

But Ara rode amid her companions feeling terribly alone.

The Gash deserved its name. A swath of scorched earth spread before them, wide enough to accommodate an army. Fifteen years earlier, the Vokkans had slashed and burned their way into the Vijerian jungle.

The jungle fought back with poisoned flora, fevers, and delirium, and in the end it was nature that prevailed. The Vokkans abandoned their project.

But the Gash remained. Despite the passage of time, nothing had sprouted, leaving the earth blackened and bare. A memorial to the violence that had been done.

It was the past, but also the future that awaited all of Saetlund should the Loresmith quest fail and Nimhea not be restored to the throne. Vokk the Devourer would never be sated. Only the overthrow of the Vokkan conquerors could save the kingdom, its people, and its very earth.

Along with that haunting knowledge, the absence of new growth, of even a hint of green among the char made Ara second-guess her decision to come this way.

All their chatter had ceased when the Gash came into view. Now they stood at its edge, their horses suddenly stomping and skittish. The broad expanse of sky was shocking after so many days in the jungle. Its stark blue glared down at the unnatural scar in the land.

Ara heard Huntress give a low growl.

"The animals do not like this place," Joar said solemnly.

Neither do I, thought Ara.

Cloud jostled her in the saddle, and Ara patted the gelding's neck, trying to soothe him.

"Lahvja, did you know nothing grew here?"

Lahvja's mouth was set in a grim line. "I've heard many things about this place, but I did not know what tales were true."

Joar nodded. "That is the nature of tales."

Gazing at the ground so bereft of life, Ara wanted to go no farther. But to backtrack after having come this far seemed unreasonable.

As if reading Ara's mind, Lahvja said, "If we're going to continue, we should do so. We must set up camp before nightfall."

Ara stiffened her spine and put her heels to Cloud. The horse gave a shrill whinny and balked, but she urged him forward, and he pranced out onto the burned soil. The other horses followed, kicking and tossing their heads with unease. Joar and Huntress took up the rear of their group.

Out of the jungle, they no longer needed to ride single file, but their group stayed in a tight line as they moved ahead one by one, keeping to one side of the Gash. Riding into the center struck Ara as a blatant, foolhardy move, though she couldn't explain why. All she knew was that her instincts told her to spend as little time in this place as possible. She wished they could push the horses into a gallop, but that would leave Joar behind. He could keep up with their mounts at a walk and even a trot, but nothing faster.

No one ventured a conversation as they rode. The jungle that edged the Gash was absent the trilling of insects and calls of birds, as if the nothing of the blackened earth had chased all life away.

Ara called a halt in the late afternoon at a flat stretch of the Gash with a pond nearby. She would have liked to make more progress—everything in her wanted to get out of this place as soon as possible—but she wasn't going to ignore Lahvja's admonition that they should set up camp before dark.

The unsettling quiet shrouded them while they pitched tents and dug a firepit. Joar and Huntress melted into the jungle in search of game for that night's dinner. Teth had taken a pair of horses to the pond to water them. He returned a few minutes later with a look of disgust on his face.

"That water is no good." His nose wrinkled. "Completely stagnant. Smells awful."

Ara smarted at his words. She'd picked this spot to camp specifically for the pond, thinking it would be useful to have a nearby source of water. It hurt more than she expected to be wrong.

Another bad choice. The thought came unbidden, and she batted it away.

"We have enough water for the horses," Ara told him.

"For now," he muttered, not bothering to meet her gaze.

Ara hated how flat his voice was, missing all the warmth and cleverness that usually spouted from the thief.

"Teth—" Ara walked toward him.

He immediately turned away from her. "I'm going for firewood."

Her chest tightened with grief, but the sadness quickly flared into anger.

How dare he act like this? He's being selfish. It's not my fault I'm the Loresmith.

The last thought was childish, but Ara held on to her anger because it felt better than regret.

And because she didn't know what else to do.

"What's wrong with Teth?"

Ara startled, jumping back. She'd been so focused on Teth that she hadn't noticed Nimhea approach.

"Sorry," Nimhea said. "Didn't mean to scare you."

"You didn't," Ara said quickly. She found it difficult to look Nimhea in the eye. "I was just . . ."

The words trailed off, but Nimhea smiled.

"You two having a lovers' spat?"

With a weak laugh, Ara replied, "Something like that."

"Don't worry about it too much." Nimhea patted her on the shoulder. "I can't imagine anything keeping the two of you apart for long."

Ara swallowed the sudden jagged lump in her throat.

Nimhea was watching her with a puzzled look.

Eager to avoid any more questions about Teth, Ara asked, "How are you feeling?"

"Sore." Nimhea lightly touched the bandages on her face. "But Lahvja says I'm healing well. The bandages will come off in another few days."

Ara's jaw clenched. She hoped her emotions weren't written on her face. The thought of Nimhea scarred, forever changed, sent a wave of guilt crashing over her.

I have to tell her.

"Nimhea—"

"I haven't told Lahvja this—she's been so attentive, and I know she wants to be reassuring." Nimhea spoke quickly, like she was making a confession. What had been a calm demeanor dissolved into a wan mask.

"But I'm afraid. What will I look like? You saw the wounds. Tell me how bad it is."

It all came rushing back to Ara. Nimhea's scream. The swamp. The fight. Nimhea lying on the ground, her face ripped open.

"If Lahvja says you're healing well . . ." Ara faltered, not knowing how to continue.

"Please," Nimhea said. "Tell me the truth."

"I think it will be . . . difficult," Ara told her. "Your wounds were severe."

And they're my fault.

Nimhea bowed her head and was silent for a moment.

"Thank you," she said finally. "I needed to hear that."

Ara took her hand. "I'm sorry."

"You have nothing to be sorry for," Nimhea replied.

So that's it. She doesn't remember.

Ara wanted to say more, but the words wouldn't come out. She was frozen with panic.

What if she can't forgive me? Will she leave?

There came a sudden rustling among the trees, and Joar appeared, stomping out of the jungle, Huntress loping at his side.

He wore an expression of bewilderment. "There is no game."

"Don't be too hard on yourself, Joar," Nimhea said. Her somber mood had vanished at Joar's appearance. "No one is lucky in a hunt every time."

Joar shook his head. "No. There is nothing to hunt. The jungle has been abandoned." Looking over the charred expanse of the Gash, he added, "The animals shun this place."

Nimhea frowned at him. "I'm sure that's not it. They're just being shy." She took the big man's arm. "Lahvja won't have trouble coming up with something for dinner that doesn't involve fresh meat."

Still unsettled by her conversation with Nimhea, Ara forced herself to let it go. The time for facing up to what she'd done would come, but for now it would have to wait. She followed the hunter and princess to meet Lahvja, and soon all three of them were chopping vegetables. The chatter and laughter that had been absent since they'd entered the Gash returned as they worked together to ready the meal, and the ache in Ara's heart began to ease. Though Nimhea had admitted her fears to Ara, the princess seemed to be genuinely in good spirits, and Joar was taking to heart his new membership in their small cadre.

Teth returned with firewood and assigned himself the task of building the cooking fire. Flames began to crackle and smoke curled in wisps, and Ara's mouth began to water at the promise of dinner.

A cry broke through the night air, a sound unlike any Ara had heard. Keening and shrill—a wolf's howl wrapped in an eagle's scream.

Lahvja suddenly dropped to her knees, gasping. Nimhea crouched beside her.

"What's wrong?"

More cries joined the first. The noise grew piercing, like a sharp point driving into her eardrums. Ara covered her ears and saw Teth do the same. Joar's face twisted with pain, but his expression was one of intense concentration. Beside him, Huntress pawed at her ears, snarling and whimpering.

The campfire caught fully, fire licking the logs. Smoke belched into the sky, taking the shape of claws that tore at the air. The shrieking cries became louder still.

Teth dropped to the ground, arms wrapped around his head. Nimhea was holding Lahvja, whose mouth was open wide as if she was screaming, but Ara could hear nothing besides the preternatural cries.

The terrible sound forced Ara to her knees beside the fire a moment later. Tears leaked from her eyes. Her skull wanted to split open.

The campfire's flames became the color of blood. Ara stared at the fire, mind driven blank by the pain. Shadows darted within the crimson, taking the shape of animals. She watched the beasts rush through the dark flames, as though they fled something terrible. Their fear seeped into her limbs; panic seized her, stealing her breath. One by one, the animals' flesh tore away in chunks until nothing was left but bone. Ara's eyes were wide with horror as painful throbs pulsed through her body. The fleeing skeletons began to crack, breaking into sharp bone shards that rose up in the bloody fire and suddenly flew at Ara's face. She screamed, throwing her arms over her eyes and rolling away, but nothing touched her.

Warily, she turned back to the fire, which was still blood red. The shadows returned, becoming animals, and the scene began to repeat itself. Her panic, which had shattered when she turned away, simmered once more.

"The fire!" Ara shouted to Joar, who was the only person still standing. "Put out the fire!"

Joar didn't move. He was still focused on the sound, but struggling against the agony of it.

Realizing he couldn't hear her, Ara struggled to her feet and ran to him. She grabbed his arm, and he blinked at her in surprise.

"We need to put out the fire!" she screamed as loud as she could.

She saw comprehension in his eyes. He crouched low and clawed through the burnt ground until he could scoop giant handfuls of dirt onto the fire. Ara grabbed Lahvja's cooking pot and stumbled to the pond. She plunged the pot into its stagnant depths, releasing a foul stench that made her gag.

When she returned to camp, the fire was struggling against Joar's attempt to suffocate it. Its smoke had become oily and sinuous. Ara dumped the pot of viscous water over the remaining flames. The answering cloud of steam and its sickening odor knocked Ara back. She tripped over Teth's legs and fell.

Joar heaped more dirt over the smoldering pile.

The shrieking all around them became a long, wavering groan and was gone. The night fell silent once more.

Ara lay on the ground, gasping. The sky above her, which had been ink black, now winked with scattered stars.

"Are you hurt?" Teth had propped himself up on his elbows and was looking at her. Her lower legs were still draped over his knees from when she'd tripped.

She quickly rolled away from him and pushed herself up.

"I'm all right," she said, though standing so quickly had left her dizzy. "You?"

His expression, which had been open and worried, quickly shuttered. "Fine."

Teth's curt tone made her wince inwardly, but she turned to the others. "Lahvja? Nimhea?"

Lahvja's head rested in Nimhea's lap. The princess stroked Lahvja's hair.

"I think we're okay," Nimhea answered. "I know that was painful for all of us, but it's affected Lahvja more severely."

In reply, Lahvja made a weak but affirmative sound.

"Hush," Nimhea told her gently. "You can explain later."

"How did you know to put out the fire?" Joar asked.

Huntress slunk up beside him, pressing her head into his leg. He rested his hand on her shoulder, and the wolf gave his knee a friendly lick.

"I—" Ara began, but looked at Lahvja, whose eyes were still shut tight, her body trembling. "We should wait to speak of it until morning. Right now we should all try to rest."

Teth threw her a sharp glance. "You think it's safe?"

"I don't know if *safe* is the right word," Ara answered carefully. "But I think we should try to sleep."

Teth appeared unhappy with her vague reply, but Nimhea and Joar both nodded. They all quietly retreated to their tents.

Ara stretched out on her bedroll, exhausted but unsure she'd be able to sleep. She'd spoken the truth—she was certain the terrors of that night were finished. But they would pass two more nights in this place, and whatever was happening to them in the Gash, she didn't think it was over.

Breakfast consisted of crusty bread, hard cheese, and dark words. Sullen clouds, heavy with rain, pressed down upon them. There was no wind, leaving the air thick and close.

Ara had passed a dreamless night in her tent. She stirred at dawn, as did her friends. Wordlessly, they'd gathered around the remains of the campfire. Lahvja's expression was strained. Despite the heat she had a cloak drawn about her, and Nimhea took over the usual task of distributing food for the meal.

"What was that last night?" Teth turned a hunk of bread over in his hands.

Ara exchanged a look with Joar.

"I'm not sure," Ara answered. "But I saw something in the fire— shapes like animals. Blood. Bones."

"You bore witness to their suffering and death." Lahvja's voice croaked.

Ara startled at the strange sound.

Nimhea urged Lahvja to take a sip of water.

"Our minds were trapped in their terror and torment." Lahvja's words were clearer now, but still gravelly. "Until the spell was broken."

"Ara and I put out the fire," Joar said, scratching his throat absentmindedly. "And the sound stopped. Did we break the spell?"

Lahvja nodded. "You must have. Fire was a weapon the Vokkans used against the jungle. Our campfire became the focus of the curse."

"Someone cursed us?" Teth spoke glibly, but his jaw tightened. "How rude."

"Not someone," Lahvja told him, pulling the cloak tighter across her shoulders. "I believe the earth itself bears a curse, and it will be visited upon us while we are here."

Joar gulped down a fistful of bread and cheese. He seemed to be the only one among them with an appetite. "Perhaps if we have no more campfire, we will be left in peace."

"It's possible," Lahvja said, biting her lip. "I know not what actions will enrage or appease the spirits here."

"I will not hunt," Joar said, then sighed. "There was no game to be found as it was."

Lahvja nodded slowly. "That is wise."

"You said the spirits perceived fire as a weapon." Ara tucked a stray lock of hair behind her ear. "The Vokkans would have used other means to clear the jungle. Swords. Axes."

"You think we should stow our weapons." Nimhea frowned as she took Ara's meaning. "That would leave us defenseless."

Ara's hands tightened on Ironbranch. Would the Loresmith stave have to be stowed away as well? It wasn't an offensive weapon, but she didn't know if that mattered. The thought of relinquishing it set her teeth on edge.

"I think we need to consider what we would be defending ourselves from," Ara replied. "Joar found the jungle emptied. We don't have to worry about predators stalking us from there. And the Vokkans aren't patrolling here."

Pushing his plate aside, Teth said, "I'm with Nimhea on this. I don't think we should stow our weapons just yet. We have no idea what else this place might throw at us."

Ara's hackles rose. She was about to reply, but Joar spoke first.

"My inclination is to agree with him and the princess." He gritted his teeth, uneasy. "Until we have more clarity as to the nature of this cursed place, we should keep our arms."

"Very well," Ara replied stiffly.

The day passed uneventfully. Rain refused to come, and Ara shifted in her saddle frequently, irritated by the sweat and damp. She lifted her face to the sky, willing the storm to come. Being soaked had to be better than this stifling heat, and the rainwater could be collected—every water source they'd come across had been like the first pond. Rank and noxious.

Cloud was likewise unhappy with the weather—and his surroundings—tossing his head and champing at the bit. Ara tried to settle him without success.

Her friends fared no better. Their mounts, stuck in foul moods, trotted with ears laid back, snorting and even snapping at one another or kicking at the packhorses.

Joar's long strides had no trouble keeping pace with the group, though he wisely gave the horses a wide berth. Huntress had abandoned them, seeking the shade—or perhaps solitude—of the jungle.

In the late afternoon, Ara called for a halt. They made camp on a rise that offered a long view of the distance they'd come across the Gash and the miles they had left to travel.

As Ara gazed northward, toward the end of this miserable trek, Teth came up beside her.

"Tomorrow night we'll be able to reach a fort the Vokkans abandoned." He wiped sweat from his brow. "It will offer additional protection . . . should we need it."

"Good." Ara risked a sidelong glance at him. "How are you?"

His lips twisted in a sour smile. "Hot. Itchy."

"Me too." Ara grimaced. "But that's not—"

"I know what you meant." He pivoted to face her. His eyes were hard. "What do you want me to say?"

She had to avert her gaze. It hurt too much to see the bitterness written on his face. "I don't know. I just . . . I want us to be okay."

"Okay." His laugh was horrible. "What exactly does 'okay' mean to you?"

Forcing herself to look at him, she said, "We're friends."

"I suppose we are." That strange smile was back. "But we were something more. Much more."

The loose easiness of his bearing was nowhere to be seen. He sat rigidly in the saddle; his every movement seemed stiff, forced.

It hurt to breathe as Ara watched him. "I know."

All she wanted to do was lean over to him and take his hand. She wanted to beg forgiveness for everything she'd said.

But Nimhea.

With a dry chuckle, Teth muttered, "I'm pining for my old life. When it was me, Fox, and pilfering. Good times."

"I don't blame you," Ara said. "I wish I could help."

"I'm sure you do," Teth replied, then looked at her sharply. "You may not like it, but I get to be angry. I will feel whatever I need to feel. I'm not going to let you down. I'm not going to turn my back on the Loresmith or the princess who must be queen, but you can't expect me to be happy."

He held her gaze for another moment and then reined Dust away.

Twisting in the saddle, he added with the flicker of a smile, "Don't worry about me. Maybe I'll start stealing things from Joar and see how long it takes him to notice. That'll make me feel better."

The sun dipped below the horizon, and darkness drenched the Gash. The clouds had not abated, and with no moon, stars, or fire to offer light, Ara and her companions were left to fumble in the darkness.

They'd pitched the tents in a tight circle and now sat together within a yet smaller circle and passed a loaf of bread around. Night brought little relief from the heat, and while Ara knew she was still sweating, the moisture on her skin seemed to increase more than the temperature warranted. She ran a hand down her arm, and her fingers came away dripping. The air felt thicker. Touching her lips, Ara found moisture there, too.

Fog. She couldn't see it, but she sensed the clouds had descended and now blanketed them.

"Ugh," Ara heard Teth say. "As if I wasn't already wet enough. I think I'm going to bed. Who wants to wager I'll get lost even though my tent is supposedly right behind me?"

Joar made a low sound that was something between a grunt and a laugh.

"Wait, friend." Lahvja's voice was tremulous. "Something about this sudden fog troubles me."

"Well, if that isn't exactly what I was hoping to hear," Teth replied. "Troubling fog: Who doesn't love it?"

"Hush, Teth." Nimhea's voice was low but firm. "I hear something."

They fell silent, waiting to catch whatever sound had caught Nimhea's attention.

The noise came suddenly, making Ara jump.

A coughing, or perhaps a rough bark. Then a snuffling. Nothing resembling the shrieks of the previous night. The sound wasn't close by, but neither was it that far off.

Ara had set Ironbranch on her right side when she sat down. Now she drew the stave into her lap. The slithering rasp of steel against leather told her that Nimhea had drawn her sword. She could only assume Joar and Teth had armed themselves as well.

The sound came again. Closer now.

Then an answering bark. Then a growl. And another.

Ara's heart gave a heavy thud.

The next sound came from above, and her head snapped up, trying to track whatever had made the noise. She squinted into the dark.

Why bother? I can't see anything.

But then her eyes did catch something. Barely. A shape swooping over the camp.

Were the clouds parting?

She peered at the sky, but no, whatever light filtered through the air wasn't coming from the moon. The light was a strange, unpleasant color. A harsh yellow that wavered, strengthening then fading like a guttering candle.

It was coming from the fog.

More noises rose in the night. The hacking bark-like sounds continued along with the snuffling. A long, stuttering whistle briefly overwhelmed the rest.

"That was a moss elk," Joar said. "I'm sure of it, but—"

"What?" Ara asked. She had to raise her voice above the growing chorus around them.

"The call was broken . . . wrong." She could hear the tension in his voice.

The unsteady whistle came again and was joined by others. New sounds shot out of the dark. Louder. Closer.

The occasional shadow passing over them became many. Birds of every size circling their camp. Ara watched their silhouettes, a frown knitting her brow. The bird shapes didn't seem right. Wings bent at angles that shouldn't have been possible. Heads drooped where necks should have held them upright.

The yellow light remained unsteady but grew brighter.

Ara gasped.

The birds, flying ever lower, were revealed in the new light—and they were diseased. At least that was what Ara thought. Bald patches. Missing feathers. Broken beaks. So many were in ravaged states that flight shouldn't have been possible.

"Senn's teeth!" Teth's shout brought Ara's gaze back to their camp.

Her stomach lurched when she saw shapes moving through the yellow fog. She turned her head.

Animals. There were animals moving through the light, dipping in and out of shadow.

The camp was surrounded.

The noise was ceaseless. Growls. Barks. Whistles. Snarls. Moaning calls. Shrill chittering. It was the song of the jungle, and yet not. This wasn't the riot of joyful sound Ara remembered from their journey to the Tangle. The cries surrounding them were jarring, stopping and starting at irregular intervals. Sounding at bizarre pitches. Gargling and belching. Suddenly strangled.

Broken. Like Joar had said.

Ara saw the moss elk first. It walked toward them with stilted steps. When the elk lifted its head to make its whistling call, Ara thought she would be sick.

The elk's throat had been ripped open. Shreds of fur and flesh hung down, slapping against its legs as it walked. Another elk appeared alongside the first. Its back was broken, spine split by a deep, bloody gash, and yet it came forward, rear legs dragging behind.

"This cannot be." Joar stared at the animals. He bowed his head, and Ara saw his body was shaking. "It must not be."

Nimhea was on her feet. She put herself between the encroaching beasts and Lahvja, who sat rigid, gazing out into the fog.

Ara pushed herself up on legs that didn't want to stand. Teth slowly rose. He had Tears of the Traitor, bow and quiver, in each hand. Joar remained on his knees.

More creatures materialized in the wavering yellow light. Ara saw snakes that had been sliced apart slithering along the perimeter of the camp. Some were missing tails, others heads. A great jungle cat with striped fur, stalking back and forth. The fur and flesh of its face had been burned away, and the empty sockets of its eyes stared balefully at Ara. Monkeys missing limbs, drenched in blood, or charred to the bone scampered by, hooting and screeching.

Wild dogs roamed in a pack whose members had been reduced to skeletons.

The animals were so close now that a wave of stench swept over the camp. Ara began to cough, then gag. She leaned against Ironbranch to keep herself upright. The smell was like that of the pond water, but immeasurably worse. A miasma of rot and ruin. The acrid odor of burnt fur and smoking flesh. The sickening sweetness of decay.

Ara could no longer discern one animal's call from another's. Their cries had become a wall of moans that rose and fell like the swells of the ocean. They pressed closer and closer.

Something bumped against Ara and she yelped, but it was only Teth. Backing away from the circling beasts, they'd run into each other. Turning further, Ara saw they were almost on top of Joar. Lahvja had crawled to the hunter. She held his hands, and her head was pressed against his. Nimhea stood guard over them, her back to Teth and Ara.

The animals continued to circle the tents. The birds swooped low enough that Ara felt the rush of air from their wings. Any creature that still had eyes fixed their gazes upon the tight group of humans. The reek of death saturated the air.

Beside Ara, Teth bent over, retching. He straightened, wiped his mouth with the back of his hand, and then, after slinging the quiver over his shoulder, he drew an arrow and notched.

All at once the animals screamed. The sound was like a physical blow. Ara stumbled, almost losing her grip on Ironbranch.

Teth swore, steadying himself so he could take aim.

"Ready?" he called.

Nimhea shouted back. "Ready!"

Her sword gleamed in the sickly yellow fog.

The elk whose throat hung open, dripping gore, snorted, lowering his head and brandishing the many spikes of his antlers.

Ara watched as Teth pointed his arrow at the elk's bowed head.

The impossibility of what was about to happen sent a shock through her limbs. There was no way that elk could be alive. What was the point of killing something that was already dead?

"Teth, wait—" Ara caught the twitch of his hand, and she was almost too late. But not quite.

She grabbed Tears of the Traitor, forcing the bow down. The arrow thunked into the earth.

"Ara, what the—"

She heard Teth's shout, but she looked at the elk. It had reared up, striking the air with its hooves, and uttered a wet, choking bellow. But it didn't charge.

Teth seized her arm. "What was that?"

"We can't kill them." Ara leaned close, making sure he could hear her over the din of animal cries. "They're already dead. How can we kill them?"

He drew back, shaking his head. "Then what are we supposed to do?"

Ara stared at him. She didn't have an answer.

"Lay your weapons down." Joar's voice boomed like thunder.

The big man looked at Ara. "Your instinct was right, Loresmith. In this place our blades and bows turn against us."

"Are you sure about this?" Teth asked, his voice tight with nerves. "In case you haven't noticed, we're surrounded."

Joar's answering smile was a shock, considering their predicament. "Lay down your bow, Loreknight, and join hands with your fellows."

As he spoke, Ara noticed that Lahvja had risen and stood beside Nimhea. The princess had sheathed her sword, and she'd taken Lahvja's hand. The summoner took one of Joar's hands. Joar reached out to Teth, and Ara accepted Nimhea's outstretched hand.

Ara turned to Teth. He looked down at her hand. She watched as his fingers reluctantly touched hers. That light caress stole Ara's breath and wrenched her heart. She closed her eyes against tears that suddenly wanted to come. When he folded her hand in his, she swallowed a sob. Her eyes were shut tight, and she was afraid to open them.

Roars, snarls, screeches, barks pounded her ears. Louder. Louder.

But then another sound joined the awful chorus. A different sound.

Low and sonorous, the new noise rumbled steadily against the chaos of the animals' cries.

Ara listened to the deep, rolling pitch, her ears following as it rose and fell. It took several minutes, but she began to recognize that it was a song.

Daring to open her eyes, Ara looked around the circle of her friends and saw Joar's lips moving. His eyes were closed, but his face lifted. Tears slid from beneath his eyelids, trailing down his cheeks and jaw before dropping to the ground.

Joar sang in a language Ara couldn't understand, but she had no trouble discerning the emotion behind his song. It was a dirge, slow and mournful. Each note bore the weight of terrible grief, a sorrow unending. The song was beautiful, yet unbearable in its sadness.

The tears that had been born of her own grief about Teth now fell because of Joar's song.

Ara wasn't the only one who cried. The faces of her friends were streaked with salt water. Teth's grip on her hand tightened. She responded by lacing her fingers through his.

Joar's lament filled the night, rising through the fog. Ara was so consumed by the heartrending melody that she barely noticed the fading of the animals' cries, nor did she realize the yellow fog was slowly dissolving until darkness covered the earth once again.

Only when Joar sounded the song's final note and the echo of his voice faded, rendering the night silent, did Ara come out of her reverie.

The animals were gone, leaving no sign that they'd ever existed.

18

iran stood outside the cell, staring at the boy who sat on a cot within. The boy stared back at him.

When Liran had pressed Zenar on his precise plans for bringing their father's reign to an end, his brother had demurred. His answer was simply "In time, in time," which was no answer at all. Zenar had, Liran surmised, revealed more than he'd intended in that meeting and regretted his words. Zenar was quick, too quick, to acquiesce to Liran's request to interview Prince Eamon on his own.

"Who are you?" Prince Eamon asked, and Liran realized he'd been watching the boy without speaking for an unusual amount of time.

He'd been thrown by how very young Eamon appeared. Younger than his eighteen years. A boy rather than a man, who could not have fully grasped the treachery Zenar had demanded of him. But perhaps his innocence had been what made the boy susceptible to Zenar's promises in the first place. His expression was earnest, and surprisingly unafraid.

"Liran, Commander of the Imperial Armies," Liran said.

"ArchWizard Zenar's brother." Eamon's eyes widened, making him appear even more childlike. "The Dark Star."

Liran frowned. It irked him to be first known by association to his younger brother, but it was the title Eamon gave him, "the Dark Star," that made Liran's skin prickle. He carried many titles, and had always regarded them like unnecessary and garish jewelry, but Eamon spoke the words as if they held significance Liran couldn't begin to comprehend.

Rolling his shoulders back, Liran began to pace in front of the cell. He found looking directly at the boy too unsettling.

"You claim to be Prince Eamon," he said. "Son of Dentroth and sister to Nimhea, Dentroth's heir."

"I *am* Eamon." The boy rose. "Why would I lie about that?"

Liran shrugged. "To gain Zenar's favor of course, or perhaps in the hope of some reward. There's no real proof you are who you say you are."

Eamon stared at him in disbelief. "But I brought Ofrit's scroll. I've been in touch with the wizards all through our journey." He paused, choking on the words. "I abandoned my sister."

Interesting. The young prince didn't hesitate before confessing the full nature of his relationship to Zenar. He could just as easily have remained silent or derided the princess for her design to reclaim the River Throne and cast the empire out of Saetlund.

"And that tells me what precisely?" Liran waved a dismissive hand, making a show of arrogance he didn't actually feel. "Fifteen years have passed since the conquest, and our scholars are still finding hidden rooms and secret caches in the libraries of Zyre and Isar. I'm certain scrolls such as the one you brought the ArchWizard have found their way into the hands of underworld operators. You're no more than an urchin from Sola, hoping to better your fortune through deceit."

Eamon's hands balled into fists, and outrage flashed through his eyes. "I am no urchin."

At that Liran smiled. He had the pride of the prince if not the bearing or confidence.

"Let's pretend for a moment that I believe you," Liran said. "Why would a prince of Saetlund ally himself with the ArchWizard of Vokk?"

The anger bled out of Eamon's gaze. "Surely Zenar will have told you."

So this was a topic the boy wanted to avoid. He was proud of his identity, but not of his actions.

"I'd like to hear what you have to say," Liran told him.

Eamon dropped back onto the cot in his cell and stared at the floor. Liran watched with growing curiosity. Not only was the boy uncomfortable with the choices he'd made, he appeared to be ashamed of them. Perhaps even to regret them.

The young prince mumbled something that Liran couldn't make out.

"Say that again."

Eamon raised his face, and there Liran saw not a hint but a world of pain. The boy didn't try to hide any of it. His expression was completely open and completely broken.

"I didn't think we could win."

"If you didn't think you could win, why bother coming to Saetlund at all?" Liran asked.

"To protect Nimhea," Eamon blurted, his cheeks reddening. "And to help myself."

"Help yourself how?"

Eamon shifted his weight. "I've always been ill. Weak. No healers could help me . . . but I thought magic could."

Liran regarded the boy thoughtfully. "And the wizards of Vokk wield the most powerful magics in the world."

Eamon began to nod, but then frowned. "I used to believe that."

"You don't any longer?" The admission surprised Liran.

The boy was looking at Liran without seeing him. His mind had gone somewhere distant.

"I've seen legends come to life." Eamon spoke quietly. "And I don't know what to believe anymore."

Liran was finding it hard to make sense of the prince. There had been no pleading or cajoling, no demands to know what fate had been decided for him. Eamon simply appeared to be resigned, but resigned to what Liran couldn't fathom.

"May I ask you a question?" Eamon's voice was so polite, Liran almost laughed.

"You may."

"What is happening to the children?"

An icy fist slammed into Liran's chest, but he managed not to visibly react to the question. When he remained silent, Eamon's brow knit together.

"I watch them file past." His gaze moved to the descending spiral steps. "They go down but never come back up." He shivered. "Sometimes at night I hear them."

Looking at Liran intently, he asked, "Why are they here?"

"I cannot tell you," Liran answered stiffly.

It was the truth. Liran knew nothing of children in the Temple of Vokk.

As commander of the imperial armies, Liran was all too familiar with the Embrace. The empire's practice of gathering the children of a conquered nation and shipping them to Vokk in order to "enfold them in the empire" had been established long before Liran's time. However effective the Embrace was at cowing populations, it was also costly in how far it went toward stoking resentment and rebellion in conquered peoples.

Liran had created an extensive proposal for his father, articulating the logic of discontinuing the Embrace for the sake of the empire's survival, but his ideas had been summarily rejected. When he asked for explanation, his father's only reply had been: "We need the children. We will always need the children."

And so the Embrace had continued with each new conquest. But Saetlund's Embrace had occurred over a decade ago. There was no reason for children to be imprisoned in the Temple of Vokk.

Whatever was taking place, Zenar had been careful to keep him from knowing.

They go down but never come back up.

Those words would haunt him until he understood their meaning. He suspected they still might after he learned the truth of what Zenar hid in the temple's bowels.

He considered pressing Eamon for more information, but didn't want to risk revealing his own ignorance on the matter. He also couldn't deny the spike of guilt he felt at knowing nothing about children being stolen and made to suffer under his watch. He should have been keeping a closer eye on Zenar's activities.

"Until next time." Liran turned away from Eamon and quickly climbed the stairs.

What is Zenar up to? Whose children are being marched past Eamon's cell?

Liran's gut told him he wouldn't get the answers he needed by confronting his brother. No, this was a mystery he'd have to unravel himself, all while ignoring the cold dread of what he might find.

He had planned to return to the war offices, but was intercepted by a servant with a summons from Zenar.

Entering the ArchWizard's office, Liran felt a fresh wave of revulsion. He'd been in this place far too often of late.

"Commander!" Zenar sat behind his desk, waving his brother into the room. "Thank you for joining us."

Us?

It was then Liran noticed that one of the chairs facing Zenar's desk was occupied by a bald, long-nosed man whose form strained against his finely tailored clothes like a sausage against its casing. The man had pale skin, a pencil of a black mustache, and wide, slack lips. His face bore a sheen of sweat despite the cool temperature of the room.

Zenar gestured to the other chair, but Liran opted to stand. Whatever this meeting was, he hoped it would be brief. If his body language could help make that happen, all the better.

Speaking to the stranger, Zenar said, "May I introduce my brother, Commander Liran. Commander, this is Fergin, the Low King of Kelden."

Liran kept his face neutral, but was surprised to learn the man's identity. He knew of the Low Kings—sometime leaders of the criminal elements of society—but dealings with them fell under the purview of the Office of Commerce. Liran bore no illusions about the corruption that fueled imperial financial dealings, and it was nothing to concern him.

"His Majesty"—Zenar only just kept the sneer out of his voice—"was recommended to me by Chancellor Pilth. A situation has developed that could be to our great advantage. In order to exploit it, I will require your assistance."

Liran briefly inclined his head to indicate interest.

"Fergin." Zenar gestured for the man to speak.

"Lord Commander." Fergin stared at Liran with black, bulging eyes. "I's here as a loyal servant of Emperor Fauld. I been true to my contracts fro' the very first. Ne'er skimming more than a bit—ya see, I has to take a bit else my men'll think I's soft—and only runnin' a few side deals, for the same reason—"

"Fergin." Zenar's cutting tone hurried the man to the point.

"Apologies, Your Lord Wizardship," Fergin babbled. "The other kings and queens, ya see, they's always too big for their britches. They's thinking they can outdo the empire. Fools they are, hearin' mad tales and then making mad deals."

Liran cleared his throat. "I'm afraid you'll need to be more specific."

"Of course, of course." Spittle gathered in the corners of the man's mouth as he spoke. "Ya see, the worst of the lot. King Lucket of Fjeri. Thinks he's so fine. He fancies himself the leader of us Low Kings, even though we's supposed to be equals. Great priggy lout that one, as if Fjeri isn't all brutes and bear shaggers."

"How colorful," Zenar murmured.

"It's no better than Kelden," Fergin said sourly. "Fruit an' fine horses we have. Fruit an' fine horses!"

"You were saying about King Lucket?" Liran prompted.

"Oh, that fiend Lucket!" Fergin spat on the rug, then froze, looking at Zenar in horror.

"It's nothing." Zenar smiled at him, then when Fergin looked about to blubber his thanks, quickly said, "Tell my brother about the alliance."

Fergin's pale face went beet red. "Alliance! It's our ruin. Lucket's goin' to bring the wrath of Fauld down on all of us, the fool. His fine words and clever talk got the other kings and queens wrapped around his finger. Help the rebellion, bah! Lost princess, rubbish!"

"Help the rebellion." Liran was suddenly very interested in what this man had to say. "What do you mean?"

"Lucket's got the Below workin' for the Resistance!" Fergin bleated. "But not me. Never me. Fergin's no fool!"

Zenar cut in. "You can see why Chancellor Pilth thought I might be interested to hear what King Fergin had to say."

"I can," Liran replied. His mind was working very quickly. He was aware of the Below's recent alliance with the Resistance, and the boon it was to them. To have it undermined would be a huge blow.

Zenar rose and went to a cabinet. He filled a crystal goblet with golden liquid. When he returned he offered it to Fergin.

"A toast to you, Your Majesty, and your continued partnership with the empire."

Fergin squinted at the goblet for a moment with suspicion, then, seeing Zenar's stern expression, thought better of it. He snatched the goblet and downed its contents. His eyes widened and he smacked his lips, apparently delighted at the taste. His wide mouth spread into a horrible, bliss-filled grin, then he slumped in the chair, rolled over, and fell face-first onto the rug.

"Dead?" Liran asked.

"Oh, no," Zenar replied, settling into his chair once more. "I just wanted to give us a bit of privacy as we discuss what to do with this information."

Liran nodded and decided he would sit after all.

19

he darkness and silence were so complete that Ara jumped when Nimhea spoke.

"What happened?" Her voice was a reverent whisper.

Lahvja answered, "We mourned, for them and with them. For that they have given us a reprieve. We will be allowed to pass through this place cursed by the Vokkans' greed and violence."

The truth of her words resonated in Ara's limbs. She had felt grief, raw and burning, unlike any sorrow she'd known. She'd been too small at the time of her father's, mother's, and grandfather's passing to know true grief. But tonight she had felt the loss of not a single life, but thousands—not only the beasts of the jungle, but the trees and vines, the flowers and creeping insects. So much life hacked apart or scorched to oblivion. The force of it had been overwhelming. If not for the hands of her companions, grasping hers so tightly, she would have swooned beneath the emotion.

Even now, she was shaken. Sorrow constricted her breath. Her muscles were weak, her knees trembling simply from the effort of keeping her upright. She felt inexplicably empty.

I must not fail. I cannot let the Vokkans destroy Saetlund.

A similar unsteadiness held sway in Teth's voice when he asked, "If my arrow had found its mark . . ."

He couldn't finish the question.

"We would likely be dead," Lahvja answered in a flat tone. "You cannot kill a spirit. Only appease it."

Silence engulfed them once more.

Several moments later, Lahvja spoke again. "We can talk of it further tomorrow, if you wish. But for now we sorely need rest."

No one answered, but Nimhea released Ara's hand. Teth did not. Their fingers remained entangled.

Ara didn't want to let go. She'd forced a change between them, drawn a line at romance. But romance wasn't what she needed, and she sensed that wasn't what Teth wanted. It was something deeper, more visceral. The simple presence of another after bearing witness to horror.

There was a shuffling of feet as the others sought their tents.

Teth gave a gentle tug on Ara's hand. She didn't object when he slowly led her through the dark. She heard the rustle of a tent flap being lifted—she didn't know if it was hers or Teth's. He released her hand, but only to move his to her shoulder, pushing down so she crouched to pass through the opening. He followed then moved past her, keeping one hand lightly on her arm as he moved. Then he took both of her wrists, pulling her down until she knelt, feeling the softness of a bedroll beneath her.

Teth moved again, this time behind her. He wrapped one arm around her waist, guiding her onto the bedroll so she stretched alongside him. Her body curled against his, the firmness of his legs and torso pressed into her, surrounding her with warmth.

He didn't speak, nor did he kiss her. His fingers didn't caress her. He only held her close, his breath soft against the crown of her head.

Ara closed her eyes, letting his embrace wash over her until the tension in her muscles eased and the lingering grief loosened its grip until, at last, sleep stole her away.

Teth was gone from the tent when Ara awoke.

The memory of what had transpired the night before, and of Teth's arms around her, sat her bolt upright. She was alone, left to wonder when he'd left her and what he'd been feeling when he slipped from the bedroll without waking her.

As to her own feelings, Ara didn't want to examine them too closely. She was horribly aware of how much she didn't like that Teth hadn't been beside her when she woke. It left a hollow cold in her stomach. Nor did she want to dissect the significance—if any—of their having spent the night, or most of it, together after she'd broken off their romance. He'd been so angry with her, yet he'd been the one to lead her here last night, to pull her into his arms.

Ara shivered at the memory of his warmth, the feel of him against her. She wished she could stop wanting that closeness from him. If they were to be friends, she had to resist the urge to be close to him, to touch him. Last night had been a lapse in judgement. No matter how much she'd needed the comfort of his embrace. She couldn't let it happen again.

Lahvja gave each of them hand-tied cloths filled with dried fruit and nuts.

"We should break our fast while we ride," she explained. "Though we've been given a reprieve, we must still make our way out of the Gash as soon as possible."

No one disagreed with her, and they were soon on their way toward the abandoned fort located on the far edge of the Gash.

As they rode north, the Gash remained an unpleasant place to travel through, but some of its overt menace seemed to have receded. While Ara didn't feel safe, she no longer sensed she was in imminent danger.

Teth reined Dust in to keep pace beside Cloud. He sighed, stealing a glance at Ara.

Ara gave him a little smile, hoping he'd take it as a peace offering.

"Do you mind if we slow down for a bit?"

"You think we should?" Ara frowned at him.

He gestured to the other riders and Joar. "Not all of us. Just you and I. We can catch up with them in a minute."

She nodded, holding Cloud back until she and Teth fell a short distance behind the rest of the group. He didn't say anything until they were out of earshot.

"I want to apologize for last night." He ran a hand over his hair, unable to look at her. "After what happened I just . . . needed to hold you."

And I needed to be held, Ara thought, but the words stuck in her throat. To admit the truth felt dangerous. Still, she didn't need him to apologize; he'd done nothing wrong. She hadn't objected when he'd led her to the tent, and she hadn't tried to enforce the boundaries she'd laid between them.

She was about to say so when he continued, "You've made it clear how you need things to be between us. And I—"

His jaw clenched, and he forced himself to look at her. "I have to respect that."

It should have been exactly what Ara wanted to hear, but instead she felt a wrench of disappointment.

What? she silently asked herself. *Do you expect him to keep pursuing you when you've told him he can't?*

Her feelings forced her to admit that she did, or at least she'd been secretly hoping he would. She wanted to know that Teth still desired her. That he loved her.

And she recognized how wretchedly unfair that was. She felt awful. A true friend would never treat him that way.

"I also want to apologize for almost getting us all killed," Teth said. "I read the situation wrong. I shouldn't have."

"No one could have known," Ara told him. "I reacted the way I did on instinct. I could have been wrong just as easily."

Shaking his head, he replied, "You don't understand. I live by my instincts. They've never put me in danger. But last night . . . I was still so angry. It twisted everything I was feeling."

"You're being too hard on yourself. We all make mistakes," she said. "There's no avoiding that."

He smiled grimly. "Like you did when you thought you were saving my life."

Ara blanched, and he swore under his breath.

"Ara . . . I'm sorry. That's exactly how I don't want to be with you. What I can't afford to be as a Loreknight. It's why I'm trying to apologize. I promise that's the last remark like that I'm going to make. I've got to let this anger go."

Unclenching her jaw, she said, "It's all right."

It wasn't. Though he didn't say the words, what Ara heard was *I'm letting you go.*

"No, it's not," he insisted. "I do want to be your friend. I promise to do a better job of it."

All she could do was nod while her heart shouted its objections as Teth moved Dust away.

Forcing her thoughts from the ache in her chest, she turned her mind to what had taken place in the Gash, and before that the Tangle. She'd come to believe each place was not simply a trial, but also a lesson. A lesson that was about both the past and the future.

Ara felt as though she was living in a tapestry partly woven, but she could begin to see threads coming together to tell a story. A story of greed, brutality, and loss that in return demanded not retribution, but healing.

A broken people, a broken land.

The Gash offered the starkest example of what the Vokkan conquest had cost Saetlund. Scorched earth where nothing would grow and the water was poison. Spirits of the slaughtered haunting the empty earth each night.

While they had made a conscious choice to traverse the Gash in hopes of avoiding any imperial encounters, Ara's bones quivered with the knowledge that she had been required to bear witness to this place and fully grasp the horrors that had been visited here.

The reality of such an abomination stood in blatant opposition to the trial she'd faced in the Tangle and the wisdom she'd gained there. She'd been required to counter madness, and the wanton devastation that had been wreaked upon the Gash embodied the madness of bloodlust and hate.

She strove to pass the giant python in peace rather than allowing fear to goad her into violence. And it had been the words of a hunter that helped her understand what she needed to do.

I hunt only to eat and kill only when attacked.

To hunt was not to destroy. Those who honored Wuldr lived in balance with nature.

Ara's instincts told her that the Vokkans hadn't waited to be attacked or provoked in any way before ravaging the Vijerian jungle.

Nor did she think they'd stopped to collect and eat what they'd killed while undertaking their mission of fire and blood.

Gazing across the Gash, Ara let the present moment fade away while the past rose up to take its place. The earth remained scorched, but it was still smoking. Carcasses, blackened and bloating, were strewn across the ground, and clouds of insects hovered in the air, thick as fog. The stench made Ara choke, forcing her to pull herself out of the awful vision.

The lesson here was not simply to comprehend what had happened, but to realize what it meant for the future. To make clear what she and the Loreknights would ultimately face. The Vokkan army was massive, its strength nearly incomprehensible, but soldiers were not the greatest threat to their cause. Nor were the wizards. Nor even the emperor himself.

It was the god.

The god from whom the founders of the empire had taken their name.

Vokk the Devourer.

Ara shuddered. This truth had been waiting in the back of her mind, ready to spring forth. And the Gash had made everything terribly clear.

Unlike the people of Saetlund, the Vokkans had never abandoned their god. They existed by the power and for the glory of Vokk. Always hungry, Vokk drove his people forward, from continent to continent, claiming and consuming until nigh all the world was his.

He had promised his brothers and sisters, the gods of Saetlund, to leave their people in peace. But he did not, could not. His hunger was as great as it was endless.

The Resistance might only be concerned with defeating an army, but the Loresmith and her companions could only win by quelling the god's destructive hunger. By stopping the ravening of the world.

But how?

The Loreknights of legend had driven back invasion after invasion, army after army, but none had faced a god. Ara didn't know if it was even possible for humans to defeat a divine being. Yet there could be no denying that the empire would only fall when its god was brought to his knees.

Despite the warmth of the day, Ara pulled out her cloak and drew it around her shoulders. Chills chased through her limbs as her conclusions overwhelmed her. She'd completed two trials, she'd learned from the gods, but nothing she'd experienced had offered the means to face and overcome an immortal being.

It was impossible.

Ara put her heels to Cloud until she took the lead of their group. She kept her gaze on the way ahead, trying to push her gloomy thoughts aside. It was better not to think at all.

20

hey reached the abandoned Vokkan fort at dusk. Though its worn timbers and rusting hinges signaled years of neglect, the structure remained largely intact and looked sound enough from the outside.

Teth called a halt when they were still a good distance from the gates.

"I'll scout first. It's best to make sure no one else has already decided to camp here."

He handed Ara Dust's reins before he slunk across the barren ground toward the fort then disappeared around one side. Several minutes passed before the gate groaned as it was pushed open. Teth stepped out and waved to them.

"You'd better come in!"

There was something pinched about his voice that Ara didn't like. It wasn't fear or a warning, but as if he'd been deeply annoyed by the fort.

Ara led the group forward. Teth had opened the gate wide enough to let the horses pass. When she rode inside, Ara was startled by the flare of torchlight.

Teth wasn't alone. Four other people waited inside the fort: two men and two women. One stood alongside Teth; the other three flanked the first. They bore the torches.

"Loresmith!" The first man hailed her with a slightly mocking note in his voice.

Something about the sound was familiar, and it took her only a moment to place it.

"Your Majesty." Ara dismounted and walked up to the Low King of Fjeri. Garbed in all black, Lucket cut a fine figure in meticulously tailored coat and trousers, a strange sight amid the ruined fort. His silver hair and neatly trimmed beard gleamed in the torchlight.

Teth silently glowered at his adoptive father.

"How nice of you to finally join us." The Low King of Fjeri smiled slowly. "We expected you yesterday."

Ara returned his smile stiffly. "Why are you here?"

Lucket's eyes danced with amusement. "Straight to business, is it? I was hoping we could at least have a drink first. My associates and I have had time to make the barracks slightly more hospitable than we found them."

"We can get to drinks after you explain yourself," she replied.

Teth failed to completely cover his explosion of laughter with a coughing fit.

Ara knew Lucket wasn't the type of man accustomed to explaining himself, but she didn't care. She and her companions had been through too much of late to indulge Lucket's humor.

Something unpleasant flashed through his gaze, but he spoke serenely. "If we must."

"Aren't you going to introduce your friends?" She gestured to the man and women standing behind him.

"No." He looked over her shoulder at the silent watchers, giving Ara the impression that Lucket's followers wouldn't engage with her or her companions unless ordered to. "But you will introduce yours. I'm aware you've lost one, and I know you've gained another, but it seems you've added yet one more. How interesting."

Nimhea came to Ara's side and fixed a steely eye on Lucket.

Not missing a beat, Lucket bowed flawlessly. "Your Highness. It's a genuine pleasure to make your acquaintance."

He gave no indication of being startled by or even interested in her bandaged face except to say, "I trust you are well."

She ignored his words, instead asking, "You're one of the supposed Low Kings I've been told about?"

"There is nothing supposed about it, Princess Nimhea," Lucket replied smoothly. "My name is Lucket, the Low King of Fjeri."

"You instigated the deal with the Resistance to help us," Nimhea said.

He spared a glance at Teth. "I have to give some credit to this one. The idea was his, but I took it to the other Low Kings, and together we agreed on the partnership."

Lahvja appeared at Nimhea's side, resting a hand on her arm. "They're not as bad as you imagine. I promise."

"Thank you, my dear," Lucket said to Lahvja. "I've been looking forward to meeting you. You're a bit of a mystery."

A playful smile appeared on Lahvja's lips as she curtsied. "That's the way I prefer it, Your Majesty."

Tilting his head as he regarded her, Lucket said, "Eni's Children are always the soul of graciousness. It's a shame, what's happening."

A sinking sensation settled beneath Ara's ribs.

Lahvja's smile vanished. "What do you mean?"

The Low King dropped his amused tone as his gaze moved over each of them in turn. "The reason I've intercepted you—partly, at least—is to bring news I decided was best delivered in person."

His calm pronouncement filled Ara with cold anticipation. Lucket wore a bland smile. It amazed her that he could remain so utterly unruffled despite the disturbing words that rolled off his lips.

Returning his attention to Lahvja, Lucket continued, "I regret to tell you that your involvement with the Loresmith has had consequences for your people. The empire has been rounding up the Imperial Players' caravans. My apologies for using that unfortunate term. I know it is abhorred among your own, but the warrants issued read thusly."

Lahvja drew a sharp breath before her shoulders slumped. "I feared such a thing might come to pass."

Nimhea whispered something in Lahvja's ear and slid her arm around the summoner's waist, which Ara watched Lucket take note of.

"Who is being rounded up?" Joar's low voice rumbled at them. He'd been hanging back, cloaked in shadows, but now he stepped into the light. Huntress was a ghost at his side, a wary growl emerging from her chest.

Lucket didn't move, but he blinked several times as he took in Joar's massive form and giant wolf guardian.

"Gotcha," Teth said under his breath, smiling.

Lucket shot an irritated glance at him before focusing again on Joar.

The Low King's eyebrows pulled together. "You're Koelli."

Joar gave a solemn nod.

Lucket kept his face blank, but given Teth's reaction when he'd realized the same about Joar's ancestry, Ara was certain Lucket stewed inside for having been caught off guard by the hunter's presence.

A master of secrets must hate surprises more than almost anything, she thought.

"I would like to know how this is possible," Lucket said in a flat voice.

"And I would like to know you better before I answer such a question," Joar replied.

Lucket's expression was unreadable as he stared at Joar. Then he suddenly pivoted to Teth.

"You haven't told your new companion of our arrangement?"

"We've been busy," Teth shot back, but quickly relented, saying to Joar, "This is Lucket, the Low King of Fjeri; perhaps you've heard of him."

Joar's expression darkened. "The Below is known to me. It is a den of iniquity, which should be shunned."

"You know, I quite like you," Nimhea said to him, laughing.

Unfazed, Lucket replied, "I've heard worse, Koelli."

"My name is Joar," the hunter growled.

"That's good to know," Lucket replied. "You're free to judge my business however you choose, but it's undeniable that you need our assistance. And I'm sure Teth has proven useful from time to time."

"From time to time, my ass," Teth muttered, then he noticed Joar's accusing stare.

"Why does this one speak of you thusly?" Joar asked.

"We're sometime associates to say the least." Spreading his hands helplessly, Teth said, "I must confess I'm an exceptional thief and hope you don't hold it against me, Joar."

"Thieves have no honor," the hunter growled.

"I remember saying that once," Nimhea remarked wistfully. "Sorry, Joar. No one listened to me then; they won't listen to you now."

A pained expression captured Teth's face. "Do you still wish me gone, Princess?"

"As if I'd tell you." Nimhea winked at him, and he grinned.

"You are joking." Joar was a picture of confusion as he took in their exchange. "I do not understand."

"Let's just say there's more to thieves than I expected," Nimhea told him.

Teth turned his lazy grin on the hunter. "You liked me before you knew I was a thief."

"I find you strange," Joar replied.

"Right, but that's not dislike."

"That's quite enough of that." Lucket snapped his fingers to reacquire their focus. "For the moment, all you need to understand is that my organization has formed a partnership with Saetlund's rebels, in the hopes of evicting the empire from our kingdom. That makes us allies."

Joar simply grunted, then said, "You haven't answered my question. Who is being rounded up?"

"If you want to continue our conversation, you'll follow me," Lucket said, turning away. "I've grown tired of standing outdoors."

With the torchbearers on either side of him, Lucket walked toward the door of one of the fort's interior structures.

"I'll take care of the horses and join you in a few minutes," Teth told Ara.

She nodded and led the others to where Lucket stood in front of the now open door, through which his companions had already passed.

"After you." Lucket gestured to the entrance.

Lucket's companions had made the barracks more than hospitable. A cheerful fire danced in the hearth and a long table had been spread with a fine linen cloth, playing host to platters of roast meat and steaming dishes from which rose mouthwatering scents.

The sight and smell of hot food made Ara's stomach rumble, reminding her that she'd only had a handful of nuts and fruit to eat that day.

"I hoped you'd join us for dinner." Lucket took a seat at the head of the table. One of his unnamed companions immediately appeared with a goblet and poured wine for the Low King. "As you can see, we have plenty to share. I'm not one to go without certain creature comforts, no matter where life takes me."

Ara chose the chair opposite Lucket. Nimhea and Lahvja settled onto the bench to her right. When Joar lowered himself on the bench to the left, the wood creaked in protest. Lucket kept a wary eye on Huntress as she nestled in beside the hearth, but otherwise made no complaint about the wolf's presence.

"Things are afoot in Five Rivers, troubling signs of what's to come," Lucket told them. "The seizing of Imperial Player caravans is one."

He leveled his gaze at Nimhea. "Prince Eamon's unexpected treachery is another."

The room became stiff with tension, and Ara's heart skittered beneath her ribs.

Nimhea's fork clattered to her plate. "You have news of my brother?"

"Indeed." Lucket dabbed the corners of his mouth with a linen napkin. "I must say, I was pleased you chose to contact us rather than go directly to the Resistance. In the Below, we tend to understand the subtleties of delicate matters such as the case of your brother."

With a brief nod, Nimhea said, "But you brought the matter to the Resistance, as we asked."

"Yes," Lucket replied. "And as you guessed, they wanted to kill him at the earliest possible moment."

Nimhea blanched, then drew a hissing breath. "Without telling me?"

"Easier to beg forgiveness than ask permission, Your Highness." Lucket's smile was little more than a thin line with the hint of a curve. "Fortunately, I convinced Suli that a hasty response wouldn't be wise.

It is paramount that we know the full reasoning behind Eamon's departure before acting."

"And you have the means to discover his motives?" Ara asked.

"Of course." He sounded a bit insulted. "The prince has already been located—he's being held at the Temple of Vokk—and an asset has been deployed to investigate the situation."

"An asset," Nimhea repeated, watching Lucket with suspicion. "What do you mean?"

"An individual with the appropriate skills to deal with a complicated set of variables," the Low King told her. "And then take whatever action is necessary."

Nimhea's eyes blazed. "Including killing him."

He replied in a flat tone. "I do not yet have a report on the status of that operation, but assassination is only one of several possibilities."

Suddenly on her feet, Nimhea scowled at him. "How can you sit there and say that to me? You're talking about my brother! My twin!"

Lucket steepled his fingers in front of his face. "Your Highness, if you plan to rule this kingdom, you'll have to get used to unpleasant news. Such is the nature of monarchy. You must also face the fact that by all appearances your brother is a traitor."

Nimhea sank back to her seat, face wan. "I know."

Lahvja leaned over and whispered in Nimhea's ear. The princess gave a tight nod, but didn't speak.

"I'll keep you apprised of the situation as it develops," Lucket said. He drained his goblet and indicated to the server to replenish his wine.

"It comes down to this: the Vokkans are actively hunting you. It's unwise to be haphazardly wandering the kingdom. I'd advise you to ensconce yourself with the Resistance as quickly as possible. They have means to keep you hidden and safe until the moment of the rebellion is at hand."

Ara shook her head. "The quest isn't finished. I still have to complete the gods' trials at three hidden sites, and to do that I have to first find those sites. We need Loreknights to take back the kingdom. I can't stop now."

"As much as these storied Loreknights might be useful to us, I have to deal in practicalities," Lucket said drily. "Perhaps you could have a word with your gods and tell them that time is of the essence."

His words took Ara by surprise. Surely, after all that had happened, Lucket didn't harbor doubts about her quest.

"One does not hurry the gods," Joar rumbled, and tore a drumstick off the roast chicken.

"Aren't you the droll fellow." Lucket watched Joar with a mildly curious expression. "Wherever did you find this one?"

"Vijeri," Ara said. "We needed a guide, and Joar offered his assistance."

"And then you decided to . . . keep him?" Lucket ventured.

"Though I'm more than glad for his companionship, the choice wasn't mine. Joar was named by Wuldr as the second Loreknight," Ara told him. "He's one of us now."

"The *second* Loreknight?" Lucket set down his goblet. "Pray tell, who is the first?"

Surprise shot through her.

He doesn't know.

No wonder Lucket had so easily dismissed her comment about Loreknights.

"You didn't tell him?" Ara stared at Teth with disbelief.

Lucket's expression remained impassive. "Tell me what?"

"I'd really rather not," Teth said, avoiding her gaze.

"You have to," Ara snapped. "Now."

With a groan, Teth turned to Lucket. "I'm the first Loreknight."

Lucket gave him an appraising look. "Your jests are usually more clever, Teth. I'm disappointed."

"This is exactly why I didn't tell him," Teth muttered, shooting a glance at Ara.

"It's not a joke, Lucket," Ara said. "Eni chose Teth, naming him Loreknight."

Lucket's expression hardened. "You expect me to believe—"

"Come with me." Teth stood up, gesturing for Lucket to follow. "I know you won't be convinced until I show you."

"I—" Lucket began to protest.

"Go with him." Ara's hard glare startled the Low King into silence.

He briefly inclined his head and followed Teth outdoors.

Lucket was silent for at least a quarter of an hour after they returned. Teth set into his meal with relish, a smug twinkle in his eye, while the Low King emptied another goblet of wine. The rest of them ate dinner quietly as little by little Lucket removed the bewildered mask that had captured his face. All the while, Lucket's followers hovered like ghosts, never speaking but always watchful.

"You'll have to pose as traders." Lucket abruptly broke his silence.

"I beg your pardon?" Ara had filled her belly to its satisfaction and a bit beyond. She didn't think she'd ever eaten so well.

"To enter the Great Market," he replied. "Medicinal herbs, spices, and potions, I think. Lahvja is Vijerian, Teth looks part Vijerian, the goods are valuable enough to warrant a"—with a delicate cough and a glance at Joar, he went on—"substantial bodyguard, and you'll only need a merchant's wagon."

The Low King appeared to be entirely himself again.

"Can't we take backroads like we did in Fjeri?" Ara asked. She didn't relish another wagon journey after the unpleasantness of the caravan in Daefrit. "It would save time."

Lucket caught her with a steady gaze. "There are no back roads in Sola."

"But—"

"You haven't studied your history, Loresmith," Lucket cut her off. "Once upon a time, Sola had gentle hills dotted with small farms. But when the kingdom was formed, the farms grew larger. Cities were born, and farmers' children sought their fortune in the new metropolises. Their children had children, and the kingdom developed quite an appetite."

He paused to smile at her. "That was all right. New generations of farmers didn't forget what Nava had taught them. They kept the land fertile and the crops varied. That ended when the Vokkans came. Soldiers need corn and oats and wheat and beans. They need them in massive quantities, and the empire prefers uniformity. Large farms were combined to become enormous imperial farms. Outside of its cities and the Great Market, Sola is now nothing but farms operated by the empire. All of the roads were built to optimize efficiency and accommodate the flow of supplies into the farms and crops out to the coasts. In case you don't know, most of Sola's crops are shipped to the empire's armies overseas, where they've been contending with rebellions.

"If you like, you can try your luck at crossing the fields themselves," he continued. "But even those only able to produce dust devils now are still well guarded. The imperials rarely show mercy to trespassers, even those claiming to have lost their way."

"So we take the major trade route," Ara said, losing patience.

"Ignorance of the past is foolish," Lucket snapped at her. "History brought you here, and you'll need its lessons if you expect to win this game."

Ara pressed her lips together and nodded, thinking that Eamon would have said the same thing but in a much nicer way. The pain of his betrayal was a reopened wound since Lucket had raised his specter.

Knowing that Eamon had indeed gone to the wizards in Five Rivers seemed to confirm the worst. Part of her had hoped that he had simply run away, possibly returning to the Ethrian Isles or else hiding out somewhere in Saetlund. Perhaps even making his way to one of the universities in Daefrit to lose himself in research.

But she didn't want to believe he was actively working against them. That he would wish them harm.

And she didn't want Eamon to die.

"You'll need better clothes." Lucket's comment brought Ara back to the moment. His gaze perused each of them, focusing on their garb. "Vijerian silk and Daefritian jewelry, for the women. Apothecaries proclaim the quality of their goods in the fineries they wear. We'll keep Teth and Joar as nondescript as possible."

"One last thing." Lucket leveled his gaze on Nimhea. "Remove your bandages."

Nimhea drew a sharp breath, and Lahvja half rose, glaring at Lucket.

Rolling his eyes, Lucket said, "Don't be tiresome. It is my business to know, in depth, your current circumstances. The extent of the princess's wounds falls under my purview."

"Is it really necessary?" Ara asked.

Lahvja had been changing Nimhea's bandages in private. Ara didn't know if Nimhea had even seen her own reflection since the attack. If she had not, Lucket's demand was invasive and cruel.

"The wound is still healing," Lahvja said sharply. "It will be bandaged for several more weeks."

"This will be but a moment's work, and do no harm," Lucket replied.

"I can describe her injuries in detail," Lahvja countered. "I've been tending to the wound."

"Seeing is believing, as they say," Lucket replied. "We can waste time arguing about it, but I'd prefer to have the matter over and done with."

Lahvja opened her mouth to protest again, but Nimhea stilled her with a gentle hand on the summoner's arm.

"It's fine," Nimhea said quietly. "Like he said, it will do no harm."

She reached up and loosened the bandages. The room went very still as she slowly unwound them. Nimhea drew a long breath and released it, then let the bandages settle onto her lap.

Ara's breath caught in her throat.

The scar began just above Nimhea's right lip. It curved just outside her nose and up her cheek, continued along the outer edge of her eye, over her forehead, and into her scalp. The wound was still angry and red, bound together by fine silk stitching.

Nimhea gazed unflinching at Lucket. After a moment, the Low King gave a brief nod.

"Thank you."

While Nimhea allowed Lahvja to rebandage her face, Lucket stood and snapped his fingers. His companions instantly materialized and just as quickly filed out the door.

"My people and I will gather the wagon and supplies in TriBridge and then return here in two nights. In the meantime, work on the backstories you'll use while operating in the Great Market. Teth will help you construct them. Commit them to memory. You can't afford mistakes. I'd prefer not to send amateurs into a situation like this, but there's no helping it."

He shot a wry glance at Joar. "Unless the gods allow substitutions?"

Joar shook his head.

Lucket barked a laugh, then gave a short bow before exiting the room. Without realizing she'd made the decision to follow him, Ara was on her feet and out the door.

"Lucket!"

He turned to face her. One of his companions pulled up short, moving quickly toward Ara. She caught the glint of a blade. Lucket waved the man off.

"Do you need something?" the Low King asked her.

"I don't care what our arrangement is, that was utterly heartless," Ara hissed at Lucket. Her stomach roiled with anger. "How dare you."

Lucket raised an eyebrow and replied, "You're speaking of the princess, I assume?"

When she simply glared at him, he blew out an indulgent sigh.

"You need to learn to look past the surface of things, Loresmith. It will stop you from embarrassing yourself."

When she scoffed, he tsk'd in reply.

"I didn't need to view the wound. A description from Lahvja would have sufficed, but that would have forestalled a necessity that all of you shirked. The princess was horribly wounded. She is disfigured. That is not a tragedy, it simply is."

"I don't understand."

"Your concern, Lahvja's tenderness, and Teth's defensiveness made it glaringly obvious each of you blames yourself in some way for the princess's injury. The more you attempted to conceal the details of what transpired, the more imperative it became for me to intervene. Your current course has been leading you to some climactic moment of revelation when Nimhea would reluctantly bare her wounds and you would fall all over yourselves trying to reassure her that nothing has changed. And that's true, *nothing has changed*, at least nothing that matters—but due to your selfish guilt you don't believe that, and your poorly hidden hand-wringing will eventually convince Nimhea she is forever altered and has lost some essential part of herself. You may not mean to do this, but that would be the result, and it would do more damage than any physical wound could.

"By inserting myself into the situation I removed all the trappings of pity and dread. I laid the situation bare and presented it for what it truly is: a warrior has been wounded in battle. That's what Nimhea is, a warrior. She needed to be reminded of that. Now, if that is all our *arrangement* dictates, then I have work to do."

Robbed of speech, Ara simply watched as Lucket and his companions rode out of the fort. She stood alone in the dark, pondering his words.

21

T here are no back roads in Sola.

Ara had never seen so many people in one place. A mass of bodies pressed northward, all destined for the Great Market. Most were on foot and brought with them carts and baskets full of wares. Some guided herds of pigs or goats or flocks of ducks, geese, or chickens.

Their wagon lurched along the choked route, surrounded by this hubbub of other travelers. Bright sunbeams streamed down on them in the warm late spring air, but a steady breeze chased away the stifling heat and humidity that had dogged their journey through Vijeri.

Sola was unlike Vijeri in so many ways. The major trade route they traveled was straight and broad, unlike the narrow, twisting trails of the jungle. The sun shone down on them unobstructed by a crush of trees and vines. Ara could turn in any direction and see for miles. The rolling hills of Sola, covered by farm fields, lay open for all to see.

It made her feel terribly exposed. They were in disguise, traveling as merchants so they could safely enter the Great Market and find the hidden worshippers of Nava who lived there. But traveling in the open air, surrounded by so many strangers, and the regular passing of imperial patrols up and down the road filled her with unease.

Shading her face with her hand, Ara strained to see the Great Market rising in the distance. It rose up amid the fields, like a great ship with sails in patchwork colors, utterly incongruous with its surroundings.

"It's always changing," Teth remarked. He'd assigned himself the task of driving the wagon, and sat comfortably, legs stretched out in front of him with the reins settled in his hands. Sitting alongside him, Ara couldn't stop herself from stealing glances at him. Her eyes drank in his finely carved profile and the strength of his arms and sureness of his hands as he guided the horses.

They were close enough that her arm too often brushed against him or their thighs pressed against each other. Each slight touch heated her blood and sent shivers over her skin.

It was intolerable, but she didn't know how to make it stop. No matter how hard she tried to keep any romantic feelings in check, her body ignored her.

"Different shapes, different colors," he continued. "It all depends on who's there. There's an original marble pavilion at the center of everything, and what's left of Nava's temple, but those are the only parts of the Great Market that stay the same."

His voice was friendly and even, hinting at no internal conflict like the one Ara battled with. She thought it must mean that when he'd agreed to a friendship and nothing more, he'd truly decided that was for the best. It made her sick with disappointment and ashamed for her hypocrisy.

Forcing her attention away from Teth, Ara waved at Joar, who walked alongside the wagon leading their riding mounts. Though admittedly not one for chatter, he seemed especially subdued in contrast to the din all around them. He briefly dipped his chin in acknowledgment of her greeting. He'd traded his kilt for trousers and wore his harness over an undyed open-collared shirt. There was no way to disguise his height and girth, but he'd donned a cowled hood of dark gray to hide his Koelli features.

It must be jarring, Ara thought. *To embark on a journey of solitude only to end up with us on this crowded road.*

She wasn't particularly unsettled by their current surroundings, but it was still surprising to find herself in a throng of travelers. Admittedly, Lucket's suggestion of disguise had been a good one. Buried amid so many people, muffled by so much noise, it was a fine way to hide in plain sight. He'd also been right about blight plaguing Sola's fields. In her mind, Sola had been a golden country. As a child, Ara had known it to be the land that fed the kingdom. Blessed by Nava and populated by people with skin of deep bronze and brown.

Sola still had golden fields, but they were broken by swaths of dry gray soil too easily picked up and cast about by the wind, and Ara was reminded of Lucket's words.

History brought you here, and you'll need its lessons if you expect to win this game.

Gazing at the stripes of gold and gray, Ara understood that what began with the Gash hadn't ended there. The empire had found yet another way to reave the earth and leave it barren.

How long would it be until all the fields were dust?

It was only a matter of time before the empire, desperate to keep its armies across the globe fed, chose to let Saetlund go hungry. Ara wondered how many other conquered kingdoms were already starving and if that was the source of their unrest and uprisings.

With a shake of her head, she silently cursed King Dentroth's naivete for believing that Saetlund would remained untouched by Vokk's insatiable appetite. His kingdom could have been ready for the onslaught but had instead been unforgivably vulnerable to conquest.

It must be hard on Nimhea, Ara thought, *to bear the conflict of claiming her inheritance while simultaneously rejecting the legacy of her father's inept rule.*

"I'm going into the wagon for a bit," Ara told Teth. Her musings pressed her toward a conversation with the princess. One she'd been avoiding, but could no longer shirk.

Teth offered her a crooked smile. "Whatever pleases milady."

She rolled her eyes at him and jumped off the seat onto the ground. Their pace on the crowded road was slow enough that it was easy to walk to the back of the wagon, open the rear door, and climb inside.

"Hello, Ara," Lahvja said as Ara ducked through the door. She reclined in Nimhea's arms, her head resting on the princess's shoulder.

Along with Lahvja's words, she was greeted by bright and pungent scents of herbs, potions, and tinctures that they would sell in the Great Market. Fortunately, their wares didn't require a great deal of space, leaving plenty of room for people to ride and rest inside the wagon. The top half of the split rear door was fastened open to allow light and fresh air in but still keep the wagon's interior dim enough to foil any prying eyes.

Hesitating, Ara asked, "Would you prefer to be alone?"

"I think we can behave," Lahvja laughed as Nimhea ran her fingers through the summoner's mahogany waves.

Ara smiled at her, then asked, "How goes it for our hidden travelers?"

"Strange to be sequestered with a giant wolf," Nimhea said from the bench where she sat beside Lahvja. "But otherwise well."

Lucket had deemed Huntress and Nimhea's bandaged face "too conspicuous" to travel in the open; thus, wolf and princess had been remanded to the interior of the wagon in daylight hours. Huntress lay on the wagon floor, her head resting on her paws. The giant wolf looked calm, but not particularly pleased about her current mode of travel. Ara wondered if the beast had ever ridden in any kind of transport prior to this. Likely not, and it spoke to Huntress's loyalty to Joar that she would obey his command to remain inside what must be a strange and uncomfortable means of travel.

As if reading Ara's thoughts, Nimhea laughed softly and said, "I'm very careful to remind myself that she's not a lovely furry rug to bury my toes in."

When Ara joined in her laughter, Huntress lifted her head and bared her teeth in a way that wasn't altogether menacing, but bore a remarkable resemblance to a grimace.

"Don't worry," Nimhea said to the wolf. "I won't forget."

With a low growl, Huntress laid her head back atop her paws and closed her eyes.

"She's an extraordinary creature," Lahvja observed in a reverent voice.

Nimhea offered her own grimace. "That's one word for it."

With a chastising cluck of her tongue, Lahvja pushed Nimhea upright. "I think I'll keep Teth company for a while. I need to stretch my legs and enjoy the sun."

"Not fair," Nimhea muttered, but happily accepted Lahvja's kiss on her cheek.

The summoner opened the back door and hopped out of the wagon, while Ara joined Nimhea on the bench. She was pleased to discover that the important road was well maintained enough to spare the ride from too many jolts or wild rocking.

"I'm surprised you wanted to leave Teth alone." Nimhea shot Ara a sidelong glance. "In fact, you seem to be leaving him alone rather frequently of late. Did you two quarrel?"

Ara's heart sank, but she steeled herself for what she had to confess. "I've been wanting to talk to you about that . . . about a lot of things."

Nimhea's brow furrowed. "That sounds ominous."

Ara couldn't keep her eyes from drifting to Nimhea's bandages. "You don't remember what happened in the swamp?"

"Thankfully I don't remember the pain or shock of receiving this wound." Her fingers gingerly brushed over her cheek. "I remember the tentacle lashing out, striking at me, but nothing else until waking in the healer's home."

Grinding her teeth, Ara forced herself to say, "Do you remember shouting for me when I went to help Teth?"

Nimhea nodded slowly and frowned, but didn't otherwise reply.

"You asked for my help, but I ignored you," Ara continued, swallowing the jagged stones that had filled her throat. "I went to Teth . . . and he didn't need my help at all. He was fine."

The princess simply gazed at Ara for several moments.

Ara hurried to fill the weighty silence. "It was wrong of me. I made a terrible choice and you suffered for it. I'm so sorry. I regret what I did so much."

"You think I should be angry with you." Nimhea spoke slowly, tilting her head to regard Ara more closely.

"Anger isn't a strong enough emotion," Ara replied. "You should be furious. I wouldn't blame you for hating me. Your wound—"

"Is terrible." Nimhea cut her off, voice tightening. "But not your fault."

"But—"

Nimhea held up her hand. "Do you think I would have left Lahvja? If she'd been the one in Teth's position, do you believe I'd have made a different choice than you did?"

Ara's heart stuttered, and she could find no words.

"I despise what happened to me." Nimhea blew out a frustrated breath. "And I wish it hadn't, but I don't blame you. Not in the least."

Rigid with disbelief at Nimhea's pronouncement, Ara said quietly, "I blame myself, and I won't stop regretting choosing Teth over my duty as Loresmith."

"What duty is that?" Nimhea asked sharply.

Ara was surprised Nimhea hadn't already come to the same conclusion she had. "That I can't favor one Loreknight over another. I have to think of the mission first, of our purpose."

Nimhea considered that, then replied, "The mission will always be important, but you're forgetting something. You may be the Loresmith, but you're still human. It's a mistake to ask yourself to be more."

"Is it?" Ara shot back. "I'm responsible for all of you. If I choose my personal feelings over the good of our company, I put everything that matters at risk."

"What you feel matters, too."

"But you could have died," Ara said, her hands balled into fists where they rested on her thighs. "If we'd lost you, the Resistance would fail and Saetlund would be lost. You're the queen our people have been waiting for."

At this Nimhea slumped against the side of the wagon. "I wonder if that's still true."

"How can you say that?" Shock rattled through Ara's bones.

"The gods haven't shown me otherwise," Nimhea said, smiling weakly. "A thief and an outsider were chosen to be Loreknights. I'm not worthy."

Gesturing to her bandages, she added, "And this. Who wants a queen with a ruined face?"

Ara shook her head, remembering Lucket's words. "Your face isn't ruined. You are still the most stunning woman I've ever known. All that injury tells me—will tell anyone—is that you're not the figurehead you were afraid people would see you as. You're a true warrior. You make sacrifices for your people."

Nimhea sighed. "It's not just that."

"What else?" Ara pressed.

"I keep thinking about how Eamon must have traveled this road," she replied. "I know I should put him out of my mind or else I should keep my fury at him alive and remind myself every day of how horrible his betrayal was and still is."

She closed her eye, and a tear slipped from beneath her lid. "But when I woke up in pain, half-blind, it wasn't Lahvja I looked for; it was Eamon."

A painful wrench seized Ara's heart.

"I miss him every day," Nimhea said softly. "Before he left I'd never spent a day without him. He was my best friend all my life. I thought he believed in me more than anyone. But he couldn't, not after what he did.

"Sometimes I think it's too much. I want to stop. I want to give everything up and go find my brother. With every breath I think about what's happened to him, where he is. I wonder if I would have ever started this journey had I known what it would cost me. I don't think I would. If that's the case, should I bother to continue?"

Ara's throat wanted to close, but she forced herself to speak. "Nimhea. I miss Eamon. I can't tell you how many times I've wished he was here and how I still hope that he's safe and unharmed. We all had come to care for him, to rely on him."

Feeling tears well in her own eyes, she drew a shuddering breath.

"His choice cut us all deeply, and knowing how I feel, I can't imagine how painful his loss is to you."

Nimhea nodded as she wept silently.

"But, Nimhea, you cannot doubt yourself. The gods' choices are as much a mystery to me as they are to you, but you are not being judged or punished. I'm certain of that. What I also know to be true is that you are vital. I believe in you. I know the people will follow you. Without you we will fail."

Nimhea's face contorted into a pained mask, and Ara took her hand. They stayed like that, silent with fingers interlaced, for a long time.

When the princess at last drew her hand from Ara's, she swiped the tracks of moisture from her cheek.

"Thank you," she said, meeting Ara's gaze.

Ara nodded, and the constriction of her throat eased.

"I'm grateful you were so forthright with me," Nimhea continued. "So let me do the same for you. Whatever this rift is between you and Teth, mend it. You're punishing him and yourself for reasons I don't believe are good enough. I can't tell you what it means to be the Loresmith, but I can't accept that denying love is demanded of you."

Ara winced at the sudden throb beneath her ribs.

Overwhelmed by Nimhea's words, her voice came out strangled. "I can't thank you for that because I don't know if I believe it."

"I don't expect you to believe . . . yet," the princess replied in a hard tone. "Only to listen."

22

Breaking into the Temple of Vokk proved far easier than Dagger expected. A number of the wizards felt safe enough leaving their balcony doors open to let the warm spring air cocoon them while they slept. That was the problem with power—it inevitably led to hubris, and hubris led to mistakes.

Saetlund had been conquered by the brawn of its armies, but the wizards dealt in magic. Magic so powerful and twisted they ruled by the people's fear of it alone, which allowed them to operate unchecked. It also made them believe they were invincible, believe they were beyond the need to take measures against thieves and assassins.

Arrogant fools.

It made Dagger wish she'd been sent to eliminate one of them, even the ArchWizard himself. The bastard.

But no. Her target was a boy . . . Well, at eighteen she supposed he was a man, but the intelligence she'd received about Prince Eamon described a slight, fragile creature prone to illness. This was no warrior prince, and given the bargain he'd made with the likes of ArchWizard Zenar, he was naive as hell. That made him a boy in Dagger's mind.

She slipped out of the slumbering wizard's chamber into the second-floor hallway. No assassin worth their salt couldn't move silently, and Dagger glided down the stairs without so much as a scrape of her shoe against marble.

The first thing she noticed about the main hall of the temple was that the walls were moving. Dagger was usually unperturbed by even the strangest sights, but something about the glossy, shivering surfaces on either side of her made her skin crawl and her stomach clench. Making a mental note that under no circumstances should she touch said walls, Dagger made her way along the hall, keeping to the shadows, until she found the entry to the bowels of the temple. Here she encountered the first obstacle to remove: two guards.

She made a quick assessment, determining these were brutes of the banal sort and not endowed with any supernatural abilities that might complicate things. Dropping into a crouch, she withdrew a pebble from her pocket. Dagger tossed it into the shadows at her back. The small stone clinked and skittered across the ebony marble floor.

The guards snapped to attention, heads swiveling toward the sound.

"I'll check it out," one of them grunted.

He lumbered toward the pebble, quickly swallowed by darkness.

When he was within Dagger's reach, she rose up like a spirit at his back. One arm wrapped around his body, plunging a needle into his thigh, while her other hand clapped over his mouth. The paralyzing agent that coated the needle worked in a matter of seconds. Dagger braced herself against the man's considerable weight and slowly eased him to the floor.

The second guard called out to his companion. Failing to get a reply, the man came into the shadows looking for him. In moments, he was on the floor, too.

Gliding noiselessly down the spiral staircase, Dagger stopped when she stood outside the single cell in the dungeon's upper reaches.

She took her time surveying the figure curled on the cot within. Even balled up as he was, she could see he was tall, but very thin. His tightly coiled body suggested fear, as if he expected to be struck.

"Prince Eamon."

He bolted upright with a gasp of alarm, blinking into the dark. "Who's there?"

"A visitor." She sidled up to his cell, knowing that in the dim light she was little more than a shadow to him.

The prince swung his feet around, resting them on the floor and sitting at his full height. The change in his posture was a study in contrasts. He no longer looked like a terrified prisoner; instead, he appeared weary. Beaten down, but not broken.

"I'm going to ask you some questions," Dagger said. "You will answer them."

Eamon didn't reply. He simply watched her.

"I could make this a much less pleasant conversation." She drew one of her namesakes.

Eamon eyed the blade, then seemed to decide something. "You're not going to torture me. You're here to either kill me or extract information, and if it's the latter, torture isn't Zenar's style. If he believes I have more to tell him, he'd want to get the information himself."

His confidence threw her off balance. She'd thought the princeling would cower at the sight of the blade. His steady resolve was a surprise. She hadn't believed he had any steel in his spine. Whatever fears he battled in his dreams, he wasn't willing to show them here.

"But maybe that means you weren't sent by Zenar." He frowned. "Then who . . ."

Even in the dim light, she could see him blanch.

"My sister?" His voice came out as a creaky whisper.

Dagger made a show of inspecting her blade. "I don't discuss clients."

His eyes wandered to her weapon, and the first hint of fear flickered over his features. "Or the Resistance." He paused, gazing at the dagger. "They'd want me dead. And I deserve it."

His words gave her pause. Something about the boy's innocence, his naked admissions of his own faults, moved her in a way no target's pleading for mercy ever had.

Eamon didn't speak for several moments. He stood up and crossed the cell until he stood just beyond her reach.

"Zenar filled my head with stories about the empire's greatness, the inevitability of its dominance. I believed the stories because I wanted to. It was easier to believe than question."

With a sigh, he bent his head. "But the children . . . they change everything."

Though his words flared through her like lightning, Dagger masked her interest.

Eamon continued, "I don't know what's happening to them, but it must be terrible."

His gaze floated to the spiral of stairs descending past his cell. "That's where they're taken. Down into the dark."

He fell silent and stared into shadows. When he turned back, Dagger was gone.

It hadn't been her intention to make her way into the man's bed.

Commander Liran was supposedly an ally, and part of Dagger's assignment was to report to him what she'd discerned about Prince Eamon as well as return to Garet with any new intelligence the man had to offer. Dagger usually would have shown her flair for drama by sitting at his desk and striking a match, knowing the sound would wake him. Or she could perch on his windowsill, letting her shadow fall over him before making a noise that was quiet but enough to rouse him from sleep.

She'd been pleased to discover that the commander of the Vokkan armies had enough sense to lock his window. But no locks could resist Dagger's manipulation. Upon seeing the commander stretched out on his bed, however, his long body composed of corded muscle and marked by interesting scars, she had changed her mind. As she approached the bedside, she took note that Commander Liran wasn't one of those offi- cers who hid in vaunted halls giving orders while his men bled and died in the field. No, this man fought side by side with his soldiers. The hard, carved strength of his body and the marks left by blades and burns attested to that.

So why had this warrior turned against his father, forsaking all the benefits he must reap from being the son of Emperor Fauld? Dagger was surprised by how much she wanted his explanation. She was viciously curious to know exactly who he was—this imperial warrior turned agent of the Resistance.

Dagger rested one knee on the edge of the bed, not yet letting any of her weight sink into the mattress. In an instant her arms were seized and she was on her back, pinned to the bed by the commander's very impressive arms.

"Who are you?" He spoke through clenched teeth.

She almost laughed, having expected this, but was still oddly grati- fied that he hadn't disappointed her by failing to notice someone had entered his bedchamber. But laughing would give him time to make her actually vulnerable.

Instead, her arms slithered from his grip—his strength no match for her litheness. Strong men had the easily exploited fault of assuming a smaller person, particularly a woman, would flounder at any display of dominance. Dagger had honed the skills to prevent that from happening.

Upon triggering a spring at her wrist, a slim blade darted out like a striking snake. It barely grazed Liran's flesh, certainly not enough to break the skin, but he froze, eyes widening. Her blade was positioned for a thrust to his heart.

Dagger smiled as she watched him swallow.

"You should let me do the talking," she said sweetly. "Now move."

Liran stared down at the woman beneath him. She was slight in figure and dressed head to toe in black but for the strand of pale-blond hair that had escaped the wrapping around her head and neck.

She was disturbingly calm and dangerously quick. He'd been sure he was in control of the situation when she'd slipped out of his grasp as easily as if his skin had been an oil slick.

She pressed him back, forcing him off the bed then backing him up into a wall.

"I'm a friend," she said, despite all evidence to the contrary.

Her voice fascinated him; it was like the purring of a cat. "If we're friends I'd appreciate you putting that away."

Her tone became matter-of-fact. "We have much to discuss. And I'd prefer to do it in a more peaceful way, though probably not as much as you would."

"Probably not."

Her blade stayed exactly where it was.

"Unfortunately," she continued, "I cannot alter our current relationship until you've answered a question."

He cleared his throat before speaking again. "What's the question?"

Her smile was suddenly as sharp as her blade. "Why are there children being held captive beneath the Temple of Vokk?"

If Liran's body had already been rigid, now it turned to stone. By Vokk's hunger, he only had one answer to give her. If she didn't believe him, this would go very badly. As much as he hated to admit it, more likely for him than her.

"I don't know."

"How can that be?" She added the tiniest pressure with the blade, and Liran grimaced.

"I only recently discovered it was happening," Liran told her, each word carrying an edge of strain. Eamon's revelation that Zenar had imprisoned children in the bowels of the temple had shocked and sickened him. He'd sworn to himself that he would uncover the reasons for their abduction and put a stop to it, but he didn't know how or when he'd find a way to do so. Maybe this stranger could help him. Her skills were impressive.

He'd never been compromised like this. Never made this vulnerable. He did not like it, but he couldn't stop himself from marveling that she'd accomplished the feat.

He continued, "Prior to that, I had no idea they were here, and I still don't know why. But I'm certain it's nothing good, as I'm certain my brother, Zenar, is behind it. It must be stopped."

He watched her jaw working. "The ArchWizard is behind the kidnappings."

Liran nodded.

Another question. "How did you find out?"

She hadn't cut him, or even nicked him. He hoped that was a good sign.

"Prince Eamon asked the same question you did," Liran answered. "That was the first I'd heard of any children in the temple."

She spent a long time searching his eyes. It felt like she was reaching inside him, and he was finding it difficult to breathe. And, impossibly, that had nothing to do with the position of her blade.

Tilting her head, she smiled again. "My assessment was the same."

Liran heard a soft *snick*, and suddenly the pressure of the blade was gone.

A breath of relief surged out of his lungs.

She walked away, settling on the edge of his bed. "I'm called Dagger."

"That's a little on the nose, isn't it?" he said with a flat smile. It occurred to him that he should arm himself, but the situation had improved a great deal, and he surmised that going for a weapon would not be in his interest at the moment.

Dagger shrugged in reply.

Liran dragged the chair at his small writing table to face her and sat down. "Why are you here, Dagger? Other than to prove you could kill me."

"I was just teasing, Commander." She had the audacity to laugh. "Come now, don't be cross."

Her behavior astonished him. He couldn't puzzle her out, and he resented the way it made her fascinating.

"I came here on assignment from our mutual friends."

So she was with the Resistance. Interesting.

"Eamon presents a possible threat," Dagger continued. "I'm here to assess whether that threat needs to be removed."

"You're an assassin," Liran murmured, his blood going cold. As far as he knew, he'd never met an assassin before, and he held an inherent distrust of the profession. As a soldier, he believed if killing had to be done it should occur on the field of battle, not in the shadows wrapped in secrecy and deception.

She rolled her eyes. "And you're one of *those*."

"I don't follow." He was fairly sure he'd just been insulted.

"Noble and narrow-minded enough not to see that stomping across fields and swinging swords will not solve particular types of problems that cannot be ignored," she sighed. "People like me are the solution to said problems."

Liran didn't reply, but his mouth set in a grim line.

She sighed, and he was shocked when she reached out to pat his cheek. "I'm sure you'll come around."

"I will do no—"

"I've determined," she cut him off, "that Eamon isn't a threat. In fact, he could be an asset, but only if he decides he doesn't deserve to die. More specifically, if he decides that he could help his sister by helping the Resistance."

He frowned at her. "That's no simple task."

"No," she agreed. Then she took his hand in hers and pressed it over her heart. His own lurched in reply. "But I believe in you."

She fluttered her lashes mockingly, and he pulled his hand back, but not quickly enough to keep the sensation of her curves pressing into his fingertips from burning into them.

"Why does it fall to me to recruit Prince Eamon?" Liran muttered.

"I would think that's obvious," Dagger replied. "You're here."

Liran scoffed. "I command armies. I don't comfort children with broken hearts."

"I'd wager you've never tried the latter," she said.

"No, but—"

"If you're terrible at it, we'll find another way." She had an infuriating habit of interrupting him. "But for the moment, you'll do."

Liran leaned toward her. He couldn't help himself. In the dim light he couldn't tell what color her eyes were, and he was embarrassingly desirous to know.

Dagger watched him, her lips curving in a languid smile. Liran's hands balled into fists.

Vokk spare me, I'm dying to touch her.

He was certain he'd lose fingers for it if he dared.

She leaned toward him, bringing their faces very close. "Do you have anything to share with me?"

He could not be drawn to her this way. She was an assassin. He despised assassins. As he tried to focus on her repellant profession instead of what he craved, it struck him that Dagger wasn't necessarily part of the Resistance. More likely, she was part of the Below.

And he absolutely did have information she needed. When he straightened, his posture stiffening, her eyes narrowed.

"The Below has been compromised," he told her. "The Low King of Sola has sold the others out to the empire. There will be raids, arrests . . ."

She drew a sharp breath. "You're certain?"

The mask of cool indifference she wore slipped for a moment, revealing stark fear. If true, the news was disastrous.

"I'm doing what I can to slow up the imperial response," he continued. "But if I interfere too much it will compromise my position here, and my ability to retain a connection with the Resistance."

"I understand." She nodded slowly. "I must go. If the Below has a traitor, it could ruin everything. If they know Lucket's plans . . ."

She stood, turning away.

"Will you come back?" He wished he didn't care what her answer was.

Dagger didn't reply at first, but she looked at him.

"I have to report back what I've learned here," Dagger finally said. "That will take some time." She paused, a smile curving one corner of her mouth. "But you'll see me again."

He had to stop himself from demanding, *When?*

"For progress reports," she added.

Liran's chest burned at his foolishness. The sooner this woman—this assassin—was out of his life, the better.

But Dagger was leaning toward him again. "And . . . because I like you," she said softly. She sounded as surprised as he felt. But that didn't stop her from brushing her lips over his.

"Yes, Commander," she whispered, breathless. "I like you very much."

Before Liran could respond, she was across the room and through the window, vanishing into the night.

23

he noise alone shook Ara to the core. A sea of people moved through the market, crowds that surged and fell back like the swells of the ocean. Shouts, laughter, hawking, braying, trilling, grunting, screeching all came together as the music of the Great Market. It took her breath away.

She once again sat beside Teth. Her mind kept returning to her conversation with Nimhea. Ara knew she needed to talk to him, but she dreaded it. She didn't know what to say or how to say it. Her feelings were wrapped up in fear and doubt.

The volatility of her emotions was only exacerbated by the intimidating task ahead. Somewhere in this chaos and din was a secret shrine to Nava. Only there could they find—or so they hoped—the location of Nava's hidden site, where the next Loresmith trial would take place. And they had to do it quickly. The sooner they were away from the Great Market, the better Ara would feel.

While Lucket's plan for their group to pose as merchants was sound, Teth alone was accustomed to disguises and hiding his identity. The rest of them were rank amateurs, and there was no guarantee that they could successfully evade notice of the many imperial soldiers who patrolled the marketplace. The entire scheme set Ara's teeth on edge.

Teth kept up calls of reassurance to the horses as the wagon fought its way along crisscrossing paths. The packhorses recruited to draw the wagon proved they were made of sturdy stuff, keeping calm despite the frequency of people darting in front of them and loud, alarming sounds.

Joar and Lahvja had the more difficult task, each leading a pair of riding mounts. These four horses were much more skittish, given to prancing and spooking amid the chaos. Ara worried that in the raging river of people, carts, and animals, they'd be separated, and she kept a careful eye on her friends and their troublesome charges.

"The market is divided by types of wares." Teth had to shout over the din. "Weavers and tailors are in the southern quarter, blacksmiths and jewelers in the northern, tanners and fur traders in the western, and the leftovers in the eastern. Food and drink are scattered throughout the market, though a good number are concentrated in a square adjacent to the pavilion. There are also legacy vendors who have coveted places within the pavilion. Those belong to the makers and merchants who have sold their wares in the Great Market for the longest time and purportedly have the finest goods."

It wasn't surprising that places in the pavilion were the most vied for. The immense marble structure gleamed white amid the patchwork of colors created by tents, wagons, and banners and loomed above everything else in the Great Market.

"So we'll be in the east with the leftovers?" Ara asked. She drew a sharp breath as Lahvja was jostled by a pair of men carrying a large crate between them, but the summoner had no trouble soothing the horses and keeping pace with their wagon.

"Yes," Teth replied. "And that's a good thing. The eastern quarter has the most turnover of merchants and isn't tied to any guilds. Our arrival shouldn't be conspicuous."

"That's good," Ara said, then asked, "Do you expect we'll actually have customers?"

She balked at the idea of frequent interactions with buyers and other vendors, but Teth grinned.

"We'd better. Haggling is one of my favorite pastimes. I'm very good at it. In fact, depending on how long we're here, I expect to make a tidy profit."

Ara scoffed at him. "I can't believe you'd even think about that."

"I'm a thief, Ara dearest. I live for the clink of shiny coins." He waggled his eyebrows at her.

She laughed and shook her head, fondly resting her hand on his forearm without thinking about it. As soon as she touched his sun-warmed skin, her pulse was afire. She knew she should snatch her hand back, but she couldn't seem to move.

Teth's eyes found hers, and Ara felt herself sinking into the amber depths of his irises. He held her gaze longer than he should have, and her breath caught. She couldn't stop thinking about what Nimhea had said.

What if she'd gotten this all wrong? Her heart longed to believe that, but her mind wasn't convinced, and she didn't know if it ever could be.

Finally able to pull her hand and eyes away from him, Ara laced her traitor fingers together. She bit her lip and stared straight ahead.

I need to talk to him. Soon. Going on like this was unbearable and unfair to both of them.

Teth returned his attention to the horses and didn't continue their conversation.

The overwhelming noise of the market suddenly seemed like nothing in comparison to the silence between them, and Ara could do nothing to stop the gnawing ache in her belly.

It took half an hour to make their way from the entrance of the Great Market to their allotted space in the eastern quarter. The leftovers, as Teth had described the vendors assigned to this quarter, were a hodgepodge of merchants, with each stand and stall striving to outmatch its neighbors with bright colors and eye-catching signs proclaiming their wares.

Teth immediately set about converting their wagon into an alchemist's stall, while Joar tended to the horses, seeking a suitable space to picket them while Huntress oversaw his endeavors. Nimhea, Lahvja, and Ara set up a living space behind the wagon with their tents, wooden folding chairs, a firepit, and cooking apparatus.

With their task completed, the three women returned to observe what changes Teth had wrought in their absence.

"My goodness," Lahvja said.

Nimhea chuckled, smiling wickedly. "It's . . . an approach."

The driver's seat and front of the wagon became stairs that rose to the wagon floor, which transformed into a platform that showcased shelves filled with glass and metal bottles and jars that winked and sparkled in the sunlight once one side of the wagon was detached and set up as a table where Teth could do his haggling. The rear door remained in place to provide a sheltered area where Lahvja could create whatever medicines and other mixtures were in demand.

Fabric in vivid scarlet striped with black and fringed with gold tassels draped the frame of the wagon. A wooden sign painted with gold leaf announced in bold, embellished letters that the Potion Palace was open for business.

"The Potion Palace?" Ara asked Teth when he strolled up to them. "Has Lucket been to many palaces?"

She kept her tone light, but staring at the garish, impromptu store, Ara felt a mounting sense of dread. This was not hiding. This was not evading notice. They would not get away with this.

He turned to admire his work. "In the Great Market, exaggeration is an effective means to an end."

"And ostentation?" Nimhea quipped, making Lahvja giggle, then throw Teth an apologetic look.

Unfazed, Teth replied, "There is a time and place for subtlety, but that is neither now nor here."

Ara moved to his side and said softly, "Are you sure this is the best idea? It's so . . ." She gestured at the converted wagon. "Loud."

Teth simply raised an eyebrow at her. "Trust me."

Joar joined them. "The horses are picketed a short distance from here in a place with good grass for grazing."

He gazed at the converted wagon for a long moment. "Are we putting on a play?"

Huntress approached the stall and sniffed around it as if perplexed by the wagon's transformation.

"I object to that question," Lahvja said. "Eni's Children perform on stages that are much more tasteful than this."

"I apologize," Joar said solemnly.

Teth smirked at them. "Insult the wagon all you want, but within the hour we'll be swarmed with customers."

Ara swallowed a wave of nausea. *Swarmed?*

"Care to wager on that?" Nimhea asked.

"Very tempting," Teth replied. "But that is a terrible bet for you, and I'd rather not take advantage of our brave, albeit naive, future queen."

Nimhea glowered at him. "Naive?"

"Only when it comes to hawking wares, Your Highness," Teth said quickly. "Please don't stick me with the pointy end of your sword."

"Don't worry, Teth." Nimhea smiled wickedly. "If I do it fast enough you'll be dead before you feel anything."

Teth blanched and backed away several steps.

"Oh, leave him be." Lahvja threaded her arm through Nimhea's. "We do need him to make sales."

From his safer vantage point, Teth called, "I'm going to prepare for said sales. You all need to get into proper clothes."

Nimhea muttered something under her breath.

"Yes, dear," Lahvja agreed. "But we'd better do as he says."

Ara absorbed their banter like it was an elixir for her anxiety. Her friends seemed confident.

If they think this will work, I should, too.

She kept telling herself that in the hopes that she would eventually believe it.

Ara knelt to open the large chest they'd received along with the wagon when Lucket and his companions returned to the abandoned fort. Nimhea and Lahvja stood on either side of her, peering over her shoulders. Even Huntress wandered over from where she'd been resting near the firepit and buried her nose in the trunk, sniffing its contents.

They'd been dressed in their usual traveling clothes, but now that it was time to play merchant, they needed to investigate the wardrobe the Low King had provided. Digging through the chest's contents, Ara found several dresses, pairs of fashionable doeskin shoes, wraps and scarves, and a smaller box containing jewelry.

The dresses were of varied sizes, and Ara divvied them out—the longest for Nimhea, those more suited for curves to Lahvja, and the shortest to herself. As she handled each piece, she marveled at the fineness of the fabrics slipping over her fingers, the susurrations they made rustling against each other, and the exquisite detail of each design.

In Rill's Pass, Ara had no need for fine clothing. She'd rarely worn dresses, and the few she owned had been simple wool for winter and muslin for summer—though her grandmother's skills as a weaver did guarantee the quality of each dress and the loveliness of embroidered details at the collars and hems. These dresses, however, were of an entirely different ilk.

The three women went to their respective tents to change. Ara spread the three dresses out on her bedroll. They were all Vijerian silk—one was sage green with long, semi-sheer sleeves and a subtle pattern of leaves and vines covering the bodice and skirt; the second was sleeveless lavender with a wrapped bodice that created a deep V at the neckline and a wide braided-leather sash at the waist; and the third was pale blue with a similar wrapped neckline but was embroidered on the bodice and had three-quarter tulip sleeves with silver thread.

Her chest pinched. Silverthread. Her family. Homesickness swept through her. She closed her eyes, willing her grandmother's face into her mind's eye, then Old Imgar's. She missed her grandmother's wit and wisdom, Imgar's stories and gruff laughter . . . even his sour moods.

When will I see them again?

The warm weather in Sola wouldn't reach the highlands for another moon, but the marks of late spring would signal summer's approach. The rivers would swell with snowmelt, and the bravest flowers would emerge from the ground and lift their faces to the lengthening sunlight.

She swallowed the hard lump in her throat and made a promise to herself that she would ask Teth to send agents from the Below to look into her family's welfare.

Ara chose the blue dress. The deep V of the neckline didn't accommodate her chemise, so she tossed it aside, then took a moment to revel in the sensual liquid pour of the silk over her skin. She used the attached ties to tighten the bodice around her chest and paused briefly at vague misgivings about the way the dress suddenly created more cleavage than she actually had. The skirt flared out from her waist and swirled around her legs when she moved.

Turning to the pieces of jewelry she'd selected, Ara picked up a silver teardrop pendant set with deep-blue lapis. She put a silver ear cuff on her left ear and several silver and copper bangles on her right wrist.

Ara emerged from the tent to find Nimhea and Lahvja waiting for her. They were an arresting sight. Ara was used to Lahvja wearing dresses, but nothing like the confection of silver draped around her now. The dress had cap sleeves fringed with black beads and a deeply cowled neckline. Its silhouette followed the curves of her body to the beaded hem that brushed over the tops of her shoes. She wore a choker of black beads strung together to resemble lace resting on her neck and collarbones.

Nimhea's transformation was nigh unbelievable. The princess wore a dress of forest green with a bodice that wrapped over one shoulder while leaving the other bare. The top half of the bodice was embroidered with copper thread on a diagonal that carried down the skirt, broadening until it circled the entire hem. A dove-gray scarf covered her head, hiding her hair and shadowing her face, and fell to her mid-back while its width pooled over her arms.

"You both look beautiful," Ara told them.

Nimhea offered a wry smile.

"As do you," Lahvja replied. "But you need to let me change your hair. Fjerian braids don't fit our disguise."

Ara's hand touched the braids coiled around the crown of her head. "I hadn't thought of that."

Lahvja smiled warmly. "It will only take a moment for me to fix."

Nimhea watched as Ara stood patiently while Lahvja unbraided her hair. The summoner combed through the black waves with her fingers then gathered the length and twisted it, securing it with a silver cuff so that Ara's hair spilled over her right shoulder.

"You still look like a Fjerian." Nimhea laughed. "But a Fjerian who'd rather be Vijerian."

When Ara blushed, Lahvja squeezed her shoulders.

"We'd be happy to adopt you."

Teth appeared from around the front of the wagon. "Are you three almost ready? We have gawkers who are going to raid the stall if we don't—"

He stopped short, staring at Ara. His jaw clenched, and the tendons of his neck tightened.

Unable to hold his gaze, Ara lowered her eyes. "We're coming. Lahvja was just finishing my hair."

She looked to Lahvja for support, but the summoner and the princess were quickly walking away.

Then Teth was beside her. Her heart stuttered. She didn't trust herself to look at him.

Clearing his throat first, he said, "Vijerian fashion suits you."

Deciding it was both ridiculous and rude to keep staring at the ground, Ara lifted her head.

Teth had changed as well, though the differences were subtle. He still wore his usual dark suede trousers, but his shirt was much finer and closer-fitting undyed linen with an open collar. The pendant bearing Eni's sign rested against his dark skin.

"Can you believe he wanted me to take it off?" Teth scoffed, after following her gaze. "Eni named me Loreknight. I'm not about to offend a god for fashion's sake."

Ara laughed. "I'm sure Eni would forgive you, but I agree with your choice."

Teth had gone quiet again, looking at her, drinking her in. His expression was pained.

"Is something wrong?" she asked as her pulse skittered.

When he met her questioning gaze, his eyes were stricken. She wanted so much to reach out to him.

"No, and yes," he murmured. "You're . . . you're more than beautiful. I don't have words for what you are."

His words stirred up all those sensations and feelings she'd been struggling to keep buried. Though she knew she shouldn't, Ara moved closer to him. She laid her fingertips against the hollow of his throat. His pulse jumped at her touch.

She took hold of Eni's pendant, resting the back of her hand on his upper chest. They stood like that for a moment that stretched out beyond bearing. Ara could feel his every heartbeat vibrate through her limbs. But he stayed very still.

An insistent ache built inside her, and she longed for Teth to put his arms around her. To possess her. She wanted her body against his, pressing tight so she could feel every contour of his chest and abdomen.

She brought her right hand up to grasp his left arm, her fingers wrapping around taut muscle.

"Teth." Longing tore through her. "I miss you."

He held her gaze. Something battled behind his eyes. She could feel the strain in his body.

I can't do this to him. I'm being unfair.

But Ara couldn't stop herself from moving closer. She brushed her lips over his.

Teth didn't move and Ara started to pull away, disappointment stinging her. But then his arms were around her and his mouth lowered to hers. The kiss began feather light. Whispers of his lips against hers. She felt the touch of his tongue and instinctively opened her mouth for him. His tongue slipped inside, and she was startled by the sound of her own unbidden moan.

The kiss deepened and his arms tightened around her, molding her body to his. She wrapped her arms around his neck. His kisses were hard, demanding. Heat curled low in her body, and her knees buckled as she melted into him. She clung to him, certain she would fall if he let her go.

Teth's lips left hers to press against her neck. His tongue flicked over her skin. He then laid a trail of searing kisses along her jaw to her temple.

"I need to know you want this," he murmured against her skin.

"I want this," she breathed. "I want you."

Ara caught his lower lip between her teeth, then kissed him. Kissed him again. And again. She became drunk with sensation. She was losing herself. Conflicting impulses raged against each other in her heart and mind.

Breaking their kiss felt like ripping herself apart, but she forced herself to pull back. Breathing hard, she cupped his face in her hands. She was shaking, her body afire but her mind chilled by doubt.

"I think I love you, Teth." Her voice cracked as tears pricked in the corners of her eyes. "But I don't know how to be the Loresmith and love you."

His eyes filled with regret. He looked away from her, giving a slow shake of his head, and let her go.

"Then learn," he said softly, stepping away.

He released a long breath and turned on his heel, heading for the wagon.

A sickening wave passed through her. *What have I done?*

Ara's limbs trembled violently, and she thought she would collapse, but suddenly Huntress was there pressing against her, helping to steady her legs. Grateful, Ara looked down into the wolf's silver eyes and found ageless wisdom.

Ara stood there, one hand buried in Huntress's fur, waiting for her pulse to stop roaring in her veins. For her skin to cool and strength to return to her limbs.

For the courage to face Teth.

She couldn't deny that despite trying to keep her feelings at bay, her desire and care for him had continued to grow. A war raged inside her; her body and heart fighting for Teth while her mind defended against their every volley.

What had Nimhea said? *You're punishing him and yourself for reasons I don't believe are good enough.*

The princess's words compelled Ara, so why was it so hard to believe they were true?

A small crowd gathered around the table where Teth had samples of the sundry goods offered by the Potion Palace. He was grinning, laughing, and chatting with his customers, handing out lists of merchandise and their prices.

Ara watched him from where she'd tucked herself at one corner of the platform. She could hardly believe what she was seeing. Teth was obviously in his element. He looked so relaxed and natural. So happy.

She didn't understand how he could so quickly alter his persona after what had just happened between them. She still felt the tremors left by his touch.

Should I go to him? Ara knew she was meant to be helping, but that last look he had given her . . .

She felt sick again. It was hard to believe that he'd want her anywhere near him. She didn't blame him. But she couldn't let herself be overwhelmed by her feelings. No matter the discomfort between her and Teth, they had to focus on finding the hidden shrine and getting the answers they needed.

As if he'd sensed Ara watching, Teth turned and waved to her.

"Ara! Come here!"

When she joined him at the table, he didn't spare her a glance. "You're going to be my runner."

He shoved a slip of paper into her hands.

"I don't—" Ara frowned at the paper.

"You don't actually have to run," Teth said with an impatient sigh. "But when I give you an order slip you need to go to the wagon and get the required items from Lahvja and Nimhea. Then bring them back here so I can sell them to the customer."

Ara nodded, deciding that he'd also determined they needed to put aside their emotions and focus on the work at hand. After explaining her task, he'd returned to engaging with the customers, using his wit and savvy to make sales.

Committing herself to her role, Ara fetched the first order. When she returned, another slip was pressed into her hand. Then another. She made her trip to the wagon and back. A pile of slips was growing beside Teth, and soon Ara was running.

Demand kept her hurrying from table to wagon for the better

part of three hours, when at last the stream of customers slowed to a trickle.

She'd barely had time to catch her breath when an imperial patrol arrived—half a dozen soldiers led by a keg of a man with a heavy brow and thick beard.

Ara turned to glance at the wagon. Nimhea and Joar had made themselves scarce. Lahvja appeared to be completely focused on her craft, not even glancing toward the table.

"Stay calm," Teth somehow murmured to her while wearing a broad smile for the benefit of the soldiers.

Ara tried to mimic the smile he wore, a feat when facing off with the approaching patrol leader, whose glower resembled a thundercloud. The leader held up his hand, and all but one of the soldiers stood in flanking positions while their commander came to the table and snapped his finger.

The soldier who'd stayed at his side looked at Teth. "Sergeant Braun requires your papers."

Ara managed to keep a straight face despite the boorish sergeant's refusal to speak for himself.

"Of course," Teth said smoothly, drawing a folded sheaf of paper from his pocket. He offered it to the sergeant, but the other man snatched it from Teth's hand.

Teth didn't lose his easy smile as the sergeant stared him down and the soldier scoured the proffered papers.

"All seems to be in order, sir."

Sergeant Braun's thick brows drew together. "You're certain."

He regarded Teth with open hostility. Teth didn't flinch.

"I assure you, Sergeant," Teth said. "All the requisite permissions are there."

"Let me see that." Braun grabbed the papers, making his second quail and go red as a beet.

Braun pored over the documents, his frown deepening. As his frustration grew, Ara's stomach clenched. It was clear this man not only *wanted* to find something wrong with the papers, he *expected* to find a problem.

But how could that be? Was it simply that the Vokkans were accustomed to finding forgeries among new traders, or did it have to with the empire's search for the Loresmith and Princess Nimhea?

She was finding it more and more difficult to maintain her composure. When Sergeant Braun shifted his glare from Teth to her, she lowered her gaze and dropped into a curtsy, hoping he'd take her for a shy young girl.

When she rose, Braun was shoving the documents back into Teth's hand.

The sergeant jerked his chin at his second and turned away.

"As you were," the other man told them, then followed his commander.

At another sharp word to the rest of the soldiers, the patrol moved off. Only when they were out of sight did Teth's smile vanish.

"I didn't like that," he said, staring after them.

"The sergeant was unpleasant," Ara agreed. The brief encounter left her skin crawling and with the lingering sense that something wasn't right.

Teth shook his head. "Not that. He was looking for something specific in the documents I gave him. I don't know what, but the fact that he anticipated finding something is more than a little troubling."

"What can we do?" Ara asked, wishing he hadn't confirmed her suspicions about the patrol's visit.

"Nothing," Teth grumbled. "All we can do is hope our business here can be concluded swiftly. I don't want to linger a moment more than we have to."

The following day passed without incident. The Potion Palace continued to draw customers, and work at the stall kept them busy until they closed for the day. Teth had been nothing but polite to her since she'd broken her own rules about their relationship. Too polite. She would have preferred his anger over the cool indifference he offered. Ara knew she had no right to complain. She could blame no one but herself. She'd earned this misery of her own making, and she hadn't been afforded the chance to fix things. During the day, managing the stall was all-consuming. At night, Teth disappeared into the market, searching for information about Nava's hidden shrine.

The third day progressed much like the second until the early afternoon. Among the small group of perusers at the table was a man with a grizzled face and skin like leather. His clothes were well worn and suited for travel, as the gnarled walking stick he bore also indicated. His eyes darted about as if uneasy to settle in one place for too long.

The man beckoned to Teth, who moved to the side of the table where he waited.

Ara attended the other customers while Teth spoke with the man, but she was able to overhear their conversation.

The stranger edged closer to Teth, lowering his voice. "I've heard you might be in the market for something."

Teth acknowledged the statement with the slightest lift of his brow.

"Something old," the man continued. "Something hard to find."

After taking a moment to casually stretch his arms, Teth replied, "We might be. What do you know about it?"

"We have mutual friends." The man scratched his beard. "Who specialize in the finding of hidden things."

He paused to give a meaningful look at the lockbox. "Dangerous work."

"Perhaps too dangerous." Teth regarded the man with a cool look.

At this the man let out a dry cackle. "Perhaps."

He paused for a moment, something like mischief glimmering in his eyes.

"I wonder if you have any bottles of Daefritian red from the Dentroth reign stashed in your stores," the man said. "It's getting harder to come by, and I've quite a thirst."

Teth scratched his chin. "I'll have to check our inventory. In the meantime, is there anything else I can get for you?"

"Sleep comes hard these days," the man replied.

"Ara," Teth said, turning to her. "Will you bring our friend two sleeping tonics?"

She nodded, making apologies to the customers she'd been helping, and hurried up the stairs to fetch the bottles, all the while wondering at the odd exchange. She knew for a fact they only had wine for themselves and certainly nothing of a special vintage. It seemed strange that Teth wouldn't simply have said so.

When she returned, Teth took her elbow and pulled her aside. "Do you think you've got the hang of this?"

He gestured to the stall and the sales table.

"Yes," she replied with more confidence than she felt. The selling bit was simple enough, but she doubted she'd be able to win customers or haggle prices like Teth had managed.

"Good. Nimhea can be your runner," Teth said. "I'm going to take a walk, and I'm not sure how long I'll be gone."

Ara glanced at the stranger then back at Teth. "Are you sure it's safe?"

"Definitely not." One side of Teth's mouth hooked up. "But this sort of thing never is."

He must have caught the sudden fear in her eyes, because he added, "You don't need to worry. Remember, this is what I do."

His voice lowered. "He used a passphrase that indicates he's an agent of the Below. It's an older code, but worth the risk."

She nodded, smiling weakly. "I'll take over until you get back."

"Here are the papers you'll need if another patrol comes by," he said. "And don't forget that Joar will tear the arms off anyone who gives you trouble. He's so quiet and still as a statue, it's easy to forget he's there. But he's there."

Teth collected a satchel from the wagon and slung it across his body. After that he went to the lockbox, filled a leather pouch with coins, and dropped the pouch into the satchel. He returned to the man, and they exchanged a few words. Teth turned to give a brief nod to Ara before the pair of them moved off into the crowd.

24

Do you think we should look for him?" Ara paced beside the fire while Lahvja prepared a dinner of braised lamb shanks with herbs and leeks, accompanied by sautéed wild greens she'd gathered as they traveled.

Teth's "walk" had stretched from the afternoon to sunset, when they'd closed up the Potion Palace for the day. It had been dark for an hour, and he had yet to appear.

"I don't think there's cause to worry yet." Nimhea sat cross-legged by the fire, watching Lahvja cook. "Teth knows what he's doing."

Ara bit her lip to stop herself from asking when the princess thought it *would* be time to be concerned about Teth's absence. She'd been on edge from the moment he left. The ebb and flow of customers at the stall had kept her occupied, but had not distracted her from speculating about the trouble Teth might get himself in. Patrols had passed by, making her all the more anxious, but none had stopped to question her or ask for documents.

Reminding herself that before she'd met him, Teth had gotten along very well in Saetlund's underworld, she forced herself to sit beside Nimhea. Her stomach rumbled with a helpful reminder that it was very much anticipating a delicious meal. Lahvja's delectable cooking would be a welcome, happy distraction.

Spooning liquid over the shanks, Lahvja announced, "They're almost ready. Joar, I'll need your assistance in a moment."

The giant man rose from where he'd been sitting with Huntress, unfolding his limbs until he reached his full size.

Lahvja looked at Ara. "I agree with Nimhea. Teth will be in his element. You need not fret."

"I'm trying." Ara laughed wryly.

"Speaking of Teth being in his element," Nimhea said. "We've made a shocking amount of money the past three days."

Lahvja began to dole out portions of lamb and greens onto plates that Joar had ready. He brought two to Ara and Nimhea and returned to Lahvja, picking up another two plates.

"I find it a bit unnerving," Lahvja told Nimhea. "I would never charge the prices Teth has been asking, but he insists I've been criminally undercharging all this time."

"Criminally?" Nimhea smirked. "Well, I suppose Teth's the expert in that area."

Joar grunted his disapproval. "I do not think we should speak of our friend's unfortunate past. It mars his character and is best forgotten."

"His past?" Ara blinked at Joar, hoping the hunter was jesting.

It became obvious he was not.

"Joar," Lahvja said gently. "I don't know that Teth's . . . unconventional trade is behind him."

With a scoff, Joar replied, "Surely now that he has been named a Loreknight he will abandon his dishonorable inclinations."

Ara had to cover her mouth to stifle a giggle. *Inclinations?*

"Ara." Joar turned to her. "It is clear you are the closest to him. Do you not think he will reform his ways?"

Her chest burned at his observation of her and Teth's relationship.

She cleared her throat before answering. "We'll see."

"There'll be no seeing about anything." Teth strode into the firelight.

Ara's heart leapt at the sight of him. She wanted to jump up and throw her arms around him, but knew she could not. Instead, she dug her fingernails into her palms.

"Joar, my good, enormous friend," Teth said, grinning at the hunter. "When Eni named me Loreknight, I was given no stipulation about abandoning my former pursuits. If my god has no trouble with my less honorable inclinations, I see no cause to reform."

A menacing sound rumbled from Joar's chest. "It is implicit in your new calling that you should reform."

"I don't deal in implications," Teth told him. "Far too risky. I'd suggest you learn to love me for who I am."

While Joar stared at him, Teth plucked the plate filled with steaming food from the hunter's large hand.

"Is this for me? Thank you. I'm ravenous."

Joar waited as Lahvja served up another plate, all the while muttering in his own language. Ara couldn't understand a word, but it was obvious the man wasn't giving Teth any compliments.

Disappointment sank into her body when Teth made himself comfortable beside Nimhea rather than sitting next to her. Resisting self-pity, Ara turned her attention to the hot meal Lahvja had prepared. She sliced into the shank, letting the mouthwatering odor of the sauce and herbs waft into her nose before taking a bite. As usual, Lahvja's dish was divine. Layers of flavor melted on her tongue and sent a shiver of pleasure through her.

Unfortunately, the sensation called to mind a much deeper pleasure she'd been captured by when in Teth's arms. She stole a glance at him, only to find him watching her, and quickly returned her gaze to her plate.

He'd been detached with her most of the day, but when she'd met his eyes she hadn't found anger. What she'd seen might have been regret, possibly longing, maybe frustration—she couldn't be sure.

Ara continued to eat, but the flavors of the dish seemed to be gone. She wondered how Teth could ever trust her. The thought that she might never feel him close because of her own indecision was unbearable.

I have to do something. I need him.

"Ara?" Teth's voice cut through the fog of her emotions. His brow was furrowed with concern.

She startled, blinking at him. Blood rushed into her cheeks as she became irrationally convinced that he'd stepped into her mind and heard everything.

Frowning, he asked, "What do you think?"

She shook her head, trying to bring herself back into the present moment.

"I'm sorry. I missed what you said."

The crease between his brows deepened. "All of it?"

"I—" Her mouth had gone very dry. "I apologize, my mind was somewhere else."

He started to ask her something, then stopped, as if reconsidering.

Lahvja came to the rescue. "Teth just explained what transpired while he was away."

Ara groaned inwardly. That was a lot to miss. Just how long had she been drifting in her own thoughts?

Lahvja gave Teth a meaningful look, and something seemed to pass between them.

"The man who approached us had information about the hidden

followers of Nava who are still here," Teth told Ara. "There's a secret temple beneath the pavilion, and a priestess of Nava resides there. If anyone can help us find the location of Nava's trial, it will be her."

"Then we should go," Ara said quickly.

"Yes." His eyes were worried again. "We agreed to that. What I was asking your opinion about is who should go. We need to attract as little attention as possible, which means we'll go to the temple at night, but someone has to stay with the wagon and be ready to get out of the market. Both roles involve risk. If we're discovered and arrested, it won't take long for the Vokkans to identify us as the vendors at the Potion Palace. Those who remain here will need to watch carefully for an increased activity of the patrols and also signs that other vendors might be quickly packing up and leaving. If word spreads that the Vokkans are planning to raid even one stall, it makes all the vendors nervous."

Ara nodding, trying to process the facts as quickly as possible. "I think you, Nimhea, and myself should go to the temple. Joar and Lahvja can have the horses ready in case we need to make a quick escape."

"I agree," Teth replied, and a bit of the concern etched onto his features faded. "There's a good chance we'll need to abandon the wagon, so, Lahvja, you should pack up whatever is most needed and leave the rest."

Turning to Joar, Teth said, "And you need to spend tomorrow finding a destrier. You need a mount, and only a warhorse will be able to carry you. There's something of a perpetual horse fair that goes on just outside the northern quarter of the Great Market. You'll be able to purchase one there."

"I prefer to walk." The look Joar leveled on Teth wasn't friendly.

Teth was unfazed. "I know you do. But we need to be able to travel faster. At a gallop."

"I run very swiftly." There was a stubborn set to Joar's formidable jaw. "I have adequate stamina."

"I'm sure your stamina is more than adequate," Teth replied solemnly, though Ara could see that he was fighting laughter. "But you cannot run as swiftly for as long or as far as a horse."

Joar glowered at him for a long moment, then said, "I cannot deny that."

"Good." Teth sounded relieved.

"So we'll keep the stall open through the day tomorrow," Ara said. "Then go to the temple after dark."

Teth nodded. "I think that's the best plan."

"I agree," Ara replied. She looked to Lahvja and Nimhea. "Your thoughts?"

Nimhea smiled. "I quite like the idea of a hidden temple and infiltration after dark."

"It's a good plan." Lahvja sighed. "Yet it leaves me uneasy."

"I never said there wouldn't be danger," Teth said defensively.

Lahvja offered him a sad smile. "I know. But the temple is hidden because its followers have been run underground, persecuted. I fear that seeking them out puts them at risk as much as ourselves. No doubt the Vokkans have already been trying to find them for some time. If we are noticed, we may lead soldiers directly to Nava's worshippers."

"There is a chance of that." Teth grimaced. "I've tried to gather intelligence about how little or how much the Vokkans know and care about a hidden shrine, but everyone I spoke to was very tight-lipped on the subject. That speaks to true fear."

"I don't think it can be helped," Ara said. "I don't like that, but we have to find Nava's hidden site. If we're cautious enough, hopefully those who still worship in the temple will be safe."

Lahvja turned away to stare into the firelight. "I shall pray for it."

The remainder of dinner passed with little conversation. A quiet but weighty tension had settled over their small camp, making a stark contrast to the ongoing sounds of music and revelry that drifted in from the never-sleeping market.

Ara knew it wasn't only the risks of their mission that troubled her friends. Lahvja's reminder that they put not only themselves but other innocents in danger clawed at her conscience. She also hated that they'd be separating in order to complete their task and sensed that the others did, too.

They had retired for the night much earlier than was their usual habit. Nimhea and Lahvja, fingers entwined, disappeared into one tent. Joar and Huntress wandered into the shadows, leaving Ara and Teth to seek their own beds. They made eye contact once, but didn't speak even to bid each other good night. Ara tried to pry any thoughts from Teth's face, but his expression was unreadable.

Inside her tent, Ara stretched out on her bedroll and knew that she wouldn't sleep anytime soon. Though she wanted to focus on what might happen in the temple, her mind always ran to Teth and the tangle of her feelings. When she'd determined they should stop their romance, she'd been sad, but confident in her choice. In the days since, that surety had crumbled. The emotional barrier she thought stood firm between them was riddled with cracks. At the slightest pressure, it gave way. First Teth's anger and then Lahvja's reprimand filled her with doubt about her choice. Nimhea's forgiveness nearly broke her with its honesty and simplicity. Finally, the torrid emotions that consumed her whenever Teth was close proclaimed the futility of her resistance.

What am I even fighting for? Ara stared at the ceiling of her tent. *My own torment?*

She imagined Teth staring at the ceiling of his own tent and craved more than anything to know what he was feeling.

I don't know how to be the Loresmith and love you.

All the muscles in her chest tightened when she thought of the words Teth had thrown back at her.

Then learn.

He'd been so full of outrage, but beneath that shield of pride she'd seen how wounded he was, the raw desperation that fueled his anger.

And she'd done that to him. The person she cared for so deeply it made her world turn over. The person she'd fallen in love with.

Suddenly it was there. The stark truth.

I was wrong.

She bolted upright. Waves of emotion crashed over her: surprise, relief, regret. So much regret.

Crawling to the flap of her tent, Ara pushed herself through, stumbling out into the dark. The campfire was reduced to embers. She glanced around, not spying Joar, nor hearing sounds from the tent Lahvja and Nimhea occupied.

Ara walked to Teth's tent. She stood outside the entrance for what felt like an eternity with her heart slamming against her ribs so hard it seemed possible they could break.

With a trembling hand, Ara grasped the flap and then ducked inside. At her appearance, Teth rolled into a crouch at one corner of the tent. She was certain he had a dagger in his hand.

"It's me." Her voice cracked when she spoke.

"Ara?" Teth relaxed onto his knees. "What are you doing here? Did something happen?"

Yes. Something. Everything.

She moved toward him, and it felt like swimming through tar. When she drew close, she lowered herself beside him. Their bodies were only a hairsbreadth apart.

"Ara." When he said her name it was so many things. A warning. A plea. A rebuke. A question.

"Teth." Her body shook. Her breath was unsteady. "I—I don't need to learn how to love you."

He went very still, and she sensed he was holding his breath.

"I know I love you." Her voice was on the verge of breaking. "But I've been afraid to, and I'm sorry. I'm so sorry."

Then she was in his arms and his lips were brushing her ear as he murmured comforting words that she barely understood. All she could do was grasp his shoulders, terrified that if she let go he would disappear. He kissed her temple and her closed eyelids.

She cupped his face in her hands and moved her lips over his in a light caress. He opened his mouth so she could taste him. The kiss deepened and he groaned. The sound sent blood rushing low in her body, made her wrap her arms around his back and drag him down until she was stretched out on his bedroll and he was above her. Her fingers twisted in his shirt, grabbing handfuls of fabric, then jerking it up until he took over the task and pulled the shirt over his head. Her hands pressed against his chest, reveling in the heat of his skin. She moved her fingers slowly, discovering the contours of his muscles, the ridges of his abdomen. The sounds he made as she touched him sent molten waves through her limbs.

He broke their kiss, bowing his head to let his tongue flick over the hollow of her throat. His lips feathered over her skin, moving down into the deep V of her bodice. She gasped. Her body moved of its own accord, lifting toward him, reaching for something it desperately wanted.

His fingers found the ties that secured her bodice and her skirt. He made quick work of the knots. Then he pulled the silk apart, baring her to the night. She drew a sharp breath as the cool air kissed her skin and gooseflesh prickled all over her body.

Teth held himself above her, no longer touching her. He was breathing hard.

"Tell me if you need me to stop," he said in a rough whisper. "I'll stop if you ask."

"Don't stop." She grasped his shoulders, pulling him toward her. "Please don't stop."

He bent to kiss her, his mouth and tongue doing extraordinary, unthinkable things to hers. But his hands. His hands. Ara didn't have words for what they were doing to her. She couldn't control the way her body reacted. She didn't want to. All she wanted to do was feel.

Until feeling wasn't enough. Her fingers found the waist of his trousers, then the buttons. She shoved the loosened garment down until he shucked them off.

And then he was there. All of him. Pressing against her in the most intimate way.

Teth kissed her gently. His fingers caressed her cheek. "Are you sure you want this?"

"I need this." She dug her fingers into his back. "I need you."

He kissed her again, slowly, exquisitely, until her body was arching against him of its own accord.

His hips moved once, carefully, and she gasped at the shock of sensation and the spear of pain. He bent his head and pressed his lips to her neck, whispering her name against her skin. He moved again, and then again, until the stars exploded.

25

ra had hoped to keep the night's events between herself and Teth for at least a little while. The night had been a revelation, and she wanted to savor her feelings before she had to share them. Unfortunately, fate had other plans.

First, having slept little over the course of the night, they didn't wake until late morning.

Second, upon waking, they discovered they weren't quite ready to leave the tent yet, and lingered there for some time, needing each other to ease their shared fears of what that night's mission would bring.

Third, they were at last drawn into the day by Huntress's incessant barking just outside the tent.

When Ara and Teth stepped into the bright morning light, not only was the wolf there, but Joar stood a few feet behind her.

At their appearance, Huntress gave another bark, this one satisfied rather than pestering, and wagged her tail. Joar looked far less happy to see them. In fact, he looked everywhere but directly at them, and Ara could swear that a blush chased across his cheeks.

"Nimhea says you must get up now." Joar spoke through clenched teeth. He didn't sound angry, just desperately uncomfortable. "They need your help. There are many buyers."

"Of course," Teth replied. "We'll be right there."

With some effort, Joar fixed Teth with a severe gaze. His features had taken on the aspects of a thundercloud.

The hunter leaned forward, baring his teeth. Taking a cue from her companion, Huntress did the same and added a growl.

Ara was impressed that Teth didn't flinch.

"Your intentions." One of Joar's hands balled into a fist that bore a terrible resemblance to the head of a war hammer. "Are they honorable?"

If Joar's expression hadn't been so full of violence, Ara might have laughed. Instead, she swallowed hard, building up the courage to step between that fist and Teth's face if need be.

"I love her." Teth stared Joar down. "Is that honorable enough for you?"

Joar froze, blinking at Teth as if he hadn't understood the words.

"I love her," Teth said again.

Ara's heart pinched with something between relief and joy.

Joar's fist relaxed, then he clapped both hands on Teth's shoulders and threw his head back to give a roar of a laugh.

Teth and Ara exchanged a look, both rather stunned at the hunter's wild shift in emotion.

"Yes!" Joar grinned at Teth. "Yes! Love is most honorable, and my heart is glad for you, my friend."

Just as quickly as his laugh had come, another shadow flitted over Joar's face. He dropped his hands from Teth's shoulders and turned to Ara.

His expression was less menacing, but deeply troubled.

"And you, Loresmith?" Joar asked her. "What is your regard for the thief?"

He glanced from Ara to Teth, as if worried Teth's heart was about to be broken.

Ara felt a wrench of guilt as she thought, *Don't worry, Joar, I stomped on Teth's heart once, but I'll do everything I can to make up for it.*

What she said aloud was: "I love him, too."

Joar took a step back, surveying them both. A slow grin spread over his face. "Good. Very good."

Huntress was wagging her tail again. She turned and gave a single bark at Joar.

"Yes." He nodded, looking at the wolf.

To Ara and Teth he said, "Now go help Nimhea and Lahvja with this business of buying and selling. I will continue to stand guard."

Joar started to walk away, then stopped, looking over his shoulder. "I hope you will finish our business here tonight. I do not like this place."

He left them.

Huntress rested on her haunches. Her tongue lolled out of her mouth, and she held Ara with an expression that was slightly reproving, but mostly delighted. Her bushy tail thumped against the ground.

Ara gazed into the wolf's eyes and could have sworn she heard Huntress's thought: *It is good that you at last understand the way things are meant to be, silly human.*

She stared at Huntress, captured by a strange idea. Perhaps Joar heard these thoughts all the time. Ara knew in her bones that the history between this beast and the hunter who'd saved her was true. That Huntress was not Eni in disguise. But every so often, especially in moments like this, Ara couldn't help but wonder.

Under cover of night, Ara, Nimhea, and Teth moved through the Great Market toward the pavilion. Though parts of the market were as lively as the whole was in the middle of the day, they kept to the quieter paths and slunk through shadows whenever they could.

The day had passed without incident. The quality of Lahvja's concoctions had spread through the market—for it couldn't have been the reasonable prices—and drawn a large crowd of buyers that didn't shrink until well after dusk. Customers' demands had kept Ara running, literally, from the wagon to the sales table for the bulk of the day. Several imperial patrols walked by, and their every appearance made Ara hold her breath until they'd gone, but none stopped to harass them in any manner. The only difference was Teth. Rather than keeping their interactions completely businesslike, he took every chance he could to be close to her. To touch her. When he handed her order slips, he let his fingers caress the underside of her wrist. He leaned in more than he needed to when he spoke to her, so his breath tickled her ear. And the smiles he gave her. Each one sent her heart tumbling and filled her with giddy bliss.

At one point, Lahvja pulled her aside and pressed an oilcloth pouch of ground herbs into Ara's hands.

"One teaspoon of this brewed like a tea, every day, until you wish to be with child," the summoner murmured. She leaned in, taking Ara's hand in hers. "I am so very happy for you both."

Ara stammered her thanks. She'd been intending to ask Lahvja for such a tisane when afforded a moment of privacy, and was deeply grateful that Lahvja had anticipated her need. The thought of having a child with Teth stirred her deeply, possibly many children, one of whom would be the next Loresmith. The broken line would be restored.

But that was for the future, when they were not so young. Certainly not until after the Resistance had, she hoped with all her being, retaken the River Throne and driven the Vokkans from Saetlund.

Ara regretted nothing about embracing her love for Teth, but these kinds of thoughts—dreams for a future that might not come to pass—brought into focus more clearly the source of her indecision about her feelings and the deep roots of her fear. They wouldn't fade away, neither the love nor the fear, but neither would Ara allow doubts to rule her.

As they passed through mostly empty streets, Teth gave signals anytime they needed to duck behind barrels or squeeze into narrow corridors to avoid being seen. Their careful movements and the coiled tension in Ara's limbs made her feel as if her body might break apart from being controlled so tightly.

After three-quarters of an hour, Teth held up his hand, and they stopped at the open door to what appeared to be a small abandoned shop.

"The entrance to the temple is hidden behind the hearth in this building," he whispered. "Follow me. No talking while we're in the tunnels."

Ara gazed at the unassuming building and bit her lip. The information provided by Teth's contact had led them here, but what lay on the other side of that door and those dirtied windows?

A dead end? A trap?

Her pulse stammered as Teth slipped into the building, while Ara and Nimhea waited for a sign from him that they should proceed. A minute passed where Ara's heart was in her throat and her ears strained for signs of a scuffle or other trouble, but then Teth returned and motioned for them to come inside.

The shop was empty save a few pieces of furniture that had been draped with cloth to keep away the dust that had since soiled the fabric to a dull brown. The floor was covered by an inch of filth. Ara worried about their having laid such a clear trail of footprints, but once Teth had opened the passageway to the underground tunnels, he ushered Ara and Nimhea inside before picking up a sack at the top of the steps leading down. He opened the sack, which was full of sand and dirt. Returning to the room, he scattered a new layer to hide their tracks.

The steps took them deep, at least another story below where most cellars would be dug. Guttering torches lit their way as Ara imagined passing beneath the streets above, and questions spun through her mind.

How many people knew of this tunnel? How strong was their belief in and loyalty to Nava?

Despite being deep in the earth, Ara felt exposed. The Great Market was a far cry from a village tucked in the Vijerian jungle or a cursed forest in the middle of the desert. She felt more trepidation here than she had at any other place this journey had taken her.

The tunnel led them not to a door, but to an opening in a wall. They stepped into a broad, square chamber framed with steps descending to a sunken floor. The stairs, floors, and walls were covered with tile featuring mosaics in vivid colors that depicted sheaves of wheat, fruit trees, bundled corn, and garden vegetables, as well as women with swollen, pregnant bellies and mothers holding infants. A row of benches faced a dais upon which sat a sculpture of Nava. The goddess knelt, her abundance of flesh carved in ebony—heavy breasts, rounded stomach, broad hips. Her hair had been painted with gold leaf, and her eyes were gleaming topaz. Her arms were outstretched, and her wide lips spread in a smile of welcome. Though Ara had shared the company of three gods, this statue was the first image of a god she'd encountered, and she was surprised by the deep emotions that shook her as she gazed upon Nava's likeness. Looking up at the goddess of Sola and Kelden, Ara felt as though she'd been wrapped in love and acceptance.

Offerings of food had been laid on the steps leading up to the dais. At the bottom of the stairs, an elderly woman dressed in a linen robe sat atop a pile of silk and velvet cushions. Men, women, and children who numbered around twenty occupied the benches or milled about the space. A few of the young women wore linen robes like that of their elder. One of these women broke from the group and came to meet them. She had dark skin, raven-black hair, and eyes that were a guileless deep, liquid brown.

"I am Mura, acolyte of Nava," the young woman said. "The holy priestess welcomes you and bids you join her."

As she led them into the room, Ara leaned over to Teth. "Did you send word we were coming?"

"I did not," he replied, giving her a look that was caught between alarm and bemusement. His eyes flicked over the room, searching for signs of danger.

Mura led them to stand before the holy priestess and then went to the elderly woman's side to help her rise. She had dark skin and eyes framed by a thick halo of tight white curls.

The holy priestess thanked Mura then lifted her hands in the manner of Nava's statue.

"Blessings of Nava, goddess of the harvest, of the fruit of the earth and the womb, be upon you. I am Bothia, holy priestess in this temple, and I bid you welcome."

Ara had never been in the presence of a holy person, and Bothia radiated a sense of light and peace. Not knowing the appropriate response, Ara bowed, and was glad when Mura nodded her approval.

Nimhea started to bow, but Bothia grasped her hand.

"No, Your Majesty," the priestess said firmly. "It is I who should bow to you."

And she did.

Nimhea drew a quick, surprised breath, and her eyes widened.

"I knew you would come." The old woman straightened, looking at each of them in turn. Her papery skin crinkled into a thousand folds when she smiled. "I told Nava I'm ready to rest, but she bade me wait for you, Loresmith, and you, my queen, and now you are here."

Her gaze moved to Teth. "You are a surprise, but I sense you are a friend."

"Holy priestess." Teth bowed.

Bothia peered at him more closely. "Ah, I see it now. Not only a friend, but a Loreknight. Our temple is honored by your presence."

Teth rubbed the back of his neck self-consciously. "I'm not that hon . . . um . . . thank you."

"Nava loves her sibling Eni, because they bring her laughter and mischief." Bothia regarded Teth with twinkling eyes. "You bring these gifts to your companions."

"I suppose that much is true," Teth replied, unable to suppress a grin.

Bothia gestured to the floor, and Ara noticed that additional cushions had been provided while they conversed.

"We praise Nava by sharing in her gifts," Bothia told them. "Please join me."

Mura helped Bothia recline in the cushions once more while Ara, Nimhea, and Teth took seats in a semicircle opposite the priestess.

Another robed woman appeared, bearing a platter of cheeses and early summer fruits.

After taking a handful of ripe berries and a slice of cheese, Ara said, "You expected us. Does that mean you know why we sought you out?"

Bothia nodded. "You search for the hidden place. The site of Nava's pain and suffering."

Ara had been enjoying the sweetness of the berries contrasted with the tang of cheese, but now her throat tightened. The memory of Ofrit, disheveled and frantic, in the Tangle haunted her. Her gaze moved to the statue of Nava that towered over them. How would the goddess's dark side manifest?

"The place is called Nava's Ire," Bothia continued. "You will find it amid the ice fens in northwest Kelden. It is a place rife with danger, and I bid you enter it with great caution."

Turning to Nimhea, the priestess said, "This task belongs to two of you. The Loresmith alone cannot ease Nava's pain. One of Nava's own children must offer her goddess succor."

Bothia winced as if with her own pain. "There are so few of us here, who dare to maintain our communion with Nava. The goddess of the hearth, of family, feels the absence of her people more keenly than Saetlund's other gods. Her grief is vast."

"How can we help her?" Nimhea asked. Her expression spoke to her disbelief that a mere mortal could aid a deity.

Ara already knew what Bothia's reply would be.

"You must discover that answer yourself as you face the perils of Nava's Ire," the priestess told Nimhea.

Teth cleared his throat, and they all looked at him. He glanced at Nava's statue hopefully. "So, this one time we were far away from where we needed to be, and Eni, or possibly Ofrit, just sent us there."

He gave the statue another meaningful look. "Is there any chance?"

Nimhea and Ara looked from Teth to the priestess, expecting Bothia to be at best aghast at this suggestion, at worst furious enough to throw them out of the temple and face Nava's wrath well before they reached her Ire.

But Bothia slapped her hands on her thighs and let out a belly-deep laugh. "A question worthy of Eni's Loreknight indeed!"

Teth smiled sheepishly.

The priestess swiped tears of mirth from her eyes. "Would I could grant your wish, friend, but alas part of this task is discovering Nava's hidden place. I have directed you as much as I am permitted."

"It was worth asking." Teth shrugged.

His impish smile suddenly vanished, and his head swiveled to the tunnels from which they'd come.

"What's wrong?" Ara asked, the hairs on the back of her neck standing at attention.

Teth's brows drew together. "I heard —"

A robed girl burst out of the tunnels, running toward them.

"Priestess—" Whatever else the girl had to say died as an arrow struck the back of her neck, ripping through her throat.

Ara, Nimhea, and Teth were on their feet. Mura moved to shield Bothia. Nimhea's sword slid from its scabbard and Teth nocked an arrow, raising Tears of the Traitor. Ironbranch felt reassuring in Ara's hands.

More arrows flew from the dark corridor, felling men, women, the old, and the young indiscriminately. The archers were hidden by shadow, but the sheer number of arrows suggested a major assault had been launched on the shrine. As the truth of it hit her, Ara's heart shattered.

This can't be happening.

Vokkan soldiers poured like ants from the corridor that led to the tunnels.

"You are under arrest for conspiracy and crimes against the empire!" one of them shouted.

They offered no quarter, cutting down anyone in their path, though few offered resistance. Blood ran down the stairs to pool in the sunken floor. The acolytes came together, forming a semicircle to block the holy priestess from the soldiers' onslaught.

Bothia grasped one of Ara's and one of Nimhea's arms. "You must leave. Now!"

"We can fight," Nimhea said through gritted teeth. "We'll hold them off until you can get to safety."

Teth nodded his agreement. His arrows were already flying, knocking down soldier after soldier, but they continued to stream out of the tunnels.

The priestess shook her head. "The time for fighting will come, but not tonight. You must flee. Nava wills it."

"But you—" Ara pleaded. It was obvious the soldiers had no interest in arresting anyone other than their targets; everyone else would be slaughtered.

Bothia cut her off. "Nava wills it."

Ara knew she couldn't argue, but tears stung her eyes as she looked into the old woman's serene face.

"Please forgive me." Ara's words came out with a sob. "I brought death to you, to everyone here."

Bothia reached out to touch Ara's cheek. "There is nothing to forgive."

Glancing at Nimhea, Ara saw the princess's cheeks were also wet with tears.

"Do not delay," Bothia told them firmly.

"Is there another way out, priestess?" Teth asked, his eyes darting around the room, hunting for a means of escape.

"There is an entrance to ruined tunnels behind the statue," the crone said, turning to point a bony finger at a fissure in the wall. "Many have collapsed, or lead nowhere. You will need light; take torches from the wall sconces. And you will need a guide—Mura will show you the way."

Mura burst into tears. "No, holy priestess, I will not leave you."

"You will do as I say."

Still weeping, Mura staggered away.

Ara reached for Bothia's hand. "Come with us."

She shook her head. "No more hiding for me. I have done what my goddess asked of me, and now I will rest. Go now and do what the gods demand. Fulfill your destiny."

Teth swore, loosing another arrow. "Go after Mura. I'll cover our escape."

Taking one of Bothia's hands, Nimhea bent to kiss it. "Nava watch over you."

"And you." Bothia laid her other hand on the crown of Nimhea's head.

Nimhea went after Mura.

"Ara, go!" Teth snapped. "There are too many of them for me to hold off."

Torn, Ara looked at Bothia, who simply nodded.

"Thank you, holy priestess," Ara murmured, and ran to catch Nimhea.

She could hear the twang of Teth's bowstring following close behind her.

Mura was at the fissure. She reached for a torch then suddenly cried out, back arching before she fell, revealing the arrow buried between her shoulder blades.

Ara came to Nimhea's side.

"We have no guide," Nimhea said bleakly.

"We have no choice," Ara answered. She grabbed the torch Mura had been reaching for and thrust it into Nimhea's hands before pushing the princess into the fissure.

Ara found another torch and plunged after Nimhea, calling to Teth over her shoulder as she did so, only to discover he was on her heels.

The tunnel differed significantly from the passages through which they'd entered the temple. It had been constructed of stone blocks that rose to meet in an arched ceiling. Some blocks had fallen, leaving gaps in the walls and ceiling. Ara eyed the tunnel warily, knowing this type of build relied on constant pressure from the stones upon one another to maintain its integrity. If too many stones fell, the entire passage was in danger of collapsing. Not to mention any single block that fell could injure or kill anyone unlucky enough to pass beneath it at the wrong time.

Rectangular alcoves featured in the walls on both sides of the passage, stacked three high, each space home to a stone sarcophagus. The tunnels were catacombs. Home only to the dead.

Ara shoved away the icy fingers of dread that settled on her shoulders.

A shallow line of water trickled along the floor. Debris cluttered the ground, broken stones, roots that had shoved their way through cracks in the floors, and bones. So many bones. Too many ways to snag a foot or turn an ankle; even so, they couldn't proceed at a cautious pace.

"Run!" Ara called to Nimhea.

The princess raced up the tunnel with Ara and Teth right behind her, water splashing as they ran. In a few minutes, her shoes were soaked. The shouts of pursuing soldiers came from behind them all too soon.

They hadn't run very far when the catacombs branched off in three directions. Each path looked the same.

"Which way?" Nimhea halted, breathing hard.

Ara shook her head, trying to catch her breath.

Teth pointed to their right. "That direction, if it continues straight, leads away from the pavilion. I think it's the best choice. You and Nimhea should go that way."

Hoping she'd misheard him, Ara didn't reply, but gave Teth a hard look.

"Where are you going?" Nimhea asked sharply.

"I'm going this way." He pointed his torch at the tunnel directly in front of them.

"Why?" Ara snapped, furious that he'd even suggest splitting up. "We stay together."

"If any of these paths is a dead end we'll be cornered," Teth replied in a measured tone. "It's better if I go a different way and make sure they follow me. That will give you the chance to find another path if the one you're taking doesn't lead to an escape."

"I don't like it," Nimhea said, frowning.

"I hate it," Ara snarled.

With a bland smile, Teth said, "I don't care."

Ara could hear the soldiers drawing closer.

"Go," Teth told them, then leveled his gaze at Ara. He lifted his hand to touch Eni's pendant where it hung at his chest. "In Eni's name I will not change my mind."

"Don't do this." Ara's voice cracked.

Teth leaned forward to lay a kiss on her temple. "It's done."

Feeling a tug on her arm, Ara turned to Nimhea. "We have to go."

Before Ara could object again, Teth had run into the tunnel ahead. He began to shout, feigning fear and confusion.

Ara bit back a curse and followed Nimhea into the tunnel to their right. Every instinct screamed at her to run back to him. She belonged with him. But the rational part of her mind knew Teth was right. His plan offered their best chance of escape.

Nimhea and Ara ran, jumping over fallen rocks and ducking under crumbling supports. They ran until Ara's lungs burned. All the while, the tunnels spoke to them in unsettling groans and creaks, a reminder that this was a place of ruin and decay. That there was no guarantee the ceiling above them and the walls around them would hold.

Nava guide our steps.

The soldiers' shouts had returned. Either they had given up searching for Teth—Ara refused to consider the possibility that he'd been captured, injured, or worse—or they'd split up and sent men in all three directions. Their voices were a good way behind, but not far enough to set Ara at ease.

"I can see light ahead!" Nimhea pointed.

In the distance, Ara could indeed make out filmy daylight, and her heart surged with relief. They'd found a way out. With any luck, Teth would evade the soldiers and find a way back to them. She only wished there were a way to tell him his instincts about the direction they should take had been correct.

I'll tell him soon, Ara reassured herself. *We'll be together again, and I'll tell him he was right.*

There was a sudden sharp crack followed by a rumbling then a roar. The ceiling crashed down in a storm of stones and choking dust, snuffing out the dim light that had sparked hope in Ara's chest. Sharp slivers of rock cut her arms, and she jumped back to avoid a slab of masonry that would have crushed her skull and fell hard onto her back. Nimhea cried out and disappeared. The princess and the promise of escape gone in the space of a heartbeat.

At first Ara couldn't breathe. Panic seized her, but she wrestled it down as she grasped that the fall had knocked the air out of her lungs. She wheezed and coughed, lungs burning from the dirtied air. Her eyes stung and watered, and she blinked until her vision cleared. Ara made herself stand, feeling twinges of pain, but nothing alarming. Streaks of blood covered her arms and hands where scrapes and abrasions were clustered, but none of the cuts were deep.

When the dust finally settled, there was a new wall of debris with no gaps to be seen. Signs of daylight had vanished, the hope of escape snatched away.

"Nimhea!" Ara's pulse pounded. She risked being heard by pursuers, but had to know if the princess was injured or worse.

No answer.

Nava, please, spare Saetlund's queen. We can't lose her. Please, merciful mother.

"Nimhea! Are you there?" Ara's voice broke, and she choked back a sob.

Not Nimhea.

Pressing close to the barrier, Ara called in a softer tone, hoping Nimhea would still be able to hear her. She couldn't risk yelling anymore. The soldiers were already closing in on her.

"Nimhea, please answer me." Salt from her tears stung the scratches on her cheeks as her fingers clawed uselessly at the pile of stones.

The princess's voice didn't come, only the scratching and cracking of shifting debris.

She can't be gone. Gods, no.

Ara forced herself to step back and examine the fall. The heap of earth and stone was packed so tightly she doubted she would be able to dig through it. It might be possible if she used Ironbranch to help, but she suspected any disturbance of the blockage would only cause another collapse.

There was no way through.

No Teth. No Nimhea.

Despair clawed at her.

No. No. No.

Shouts came from the tunnel at Ara's back. The soldiers would find her in a matter of minutes. They were too close for her to attempt going back to search for another branch of the tunnels. All she could do was hide. After a quick glance at her surroundings, it was obvious there was only one place to tuck herself away.

Ara snuffed her torch out in the dirt then shoved it as far into the pile of debris as she could, hoping it would appear to be just another piece of the collapsed tunnel. Turning to the nearest sarcophagus, she hauled herself onto the ledge of the alcove that held it. She crawled over the coffin and wedged herself into the crevice behind it. For the first time in her life, she thanked the gods she was small. Not only was the sarcophagus much longer than her body, but had she been any larger she couldn't have fit into the space between the coffin and the alcove wall.

The soldiers' voices were very close now. The light of their torches reached into the alcove, and Ara willed herself to be as immovable at the sarcophagus hiding her. She heard them talk as they examined the collapsed tunnel, and she sent up a plea to Eni that none of them would have the skill to judge how recent it had been.

"Are you sure you heard someone?" one of the soldiers asked.

"Yes," came a surly reply. "I know what I heard."

"I'd wager whoever you heard is under that heap," a third voice said with a snicker. "And no trouble of ours now."

"I'll decide what's our trouble and what's not, Jenkins," the first soldier, presumably their commander, barked. "Now see what you can do about that pile."

Jenkins muttered something under his breath, but soon Ara heard grunts and scraping as the soldiers tried to dismantle the collapsed stone blocking the tunnel.

As they lingered, sweat beaded on Ara's brow, as she feared discovery. In her own mind her breath sounded like a bellows, and every heartbeat was as loud as a hammer striking hot iron.

But after several minutes their grumbling grew louder, and the commander gave the order to abandon their attempt to clear the debris. She bit her lip when they decided to turn back. The torchlight faded long before the soldiers' voices did.

Ara forced herself to stay hidden an unbearably long time after silence surrounded her. She hoped long enough that the soldiers had quit the tunnels altogether. Wriggling from her hiding spot, Ara made her way out of the alcove. Her cramped muscles shrieked as she stretched them. With the absence of her torch, the tunnel was dark as pitch.

She moved as quickly as she could, given she couldn't see, using Ironbranch to sweep the ground in front of her to help her avoid debris, following the shape of the tunnel, finding other tunnels branching off. Her heart pounded as she turned one corner, then another. She didn't know where she was going.

Thoughts of Teth and Nimhea dogged her steps, making her falter, adding more weight to the weariness. Injured, captured, dead. Images of the worst things that could have happened to them wrapped around her mind like chains, trying to drag her down and imprison her with the dead.

She turned her focus to her feet, to each step she took, and to Ironbranch showing her the safest path. She walked and walked until it felt like she'd been wandering for miles. There was nothing to do but keep walking. She stopped only when she thought she felt a whisper of air lift the tendrils of hair that had escaped her plait. As soon as it was there it was gone. Ara froze, waiting, silently begging the tunnel to breathe again.

A minute passed. Then another. Her chest cramped with disappointment.

But there it was, fresh and sweetly scented, pushing through the otherwise stale air. It came from her left.

Ara turned and moved in the direction of the trickle of air. She pushed forward. Hope edged in, making her imagine the tunnel was getting lighter. Then she wasn't imagining it. She could see Ironbranch in her hands and the slope of the tunnel pitching up. The dead no longer filled the walls; there was only stone. The light grew, and Ara's blood surged with relief. Soon it would be safe enough to run.

Suddenly there was a figure in front of her, blocking the way. Ara jumped back. It took all her will to stop herself from striking him with Ironbranch. She braced herself, waiting for his attack, but instead of lunging at her, the figure said:

"Thank Nava."

She had not expected to hear those words. More than that, something about the man's voice was familiar. She squinted in the dim light, but couldn't make out his features.

"Are you hurt at all?" he asked.

"No."

"Then let us hurry," the man urged. "It isn't far to the surface."

"What about my friends?" Ara asked.

He turned away without answering and moved up the tunnel with long strides. Infuriated, but seeing no better option, she followed.

The tunnel grew brighter as they climbed. In the distance a sliver of light grew larger and larger. The tunnel transformed into a cavern, and at the apex of the slope a long crevice, wide enough for even a large person to crawl through, split a rock wall.

The man passed nimbly through the crevice. Ara paused for a beat, then scrambled through the rock face. Sunlight greeted her as she emerged from the cavern. She shaded her eyes against its brightness.

A familiar whicker called to her, and Ara was surprised to see Cloud standing beside another horse.

"I was able to retrieve your mount." The man stood to her side. "Nava has been known to reward the hopeful in dark times."

With her eyesight adjusted to the sunlight, Ara could see him properly. It took her a moment to place the light brown hair and hazel eyes set in a fair-skinned Keldenese face. The twitch of a smile in the corners of his mouth and the sardonic gaze when he realized she was trying to remember him settled it.

"Ioth."

The Resistance leader from Kelden grinned at her. "I'm honored that I didn't have to tell you my name a second time, Loresmith."

Her eyebrows lifted at his use of her title. "You're taking me seriously now."

"After what's been reported, we had little choice," Ioth replied. "I confess I still find your companions' tales hard to believe, but neither do I doubt they speak the truth."

Ara's breath caught. "Teth and Nimhea were in the tunnels with me. What happened to them?"

Ioth grimaced. "My companions are searching for them, but when we parted, the princess and the thief were still missing."

Her throat felt raw. "How did you know we were in trouble?"

"We received intelligence that the Below had been compromised and knew you were in immediate danger," Ioth told her, failing to answer her question. "I came with three of Lucket's agents to get you out of the market."

"What do you mean the Below has been compromised?" Her expression was bleak.

That could mean so many things, none of them good. Had the Vokkans simply been given the location of Nava's shrine, or did they have specific orders to hunt down Nimhea, the heir to the River Throne, Teth, the adopted son of the Low King who'd struck an alliance, or herself, the Loresmith? Each of them represented a different kind of prize. Ara closed her eyes against the pain and fear of knowing Teth or Nimhea, or both, could have been taken by the Vokkans.

She forced herself to look at Ioth, who was watching her with an expression of concern. "Tell me."

The roughness of his voice made plain his own devastation at the news. "One of the Low Kings forfeited the others, hoping to gain the empire's favor. Vokkan soldiers have been raiding hideouts, ransacking safe houses, and arresting anyone they can get their hands on."

Iron bands tightened around Ara's chest, making it hard to breathe. What did that mean for Lucket? For Teth—if he hadn't been captured already, or killed? And the Resistance—she didn't know if it could recover from such a blow. If the Below's secrets now belonged to the empire, they would be able to find Resistance hideouts and agents. The rebellion would be crushed before it could raise an army. And her own quest . . . how could she carry on without her friends? Did the Loreknights even matter without Nimhea on the throne? It could be the end of everything.

Ara fell back against the stony hillside. She couldn't speak. She could barely breathe. Black spots clouded her vision. Leaning her head back, she struggled for control of the chaos in her mind and the wrenching of her heart. With great effort she caught her breath, opened her eyes, and made herself focus on Ioth. Only Ioth.

He turned toward her, leaning his side against the rock face, and after gauging her expression, he continued his story. "When we reached your trading stall, the summoner and the Koelli were already gone, and I don't know if they've been found yet. Your horses were still picketed nearby. You, the princess, and the thief had made your way to the temple by the time we discovered where the empire's raid was focused."

A flash of anger made her want to remind Ioth that her friends had names, but she held her tongue.

So Lahvja and Joar were already gone. She could only hope that they'd escaped rather than being captured.

"We couldn't reach the temple ahead of the soldiers." Ioth grimaced. "And we could do nothing but wait until they'd finished the raid. One of the temple acolytes managed to escape and crawled out of the tunnels. She was wounded, but she was able to tell us that there were two paths of escape through the catacombs. That's why I'm here. Now we need to rendezvous with the others and hope they've found your friends."

Ara nodded. Her throat was tight at the thought that her friends might not be found.

I'm the only one.

He walked to Cloud, led the gelding to Ara, and handed her the reins.

"We need to go."

Cloud nuzzled Ara's hand, but she couldn't take comfort in the gentle touch.

Ara ground her teeth. No matter how viciously fear attacked her, she couldn't give in. Numbness crept over her, and her heart hardened until it was a stone. It had to be this way if she wanted to carry on. And she had to carry on.

Taking a fistful of Cloud's mane, Ara swung up into the saddle and nodded to Ioth.

"Let's go."

26

ra turned back to gaze at the hulk of the Great Market fading in the distance. She twisted in the saddle every few minutes, searching the road behind them for any signs of her friends among the northbound travelers on the road.

It didn't matter that she was distracted from the way ahead. Cloud knew to follow Ioth's mount as he led them to a rendezvous site where the others, if they had escaped the Great Market, would meet them.

With each passing mile, Ara's blood grew colder; she couldn't stop herself from feeling like she was abandoning her companions no matter how irrational that impulse was. Ioth had assured her that they'd reach the meeting point around sunset, but she couldn't keep her focus on the way ahead. Her heart wasn't with her on the road; she'd left it with her friends.

Treachery. The revelation was like a saw on her bones. That one of the Low Kings had turned against the others. She couldn't fathom the magnitude of it. *Compromised* wasn't a strong enough word for what had happened. It was a gutting, sickening betrayal. Despite the hardships and trials she'd faced, Ara understood now that she'd begun to embrace hope. She would be Loresmith. Nimhea would be queen. The Vokkans would be forced out of Saetlund.

But the act of this traitor crushed her budding dreams.

Horrible questions chased after one another in her mind:

What if Joar and Lahvja haven't gotten out of the city?

What if Nimhea is lost or captured or worse?

What if Teth—

She wouldn't finish the question of Teth; even considering that something might have happened to him was too much to bear.

So she stopped herself and tried to clear her mind, willing it to be blank as her horse walked north until, inevitably, she turned to look back again.

Ioth turned off the main road, leading the way down a short path that ended in front of a small farmstead that had been converted to an inn. They took their horses to the stables, but he didn't head back to the inn. Instead, he led Ara to an outbuilding behind the barn.

Pausing in front of the door, Ioth rapped on the wood in a strange staccato pattern and then waited. A few moments later, the door opened an inch and a woman's voice floated out.

"Do you like your cider tart or sweet?"

"Neither," Ioth replied. "I prefer it hard."

The door swung open just enough to give them entrance. Sunlight filtered through slats in the walls, revealing a storage shed filled with abandoned, rusting farm tools. Ara recognized the woman who'd let them in as one of Lucket's agents who'd been with him at the fort north of the Gash.

"Loresmith." The woman inclined her head briefly. "Glad you made it."

Ara barely remembered to be polite. "Thank you. What about the others?"

"No word yet," the woman answered. "You're the first to arrive."

Biting her lip, Ara could do nothing to quell her disappointment.

"My name is Elin." The woman made a careful study of Ara's face. "There's a table and chairs at the back of the shed. I'll go to the inn and scrounge up something for you to eat."

Ara nodded, not trusting herself to speak. She didn't object when Ioth guided her to one of the chairs.

"How bad were the raids?" Ara asked him. It hadn't been safe to discuss recent events while they were on the road.

Passing a hand over his weary face, Ioth replied, "It would have been much worse if we hadn't received a warning from the Dove."

Ara nodded. "Your man with the Vokkans."

"Word arrived only a few hours ahead of the soldiers," Ioth told her. "The Low Kings did their best to evacuate their hideouts and protect their agents, but hundreds of arrests have been made and countless assets stolen. We lost the Low Queen of Sola. She was still burning documents when the raid hit her hideout, and she wasn't able to escape."

Ara rested her elbows on the table. "What does it mean for the Resistance?"

"It's hard to say," Ioth replied, choosing his words carefully. "Obviously nothing good, but as far as how bad it is, only time will tell. We don't know what records the Vokkans got their hands on, how much we've been compromised."

Her expression must have been worrying, because he reached over to briefly cover her hand with his.

"We don't despair, and we don't lose hope. When you're part of the Resistance, you expect to get knocked down. Some hits hurt more than others, but we always get back up."

She offered him a weak smile.

Another syncopated knocking sounded at the door. Ioth stood up and went to answer it. Ara expected that it was Elin returning with food, but Ioth didn't immediately give entry to the knocker. Instead, he ran through the same exchange of phrases they had upon arrival.

When Ioth opened the door and stepped back, a man and a woman entered followed by—

"Nimhea!" Ara leapt out of the chair so quickly it toppled to the ground. She threw herself at Nimhea and flung her arms around the princess. "Thank Nava you're all right."

Nimhea squeezed her tight. "After the tunnel collapsed I was so afraid. I couldn't hear you. I didn't know if you'd been hurt. I tried to dig my way back, but it was impossible."

"I know." Ara stepped back, but kept Nimhea's hands in hers. "I tried, too."

Turning her head, Nimhea searched the space. Her face drew into a tight, bleak mask. "No one else?"

"Not yet." The fear in her voice was mirrored in Nimhea's gaze.

Ioth joined them, bowing to the princess. "Your Majesty."

Nimhea scrutinized him for a moment, then said, "Ioth of Kelden. I'm glad to see you again."

"Not as glad as I am to see you," Ioth replied. "We feared the worst."

Nimhea's jaw clenched when she nodded.

Another knocking came at the door, and Ara's heart leapt into her throat, but this time it was Elin with a tray of hot tea and sandwiches.

Ara and Nimhea settled at the table and drank cups of tea, but only nibbled at the sandwiches. It was easy for Ara to assume that, just as her own had been for hours, Nimhea's stomach was in knots. They spoke little, knowing all they had to say was how afraid they were for their missing friends.

Ioth joined them, telling Nimhea what he'd already told Ara about the raids on the Below and their impact on the Resistance. Then Ara listened as the two of them fell into conversation about the activities of the Resistance in the weeks since Nimhea had left them.

Lanterns were lit as sunlight faded. The deeper the shadows grew, the tighter the fist became around Ara's heart.

"We can hope they arrive in the night or tomorrow morning," Ioth finally said. "But you should both try to rest. I'll set up bedrolls. You don't have to worry about taking a watch. We'll see to that."

Ara's knee-jerk reaction was to dismiss the suggestion, but she realized there was no point. She might not be able to sleep, given the circumstances, but there was no reason to insist on sitting in a chair all night.

Ioth brought the bedrolls, and Elin surprised them with pillows from the inn. When Ara's head sank into the down, she stifled a moan of pleasure. She'd forgotten how lovely a pillow could feel, especially after weeks of resting her head on rolled-up clothing.

Despite being certain fear would keep her awake, physical exhaustion won out over anxiety. Within minutes of stretching out on the bedroll, Ara had fallen into a dreamless sleep.

No knocks came in the night. Nor did anyone appear while they broke their fast shortly after sunrise.

At midmorning, Ioth came to Ara and Nimhea, wearing a grave expression.

"We shouldn't linger here," he told them. "Staying too long in any place is too much of a risk."

Ara bowed her head against a wave of grief. She knew he was right, but the thought of leaving without knowing what had befallen Teth, Lahvja, and Joar was unbearable.

"Will we go to another rendezvous point and wait there?" Nimhea asked.

Before Ioth could answer, Ara lifted her face and said, "No."

Both of them looked at her in surprise.

"Nimhea," Ara said, a stony resolve filling her. "We have to go on. Without them."

The princess stared at her. "But we can't . . . Lahvja . . . I need her."

"I know." Ara rested her hand over Nimhea's. Her voice trembled with grief. "I know."

Taking in a deep breath, Ara pressed on. "But we must. Bothia told us that the trial in Nava's Ire is for you and me. We can't wait for them, especially now that the Below has been invaded. Lahvja would want us to go on. You know that."

Nimhea looked away.

"You're going to Nava's Ire?" Ioth asked sharply. His face had taken on a gray pallor.

"Yes," Ara told him. "It's the site of the next Loresmith trial. You know it?"

She watched his throat work as he swallowed. "Senn's teeth. I didn't think it was real."

He shook his head as if trying to get his bearings. "Nava's Ire is a place that children are warned about. Behave badly enough and Nava's shadow will come to take you away and make you live in her Ire with all the other bad children. It's supposed to be a place that is always cold, always lonely, where spring never comes."

"Lovely," Nimhea murmured, her eyes still averted. She was gripping Ara's hand so tightly it was painful, but Ara didn't pull away.

Ara kept her gaze on Ioth. "Do you know where it is?"

"Like I told you, I didn't think it was real," Ioth replied. "But I can take you to people who might know. If anyone does know, it will be the fisherfolk of the fens."

Turning back to the princess, Ara said, "I don't want to leave them either, but it is what we must do."

Unbidden, her last exchange with Teth intruded on her thoughts. Her pleading with him not to lead the Vokkans down a different tunnel. The brush of his lips just before he disappeared into the dark.

Where are you, Teth?

Even suggesting the plan felt like a betrayal. If only there was some news, some scrap of information that hinted at her missing friends' safety. But they couldn't wait.

Nimhea was silent for several heartbeats before she nodded. "I know."

The marsh spread before them, a sullen mat of greens and grays dusted by hoarfrost. The longer Ara stared at it, the more she wished their destination was anywhere else. In the far distance she could spot the frigid ocean that spilled salt water into the broad, flat expanse, etching out a maze of streams and pools amid spiked grasses and stunted trees.

The place where spring never comes.

The days and nights that passed on their journey from Sola into Kelden had been interminable. Had Ara been in a less stark state of mind, she probably would have enjoyed the transition from golden fields into rolling green hills that hosted orchards and hid lakes of deep blue. Ioth took pride in his homeland, pointing out sites of interest and offering impromptu history lessons about the province. She tried to listen but her thoughts insisted on running either to what lay ahead or what they'd left behind.

The same dream visited her night after night. She'd awaken to find Teth kneeling beside her bedroll, pulling her close, whispering that he was okay, and the sweetest relief spilled through her limbs. Then she would truly wake and realize he wasn't there. Every dream left her with a deeper sense of loss.

Nimhea felt the same loss. Ara could see the strain on her face and sometimes noticed a red-rimmed, glistening eye. They didn't speak of it. They didn't have to.

Ioth seemed happy to do all the talking.

Now that they'd stopped on a rise to take in the whole of the ice fens, he pointed to a cluster of buildings in the valley below.

"That's the village."

Compared to the dullness of the surrounding environs, the lively hues of the village looked like a pile of gemstones strewn across dirt. The sight of it lifted Ara's spirits, if only briefly.

The temperature plummeted as they descended toward the fens. What had been a warm, sunny day became chilled and blustery. Ara began to shiver. The air was much colder than it should have been for the season, but she sensed that in this place the weather of the outside world had little impact. The frozen air's touch reminded her of iron left outside in deep winter. Of metal so cold it would tear skin from your fingers. She tightened her cloak around her. The sudden cold wasn't merely unpleasant, it struck her as a disturbing harbinger of things to come.

They reached the village in the late afternoon; it consisted of a row of houses built of clapboard with black-shingled roofs that rose to a high peak. The houses were painted in bright hues that Ara perceived to be a sort of armor against the brooding colors of the fens. A rainbow wall that refused to be smothered by sullen clouds. The houses lined up smartly along a wooden dock that stretched the entire length of the village. A dozen or more shallow-bottomed boats bobbed and strained at their ties to the dock. At the center of the row of houses sat a building only slightly larger than the houses, bearing a whitewashed sign with sky-blue lettering declaring it Frog's Folly Tavern and Inn.

A blast of warmth wrapped around Ara as they entered Frog's Folly. The main room held modest groupings of tables and chairs along with the source of welcome heat—a giant stone hearth in which a peat fire smoldered. Ara felt as if she'd been wrapped in one of her grandmother's quilts. A welcoming atmosphere suffused the space. The walls were clad with polished burled wood in hues of dark honey. Vases filled with wildflowers graced every table. The scent of freshly baked bread wafted through the air, making Ara's mouth water. Everything about Frog's Folly whispered of home, of family. It made her heart ache at the same time she took comfort from it.

One of the tables near the hearth was occupied by a middle-aged man and woman and an older man with a white beard that rivaled a shrub. All three wore heavy flannel shirts and chest-high oilcloth waders. Their boisterous conversation ceased at the appearance of strangers.

"Good day to you." Ioth stepped forward. "We're in need of a boat and guide into the fens."

The tablemates exchanged looks.

"What ye be wantin' in the fens?" the woman asked. Her light brown hair was pulled tight in a knot at the nape of her neck, and her expression was curious rather than unfriendly.

When Ioth hesitated, Ara said, "We seek Nava's Ire."

Silence fell like speech had been stolen from the room. It was a long time before someone spoke.

"Nae," the man with the bushy white beard said at last. His bright blue eyes were full of warning. "Ye're not wantin' to go there, and there's none here fool enough to take ye."

His companions nodded, watching the three visitors with disbelief.

The middle-aged man cleared his throat. Bits of straw-colored hair poked out from beneath his woolen cap. "If ye're adventure seeking, I can tell ye of fine rivers and holes full of plump tasty fish that'll give ye a fine battle if ye snag them."

"Or ye could climb Hill o' Hunt, where ye can see for miles and miles and in the night watch the dancing rainbows Nava paints onto the sky," the woman added. She rose and tossed another peat brick into the fire.

The bearded man nodded enthusiastically. "Aye. All good ways to pass the time. But Nava's Ire. No. Ye'll find nothin' there but trouble. Mind ye, this is our home, and we never set foot in that wicked place."

"Perhaps someone could draw us a map and rent us a boat," Nimhea suggested.

The three villagers gaped at her, then collapsed into gales of laughter.

"A map!" The middle-aged man banged the table with his fist. "Och, that's brilliant!"

Ara waited with rising irritation until their laughter subsided.

"What's wrong with asking for a map?" Nimhea snapped. It was clear she was just as irked and impatient as Ara.

The villagers fell into laughter again, but Ioth cleared his throat.

"Fens aren't like other environments," he said quietly to Ara and Nimhea. "They're filled with floating clumps of earth, some the size of your hand, others large enough to be called islands, that shift with the current and the wind. A map drawn right now could very well be useless a few hours later."

"Oh," Nimhea said, chagrined.

Ara ground her teeth. "But if the fens are always changing, how could one of them guide us?"

"It takes years of experience," Ioth replied. "But the fisherfolk can learn the patterns of the fens, read the currents, know how the weather will move the canals."

His answer didn't make Ara feel any better. How could they convince these people to help them?

If it came down to it, Nimhea could intimidate the villagers with her sword, but the folk living in this place didn't deserve even the threat of violence.

A stout woman with silver-streaked brown hair and cheeks red as plums burst into the room wielding a large wooden spoon like a cudgel.

"What's all this fuss about? I canna cook when ye keep breakin' me concentration."

She caught sight of Ara, Nimhea, and Ioth and smiled.

"Guests! Och, we ne'er get guests in these dark times." She clapped her hands with delight. "I's a fair cook if I do say so meself. I can offer ye turtle soup, baked fish, and me famous brown bread. And, of course, frog legs. They're the house specialty."

Glaring at the trio sitting before her, with particular rancor for Bushy Beard, she said, "Have ye not invited them to sit down? Where's yer manners, husband?"

"They dinna want to sit!" Bushy Beard objected. "They've come with a mad notion of findin' Nava's Ire."

The cook gasped, then fixed her eyes on her new guests and shook her spoon at them. "Ye've no business in Nava's Ire! 'Tis a sacred place, but a cursed one."

"Please," Ara said, exasperated. "We know it is a holy site and also a place of sorrow. The gods have guided us here, and it is Nava's will that we find her Ire."

"Nava's will?" The red-faced cook took her time looking Ara up and down, then Nimhea. Her forehead wrinkled as she scrutinized the princess. She took a step closer, then another. "Ye. The tall one. Push yer hood back."

Nimhea shot a glance at Ara, who gave a brief nod. What choice did they have?

When the princess pulled back her hood, it was easy to glimpse the flaming roots that had grown in since her hair was last dyed.

The cook's eyes widened, and she sucked in a gasping breath. "It's ye! I canna believe it. I heard the rumors but . . ."

She dropped into a curtsy and at the same time batted Bushy Beard on the shoulder.

"Get on yer feet and bow, ye eejit!"

"What are ye on about, woman?" Bushy Beard rubbed his shoulder.

"It's *her*," the cook hissed through her teeth, holding the curtsy. "Princess Nimhea. The lost heir."

Bushy Beard didn't leave his chair, but stared at his wife, then Nimhea, then his wife. The other man and woman drew sharp breaths, then rose to bow and curtsy to the princess, exchanging looks of wonder and disbelief.

"Pardon me husband, Yer Highness." The cook's curtsy began to wobble. "My husband, Tymas, he's a right fool sometimes. The others are me son, Neff, and me daughter-in-law, Allamae."

Nimhea stepped forward and took the woman's hands, guiding her to her feet. "I'm honored, but you needn't make a fuss."

She took the time to smile and nod at each of them in turn. "Thank you for welcoming us to your village."

The cook's already red face managed to become even redder. "We're loyal to the River Throne, we are. Always have been. Those Vokkans said you were dead, but I didna believe it. Didna I tell ye, Tymas? And to think ye'd appear in our little village after all this time. Blessed by Nava we are, surely."

Through this exchange, Bushy Beard, aka Tymas, had been watching his wife and Nimhea with rising alarm. He suddenly jumped up and bowed so swiftly and deeply that Ara worried he would tip over.

"Forgive an ignorant man, Yer Highness," he blabbered, blue eyes shining with awe. "'Tis my own shame that I didna recognize you. Ye's a legend in these parts."

"Please, sit down," Nimhea told the three at the table.

They did so, but continued to stare at her with wide eyes.

"Now that you know who I am," Nimhea said, "will you take us into the fens?"

The three tablemates exchanged disconcerted glances and shifted uneasily in their seats.

Neff took his cap off, twisting it in his hands. "It's nae so simple, Yer Highness—"

"Course they will," the cook pronounced, cutting her son off. "My name is Dilia, and my family is at yer service."

"You have my deepest gratitude." Nimhea smiled at her. "My companions are Ara and Ioth."

Tymas eyed Ioth. "Ye're Kelden born. Ye don't happen to be Ioth Glenelk."

"I am." Ioth held the man's inquisitive gaze.

"Heard things about ye." Tymas leaned forward, resting his elbows on his thighs. "Interestin' things."

Ioth replied with a bland smile.

Neff and Allamae had bent their heads together and were whispering furiously.

"Huld yer whisht," Tymas said to them. "There's no need to draw straws. I'll guide them."

The pair stammered with embarrassment, but also looked immensely relieved.

"Thank you, Tymas," Nimhea said. "We'd like to leave immediately."

Tymas shook his head, frowning. "If ye go out yet this afternoon ye'll not make it back before dark. No one in their right mind risks the fens after sunset."

"We don't have a choice," Ara told him, and Nimhea affirmed her statement with a nod.

He sighed, scratching his beard. "I'll take ye as far as the first split. That's where ye'll have to continue on foot to reach the Ire."

Lowering his gaze, he said, "Forgive me, Yer Highness, but I canna follow ye there. I've me wife, me son and daughter-in-law, two more daughters, and my first grandchild on the way."

Allamae blushed, her hand moving to a belly that hadn't yet revealed her coming child.

"Don't apologize," Nimhea said crisply. "We wouldn't have let you take us all the way even if you insisted."

Tymas gave her a grateful smile. He cast a nervous glance at his wife, but she appeared happy with the arrangement.

Pushing up from his chair, Tymas gestured for them to follow him out the back door. His punt was tied to the dock right behind Frog's Folly.

"Good ye've got a walking stick." He jabbed a finger at Ironbranch. "Ye need to test the ground before each step ye take. Wha' looks solid enough is often not."

He looked at Nimhea. "Do ye have one, Princess? If not, I'll lend ye one of mine."

"I'd be grateful," Nimhea replied.

Tymas nodded and went back to the tavern.

Ara expected Ioth to object when she told him he needed to stay in the village, but he was quick to agree.

"If your friends are found, they'll be brought here," he said by way of explanation. "And I need to keep an eye on the villagers. In a place like this I doubt you'll find anyone loyal to the Vokkans, but it's best to be cautious."

When he saw Ara was at a loss for words, he added, "Besides, I'm a leader of the Resistance. We don't go on magical quests. I'll be here when you get back."

He grinned, and she laughed.

Tymas returned with a slender, gnarled walking stick and handed it to Nimhea. His wife followed with a bundle of flannels and three lanterns.

"'Twill be fearsome cold come nightfall," Dilia said, pushing supplies into their arms.

Tymas stepped lightly into the boat, gathering up nets and fishing poles and spears. He handed his work tools to Dilia, then helped Ara and Nimhea board the punt. The wooden boat was long and shallow, with enough room to accommodate the two young women, but only just. Tymas untied the boat and stood upon the platform at its stern, and after blowing a kiss to Dilia, pushed the boat away from the dock through the shallow waters.

The punt slid into one of the strangest places Ara had encountered. The fens didn't swallow them so much as they seemed to curl around them subtly, reeds and grasses whispering all the while. Canals wound through spits of land, islands, and floating mounds of earth. All featured plants that seemed trapped in a state of decay, but were clearly still alive. The scent of the fens wasn't what Ara expected. She'd anticipated odors similar to the swamp in Vijeri, but here the air was rich with peat, cut by the sharpness of brackish water, all of it crisped by frost. The damp cold crawled beneath Ara's cloak, and she was grateful for the flannel Dilia had loaned her.

Tymas was silent as he poled along the canals, and Ara sensed his taciturn state was a requirement for successfully navigating the fens. Nimhea remained quiet as well, her expression set with determination.

Two hours passed before Tymas maneuvered the punt toward what looked like a substantial outcrop of solid ground. He pushed the boat forward until its bow brushed up against the shore.

"This is the split," he told them. "'Tis a wedge of land that divides the fens in two, and by all accounts 'tis the beginning of the path to Nava's Ire. Mind ye, no one has ever followed that path to its end or at least come back to tell of it."

Nimhea led the way out of the punt, tentatively testing the ground before stepping onto it. Ara followed.

"Thank you," Nimhea said to Tymas.

Tymas nodded, and his gaze slipped to the west where the sun was poised to sink over the horizon.

"I's decided to stay here for an hour past sunset."

Nimhea opened her mouth to object, but he shook his head.

"When ye find yerself in darkness, ye may have a change of heart, and if ye do, come back straightaway. I know the fens well enough to make my way with a lantern."

Pressing her lips into a thin line, Nimhea nodded. "We're indebted to you."

"Mind how ye go," Tymas urged, blushing at Nimhea's words. "The split is said to be solid, but the fens like to play tricks."

Layered in flannels, bearing lanterns and walking sticks, Ara and Nimhea set off on the path to Nava's Ire.

Within a quarter of an hour it was dark. The lanterns provided a good amount of light, but their pace was glacial as they prodded the earth to ensure it wouldn't sink under their weight. Clouds had moved in, blocking out the night sky and any hope of moonlight.

With the sun gone and stars hidden, it was impossible to know what direction they traveled. With each step, Ara's doubts about their decision to be here after nightfall grew. When she stumbled and fell to one side of the path, the ground beneath her hands and chest squelched, sinking and sucking at her. She shrieked before Nimhea pulled her back onto solid ground.

Tymas had been right. They were fools to attempt this search in the dark.

"We should go back to the punt," Ara said, breathless and defeated. "We'll come back tomorrow at first light."

"You'll get no argument from me." Nimhea sounded relieved, but when she turned around her breath caught.

"Ara."

Ara peered around Nimhea into the lantern light that shone on the way they'd come.

The path was gone. Where a moment ago solid ground had offered passage, murky water now blocked the way.

There would be no going back.

27

The fens' cruel mischief started only a few minutes after they'd realized there was no way to retrace their steps and put aside their journey until daylight. Ara and Nimhea continued forward, lanterns casting pools of light around them as they walked. The world around them was alive with sounds. Frogs croaked, fish splashed. The grasses murmured, and reeds stirred. These natural noises gave Ara slight reassurance, reminding her that as strange as the fens might be to her, they were behaving as they should.

But then the mists had risen from the cold waters, and the fens began to speak.

Ara heard it first. A voice piercing the dark. A voice that made her heart leap.

"Ara!" Teth called out. He was somewhere out there in the dark, but she couldn't make out a light. "Ara, I can't find you!"

Mist that curled around her ankles climbed up to her thighs. Her pulse slammed through her veins.

"Teth!" Ara turned in a circle, searching for any sign of him. "I'm here!"

"Ara!" The sound of his voice was so warm, so familiar, it wrapped around her. Lulling her into a sweet calm with a promise that all would be well if only she could reach him.

He can't be far away. It will only take a moment to find him.

She took a step in the direction of his voice.

Nimhea's hand clamped down on her shoulder. "What are you doing?"

"Teth's here." Ara pulled away from her, impatient. "I think he's this way."

She took another step, but Nimhea grabbed her arm, halting her progress.

"Look down," Nimhea said through clenched teeth.

Ara shot an irritated glance at the princess then looked down. Her left foot had sunk into the bog, submerged to her ankle. She hadn't even noticed. Strangely, the evident danger didn't deter her, and she tried to take another step.

Nimhea held her back. "Stop!"

"But it's Teth," Ara shot back. "He's trying to find us."

"Ara, what are you talking about?" Nimhea searched her friend's face. "Why are you talking about Teth?"

Ara seethed, desperate to continue her search. "Don't you hear him?"

Even now she could hear Teth calling her name. He sounded close. If she could only walk a little ways into the fens he'd be able to see the light of her lantern.

Nimhea dragged Ara back onto the path. Sudden rage lashed Ara, and she struggled against Nimhea's tight hold.

"Let me go!"

"Ara." Nimhea's grip tightened. "There is no voice. Teth is not out there."

"But—" Ara shook her head. Teth's calls grew louder. "He is. He's shouting my name."

"No." Nimhea locked her in a fierce gaze. "He is not."

Ara's mind grew frenzied. She heard Teth. She knew he was near. Why couldn't Nimhea hear him?

Nimhea's eyes suddenly grew large, and her gaze swiveled away. "Lahvja?"

"What?" Ara frowned. She couldn't fathom why Nimhea would suddenly bring up their friend when Teth was obviously so close.

Dropping Ara's arm, Nimhea face twisted with grief and confusion. "I hear Lahvja, but . . . it can't be."

Nimhea's voice throbbed with agony. "She's hurt. She needs help." Shaking her head, the princess closed her eyes. "No. It can't be her. She's not here."

Ara watched Nimhea struggle with her emotions; all the while she could still hear Teth calling out for her . . . but she could not hear Lahvja at all.

Then she noticed a subtle glassiness in Nimhea's eyes and remembered the way Teth's voice ensnared her, dulling her mind to the present moment and the dangers of the fens. She wanted Teth—to know he was safe, to hold him—more than anything. Nimhea's feelings for Lahvja were the same. They were both being lured to the same trap, but with differing bait.

"You're right." Knowing how hard it was to ignore Teth's voice, Ara could only pray that her words got through to Nimhea. "It's not real. You can't hear Teth, and I can't hear Lahvja."

"We hear who we most want to." Nimhea's voice dropped to a whisper.

Teth's voice abruptly fell silent. The startled expression on Nimhea's face told Ara that Lahvja had stopped calling out, too.

Ara pulled Nimhea into an embrace. They leaned on each other, both of them shaking, understanding their shared torment. The unbearable longing for what they'd lost.

When both their breathing had steadied, Ara stepped back. "I think we've reached Nava's Ire."

"Then it's Nava who's doing this," Nimhea said in horror. "She made those voices. We're here to help her. Why would she try to hurt us?"

"We have to remember that this isn't Nava's true self," Ara replied, struggling against her own fear. "Her Ire manifests the opposite of all the good she is. Think about what Ioth said about the children's stories. It wasn't Nava who kidnapped children to bring them here, it was Nava's shadow. When I encountered Ofrit in the Tangle, he put me in terrible danger, and it made him laugh. I found no malice in it; he simply didn't seem able to stop himself."

"Bothia said this is the place of Nava's suffering," Nimhea murmured. Her expression was fearful, but there was compassion in her voice.

Ara nodded. "Here she exists in grief and rage."

"And I have to heal her somehow," Nimhea said, pinching the bridge of her nose. "I don't know how to do that."

"I didn't either," Ara told her. "But it came to me when I faced the god. I hope it will be the same for you."

Nimhea turned away from Ara, lifting her lantern over the path ahead. "Then we must find her."

They continued forward, and no voices rose from the fens. Instead, Nava's Ire fell silent. All the animal calls and insect noises vanished. Even the susurrations of the wind-tossed grasses ceased.

The mists continued to climb, wrapping around Ara's thighs, then her waist and chest.

"Nimhea, I think we should—"

She'd been about to say they should walk hand in hand, but before she could finish her sentence the mist closed around her, and Nimhea was gone.

"Nimhea!"

The princess should have been only a few feet ahead, but she didn't respond to Ara's shout.

"Nimhea, wait!"

It was like the catacombs, but somehow more frightening. The tunnel collapse had terrified Ara, but it had been caused by natural forces. This mist that had suddenly isolated her was the work of a goddess.

They needed to find Nava, but what could they do if Nava didn't want to be found?

Cocooned by mist, Ara struggled to see her feet, much less the path.

She crouched and waited, listening for signs of Nimhea.

Listening for anything.

There was nothing. Nothing but mists and silence. And her thoughts.

Images seeped into her mind.

Teth broken and bleeding.

Lahvja weeping.

Joar and Huntress dead.

These visions turned like a water mill, one horrible picture giving way to another and another.

Ara couldn't stop them. Despair latched on to her like a leech draining her hope. Grief followed close behind, nesting in her hollowed-out soul. She dropped her lantern, wrapped her arms around her body, and tucked her head into her knees.

So cold.

So alone.

Whispers joined the images.

They will never come back to you.

You lost them.

You killed them.

You failed.

Ara sobbed.

"No." She choked out the word.

You failed.

"No." Her tears ran hot against the cold air.

You failed.

"No!" Ara shot to her feet as her grief burst into flames and became rage.

Taking Ironbranch from its harness, she swung it wildly through the mist.

She wanted to hurt something.

She swung again.

She wanted to destroy something. Anything.

Ara lifted Ironbranch overhead and swung it like an ax, slamming the stave into the ground. The impact reverberated through her limbs, but didn't bring the relief she sought.

She let out a scream of fury and defeat, then planted Ironbranch onto the ground and leaned into it.

I feel so helpless. I can't bear it.

Another sob was wrenched from her throat.

I can't bear it.

Ara fell to her knees. So much anger, so much sorrow. The raw emotions twisted her gut and made her bones ache. She'd never felt such anguish.

A murmur of reason pushed against the pain.

You haven't lost them. You haven't failed them. You simply don't know what's happened to them.

Ara clung to those thoughts hard, needing them to keep the poisoned whispers at bay. The force of them was so strong, they were more than she had ever imagined she could feel, like they would rip her apart.

Her grief is vast.

Bothia's words joined the quiet voice of reason.

Ironbranch had fallen to Ara's side. She took up the stave and used it to help her stand.

Not all of this grief is mine, Ara realized.

In this place where the goddess suffers, her sorrow and fury have amplified my own.

Taking Ironbranch in both hands, she lifted her chin.

I have hope.

Ara spoke in a clear, strong voice. "I am the Loresmith, and I will not bow or break. I am here because Nava wills it. The gods will it."

The mists around her shuddered.

"Show me the path. Take me to Nava, the Sower, the Mother. She must be restored so that Saetlund may be reborn."

The air began to shimmer and pulse. Silver ripples chased through it as it brightened. The growing light brought warmth with it, pushing back the chill that plagued her bones. Slowly, the mist parted like curtains, drawing back to reveal the way ahead. It was not the path she and Nimhea had been following. The earth beneath her feet was no longer springy and damp, but dry and hard-packed like the road in Sola. Bright light shone through the mists as Ara started on the path, but she didn't think it was sunlight. She followed the path until the mists parted again, this time revealing a wide clearing.

Inside the clearing walked Nava.

The goddess wasn't immense in size like the statue in the temple. To Ara she looked to be slightly taller than Nimhea, and where Nimhea had the lean hardness of an athlete, Nava's body was all swells and curves. Her golden hair fell dull and lank over her shoulders. There was no gleam in her dark skin.

Nava walked in a circle. She walked and wept.

As Ara watched, the space around the goddess changed. One scene melting into the next.

The goddess wept as she walked through cornstalks gray with blight. The earth was like chalk, spinning up dust tornadoes. Nava seized an ear of corn, only to have it crumble to ash in her hand.

Cornstalks faded away, then the clearing was filled with bodies. Blood flowed from horrible wounds as the dying moaned and cried for help. The dead stared glassy-eyed into oblivion.

Nava carried the body of a child in her arms.

The child faded away, and the field and its carnage disappeared, replaced by a room full of crowded cells. Children whimpered and stretched pleading hands through the bars. Their faces were dirty and tear-streaked. Nava reached for the children, but darkness swallowed them.

One image following another. Endless sorrow. The absence of hope kindling rage.

The power of Nava's emotions radiated out, and Ara flinched against their devastation.

Someone else stepped into the clearing.

"Nimhea." Ara gasped as the princess strode toward the goddess without hesitation.

When Ara thought to join Nimhea, it was as if the princess sensed her presence and shot her a warning glance.

Whatever Nimhea intended to do, she would do it alone. Ara remained still.

Nava was walking through the aftermath of war, again carrying a dead child. Nimhea stepped directly in her path.

The goddess stopped and stared at the princess. Nimhea stood her ground.

The bodies disappeared, as did the child in Nava's arms. Pressure began to build in the clearing like the thickening of air before a storm. The mists turned black, and flashes of electricity chased through them. The earth beneath Ara's feet rumbled, and she had to brace herself with Ironbranch to keep herself upright.

Nimhea went down on one knee, but not because she'd fallen. Looking up into Nava's face, the princess reached out and took the goddess's hand. At the touch, the fiery roots of Nimhea's hair spread through her tresses, banishing the dye, and the princess was once again crowned by flame.

Everything went still, as if the world held its breath.

The goddess stared at the princess. Nimhea held her gaze and began to speak.

Ara couldn't hear what she was saying, but when Nimhea fell silent and pressed a kiss to Nava's hand, the goddess reached out and gathered the princess into her arms, holding her like a priceless gift. Then Nava stood and helped Nimhea to her feet.

Holding her hand out to Ara, Nava said, "Come, Loresmith, we have need of you."

Like Nimhea, the goddess had also transformed. Her lifeless hair was a golden cloud of tight curls. Her dark skin glowed with vitality, and her smile was like sunshine.

When Ara took her hand, feelings of happiness and contentment washed away her fears. She was filled with hope and gratitude. She didn't notice when the mist and the clearing vanished, but she couldn't miss the appearance of a place she'd come to think of as an odd sort of home.

"What is this place?" Nimhea whispered.

Ara was startled to see the princess still beside the goddess. "This is the Loresmith Forge."

Nimhea gasped, taking in her surroundings with wonder. "Are those stars?"

"They are," Nava answered. "But not the stars of your sky."

The goddess turned to Ara. "There are things the princess and I must speak of. Here is what I require of you."

A scroll appeared in her hand that she passed to Ara.

Taken aback, Ara could only manage to nod. No other god had given her instructions. For Eni and Wuldr, the image of what she needed to create had manifested inside her.

A small garden appeared, abundant with fragrant flowers of all colors, at the center of which bubbled a fountain. Two throne-like chairs had been placed upon a dais nearby, ideal for viewing the fountain. Nava gestured for Nimhea to sit before taking the other chair for herself.

Leaving goddess and princess to converse, Ara went to the forge and opened the scroll. The moment she saw the design, she was grateful that Nava had provided it. The piece was like nothing Ara had crafted, and she guessed that the intricate details inscribed on its surface imbued it with powers she could only begin to grasp. The molds were complex. Timing was essential to correctly gauge the cooling of metal so it could be bent into curves. Pieces had to be joined. She would shape and hammer and etch and polish until it was complete.

In contrast to Tears of the Traitor and StormSong, Ara wouldn't need godswood for this task. Instead, she gathered bricks of gold that were stacked near the worktable and began melting them down.

She needn't have worried that Nimhea's presence would be a distraction. As she began to work, everything fell away. It was only the fire and molten gold, the anvil and the hammer. Ara danced to the rhythms of her craft.

When she stopped to eat, Nava and Nimhea joined her, but when she slept they disappeared, and Ara couldn't fathom where they had gone. After she began to work again, they once again sat in the garden.

The piece began to take shape. A perfect circle. Valleys and peaks.

She turned to the etching, using beeswax to create a ground. With painstaking care, she carved the symbols from Nava's design into the wax. She knew instinctively that even the slightest error in replication would render the piece worthless. The only symbols she recognized were those of Saetlund's five gods, but the others seemed to be writing in a language unknown to Ara. The writing covered the entire surface of the piece, and Ara had to take several breaks when the focus required of her made her head ache.

When at last the carving was complete, Ara used an acid bath to transfer the design onto the piece. With the etching complete, Ara set to polishing. It was the final step.

When the piece gleamed and Ara knew it was ready, a velvet pillow appeared on her worktable. Nestling the piece into red velvet, she smiled at the light the gold threw back at her. As she approached the garden, Nava rose and gestured for Nimhea to stand.

During their time in the Loresmith Forge, Ara had noticed a change coming over the princess. She bore herself with a new confidence. Her mood was lighter, happier, but remained girded by steel. When she stood on the dais, she looked regal.

Ara presented the pillow to Nava. "I give you Restoration."

Nava took up the crown and lifted it. Its gold band rose into five symmetrical peaks, each peak bearing a symbol of the gods. The entirety of the band was inscribed with the unknown writing.

"Your work exceeds my expectations, Loresmith. I thank you."

Ara bowed to the goddess. "I am honored."

Nava turned to Nimhea. Without being asked, the princess knelt.

"Nimhea, Flamecrowned, I name you Loreknight and Queen. Restorer of the River Throne."

Nava laid the crown on Nimhea's head, and it was instantly alight with flames. Fire of gold, orange, red, and blue danced over its surface but did no harm to the princess.

"It feels as if it weighs nothing," Nimhea murmured. She smiled up at the goddess. Her cheeks were wet with tears, but only joy shone in her eyes.

"If it pained you, it would be a poor gift." Nava laughed, then her dancing eyes grew solemn. "You are the realm's rightful ruler, and you shall be its protector. It is time for you to take your place. When you wear this crown, no harm can come to you."

Nimhea's eyes widened.

"More than that," the goddess continued, "you are the protector of your peers. When this crown sits upon your head and you fight beside them, neither shall your fellow Loreknights come to harm. No weapon will touch them, nor spell assault them."

"My reign will honor you, Nava," Nimhea said. "And every day I rule, I will strive to heal Saetlund, its people, and the earth that sustains us."

"Rise, Queen Nimhea."

Nimhea stood, and Nava leaned forward to press a kiss to the princess's cheeks. "My love and blessings go with you, my child."

Nava turned her attention to Ara once more. "Loresmith, you have faced my trial and succeeded, and you have more trials to come." Nava touched her cheek, and Ara was suffused with the knowledge that she was loved. "Yet I must give you another task."

"I am your servant, Nava," Ara replied.

"You saw the depth of my grief. Know it is born of the past but also the present. The children, suffering, prisoned; they are the present," Nava said, and for a moment grief wracked her features. "You must save them before he becomes."

Cold fingers wrapped around Ara's neck at Nava's last three words. *Before he becomes.*

Nimhea asked the question trapped in Ara's throat. "Before who becomes what?"

Nava didn't answer, instead smiling at them and resting her other hand on Nimhea's cheek.

The world around them dissolved.

Ara and Nimhea stood on the dock behind the Frog's Folly, and Tymas fell over.

"Ye're—ye're here!" He gripped the side of his boat and waited for its wild rocking to cease. "It canna be. Ye had no punt."

Ara reconciled herself to the fact that a moment earlier they had been in Nava's Ire and now they were in the fishing village with the morning sun shining down on them.

"We had an extraordinary kind of help," she told Tymas.

The fisherman's eyes widened, and he stared at the pair of them.

"In all me days," he said softly. "I ne'er believed such a thing could happen."

Pulling his gaze away, he returned to the task of tying his boat to the dock.

"Are you just now getting back?" Nimhea asked.

"Aye," Tymas said, sounding abashed. "I couldna bring meself to leave ye in that treacherous place. Stayed there all night I did. When ye didna come back at dawn, I came back to the village, thinkin' to roust up the other fisherfolk to search for ye."

"Thank you, Tymas," Ara said, deeply touched.

He ducked his head and didn't reply.

"Tymas!" Dilia burst out of the tavern's back door. "Ye're back, thank Nava! I been fearin' the worst for ye. Me poor heart."

She stumbled to a halt when confronted with the sight of Ara and Nimhea. "Me husband brought ye back, did he? He's a blessed soul for that. Did ye find what ye were searchin' for?"

Tymas climbed onto the dock. "I didna bring them back. They just appeared on the dock. 'Tis magic, that is."

"Nae," Dilia scoffed.

"Ye see 'em here, don't ye?" he replied. "By Nava, they didna come back in this boat."

"By Nava indeed," Nimhea said with a sly grin, and Ara laughed.

Flustered, Dilia changed the subject. "Ye'll nae believe it, Tymas. We hae *more* guests!"

Ara's pulse skipped, and she heard Nimhea draw a sharp breath. They exchanged a quick glance before rushing to the door and into the tavern.

Nimhea gave a shriek of joy. "Lahvja!"

Princess and summoner flew into each other's arms and fell into a storm of laughter, sobs, and kisses.

"I will not receive such a welcome, I think." Joar smiled at Ara. Huntress stood beside him, wagging her tail.

Ara went to him. "I do want to hug you."

She wrapped her arms around him and laughed when he lifted her off her feet.

"It is good to see you, little Loresmith," he said, setting her down.

Huntress barked, and Ara knelt beside the huge wolf, scratching her head and receiving a sloppy kiss as thanks.

Ara wiped off her face and stepped back to look at the newly arrived trio. They looked tired, but otherwise well. She felt a swell of relief, but also a little withering of her spirit at the one who was still missing.

Where are you, Teth? Her heart gave a painful wrench. *I need you.*

Lahvja and Nimhea had finished reassuring each other that they were alive, and Lahvja came to hug Ara.

"You have completed another trial." The summoner smiled at her. "Well done."

Ara smiled back. "Nimhea did most of the work."

"How did you get out of the Great Market?" Nimhea asked.

"Joar did most of the work," Lahvja replied, grinning at Ara. "Huntress warned us. She sensed something was amiss, and Joar went to get our horses. He came back just before the soldiers swarmed our camp."

Ara looked at her with alarm. "But you weren't captured."

"Like I said," Lahvja told her. "Joar did most of the work. Those axes of his are astonishing. Did you know they sing and make blizzards?"

When Ara lifted one eyebrow, Lahvja laughed. "Oh. Of course you did, no matter. By the time he cut down the first dozen, the others backed off enough for us to flee on horseback. If they gave chase, I think it was with little enthusiasm. They never caught up."

"Thank Nava." Nimhea kissed Lahvja's temple.

"I've been thanking her with every breath. Even more so since I set eyes on you a few minutes ago." Lahvja laughed, pressing a light kiss to Nimhea's lips.

Then she looked at Ara, and her eyes grew serious. "But no news of Teth?"

"I was going to ask you the same." Ara's shoulders slumped.

Ioth had been standing aside during their reunion, but now he joined them. "They didn't come with agents of the Below as I expected. We won't know anything further of Teth until those agents arrive, or he does."

Ara's lips set in a grim line, and she nodded, fighting another wave of grief.

Where are you?

"If agents didn't bring you here, how did you know where to find us?" Nimhea asked, threading her arm through Lahvja's.

"We had a visit from an old friend." Lahvja beamed at them. "Fox!"

"Fox!" Ara and Nimhea exclaimed at once.

Joar grumbled, "I did not understand the antics of that beast nor why Lahvja started laughing and clapping her hands. I have seen many foxes, and I have never wanted to clap."

"I was so happy to see Fox, I not only clapped, I cried," Lahvja added.

"Nor have I ever been told I must follow a fox for miles and miles," Joar muttered with irritation.

Ara's brow crinkled, and she asked Lahvja, "You did explain to him that Fox is Eni."

"Eventually," the summoner replied, eyes twinkling. "But I enjoyed his grumpiness for a while before I did. Joar is very funny when he's grumpy."

"I am not." Joar crossed his arms over his chest.

Lahvja patted his bulging bicep fondly. "Oh you are. You just don't know it."

"Is Eni still here?" Ara asked anxiously. As Teth's patron, the god might know what had happened to him.

"No," Lahvja answered. "As soon as we reached the village, Fox ran off. Fox led us here, but Eni did not speak to us."

"Ye must be starvin'!" Dilia trundled into the inn, pushed two tables together, and herded them to chairs.

Eyeing Joar, she said, "Ye're the largest man I e'er seen. I best bring a boatload of a meal for ye."

"Yes." Joar looked pleased.

"It's a little early for me." Ioth excused himself. "I'm going to check on the horses while you catch up."

Every platter, plate, bowl, and basket Dilia brought them was picked clean within minutes. Ara was ravenous, and her companions stuffed themselves with food with equal fervor.

When they leaned back in their chairs, bellies sated, only Joar glanced toward the kitchen as if hoping for more.

He caught Ara eyeing him and shrugged. "I did not hunt on the way here."

"That chowder was superb." Lahvja sighed with contentment. "I need to ask Dilia for the recipe."

Nimhea rested her elbows on the table. She let her eyes rest on Lahvja, and Ara was surprised to see pain in the princess's gaze.

Turning to the rest of them, Nimhea said, "I came to understand something in Nava's Ire. It affects all of us."

Lahvja's brow crinkled with concern. "Is something wrong?"

"No," Nimhea replied. "Something is necessary. I need to fulfill my duty and become a leader of the people."

Ara's chest tightened as she anticipated what the princess would say next.

"When we leave this place, I'll go with Ioth to the Resistance," Nimhea told them. "They need me, and the Resistance is where I belong."

Her words settled around the table, and for a few minutes it was quiet. Lahvja took Nimhea's hand and gripped it tightly.

Joar spoke first. "I think this is wise. You will be their queen."

"The rumors that I've returned have set a fire in the hearts of Saetlund's people," Nimhea said, a smile flashing on her face. "The truth that I'm here could be the key to gaining the allies and hopefully mitigating the harm done by our loss of the Below."

Ara nodded slowly. "And Nava told you it was time to take your place."

"She did," Nimhea replied in a quiet voice.

"If it is Nava's will, you must go," Lahvja said stiffly. Her olive skin paled with strain. "But we cannot go with you."

"I know." Nimhea gave her a sad smile. "Where will you go?"

Lahvja tore her gaze away from the princess to look at Ara and Joar. "We must continue to the next hidden site, that of the twins. To find it, we will go to the Well."

"Make the pilgrimage," Ara said with awe.

The pilgrimage to the Well of the Twins had been outlawed by the empire the year Ara was born, but her grandmother told her that even before the ban, few dared venture to the holy site. The climb into the mountain peaks was too treacherous, the weather too unpredictable.

The idea of making it herself was intimidating, but the path to the Well was so near Rill's Pass. She might have a chance to see her grandmother and Old Imgar. To go home. That possibility filled her with joy. It would mean so much to her to be with her loved ones. To tell them everything that had happened since she'd left. She hoped she would make them proud.

With all of her being, she hoped Teth would be with her. She wanted him to see the places she'd loved as a child and meet her family.

Nava, please let him be safe. Eni, please bring your chosen back to me.

"It will be good to return to the mountains." Joar had a wistful expression, which looked strange on the warrior's usually stern face. "I regard them as my home."

Lahvja's voice was laden with sorrow, but she smiled at him. "We will need your experience to survive the trek. The way is difficult."

"That is all the more exciting!" Joar looked like a child who had just received a gift and couldn't wait to open it.

"Then it's decided," Nimhea said. "When Ioth is ready to leave, I'll go with him, and you'll go to the Well."

"I think we should take Elke's Pass into the mountains," Ara said. "We could travel through the Fjeri lowlands to come at the pilgrimage from the south, but there are less likely to be patrols in the mountains. The empire is chasing us now, and we must do our best to stay hidden."

The others nodded their agreement.

Ara paused, heart in her throat, then added, "But we'll wait for Teth."

"He's not coming." Ioth stood a few feet away wearing a bleak expression. Lucket's agent Elin hovered behind him.

The truth of it unfolded in Ara's mind before he spoke. Nightmare emotions born in Nava's Ire roared through her. Her eyes wanted to squeeze shut and she needed to scream, but she made herself remain still when Ioth said:

"Teth was taken."

iran had spent more time in the Temple of Vokk over the last several weeks than he had in the entirety of his fifteen years in Saetlund. He found the place more vile than ever.

Each time he entered the building, he seemed to notice some new noxious odor or catch some nameless thing squirming in the shadows out of the corner of his eye, only to have it disappear when he tried to discern what it was. Every horror hounded Liran, a reminder that he should have paid closer attention, intervened sooner.

Upon entering the ArchWizard's office, Liran was startled by his brother's haggard appearance. Zenar's already pale skin was ashen and stretched too tight, putting the contours of his skull on display. His fingernails had grown long, curving like talons.

When Liran approached Zenar's desk, his brother stared at him with red-rimmed eyes.

"It has begun." Despite his wretched appearance, the ArchWizard looked exultant.

Rather than speak, Liran decided to wait for an explanation. There was a frenzied sheen to Zenar's gaze that told Liran to be extremely cautious in the conversation.

Zenar picked up a letter from his desk and shook it at Liran. "He is coming. At last. He is coming to me!"

Again, Liran stayed silent as Zenar bared his teeth in what might have been a smile.

He threw the letter at Liran. "It's all falling into place."

After retrieving the letter from the floor, Liran smoothed the wrinkled sheaf of paper and quickly read its contents. The letter was from their father. Fauld the Ever-Living had set sail for Saetlund. He would be here just after the next moon.

Liran held his emotions in check while his mind reeled. He hadn't seen his father in years. The emperor's attentions were supposed to be focused on the increasing unrest in other imperial territories. Why would his plans suddenly change?

"Did you do this?" Liran placed the letter back on the desk, hoping he hid the edge of anger in the question.

Zenar shook his head. "No . . . well, perhaps. It was not my intention to draw our father here, but it suits my purpose."

"Then why is he coming, if not at your request?" Liran didn't need this. Too much was already happening. Imperial raids on the Below had made the Resistance vulnerable. They needed time to shore themselves up before taking the next step.

And Liran needed to know more. The letter said nothing about whether their father was bringing reinforcements or soldiers of any number with him. Any infusion of troops whose loyalties lay with the emperor could quash the rebels' chance at a coup.

"I believe he senses that I am close." Zenar sounded triumphant. "He plans to stop me, but he won't arrive in time. The key will be mine, and Fauld the Ever-Living cannot prevent his downfall."

He picked up the chalice sitting on his desk and went to the wall, filling it with black ooze.

"Are you going to tell me what this key is?" Liran fought through a wave of nausea as Zenar took sips from the chalice. The dark substance seemed to crawl over his lips and into his mouth.

Zenar studied his brother's face, then set the chalice down. "Yes. Now that Father is coming, you should know what I've discovered, what I've labored at for years. It's what makes our victory possible, and I want to assure you that we will win. Against the two of us, Father has no chance."

"Father is untouchable because he's tethered to Vokk," Liran said. "When Father comes, Vokk comes with him. Do you actually believe you can best our god?"

"I don't." Zenar's mouth spread in a skeletal grin. "I won't need to."

Liran frowned at the ArchWizard.

"Don't you see, brother? Our god is the Devourer," Zenar said. "All I must do is show Vokk that I'm hungrier than Father. Much, much hungrier."

He retrieved the chalice and drained its contents. "Follow me."

Zenar led his brother out of the office and into the main corridor. Cold dread began to build in Liran's chest when Zenar passed through the door leading to the temple's lower chambers. With each step into the spiral, Liran's gut clenched.

"Your Highness." The ArchWizard waved nonchalantly at the prince in his cell.

Liran gave the boy a brief nod but couldn't meet his gaze. A sudden fear had taken hold of him, the kind of fear one experiences only as a child. He was walking into a nightmare and knew there would be no waking up.

"Weren't you ever curious, Liran?" Zenar spoke in a light tone. "About the true reason for the Embrace?"

"The reasons were clear enough," Liran answered. It was a half-truth. As much as he despised the Embrace, it was an effective tool of conquest, but beneath that rationale he couldn't help but be suspicious about the emperor's insistence on it in territory after territory.

Even kingdoms that surrendered immediately when facing Vokk's armies, offering no resistance, did not escape the Embrace. He didn't like Zenar's suggestion that something else compelled their father to institute its practice. He didn't like it at all.

Zenar laughed and turned to grin at Liran. "That's always been your problem, you know. Lack of imagination."

The steps twisted down and down. They passed other cells, some occupied, others empty. The deeper they descended, the worse the state of the prisoners was.

New sounds reached Liran's ears. Shrill, desperate keening. Choked sobs. Groans of pain. A chorus of fear without hope.

The spiral staircase came to an end. Torchlight from sconces that ringed the room revealed a chamber that was empty save a door. Zenar withdrew a key from his long silk coat.

Liran's throat closed. He didn't want to see what was behind the door. It hid whatever made those hellish sounds. It muffled the odious smells within.

Don't. Liran pleaded silently with his brother. *Don't.*

Zenar turned the key in the lock and pulled the door open.

Liran doubled over when the smell hit him. It was familiar. He'd caught whiffs of it in the temple. But this, this was a sea of stale sweat, excrement, and vomit. He couldn't stop the dry heaves that wrenched his gut and turned away, bracing himself against the stairs' railing.

When he finally wrestled his stomach under control, Liran straightened to find Zenar watching him with an amused expression.

"You grow accustomed to it."

Liran would never believe it was possible to be unaffected by the noisome air. He could barely keep himself from gagging at each breath.

Zenar gestured to the open door. "After you."

Liran made it as far as the threshold. He thought he'd seen the worst of humanity in war, but this, this was a nightmare beyond imagining. Oily smoke choked the air and made the miasma of repulsive scents even worse.

The corridor in front of him was lined on both sides with iron cages. Skinny limbs and tiny hands stretched through the bars. Every cage was crowded with children, pressed together, crawling over one another to get away from the ankle-deep filth rising from the cage floors. The children's clothes were little more than rags hanging off skeletal bodies, their skin covered with grime and open, festering sores. The corridor went on and on and on, until the cages stretched beyond sight.

The children in the nearest cages stared at him, eyes wide with fear. Liran realized that from the moment the door had opened, the wails and cries had stopped, the corridor growing quiet save a few whimpers and muffled sobs.

Fear outweighs their suffering. What is it they've seen that is so much more terrible than the pain and misery of this place?

"What. Is. This." Liran forced the words through clenched teeth. He wanted to wrap his hands around Zenar's throat and strangle him. He was beginning to believe it would ultimately come to that. Zenar would have to die. Anyone who could do this had to die.

Not yet. A small voice whispered in his mind. *Not yet.*

If Zenar noted Liran's distress, he was unfazed by it.

He strolled to the nearest cage. The children shrank away, piling on top of one another, to avoid Zenar's reach. But there was no escape. Zenar's fingers closed on a tiny wrist and dragged a whimpering girl, who couldn't be more than five, to the bars. He stretched his other hand through the bars to stroke the girl's matted hair in a sick mockery of affection.

"This, my dear brother," Zenar crooned, "is the key to eternal life."

ACKNOWLEDGMENTS

very book has a family, and with each new tale I am grateful for all the work and support of mine at Philomel and Penguin Young Readers. I'm especially indebted to Kenneth Wright and Jill Santopolo for their faith and encouragement. Kelsey Murphy guided this book from its rough beginnings, and her insights kept me from getting lost. Thank you to Cheryl Eissing, Krista Ahlberg, Tessa Meischeid, Felicity Vallence, Eileen Kreit, and the marketing and publicity teams at PYR. My agent, Charlie Olsen, is tireless and always keeps me smiling. The Robertsons and Otrembas surround me with love that makes writing possible. This book is dedicated to Katie Saarinen Buhrandt, my best friend from age five, who knows what real magic is. To my husband, Eric—thank you for understanding when mid-conversation I drift into other worlds.